Ripping

Ripping Publishing
PO Box 286
Epsom, Surrey,
England KT19 9YG

Copyright © Edward E. Smith 1950

Copyright © Street & Smith Publications, Inc.

Bookcover design © Warren James Palmer &
Neil Stuart Lawson1997

Published by Ripping Publishing

Twelve previous printings.

This edition 1997.

First Lensman
ISBN 1 899884 13 0

Printed by Cox & Wyman Ltd, Reading

A word in your ear!

Well here it is! We're more proud than we can say, to present to you…the legendary and classic E.E Doc Smith Lensman series! Welcome to a universe of high adventure, square-jawed heroes, valve technology, fishbowl helmets and streamlined rocket-ships!

When we first considered the concept of reprinting and recreating the types of heroes once found on the back of cigarette cards; 'Doc' Smith's classic Lensman series was the top of our acquisition list!

Politically incorrect?—Yes!

Technically dated?—Definitely!

Simplistic and naïve?—Maybe!

Absolutely Ripping?—Without question!

Often called the 'Father of Space Opera' E.E Doc Smith wrote Triplanetary the first of the Lensman series in 1934 and it was initially printed in one of the American pulp SF magazines of that period. The other titles in the series were written in the late 30's and 40's.

Judged solely on entertainment value, it is our opinion that the Lensman series out-performs almost anything available in contemporary Science Fiction. However, it's very important that when reading the Lensman series you realise the period in which the books were written.

The world at that time was a political maelstrom of Fascism and Communism, overshadowed by a looming second World War. To many at that time, the United States of America appeared an island of strength and honour—willing to drop everything to defend freedom, democracy and the dollar.

The world has changed considerably since then—although it's just as confusing. Undoubtedly, we are all a lot more cynical about our lives and political masters. Which is why some sixty years later, it's kind of nice to imagine that somewhere out there among the stars, are people still willing to fight for freedom, democracy and American apple pie!

Here it is; the original star-war saga. It ain't Shakespeare, but it is one hell of a *Ripping* Yarn!

Warren James Palmer

100612,3072@compuserve.uk

Sikmon Shinerock

You can also contact us at our website—

Ripping.com.UK

About the Author

Edward Elmer Smith was born in the United Stated in 1890 and died in 1965. Often called the *'Father of Space Opera'*, he became known as *'Doc'* Smith because of his PhD and work as a food chemist. He first became well known as a writer during the period 1928 to 1945 when he was greatly influential in the pulp SF magazines of that period. However, he found his popularity fading after the second world war possibly due to the new world order emerging at that time. The simpler prewar days appeared to be gone forever and much of the pulp SF fiction with it.

However, his works were reprinted by small specialist publishing houses in the late 40's and 50's and they attracted an ever-growing readership of new readers. By the time of his death in 1965 new generations of SF fans had made EES a bestselling writer firstly in the USA then later in the UK.

The *Lensman* series is seen by many as E.E 'Doc' Smith's most definitive work with its theme of a hierarchical order to the universe. The first in the series was written in 1934 which explains why part of the first section of *Triplanetary* takes place at the Western Front during the first world war of 1914-1918. Before WWII, this was known as the 'Great War' and was a great influence on writers at that time. The remainder of the series were written in a period from 1937 to 1948 except for *Masters of the Vortex*. This title was completed some time later and although it takes place in the Lensman universe, it is outside the central plot.

E.E 'Doc' Smith also wrote the *Skylark* series which he began work on in 1915. The *Family d'Alembert* series was also attributed to EES but was derived posthumously from incomplete manuscripts by Stephen Goldin. The *Lensman* series is undoubtedly a classic and to the best of our knowledge, this is the twelfth time it has been printed in its entirety.

BOOK TWO

FIRST LENSMAN

CHAPTER 1

The visitor, making his way unobserved through the crowded main laboratory of The Hill, stepped up to within six feet of the back of a big Norwegian seated at an electrono-optical bench. Drawing an automatic pistol, he shot the apparently unsuspecting scientist seven times, as fast as he could pull the trigger; twice through the brain, five times, closely spaced, through the spine.

'Ah, Gharlane of Eddore, I have been expecting you to look me up. Sit down.' Blonde, blue-eyed Dr. Nels Bergenholm, completely undisturbed by the passage of the stream of bullets through his head and body, turned and waved one huge hand at a stool beside his own.

'But those were not ordinary projectiles!' the visitor protested. Neither person—or rather, entity—was in the least surprised that no one else had paid any attention to what had happened, but it was clear that the one was taken aback by the failure of his murderous attack. 'They should have volatilised that form of flesh—should at least have blown you back to Arisia, where you belong.'

'Ordinary or extraordinary, what matter? As you, in the guise of Grey Roger, told Conway Costigan a short time since, "I permitted that, as a demonstration of futility." Know, Gharlane, once and for all, that you will no longer be allowed to act directly against any adherent of Civilisation, wherever situate. We of Arisia will not interfere in person with your proposed conquest of the two galaxies as you have planned it, since the stresses and conflicts involved are necessary—and, I may add, sufficient—to produce the Civilisation which must and shall come into being. Therefore, neither

will you, or any other Eddorian, so interfere. You will go back to Eddore and you will stay there.'

'Think you so?' Gharlane sneered. 'You, who have been so afraid of us for over two thousand million Tellurian years that you dared not let us even learn of you? So afraid of us that you dared not take any action to avert the destruction of any one of your budding Civilisations upon any one of the worlds of either galaxy? So afraid that you dare not, even now, meet me mind to mind, but insist upon the use of this slow and unsatisfactory oral communication between us?'

'Either your thinking is loose, confused, and turbid, which I do not believe to be the case, or you are trying to lull me into believing that you are stupid.' Bergenholm's voice was calm, unmoved. 'I do not *think* that you will go back to Eddore; I know it. You, too, as soon as you have become informed upon certain matters, will know it. You protest against the use of spoken language because it is, as you know, the easiest, simplest, and surest way of preventing you from securing any iota of the knowledge for which you are so desperately searching. As to a meeting of our two minds, they met fully just before you, operating as Grey Roger, remembered that which your entire race forgot long ago. As a consequence of that meeting I so learned every line and vibration of your life pattern as to be able to greet you by your symbol, Gharlane of Eddore, whereas you know nothing of me save that I am an Arisian, a fact which has been obvious from the first.'

In an attempt to create a diversion, Gharlane released the zone of compulsion which he had been holding; but the Arisian took it over so smoothly that no human being within range was conscious of any change.

'It is true that for many cycles of time we concealed our existence from you.' Bergenholm went on without a break. 'Since the reason for that concealment will

still further confuse you, I will tell you what it was. Had you Eddorians learned of us sooner you might have been able to forge a weapon of power sufficient to prevent the accomplishment of an end which is now certain.

'It is true that your operations as Lo Sung of Uighar were not constrained. As Mithridates of Pontus—as Sulla, Marius, and Nero of Rome—as Hannibal of Carthage—as those self-effacing wights Alcixerxes of Greece and Menocoptes of Egypt—as Genghis Khan and Attila and the Kaiser and Mussolini and Hitler and the Tyrant of Asia—you were allowed to do as you pleased. Similar activities upon Rigel Four, Velantia, Palain Seven, and elsewhere were also allowed to proceed without effective opposition. With the appearance of Virgil Samms, however, the time arrived to put an end to your customary pernicious, obstructive, and destructive activities. I therefore interposed a barrier between you and those who would otherwise be completely defenceless against you.'

'But why now? Why not thousands of cycles ago? And why Virgil Samms?'

'To answer those questions would be to give you valuable data. You may—too late—be able to answer them yourself. But to continue: you accuse me, and all Arisia, of cowardice; an evidently muddy and inept thought. Reflect, please, upon the completeness of your failure in the affair of Roger's planetoid; upon the fact that you have accomplished nothing whatever since that time; upon the situation in which you now find yourself.

'Even though the trend of thought of your race is basically materialistic and mechanistic, and you belittle ours as being "philosophic" and "impractical", you found—much to your surprise—that your most destructive physical agencies are not able to affect

even this form of flesh which I am now energising, to say nothing of affecting the reality which is I.

'If this episode is the result of the customary thinking of the second-in-command of Eddore's Innermost Circle...but no, my visualisation cannot be that badly at fault. Overconfidence—the tyrant's innate proclivity to underestimate an opponent—these things have put you in a false position; but I greatly fear that they will not operate to do so in any really important future affair.'

'Rest assured that they will not!' Gharlane snarled. 'It may not be—exactly—cowardice. It is, however, something closely akin. If you could have acted effectively against us at any time in the past, you would have done so. If you could act effectively against us now, you would be acting, not talking. That is elementary—self-evidently true. So true that you have not tried to deny it—nor would you expect me to believe you if you did.' Cold black eyes stared level into icy eyes of Norwegian blue.

'Deny it? No. I am glad, however, that you used the word "effectively" instead of "openly"; for we have been acting effectively against you ever since these newly-formed planets cooled sufficiently to permit of the development of intelligent life.'

'What? You have? How?'

'That, too, you may learn—too late. I have now said all I intend to say. I will give you no more information. Since you already know that there are more adult Arisians than there are Eddorians, so that at least one of us can devote his full attention to blocking the direct effort of any one of you, it is clear to you that it makes no difference to me whether you elect to go or to stay. I can and I will remain here as long as you do; I can and I will accompany you whenever you venture out of the volume of space

protected by Eddorian screen, wherever you go. The election is yours.'

Gharlane disappeared. So did the Arisian—instantaneously. Dr. Nels Bergenholm, however, remained. Turning, he resumed his work where he had left off, knowing exactly what he had been doing and exactly what he was going to do to finish it. He released the zone of compulsion, which he had been holding upon every human being within sight or hearing, so dextrously that no one suspected, then or ever, that anything out of the ordinary had happened. He knew these things and did these things in spite of the fact that the form of flesh which his fellows of the Triplanetary Service knew as Nels Bergenholm was then being energised, not by the stupendously powerful mind of Drounli the Moulder, but by an Arisian child too young to be of any use in that which was about to occur.

Arisia was ready. Every Arisian mind capable of adult, or of even near-adult thinking was poised to act when the moment of action should come. They were not, however, tense. While not in any sense routine, that which they were about to do had been foreseen for many cycles of time. They knew exactly what they were going to do, and exactly how to do it. They waited.

'My visualisation is not entirely clear concerning the succession of events stemming from the fact that the fusion of which Drounli is a part did not destroy Gharlane of Eddore while he was energising Grey Roger,' a young Watchman, Eukonidor by symbol, thought into the assembled mind. 'May I take a moment of this idle time in which to spread my visualisation, for enlargement and instruction?'

'You may, youth.' The Elders of Arisia—the mightiest intellects of that tremendously powerful race—fused their several minds into one mind and

gave approval. 'That will be time well spent. Think on.'

'Separated from the other Eddorians by inter-galactic distance as he then was, Gharlane could have been isolated and could have been destroyed,' the youth pointed out, as he somewhat diffidently spread his visualisation in the public mind. 'Since it is axiomatic that his destruction would have weakened Eddore somewhat and to that extent would have helped us, it is evident that some greater advantage will accrue from allowing him to live. Some points are clear enough: that Gharlane and his fellows will believe that the Arisian fusion could not kill him, since it did not; that the Eddorians, contemptuous of our powers and thinking us vastly their inferiors, will not be driven to develop such things as atomic-energy-powered mechanical screens against third-level thought until such a time as it will be too late for even those devices to save their race from extinction; that they will, in all probability, never even suspect that the Galactic Patrol which is so soon to come into being will in fact be the prime operator in that extinction. It is not clear, however, in view of the above facts, why it has now become necessary for us to slay one Eddorian upon Eddore. Nor can I formulate or visualise with any clarity the techniques to be employed in the final wiping out of the race; I lack certain fundamental data concerning events which occurred and conditions which obtained many, many cycles before my birth. I am unable to believe that my perception and memory could have been so imperfect—can it be that none of that basic data is, or ever has been available?'

'That, youth, is the fact. While your visualisation of the future is of course not as detailed nor as accurate as it will be after more cycles of labour, your background of knowledge is as complete as that of any other of our number.'

'I see.' Eukonidor gave the mental equivalent of a nod of complete understanding. 'It is necessary, and the death of a lesser Eddorian—a Watchman—will be sufficient. Nor will it be either surprising or alarming to Eddore's Innermost Circle that the integrated total mind of Arisia should be able to kill such a relatively feeble entity. I see.'

Then silence; and waiting. Minutes? Or days? Or weeks? Who can tell? What does time mean to any Arisian?

Then Drounli arrived; arrived in the instant of his leaving The Hill—what matters even intergalactic distance to the speed of thought? He fused his mind with those of the three other Moulders of Civilisation. The massed and united mind of Arisia, poised and ready, awaiting only his coming, launched itself through space. That tremendous, that theretofore unknown concentration of mental force arrived at Eddore's outer screen in practically the same instant as did the entity that was Gharlane. The Eddorian, however, went through without opposition; the Arisians did not.

Some two thousand million years ago, when the Coalescence occurred—the event which was to make each of the two interpassing galaxies teem with planets—the Arisians were already an ancient race; so ancient that they were even then independent of the chance formation of planets. The Eddorians, it is believed, were older still. The Arisians were native to this, our normal space-time continuum; the Eddorians were not.

Eddore was—and is—huge, dense, and hot. Its atmosphere is not air, as we of small, green Terra, know air, but is a noxious mixture of gaseous substances known to mankind only in chemical laboratories. Its hydrosphere, while it does contain

some water, is a poisonous, stinking, foully corrosive, slimy and sludgy liquid.

And the Eddorians were as different from any people we know as Eddore is different from the planets indigenous to our space and time. They were, to our senses, utterly monstrous; almost incomprehensible. They were amorphous, amoeboid, sexless. Not androgynous or parthenogenetic, but absolutely sexless; with a sexlessness unknown in any Earthly form of life higher than the yeasts. Thus they were, to all intents and purposes and except for death by violence, immortal; for each one, after having lived for hundreds of thousands of Tellurian years and having reached its capacity to live and to learn, simply divided into two new individuals, each of which, in addition to possessing in full its parent's mind and memories and knowledges, had also a brand-new zest and a greatly increased capacity.

And, since life was, there had been competition. Competition for power. Knowledge was worthwhile only insofar as it contributed to power. Warfare began, and aged, and continued; the appallingly efficient warfare possible only to such entities as those. Their minds, already immensely powerful, grew stronger and stronger under the stresses of internecine struggle.

But peace was not even thought of. Strife continued, at higher and even higher levels of violence, until two facts became apparent. First, that every Eddorian who could be killed by physical violence had already died; that the survivors had developed such tremendous powers of mind, such complete mastery of things physical as well as mental, that they could not be slain by physical force. Second, that during the ages through which they had been devoting their every effort to mutual extermination, their sun had begun markedly to cool; that their planet would very soon become so cold that it would be impossible for them ever again to live their normal physical lives.

Thus there came about an armistice. The Eddorians worked together—not without friction—in the development of mechanisms by the use of which they moved their planet across light-years of space to a younger, hotter sun. Then, Eddore once more at its hot and reeking norm, battle was resumed. Mental battle, this time, that went on for more than a hundred thousand Eddorian years; during the last ten thousand of which not a single Eddorian died.

Realising the futility of such unproductive endeavour, the relatively few survivors made a peace of sorts. Since each had an utterly insatiable lust for power, and since it had become clear that they could neither conquer nor kill each other, they would combine forces and conquer enough planets—enough galaxies—so that each Eddorian could have as much power and authority as he could possibly handle.

What matter that there were not that many planets in their native space? There were other spaces, an infinite number of them; some of which, it was mathematically certain, would contain millions upon millions of planets instead of only two or three. By mind and by machine they surveyed the neighbouring continua; they developed the hyper-spatial tube and the inertialess drive; they drove their planet, space-ship-wise, through space after space after space.

And thus, shortly after the Coalescence began, Eddore came into our space-time; and here, because of the multitudes of planets already existing and the untold millions more about to come into existence, it stayed. Here was what they wanted since their beginnings; here were planets enough, here were fields enough for the exercise of power, to sate even the insatiable. There was no longer any need for them to fight each other; they could now co-operate whole-heartedly—as long as each was getting more—and *more* and MORE!

Enphilistor, a young Arisian, his mind roaming eagerly abroad as was its wont, made first contact with the Eddorians in this space. Inoffensive, naive, innocent, he was surprised beyond measure at their reception; but in the instant before closing his mind to their vicious attacks, he learned the foregoing facts concerning them.

The fused mind of the Elders of Arisia, however, was not surprised. The Arisians, while not as mechanistic as their opponents, and innately peaceful as well, were far ahead of them in the pure science of the mind. The Elders had long known of the Eddorians and of their lustful wanderings through plenum after plenum. The Visualisations of the Cosmic All had long since forecast, with dreadful certainty, the invasion which had now occurred. They had long known what they would have to do. They did it. So insidiously as to set up no opposition they entered the Eddorians' minds and sealed off all knowledge of Arisia. They withdrew, tracelessly.

They did not have much data, it is true; but no more could be obtained at that time. If any one of those touchy suspicious minds had been given any cause for alarm, any focal point of doubt, they would have had time in which to develop mechanisms able to force the Arisians out of this space before a weapon to destroy the Eddorians—the as yet incompletely designed Galactic Patrol—could be forged. The Arisians could, even then, have slain by mental force alone all the Eddorians except the All-Highest and his Innermost Circle, safe within their then impenetrable shield; but as long as they could not make a clean sweep they could not attack—then.

Be it observed that the Arisians were not fighting for themselves. As individuals or as a race they had nothing to fear. Even less than the Eddorians could they be killed by any possible application of physical force. Past masters of mental science, they knew that

no possible concentration of Eddorian mental force could kill any one of them. And if they were to be forced out of normal space, what matter? To such mentalities as theirs, any given space would serve as well as any other.

No, they were fighting for an ideal; for the peaceful, harmonious, liberty-loving Civilisation which they had envisaged as developing throughout, and eventually entirely covering the myriads of planets of two tremendous Island Universes. Also, they felt a heavy weight of responsibility. Since all these races, existing and yet to appear, had sprung from and would spring from the Arisian life-spores which permeated this particular space, they all were and would be, at bottom, Arisian. It was starkly unthinkable that Arisia would leave them to the eternal dominance of such a rapacious, such a tyrannical, such a hellishly insatiable breed of monsters.

Therefore the Arisians fought; efficiently if insidiously. They did not—they could not—interfere openly with Eddore's ruthless conquest of world after world; with Eddore's ruthless smashing of Civilisation after Civilisation. They did, however, see to it, by selective matings and the establishment of blood-lines upon numberless planets, that the trend of the level of intelligence was definitely and steadily upward.

Four Moulders of Civilisation—Drounli, Kriedigan, Nedanillor, and Brolenteen, who, in fusion, formed the "Mentor of Arisia" who was to become known to every wearer of Civilisation's Lens—were individually responsible for the Arisian programme of development upon the four planets of Tellus, Rigel IV, Velantia, and Palain VII. Drounli established upon Tellus two principal lines of blood. In unbroken male line of descent the Kinnisons went back to long before the dawn of even mythical Tellurian history. Kinnexa of Atlantis, daughter of one Kinnison and sister of another, is the first of the blood to be named in these

annals; but the line was then already old. So was the other line; characterised throughout its tremendous length, male and female, by peculiarly spectacular red-bronze-auburn hair and equally striking gold-flecked, tawny eyes.

Nor did these strains mix. Drounli had made it psychologically impossible for them to mix until the penultimate stage of development should have been reached.

While that stage was still in the future Virgil Samms appeared, and all Arisia knew that the time had come to engage the Eddorians openly, mind to mind. Gharlane-Roger was curbed, savagely and sharply. Every Eddorian, wherever he was working, found his every line of endeavour solidly blocked.

Gharlane, as has been intimated, constructed a supposedly irresistible weapon and attacked his Arisian blocker, with results already told. At that failure Gharlane knew that there was something terribly amiss; that it had been amiss for over two thousand million Tellurian years. Really alarmed for the first time in his long life, he flashed back to Eddore; to warn his fellows and to take counsel with them as to what should be done. And the massed and integrated force of all Arisia was only an instant behind him.

Arisia struck Eddore's outermost screen, and in the instant of impact that screen went down. And then, instantaneously and all unperceived by the planet's defenders, the Arisian forces split. The Elders, including all the Moulders, seized the Eddorian who had been handling that screen—threw around him an impenetrable net of force—yanked him out into intergalactic space.

Then, driving in resistlessly, they turned the luckless wight inside out. And before the victim died under their poignant probings, the Elders of Arisia learned everything that the Eddorian and all of his ancestors had ever known. They then withdrew to Arisia, leaving their younger, weaker, partially-developed fellows to do whatever they could against mighty Eddore.

Whether the attack of these lesser forces would be stopped at the second, the third, the fourth, or the innermost screen; whether they would reach the planet itself and perhaps do some actual damage before being driven off; was immaterial. Eddore must be allowed and would be allowed to repel that invasion with ease. For cycles to come the Eddorians must and would believe that they had nothing really to fear from Arisia.

The real battle, however, had been won. The Arisian visualisations could now be extended to portray every essential element of the climactic conflict which was eventually to come. It was no cheerful conclusion at which the Arisians arrived, since their visualisations all agreed in showing that the only possible method of wiping out the Eddorians would also of necessity end their own usefulness as Guardians of Civilisation.

Such an outcome having been shown necessary, however, the Arisians accepted it, and worked toward it, unhesitatingly.

CHAPTER 2

As has been said, The Hill, which had been built to be the Tellurian headquarters of the Triplanetary Service and which was now the headquarters of the half-organised Solarian Patrol, was—and is—a truncated, alloy-sheathed, honeycombed mountain. But, since human beings do not like to live eternally underground, no matter how beautifully lighted or how carefully and comfortably air-conditioned the dungeon may be, the Reservation spread far beyond the foot of that grey, forbidding, mirror-smooth cone of metal. Well outside that far-flung Reservation there was a small city; there were hundreds of highly productive farms; and, particularly upon this bright May afternoon, there was a Recreation Park, containing, among other things, dozens of tennis courts.

One of these courts was three-quarters enclosed by stands, from which a couple of hundred people were watching a match which seemed to be of some little local importance. Two men sat in a box which had seats for twenty, and watched admiringly the pair who seemed in a fair way to win in straight sets the mixed-doubles championship of the Hill.

'Fine-looking couple, Rod, if I do say so myself, as well as being smooth performers.' Solarian Councillor Virgil Samms spoke to his companion as the opponents changed courts. 'I still think, though the young hussy ought to wear some clothes—those white nylon shorts make her look nakeder even than usual. I told her so, too, the jade, but she keeps on wearing less and less.'

'Of course,' Commissioner Roderick K. Kinnison laughed quietly. 'What did you expect? She got her

hair and eyes from you, why not your hard-headedness, too? One thing, though, that's all to the good—she's got what it takes to strip ship that way, and most of 'em haven't. But what I can't understand is why they don't...' He paused.

'I don't either. Lord knows we've thrown them at each other hard enough, and Jack Kinnison and Jill Samms would certainly make a pair to draw to. But if they won't...but maybe they will yet. They're still youngsters, and they're friendly enough.'

If Samms Pere could have been out on the court, however, instead of in the box, he would have been surprised; for young Kinnison, although smiling enough as to face, was addressing his gorgeous partner in terms which carried little indeed of friendliness.

'Listen, you bird-brained, knot-headed, grand-standing half-wit!' he stormed, voice low but bitterly intense. 'I ought to beat your alleged brains out! I've told you a thousand times to watch your own territory and *stay out of mine!* If you had been where you belonged, or even taken my signal, Frank couldn't have made that thirty-all point; and if Lois hadn't netted she'd've caught you flat-footed, a kilometre out of position, and made it deuce. What do you think you're doing, anyway—playing tennis or seeing how many innocent bystanders you can bring down out of control?'

'What do *you* think?' the girl sneered, sweetly. Her tawny eyes, only a couple of inches below his own, almost emitted sparks. 'And just look at who's trying to tell who how to do what! For your information, Master Pilot John K. Kinnison, I'll tell you that just because you can't quit being "Killer" Kinnison even long enough to let two good friends of ours get a point now and then, or maybe even a game, is no reason

why I've got to turn into "Killer" Samms. And I'll also tell you...'

'You'll tell me nothing, Jill—I'm telling you! Start giving away points in anything and you'll find out some day that you've given away too many. I'm not having any of that kind of game—and as long as you're playing with me you aren't either—or else. If you louse up this match just once more, the next ball I serve will hit the tightest part of those fancy white shorts of yours—right where the hip pocket would be if they had any—and it'll raise a welt that will make you eat off of the mantel for three days. So watch your step!'

'You insufferable lug! I'd like to smash this racket over your head! I'll do it, too, and walk off the court, if you don't...'

The whistle blew. Virgilia Samms, all smiles, toed the base-line and became the personification and embodiment of smoothly flowing motion. The ball whizzed over the net, barely clearing it—a sizzling service ace. The game went on.

And a few minutes later, in the shower room, where Jack Kinnison was carolling lustily while plying a towel, a huge young man strode up and slapped him ringingly between the shoulder blades.

'Congratulations, Jack, and so forth. But there's a thing I want to ask you. Confidential, sort of...?'

'Shoot! Haven't we been eating out of the same dish for lo, these many moons? Why the diffidence all of a sudden, Mase? It isn't in character.'

'Well...it's...I'm a lip-reader, you know.'

'Sure. We all are. What of it?'

'It's only that...well, I saw what you and Miss Samms said to each other out there, and if that was lovers' small talk I'm a Venerian mud-puppy.'

'*Lovers!* Who the hell ever said we were lovers?...Oh, you've been inhaling some of dad's balloon-juice. *Lovers!* Me and that red-headed stinker—that jelly-brained sapadilly? *Hardly!*'

'Hold it, Jack!' The big officer's voice was slightly edged. 'You're off course—a hell of a long flit off. That girl has got everything. She's the class of the Reservation—why, she's a regular twelve-nineteen!'

'Huh?' Amazed, young Kinnison stopped drying himself and stared. 'You mean to say you've been giving her a miss just because...' He had started to say "because you're the best friend I've got in the System," but he did not.

'Well, it would have smelled slightly cheesy, I thought.' The other man did not put into words, either, what both of them so deeply knew to be the truth. 'But if you haven't got...if it's OK with you, of course...'

'Stand by for five seconds—I'll take you around.'

Jack threw on his uniform, and in a few minutes the two young officers, immaculate in the space-black-and-silver of the Patrol, made their way towards the women's dressing rooms.

'...but she's all right, at that...in most ways...I guess.' Kinnison was half-apologising for what he had said. 'Outside of being chicken-hearted and pig-headed, she's a good egg. She really qualifies...most of the time. But I wouldn't have her, bonus attached, any more than she would have me. It's strictly mutual. You won't fall for her, either, Mase; you'll want to pull one of her legs off and beat the rest of her to death with it inside of a week—but there's nothing like finding things out for yourself.'

In a short time Miss Samms appeared; dressed somewhat less revealingly than before in the blouse and kilt which were the mode of the moment.

'Hi, Jill! This is Mase—I've told you about him. My boat-mate, Master Electronicist Mason Northrop.'

'Yes, I've heard about you, 'Troncist—a lot.' She shook hands warmly.

'He hasn't been putting tracers on you, Jill, on accounta he figured he'd be poaching. Can you feature that? I straightened him out, though, in short order. Told him why, too, so he ought to be insulated against any voltage you can generate.'

'Oh, you did? How sweet of you! But how...oh, those?' She gestured at the powerful prism binoculars, a part of the uniform of every officer of space.

'Uh-huh.' Northrop wriggled, but held firm.

'If I'd only been as big and husky as you are,' surveying admiringly some six feet two of altitude and two hundred odd pounds of hard meat, gristle, and bone, 'I'd have grabbed him by one ankle, whirled him around my head, and flung him into the fifteenth row of seats. What's the matter with him, Mase, is that he was born centuries and centuries too late. He should have been an overseer when they built the pyramids—flogging slaves because they wouldn't step just so. Or better yet, one of those people it told about in those funny old books they dug up last year—liege lords, or something like that, remember? With the power of life and death—"high, middle, and low justice", whatever that was—over their vassals and their families, serfs, and serving-wenches. *Especially* serving-wenches! He likes little, cuddly baby-talkers, who pretend to be utterly spineless and completely brainless—eh, Jack?'

'Ouch! Touch, Jill—but maybe I had it coming to me, at that. Let's call it off, shall we? I'll be seeing you two, hither or yon.' Kinnison turned and hurried away.

'Want to know why he's doing such a quick flit? Jill grinned up at her companion; a bright, quick grin.

'Not that he was giving up. The blonde over there—the one in rocket red. Very few blondes can wear such a violent shade. Dimples Maynard.'

'And is she... er...?'

'Cuddly and baby-talkish? Uh-uh. She's a grand person. I was just popping off; so was he. You know that neither of us really meant half of what we said...or...at least...' Her voice died away.

'I don't know whether I do or not,' Northrop replied, awkwardly but honestly. 'That was savage stuff if there ever was any. I can't see for the life of me why you two—two of the world's finest people—should have to tear into each other that way. Do you?'

'I don't know that I ever thought of it like that.' Jill caught her lower lip between her teeth. 'He's splendid, really, and I like him a lot—usually. We get along perfectly most of the time. We don't fight at all except when we're too close together... and then we fight about anything and everything... say, suppose that that could be it? Like charges, repelling each other inversely as the square of the distance? That's about the way it seems to be.'

'Could be, and I'm glad.' The man's face cleared. 'And I'm a charge of the opposite sign. Let's go!'

And in Virgil Samms' deeply buried office, Civilisation's two strongest men were deep in conversation.

'...troubles enough to keep four men of our size awake nights.' Samms' voice was light, but his eyes were moody and sombre. 'You can probably whip yours, though, in time. They're mostly in one solar system; a short flit covers the rest. Languages and customs are known. But how—*how*—can legal processes work efficiently—work at all, for that

matter—when a man can commit a murder or a pirate can loot a space-ship and be a hundred parsecs away before the crime is even discovered? How can a Tellurian John Law find a criminal on a strange world that knows nothing whatever of our Patrol, with a completely alien language—maybe no language at all—where it takes months even to find out who and where—if any—the native police officers are? But there must be a way, Rod—there's *got* to be a way!' Samms slammed his open hand resoundingly against his desk's bare top. 'And by God I'll find it—the Patrol *will* come out on top!'

' "Crusader" Samms, now and forever!' There was no trace of mockery in Kinnison's voice or expression, but only friendship and admiration. 'And I'll bet you do. Your Interstellar Patrol, or whatever...'

'Galactic Patrol. I know what the name of it is going to be, if nothing else.'

'... is just as good as in the bag, right now. You've done a job so far, Virge. This whole system, Nevia, the colonies on Aldebaran II and other planets, even Valeria, as tight as a drum. Funny about Valeria, isn't it...'

There was a moment of silence, then Kinnison went on:

'But wherever diamonds are, there go Dutchmen. And Dutch women go wherever their men do. And in spite of medical advice, Dutch babies arrive. Although a lot of the adults died—three G's is no joke—practically all of the babies keep on living. Developing bones and muscles to fit—walking at a year and a half old—living normally—they say that the third generation will be perfectly at home there.'

'Which shows that the human animal is more adaptable than some ranking medicos had believed, is all. Don't try to side-track me, Rod. You know as

well as I do what we're up against; the new headaches that interstellar commerce is bringing with it. New vices—drugs—thionite, for instance; we haven't been able to get an inkling of an idea as to where that stuff is coming from. And I don't have to tell you what piracy has done to insurance rates.'

'I'll say not—look at the price of Aldebaranian cigars, the only kind fit to smoke! You've given up, then, on the idea that Arisia is the pirates' GHQ?'

'Definitely. It isn't. The pirates are even more afraid of it than tramp spacemen are. It's out of bounds—absolutely forbidden territory, apparently—to everybody, my best operatives included. All we know about it is the name—Arisia—that our planetographers gave it. It is the first completely incomprehensible thing I have ever experienced. I am going out there myself as soon as I can take the time—not that I expect to crack a thing that my best men couldn't touch, but there have been so many different and conflicting reports—no two stories agree on anything except in that no one could get anywhere near the planet—that I feel the need of some first-hand information. Want to come along?'

'Try to keep me from it!'

'But at that, we shouldn't be too surprised,' Samms went on, thoughtfully. 'Just beginning to scratch the surface as we are, we should expect to encounter peculiar, baffling—even completely inexplicable things. Facts, situations, events, and beings for which our one-system experience could not possibly have prepared us. In fact, we already have. If, ten years ago, anyone had told you that such a race as the Rigellians existed, what would you have thought? One ship went there, you know—once. One hour in any Rigellian city—one minute in a Rigellian automobile—drives a Tellurian insane.'

'I see your point.' Kinnison nodded. 'Probably I would have ordered a mental examination. And the Palainians are even worse. People—if you can call them that—who live on Pluto and *like* it! Entities so alien that nobody as far as I know, understands them. But you don't have to go even that far from home to locate a job of unscrewing the inscrutable. Who, what, and why—and for how long—was Grey Roger? And, not far behind him, is this young Bergenholm of yours. And by the way, you never did give me the low-down on how come it was the "Bergenholm", and not the "Rodebush-Cleveland", that made trans-galactic commerce possible and caused nine-tenths of our headaches. As I get the story, Bergenholm wasn't—isn't—even an engineer.'

'Didn't I? Thought I did. He wasn't, and isn't. Well, the original Rodebush-Cleveland free drive was a killer, you know...'

'*How* I know!' Kinnison exclaimed, feelingly.

'They beat their brains out and ate their hearts out for months, without getting it any better. Then, one day, this kid Bergenholm ambles into their shop—big, awkward, stumbling over his own feet. He gazes innocently at the thing for a couple of minutes, then says:

'Why don't you use uranium instead of iron and rewind it so it will put out a wave-form like this, with humps here, and here; instead of there, and there?' and he draws a couple of free-hand, but really beautiful curves.

' "Why should we?" they squawk at him.

' "Because it will work that way," he says, and ambles out as unconcernedly as he came in. Can't—or won't—say another word.

'Well in sheer desperation, they tried it—and it WORKED! And nobody has ever had a minute's

trouble with a Bergenholm since. That's why Rodebush and Cleveland both insisted on the name.'

'I see; and it points up what I just said. But if he's such a mental giant, why isn't he getting results with his own problem, the meteor? Or is he?'

'No...or at least he wasn't as of last night. But there's a note on my pad that he wants to see me sometime today—suppose we have him come in now?'

'Fine! I'd like to talk to him, if it's OK with you and with him.'

The young scientist was called in, and was introduced to the Commissioner.

'Go ahead, Doctor Bergenholm,' Samms suggested then. 'You may talk to both of us, just as freely as though you and I were alone.'

'I have, as you already know, been called psychic,' Bergenholm began, abruptly. 'It is said that I dream dreams, see visions, hear voices, and so on. That I operate on hunches. That I am a genius. Now I very definitely am *not* a genius—unless my understanding of the meaning of that word is different from that of the rest of mankind.'

Bergenholm paused. Samms and Kinnison looked at each other. The latter broke the short silence.

'The Councillor and I have just been discussing the fact that there are a great many things we do not know; that with the extension of our activities into new fields, the occurrence of the impossible has become almost a commonplace. We are able, I believe, to listen with open minds to anything you have to say.'

'Very well. But first, please know that I am a scientist. As such, I am trained to observe; to think calmly, clearly, and analytically; to test every hypothesis. I do not believe at all in the so-called supernatural. This universe did not come into being, it does not continue

to be, except by the operation of natural and immutable laws. And I mean *immutable*, gentlemen. Everything that has ever happened, that is happening now, or that is ever to happen, was, is, and will be statistically connected with its predecessor event and with its successor event. If I did not believe that implicitly, I would lose all faith in the scientific method. For if one single "supernatural" event or thing had ever occurred or existed it would have constituted an entirely unpredictable event and would have initiated a series—a succession—of such events; a state of things which no scientist will or can believe possible in an orderly universe.

'At the same time, I recognise the fact that I myself have done things—caused events to occur, if you prefer—that I cannot explain to you or to any other human being in any symbology known to our science; and it is about an even more inexplicable—call it "hunch" if you like—that I asked to have a talk with you today.'

'But you are arguing in circles,' Samms protested. 'Or are you trying to set up a paradox?'

'Neither. I am merely clearing the way for a somewhat startling thing I am to say later on. You know, of course, that any situation with which a mind is unable to cope; a really serious dilemma which it cannot resolve; will destroy that mind—frustration, escape from reality, and so on. You also will realise that I must have become cognizant of my own peculiarities long before anyone else did or could?'

'Ah, I see. Yes, of course.' Samms, intensely interested, leaned forward. 'Yet your present personality is adequately, splendidly integrated. How could you possibly have overcome—reconciled—a situation so full of conflict?'

'You are, I think, familiar with my parentage?' Samms, keen as he was, did not consider it noteworthy

that the big Norwegian answered his question only by asking one of his own.

'Yes…oh, I'm beginning to see…but Commissioner Kinnison has not had access to your dossier. Go ahead.'

'My father is Dr. Hjalmar Bergenholm. My mother, before her marriage, was Dr. Olga Bjornson. Both were, and are, nuclear physicists—very good ones. Pioneers, they have been called. They worked, and are still working, in the newest, outermost fringes of the field.'

'Oh!' Kinnison exclaimed. 'A mutant? Born with second sight—or whatever it is?'

'Not second sight, as history describes the phenomenon, no. The records do not show that any such faculty was ever demonstrated to the satisfaction of any competent scientific investigator. What I have is something else. Whether or not it will breed true is an interesting topic of speculation, but one having nothing to do with the problem now in hand. To return to the subject, I resolved my dilemma long since. There is, I am absolutely certain, a science of the mind which is as definite, as positive, as immutable of law, as is the science of the physical. While I will make no attempt to prove it to you, I *know* that such a science exists, and that I was born with the ability to perceive at least some elements of it.

'Now to the matter of the meteor of the Patrol. That emblem was and is purely physical. The pirates have just as able scientists as we have. What physical science can devise and synthesize, physical science can analyse and duplicate. There is a point, however, beyond which physical science cannot go. It can neither analyse nor imitate the tangible products of that which I have so loosely called the science of the mind.

'I know, Councillor Samms, what the Triplanetary Service needs; something vastly more than its meteor. I also know that the need will become greater and greater as the sphere of action of the Patrol expands. Without a really efficient symbol, the Solarian Patrol will be hampered even more than the Triplanetary Service; and its logical extension into the Space Patrol, or whatever that larger organisation may be called, will be definitely impossible. We need something which will identify any representative of Civilisation, positively and unmistakably, wherever he may be. It must be impossible of duplication, or even of imitation, to which end it must kill any unauthorised entity who attempts imposture. It must operate as a telepath between its owner and any other living intelligence, of however high or low degree, so that mental communication, so much clearer and faster than physical, will be possible without the laborious learning of language; or between us and such peoples as those of Rigel Four or of Palain Seven, both of whom we know to be of high intelligence and who must already be conversant with telepathy.'

'Are you or have you been, reading my mind?' Samms asked quietly.

'No,' Bergenholm replied flatly. 'It is not and has not been necessary. Any man who can think, who has really considered the question, and who has the good of Civilisation at heart, must have come to the same conclusions.'

'Probably so, at that. But no more side issues. You have a solution of some kind worked out, or you would not be here. What is it?'

'It is that you, Solarian Councillor Samms, should go to Arisia as soon as possible.'

'Arisia!' Samms exclaimed, and:

'Arisia! Of all the hells in space, why Arisia? And how can we make the approach? Don't you know that *nobody* can get anywhere near that damn planet?'

Bergenholm shrugged his shoulders and spread both arms wide in a pantomime of complete helplessness.

'How do you know—another of your hunches?' Kinnison went on. 'Or did somebody tell you something? *Where* did you get it?'

'It is not a hunch,' the Norwegian replied, positively. 'No one told me anything. But I *know*—as definitely as I know that the combustion of hydrogen in oxygen will yield water—that the Arisians are very well versed in that which I have called the science of the mind; that if Virgil Samms goes to Arisia he will obtain the symbol he needs; that he will never obtain it otherwise. As to *how* I know these things...I can't...I just...I *know* it, I tell you!'

Without another word, without asking permission to leave, Bergenholm whirled around and hurried out. Samms and Kinnison stared at each other.

'Well?' Kinnison asked, quizzically.

'I'm going. Now. Whether I can be spared or not, and whether you think I'm out of control or not. I believe him, every word—and besides, there's the Bergenholm. How about you? Coming?'

'Yes. Can't say that I'm sold one hundred percent; but, as you say, the Bergenholm is a hard fact to shrug off. And at minimum rating, it's got to be tried. What are you taking? Not a fleet, probably—the *Boise*? Or the *Chicago*?' It was the Commissioner of Public Safety speaking now, the Commander-in-Chief of the Armed Forces. 'The *Chicago*, I'd say—the fastest and strongest thing in space.'

'Recommendation approved. Blast-off; twelve hundred hours tomorrow!'

CHAPTER 3

The superdreadnought *Chicago*, as she approached the imaginary but nevertheless sharply defined boundary, which no other ship had been allowed to pass, went inert and crept forward, mile by mile. Every man, from Commissioner and Councillor down, was taut and tense. So widely variant, so utterly fantastic, were the stories going around about this Arisia that no one knew what to expect. They expected the unexpected—and got it.

'Ah, Tellurians, you are precisely on time.' A strong, assured, deeply resonant pseudo-voice made itself heard in the depths of each mind aboard the tremendous ship of war. 'Pilots and navigating officers, you will shift course to one seventy eight dash seven twelve fifty three. Hold that course, inert, at one Tellurian gravity of acceleration. Virgil Samms will now be interviewed. He will return to the consciousness of the rest of you in exactly six of your hours.'

Practically dazed by the shock of their first experience with telepathy, not one of the *Chicago's* crew perceived anything unusual in the phraseology of that utterly precise, diamond-clear thought. Samms and Kinnison, however, precisionists themselves, did. But, warned although they were and keyed up although they were to detect any sign of hypnotism or of mental suggestion, neither of them had the faintest suspicion, then or ever, that Virgil Samms did not as a matter of fact leave the *Chicago* at all.

Samms *knew* that he boarded a lifeboat and drove it towards the shimmering haze beyond which Arisia was. Commissioner Kinnison *knew*, as surely as did every other man aboard, that Samms did those things,

because he and the other officers and most of the crew watched Samms do them. They watched the lifeboat dwindle in size with distance; watched it disappear within the peculiarly iridescent veil of force which their most penetrant ultra-beam spy-rays could not pierce.

They waited.

And, since every man concerned *knew*, beyond any shadow of doubt and to the end of his life, that everything that seemed to happen actually did happen, it will be so described.

Virgil Samms, then, drove his small vessel through Arisia's innermost screen and saw a planet so much like Earth that it might have been her sister world. There were the white ice-caps, the immense blue oceans, the verdant continents partially obscured by fleecy banks of cloud.

Would there, or would there not, be cities? While he had not known at all exactly what to expect, he did not believe that there would be any large cities upon Arisia. To qualify for the role of *deus ex machina*, the Arisian with whom Samms was about to deal would have to be a superman indeed—a being completely beyond man's knowledge or experience in power of mind. Would such a race of beings have need of such things as cities? They would not. There would be no cities.

Nor were there. The lifeboat flashed downward—slowed—landed smoothly in a regulation dock upon the outskirts of what appeared to be a small village surrounded by farms and woods.

'This way, please.' An inaudible voice directed him toward a two-wheeled vehicle which was almost, but not quite, like a Dillingham roadster.

This car, however, took off by itself as soon as Samms closed the door. It sped smoothly along a

paved highway devoid of all other traffic, past farms and past cottages, to stop of itself in front of the low, massive structure which was the centre of the village and, apparently, its reason for being.

'This way, please,' and Samms went through an automatically-opened door; along a short, bare hall; into a fairly large central room containing a vat and one deeply-upholstered chair.

'Sit down, please.' Samms did so, gratefully. He did not know whether he could have stood up much longer or not.

He had expected to encounter a tremendous mentality; but this was a thing far, far beyond his wildest imaginings. This was a brain—just that— nothing else. Almost globular; at least ten feet in diameter; immersed in and in perfect equilibrium with a pleasantly aromatic liquid—a BRAIN!

'Relax,' the Arisian ordered, soothingly, and Samms found that he *could* relax. 'Through the one you know as Bergenholm I heard of your need and have permitted you to come here this once for instruction.'

'But this...none of this...it isn't...it *can't* be real!' Samms blurted. 'I am—I must be—imagining it...and yet I know that I *can't* be hypnotised—I've been psychoed against it!'

'What is reality?' the Arisian asked, quietly. 'Your profoundest thinkers have never been able to answer that question. Nor, although I am much older and a much more capable thinker than any member of your race, would I attempt to give you its true answer. Nor, since your experience has been so limited, is it to be expected that you could believe without reservation any assurances I might give you in thoughts or in words. You must, then, convince yourself—definitely, by means of your own five senses—that I and everything about you are real, as you understand

reality. You saw the village and this building; you see the flesh that houses the entity which is I. You feel your own flesh; as you tap the woodwork with your knuckles you feel the impact and hear the vibrations as sound. As you entered this room you must have perceived the odour of the nutrient solution in which and by virtue of which I live. There remains only the sense of taste. Are you by any chance either hungry or thirsty?'

'Both.'

'Drink of the tankard in the niche yonder. In order to avoid any appearance of suggestion I will tell you nothing of its contents except the one fact that it matches perfectly the chemistry of your tissues.'

Gingerly enough, Samms brought the pitcher to his lips—then, seizing it in both hands, he gulped down a tremendous draught. It was GOOD! It smelled like all the appetizing kitchen aromas blended into one; it tasted like all of the most delicious meals he had ever eaten; it quenched his thirst as no beverage had ever done. But he could not empty even that comparatively small container—whatever the stuff was, it had a satiety value immensely higher even than old, rare, roast beef! With a sigh of repletion Samms replaced the tankard and turned again to his peculiar host.

'I am convinced. That was real. No possible mental influence could so completely and unmistakably satisfy the purely physical demands of a body as hungry and as thirsty as mine was. Thanks, immensely, for allowing me to come here, Mr...?'

'You may call me Mentor. I have no name, as you understand the term. Now, then, please think fully— you need not speak—of your problems and of your difficulties; of what you have done and of what you have it in mind to do.'

Samms thought, flashingly and cogently. A few minutes sufficed to cover Triplanetary's history and the beginning of the Solarian Patrol; then, for almost three hours, he went into the ramifications of the Galactic Patrol of his imaginings. Finally he wrenched himself back to reality. He jumped up, paced the floor, and spoke.

'But there's a vital flaw, one inherent and absolutely ruinous fact that makes the whole thing impossible!' he burst out, rebelliously. 'No one man, or group of men, no matter who they are, can be trusted with that much power. The Council and I have already been called everything imaginable; and what we have done so far is literally nothing at all in comparison with what the Galactic Patrol could and must do. Why, I myself would be the first to protest against the granting of such power to anybody. Every dictator in history, from Philip of Macedon to the Tyrant of Asia, claimed to be—and probably was, in his beginnings—motivated solely by benevolence. How am I to think that the proposed Galactic Council, or even I myself, will be strong enough to conquer a thing that has corrupted utterly every man who has ever won it? Who is to watch the watchmen?'

'The thought does you credit, youth,' Mentor replied, unmoved. 'That is one reason why you are here. You, of your own force, can not know that you are in fact incorruptible. I, however, know. Moreover, there is an agency by virtue of which that which you now believe to be impossible will become commonplace. Extend your arm.'

Samms did so, and there snapped around his wrist a platinum-iridium bracelet carrying, wristwatch-wise, a lenticular something at which the Tellurian stared in stupified amazement. It seemed to be composed of thousands—millions—of tiny gems, each of which emitted pulsatingly all the colours of the spectrum; it

was throwing out—broadcasting—a turbulent flood of writhing, polychromatic light!

'The successor to the golden meteor of the Triplanetary Service,' Mentor said, calmly. 'The Lens of Arisia. You may take my word for it, until your own experience shall have convinced you of the fact, that no one will ever wear Arisia's Lens who is in any sense unworthy. Here also is one for your friend, Commissioner Kinnison; it is not necessary for him to come physically to Arisia. It is, you will observe, in an insulated container, and does not glow. Touch its surface, but lightly and very fleetingly, for the contact will be painful.'

Samms' finger-tip barely touched one dull, grey, lifeless jewel: his whole arm jerked away uncontrollably as there swept through his whole being the intimation of an agony more poignant by far than any he had ever known.

'Why—it's alive!' he gasped.

'No, it is not really alive, as you understand the term...' Mentor paused, as though seeking a way to describe to the Tellurian a thing which was to him starkly incomprehensible. 'It is, however, endowed with what you might call a sort of pseudo-life; by virtue of which it gives off its characteristic radiation while, and only while, it is in physical circuit with the living entity— the ego, let us say—with whom it is in exact resonance. Glowing, the Lens is perfectly harmless; it is complete— saturated—satiated—fulfilled. In the dark condition it is, as you have learned, dangerous in the extreme. It is then incomplete—unfulfilled—frustrated—you might say seeking or yearning or demanding. In that condition its pseudo-life interferes so strongly with any life to which it is not attuned that that life, in a space of seconds, is forced out of this plane or cycle of existence.'

'Then I—I alone—of all the entities in existence, can wear this particular Lens?' Samms licked his lips and stared at it, glowing so satisfyingly and contentedly upon his wrist. 'But when I die, will it be a perpetual menace?'

'By no means. A Lens cannot be brought into being except to match some one living personality; a short time after you pass into the next cycle your Lens will disintegrate.'

'Wonderful!' Samms breathed, in awe. 'But there's one thing...these things are...priceless, and there will be millions of them to make...and you don't...'

'What will we get out of it, you mean?' The Arisian seemed to smile.

'Exactly.' Samms blushed, but held his ground. 'Nobody does anything for nothing. Altruism is beautiful in theory, but it has never been known to work in practice. I will pay a tremendous price—any price within reason or possibility—for the Lens; but I will have to know what that price is to be.'

'It will be heavier than you think, or can at present realise; although not in the sense you fear.' Mentor's thought was solemnity itself. 'Whoever wears the Lens of Arisia will carry a load that no weaker mind could bear. The load of authority; of responsibility; of knowledge that would wreck completely any mind of lesser strength. Altruism? No. Nor is it a case of good against evil, as you so firmly believe. Your mental picture of glaring white and of unrelieved black is not a true picture. Neither absolute evil nor absolute good do or can exist.'

'But that would make it still worse!' Samms protested. 'In that case, I can't see any reason at all for your exerting yourselves—putting yourselves out—for us.'

'There is, however, reason enough; although I am not sure that I can make it as clear to you as I would wish. There are in fact three reasons; any one of which would justify us in exerting—would compel us to exert—the trivial effort involved in the furnishing of Lenses to your Galactic Patrol. First, there is nothing either intrinsically right or intrinsically wrong about liberty or slavery, democracy or autocracy, freedom of action or complete regimentation. It seems to us, however, that the greatest measure of happiness and of well-being for the greatest number of entities, and therefore the optimum advancement toward whatever sublime Goal it is toward which this cycle of existence is trending in the vast and unknowable Scheme of Things, is to be obtained by securing for each and every individual the greatest amount of mental and physical freedom compatible with the public welfare. We of Arisia are only a small part of this cycle; and, as goes the whole, so goes in greater or lesser degree each of the parts. Is it impossible for you, a fellow citizen of this cycle-universe, to believe that such fulfillment alone would be ample compensation for a much greater effort?'

'I never thought of it in that light...' It was hard for Samms to grasp the concept; he never did understand it thoroughly. 'I begin to see, I think... at least, I believe you.'

'Second, we have a more specific obligation in that the life of many, many worlds has sprung from Arisian seed. Thus, in loco parentis, we would be derelict indeed if we refused to act. And third, you yourself spend highly valuable time and much effort in playing chess. Why do you do it? What do you get out of it?'

'Why, I...uh...mental exercise, I suppose...I like it!'

'Just so. And I am sure that one of your very early philosophers came to the conclusion that a fully competent mind, from a study of one fact or artifact

belonging to any given universe, could construct or visualise that universe, from the instant of its creation to its ultimate end?'

'Yes. At least, I have heard the proposition stated, but I have never believed it possible.'

'It is not possible simply because no fully competent mind ever has existed or ever will exist. A mind can become fully competent only by the acquisition of infinite knowledge, which would require infinite time as well as infinite capacity. Our equivalent of your chess, however, is what we call the 'Visualisation of the Cosmic All'. In my visualisation a descendant of yours name Clarrissa MacDougall will, in a store called Brenleer's upon the planet…but no, let us consider a thing nearer at hand and concerning you personally, so that its accuracy will be subject to check. Where you will be and exactly what you will be doing, at some definite time in the future. Five years, let us say?'

'Go ahead. If you can do that you're good.'

'Five Tellurian calendar years then, from the instant of your passing through the screen of 'The Hill' on this present journey, you will be…allow me, please, a moment of thought…you will be in a barber shop not yet built; the address of which is to be fifteen hundred fifteen Twelfth Avenue, Spokane, Washington, North America, Tellus. The barber's name will be Antonio Carbonero and he will be left-handed. He will be engaged in cutting your hair. Or rather, the actual cutting will have been done and he will be shaving, with a razor trade-marked "Jensen-King-Byrd", the short hairs in front of your left ear. A comparatively small, quadrupedal, greyish-striped entity, of the race called "cat"—a young cat, this one will be, and called Thomas, although actually of the female sex—will jump into your lap, addressing you pleasantly in a language with which you yourself are only partially familiar. You call it mewing and purring, I believe?'

'Yes,' the flabbergasted Samms managed to say. 'Cats do purr—especially kittens.'

'Ah—very good. Never having met a cat personally, I am gratified at your corroboration of my visualisation. This female youth erroneously called Thomas, somewhat careless in computing the elements of her trajectory, will jostle slightly the barber's elbow with her tail; thus causing him to make a slight incision, approximately three millimetres long, parallel to and just above your left cheekbone. At the precise moment in question, the barber will be applying a styptic pencil to this insignificant wound. This forecast is, I trust, sufficiently detailed so that you will have no difficulty in checking its accuracy or its lack thereof?'

'Detailed! Accuracy!' Samms could scarcely think. 'But listen—not that I want to cross you up deliberately, but I'll tell you now that a man doesn't like to get sliced by a barber, even such a little nick as that. I'll remember that address—and the cat—and I'll never go into the place!'

'Every event does affect the succession of events,' Mentor acknowledged, equably enough. 'Except for this interview, you would have been in New Orleans at that time, instead of in Spokane. I have considered every pertinent factor. You will be a busy man. Hence, while you will think of this matter frequently and seriously during the near future, you will have forgotten it in less than five years. You will remember it only at the touch of the astringent, whereupon you will give voice to certain self-derogatory and profane remarks.'

'I ought to,' Samms grinned; a not-too-pleasant grin. He had been appalled by the quality of mind able to do what Mentor had just done; he was not more than appalled by the Arisian's calm certainty that what he had foretold in such detail would in every detail come to pass. 'If, after all this Spokane—let a tiger-striped kitten jump into my lap—let a left-handed

Tony Carbonero nick me—uh-uh, Mentor, UH-UH! If I do, I'll deserve to be called everything I can think of!'

'These that I have mentioned, the gross occurrences, are problems only for inexperienced thinkers.' Mentor paid no attention to Samms' determination never to enter that shop. 'The real difficulties lie in the fine detail, such as the length, mass, and exact place and position of landing, upon apron or floor, of each of your hairs as it is severed. Many factors are involved. Other clients passing by— opening and shutting doors—air currents—sunshine— wind—pressure, temperature, humidity. The exact fashion in which the barber will flick his shears, which in turn depends upon many other factors—what he will have been doing previously, what he will have eaten and drunk, whether or not his home life will have been happy... you little realise, youth, what a priceless opportunity this will be for me to check the accuracy of my visualisation. I shall spend many periods upon the problem. I cannot attain perfect accuracy, of course. Ninety nine point nine nines per cent, let us say...or perhaps ten nines...is all that I can reasonably expect...'

'But, Mentor!' Samms protested. 'I can't help you on a thing like that! How can I know or report the exact mass, length, and orientation of single hairs?'

'You cannot; but, since you will be wearing your Lens, I myself can and will compare minutely my visualisation with the actuality. For know, youth, that wherever any Lens is, there can any Arisian be if he so desires. And now, knowing that fact, and from your own knowledge of the satisfactions to be obtained from chess and other such mental activities, and from the glimpses you have had into my own mind, do you retain any doubts that we Arisians will be fully compensated for the trifling effort involved in

furnishing whatever number of Lenses may be required?'

'I have no more doubts. But this Lens...I'm getting more afraid of it every minute. I see that it is a perfect identification; I can understand that it can be a perfect telepath. But is it something else, as well? If it has other powers...what are they?'

'I cannot tell you; or, rather, I will not. It is best for your own development that I do not, except in the most general terms. It has additional qualities, it is true; but, since no two entities ever have the same abilities, no two Lenses will ever be of identical qualities. Strictly speaking, a Lens has no real power of its own; it merely concentrates, intensifies, and renders available whatever powers are already possessed by its wearer. You must develop whatever powers are already possessed by its wearer. You must develop your own powers and your own abilities; we of Arisia, in furnishing the Lens, will have done everything that we should do.'

'Of course, sir; and much more than we have any right to expect. You have given me a Lens for Roderick Kinnison; how about the others? Who is to select them?'

'You are, for a time.' Silencing the man's protests, Mentor went on: 'You will find that your judgement will be good. You will send to us only one entity who will not be given a Lens, and it is necessary that that one entity should be sent here. You will begin a system of selection and training which will become more and more rigorous as time goes on. This will be necessary; not for the selection itself, which the Lensmen themselves could do among babies in their cradles, but because of the benefits thus conferred upon the many who will not graduate, as well as upon the few who will. In the meantime you will select the

candidates; and you will be shocked and dismayed when you discover how few you will be able to send.

You will go down in history as First Lensman Samms; the Crusader, the man whose wide vision and tremendous grasp made it possible for the Galactic Patrol to become what it is to be. You will have highly capable help, of course. The Kinnisons, with their irresistible driving force, their indomitable will to do, their transcendent urge; Costigan, back of whose stout Irish heart lie Erin's best of brains and brawn; your cousins George and Ray Olmstead; your daughter Virgilia...'

'Virgilia! Where does she fit into this picture? What do you know about her—and how?'

'A mind would be incompetent indeed who could not visualise, from even the most fleeting contact with you, a fact which has been in existence for some twenty three of your years. Her doctorate in psychology; her intensive studies under Martian and Venerian masters—even under one reformed Adept of North Polar Jupiter—of the involuntary, uncontrollable, almost unknown and hence highly revealing muscles of the face, the hands, and other parts of the human body. You will remember that poker game for a long time.'

'I certainly will.' Samms grinned, a bit shamefacedly. 'She gave us clear warning of what she was going to do, and then cleaned us out to the last millo.'

'Naturally. She has, all unconsciously, been training herself for the work she is destined to do. But to resume; you will feel yourself incompetent, unworthy—that, too, is a part of a Lensman's Load. When you first scan the mind of Roderick Kinnison you will feel that he, not you, should be the prime mover in the Galactic Patrol. But know now that no mind, not even the most capable in the universe, can either visualise truly or truly

evaluate itself. Commissioner Kinnison, upon scanning your mind as he will scan it, will know the truth and will be well content. But time presses; in one minute you leave.'

'Thanks a lot...thanks.' Samms got to his feet and paused, hesitantly. 'I suppose that it will be all right...that is, I can call on you again, if...?'

'No,' the Arisian declared, coldly. 'My visualisation does not indicate that it will ever again be either necessary or desirable for you to visit or to communicate with me or with any other Arisian.'

Communication ceased as though a solid curtain had been drawn between the two. Samms strode out and stepped into the waiting vehicle, which whisked him back to his lifeboat. He blasted off; arriving in the control room of the Chicago precisely at the end of the sixth hour after leaving it.

'Well, Rod, I'm back...' he began, and stopped; utterly unable to speak. For at the mention of the name Samms' Lens had put him fully en rapport with his friend's whole mind; and what he perceived struck him—literally and precisely—dumb.

He had always liked and admired Rod Kinnison. He had always known that he was tremendously able and capable. He had known that he was big; clean; a square shooter; the world's best. Hard; a driver who had little more mercy on his underlings in selected undertakings than he had on himself. But now, as he saw spread out for his inspection Kinnison's ego in its entirety; as he compared in fleeting glances that terrific mind with those of the other officers—good men, too, all of them—assembled in the room; he knew that he had never even begun to realise what a giant Roderick Kinnison really was.

'What's the matter, Virge?' Kinnison exclaimed, and hurried up, both hands outstretched. 'You look like you're seeing ghosts! What did they do to you?'

'Nothing—much. But "ghosts" doesn't half describe what I'm seeing right now. Come into my office, will you, Rod?'

Ignoring the curious stares of the junior officers, the Commissioner and the Councillor went into the latter's quarters, and in those quarters the two Lensmen remained in close consultation during practically all of the return trip to Earth. In fact, they were still conferring deeply, via Lens, when the Chicago landed and they took a ground-car into The Hill.

'But who are you going to send first, Virge?' Kinnison demanded. 'You must have decided on at least some of them, by this time.'

'I know of only five, or possibly six, who are ready,' Samms replied, glumly. 'I would have sworn that I knew of a hundred, but they don't measure up. Jack, Mason Northrop, and Conway Costigan, for the first load. Lyman Cleveland, Fred Rodebush, and perhaps Bergenholm—I haven't been able to figure him out, but I'll know when I get him under my Lens—next. That's all.'

'Not quite. How about your identical-twin cousins, Ray and George Olmstead, who have been doing such a terrific job of counter-spying?'

'Perhaps...Quite possibly.'

'And if I'm good enough, Clayton and Schweikert certainly are, to name only two of the commodores. And Knobos and DalNalten. And above all, how about Jill?'

'Jill? Why, I don't...she measures up, of course, but... but at that, there was nothing said against it, either...I wonder...'

'Why not have the boys in—Jill, too—and thrash it out?'

The young people were called in; the story was told; the problem stated. The boys' reaction was instantaneous and unanimous. Jack Kinnison took the lead.

'Of course Jill's going, if anybody does!' he burst out vehemently. 'Count her out, with all the stuff she's got? Hardly!'

'Why, Jack! This, from you?' Jill seemed highly surprised. 'I have it on excellent authority that I'm a stinker; a half-witted one, at that. A jelly-brain, with come-hither eyes.'

'You are, and a lot of other things besides.' Jack Kinnison did not back up a millimetre, even before their fathers. 'But even at your sapadilliest your half wits are better than most other people's whole ones; and I never said or thought that your brain couldn't function, whenever it wanted to, back of those sad eyes. Whatever it takes to be a Lensman, sir,' he turned to Samms, 'she's got just as much of as the rest of us. Maybe more.'

'I take it, then, that there is no objection to her going?' Samms asked.

There was no objection.

'What ship shall we take, and when?'

'The Chicago. Now.' Kinnison directed. 'She's hot and ready. We didn't strike any trouble going or coming, so she didn't need much servicing. Flit!'

They flitted, and the great battleship made the second cruise as uneventfully as she had made the first. The Chicago's officers and crew knew that the young people left the vessel separately; that they returned separately, each in his or her lifeboat. They met, however, not in the control room, but in Jack

Kinnison's private quarters; the three young Lensmen and the girl. The three were embarrassed; ill at ease. The Lenses were—definitely—not working. Not one of them would put his Lens on Jill, since she did not have one...

The girl broke the short silence.

'Wasn't she the most perfectly beautiful thing you ever saw?' she breathed. 'In spite of being over seven feet tall? She looked to be about twenty—except her eyes—but she must have been a hundred, to know so much—but what are you boys staring so about?'

'She!' Three voices blurted as one.

'Yes. She. Why? I know we weren't together, but I got the impression, some way or other, that there was only the one. What did you see?'

All three men started to talk at once, a clamour of noise; then all stopped at once.

'You first, Spud. Whom did you talk to, and what did he, she, or it say?' Although Conway Costigan was a few years older than the other three, they all called him by nickname as a matter of course.

'National Police Headquarters—Chief of the Detective Bureau,' Costigan reported, crisply. 'Between forty three and forty five; six feet and half an inch; one seventy five. Hard, fine, keen, a Big Time Operator if there ever was one. Looked a lot like your father, Jill; the same dark auburn hair, just beginning to grey, and the same deep orange-yellow markings in his eyes. He gave me the works; then took this Lens out of his safe, snapped it onto my wrist, and gave me two orders—get out and stay out.'

Jack and Mase stared at Costigan, at Jill, and at each other. Then they whistled in unison.

'I see this is not going to be a unanimous report, except possibly in one minor detail,' Jill remarked. 'Mase, you're next.'

'I landed on the campus of the University of Arisia,' Northrop stated, flatly. 'Immense place—hundreds of thousands of students'. They took me to the Physics Department—to the private laboratory of the Department Head himself. He had a panel with about a million meters and gauges on it; he scanned and measured every individual component element of my brain. Then he made a pattern, on a milling router just about as complicated as his panel. From there on, of course, it was simple—just like a dentist making a set of china choppers or a metallurgist embedding a test-section. He snapped a couple of sentences of directions at me, and then said "Scram!" That's all.'

'Sure that was all?' Costigan asked. 'Didn't he add "and stay scrammed"?'

'He didn't say it, exactly, but the implication was clear enough.'

'The one point of similarity,' Jill commented. 'Now you, Jack. You have been looking as though we were all candidates for canvas jackets that lace tightly up the back.'

'Uh-uh. As though maybe I am. I didn't see anything at all. Didn't even land on the planet. Just floated around in an orbit inside that screen. The thing I talked with was a pattern of pure force. This Lens simply appeared on my wrist, bracelet and all, out of thin air. He told me plenty, though, in a very short time— his last word being for me not to come back or call back.'

'Hm...m...m.' This of Jack's was a particularly indigestible bit, even for Jill Samms.

'In plain words,' Costigan volunteered, 'we all saw exactly what we expected to see.'

'Uh-uh,' Jill denied. 'I certainly did not expect to see a woman...no; what each of us saw, I think, was what would do us the most good—give each of us the highest possible lift. I am wondering whether or not there was anything at all really there.'

'That might be it, at that.' Jack scowled in concentration. But there must have been something there—these Lenses are real. But what makes me mad is that they wouldn't give you a Lens. You're just as good a man as any one of us—if I didn't know it wouldn't do a damn bit of good I'd go back there right now and...'

'Don't pop off so, Jack!' Jill's eyes, however, were starry. 'I know you mean it, and I could almost love you, at times—but I don't need a Lens. As a matter of fact, I'll be much better off without one.'

'Jet back, Jill!' Jack Kinnison stared deeply into the girl's eyes—but still did not use his Lens. 'Somebody must have done a terrific job of selling, to make you believe that...or are you sold, actually?'

'Actually. Honestly. That Arisian was a thousand times more of a woman than I ever will be, and she didn't wear a Lens—never had worn one. Women's minds and Lenses don't fit. There's a sex-based incompatibility. Lenses are as masculine as whiskers—and at that, only a very few men can ever wear them, either. Very special men, like you three and Dad and Pops Kinnison. Men with tremendous force, drive, and scope. Pure killers, all of you; each in his own way, of course. No more to be stopped than a glacier, and twice as hard and ten times as cold. A woman simply can't have that kind of a mind! There is going to be a woman Lensman some day—just one—but not for years and years; and I wouldn't be in her shoes for anything. In this job of mine, of...'

'Well, go on. What is this job you're so sure you are going to do?'

'Why, I don't know!' Jill exclaimed, startled eyes wide. 'I thought I knew all about it, but I don't! Do you, about yours?'

They did not, not one of them; and they were all as surprised at that fact as the girl had been.

'Well, to get back to this Lady Lensman who is going to appear some day, I gather that she is going to be some kind of a freak. She'll have to be, practically, because of the sex-based fundamental nature of the Lens. Mentor didn't say so, in so many words, but she made it perfectly clear that...'

'Mentor!' the three men exclaimed.

Each of them had dealt with Mentor!

'I am beginning to see,' Jill said, thoughtfully. 'Mentor. Not a real name at all. To quote the Unabridged verbatim—I had occasion to look the word up the other day and I am appalled now at the certainty that there was a connection—quote; Mentor, a wise and faithful counsellor; unquote. Have any of you boys anything to say? I haven't; and I am beginning to be scared blue.'

Silence fell; and the more they thought, those three young Lensmen and the girl who was one of the two human women ever to encounter knowingly an Arisian mind, the deeper that silence became.

CHAPTER 4

'So you didn't find anything on Nevia.' Roderick Kinnison got up, deposited the inch-long butt of his cigar in an ashtray, lit another, and prowled about the room; hands jammed deep into breeches pockets. 'I'm surprised. Nerado struck me as being a B.T.O...I thought sure he'd qualify.'

'So did I.' Samms' tone was glum. 'He's Big Time, and an Operator; but not big enough, by far. I'm—we're both—finding out that Lensman material is damned scarce stuff. There's none on Nevia, and no indication whatever that there ever will be any.'

'Tough...and you're right, of course, in your stand that we'll have to have Lensmen from as many different solar systems as possible on the Galactic Council or the thing won't work at all. So damned much jealousy—which is one reason why we're here in New York instead of out at The Hill, where we belong—we've found that out already, even in such a small and comparatively homogeneous group as our own system—the Solarian Council will not only have to be made up mostly of Lensmen, but each and every inhabited planet of Sol will have to be represented—even Pluto, I suppose, in time. And by the way, your Mr. Saunders wasn't any too pleased when you took Knobos of Mars and DalNalten of Venus away from him and made Lensmen out of them—and put them miles over his head.'

'Oh, I wouldn't say that... exactly. I convinced him ... but at that, since Saunders is not Lensman grade himself, it was a trifle difficult for him to understand the situation completely.'

'You say it easy—"difficult" is not the word I would use. But back to the Lensman hunt.' Kinnison scowled blackly. 'I agree, as I said before, that we need non-human Lensmen, the more the better, but I don't think much of your chance of finding any. What makes you think...Oh, I see...but I don't know whether you're justified or not in assuming a high positive correlation between a certain kind of mental ability and technological advancement.'

'No such assumption is necessary. Start anywhere you please, Rod, and take it from there; including Nevia.'

'I'll start with known facts, then. Interstellar flight is new to us. We haven't spread far, or surveyed much territory. But in the eight solar systems with which we are most familiar there are seven planets—I'm not counting Valeria—which are very much like Earth in point of mass, size, climate, atmosphere, and gravity. Five of the seven did not have any intelligent life and were colonised easily and quickly. The Tellurian worlds of Procyon and Vega became friendly neighbours— thank God we learned something on Nevia—because they were already inhabited by highly advanced races: Procia by people as human as we are, Vegia by people who would be so if it weren't for their tails. Many other worlds of these systems are inhabited by more or less intelligent non-human races. Just how intelligent they are we don't know, but the Lensmen will soon find out.

'My point is that no race we have found so far has had either atomic energy or any form of space-drive. In any contact with races having space-drives we have not been the discoverers, but the discovered. Our colonies are all within twenty six light-years of Earth except Aldebaran II, which is fifty seven, but which drew a lot of people, in spite of the distance, because it was so nearly identical with Earth. On the other hand, the Nevians, from a distance of over a hundred light-

years, found us...implying an older race and a higher development—but you just told me that they would never produce a Lensman!'

'That point stopped me, too, at first. Follow through; I want to see if you arrive at the same conclusion I did.'

'Well...I...I...' Kinnison thought intensely, then went on: 'Of course, the Nevians were not colonising; nor, strictly speaking, exploring. They were merely hunting for iron—a highly organised, intensively specialised operation to find a raw material they needed desperately.'

'Precisely,' Samms agreed.

'The Rigellians, however, were surveying, and Rigel is about four hundred and forty light-years from here. We didn't have a thing they needed or wanted. They nodded at us in passing and kept on going I'm still on your track?'

'Dead centre. And just where does that put the Palainians?'

'I see... you may have something there, at that. Palain is so far away that nobody knows even where it is—probably thousands of light-years. Yet they have not only explored this system; they colonised Pluto long before our white race colonised America. But damn it, Virge, I don't like it—any part of it. Rigel Four you may be able to take, with your Lens—even one of their damned automobiles, if you stay solidly en rapport with the driver. But Palain, Virge! Pluto is bad enough, but the home planet! You can't. Nobody can. It simply can't be done!'

'I know it won't be easy,' Samms admitted, bleakly, 'but if it's got to be done, I'll do it. And I have a little information that I haven't had time to tell you yet. We discussed once before, you remember, what a job it was to get into any kind of communication with the

Palainians on Pluto. You said then that nobody could understand them, and you were right—then. However, I re-ran those brain-wave tapes, wearing my Lens, and could understand them—the thoughts, that is—as well as though they had been recorded in precisionist-grade English.'

'What?' Kinnison exclaimed, then fell silent. Samms remained silent. What they were thinking of Arisia's Lens cannot be expressed in words.

'Well, go on,' Kinnison finally said. 'Give me the rest of it—the stinger that you've been holding back.'

'The messages—as messages—were clear and plain. The backgrounds, however, the connotations and implications, were not. Some of their codes and standards seem to be radically different from ours—so utterly and fantastically different that I simply cannot reconcile either their conduct or their ethics with their obviously high intelligence and their advanced state of development. However, they have at least some minds of tremendous power, and none of the peculiarities I deduced were of such a nature as to preclude Lensmanship. Therefore I am going to Pluto; and from there—I hope—to Palain Seven. If there's a Lensman there, I'll get him.'

'You will, at that,' Kinnison paid quiet tribute to what he, better than anyone else, knew that his friend had.

'But enough of me—how are you doing?'

'As well as can be expected at this stage of the game. The thing is developing along three main lines. First, the pirates. Since that kind of thing is more or less my own line I'm handling it myself, unless and until you find someone better qualified. I've got Jack and Costigan working on it now.

'Second; drugs, vice, and so on. I hope you find somebody to take this line over, because, frankly, I'm

in over my depth and want to get out. Knobos and DalNalten are trying to find out if there's anything to the idea that there may be a planetary, or even inter-planetary, ring involved. Since Sid Fletcher isn't a Lensman I couldn't disconnect him openly from his job, but he knows a lot about the dope-vice situation and is working practically full time with the other two.

'Third; pure—or rather, decidedly impure—politics. The more I studied that subject, the clearer it became that politics would be the worst and biggest battle of the three. There are too many angles I don't know a damned thing about, such as what to do about the succession of foaming, screaming fits your friend Senator Morgan will be throwing the minute he finds out what our Galactic Patrol is going to do. So I ducked the whole political line.

'Now you know as well as I do—better, probably—that Morgan is only the Pernicious Activities Committee of the North American Senate. Multiply him by the thousands of others, all over space, who will be on our necks before the Patrol can get its space-legs, and you will see that all that stuff will have to be handled by a Lensman who, as well as being a mighty smooth operator, will have to know all the answers and will have to have plenty of guts. I've got the guts, but none of the other prime requisites. Jill hasn't, although she's got everything else. Fairchild, your Relations ace, isn't a Lensman and can never become one. So you can see quite plainly who has got to handle politics himself.'

'You may be right...but this Lensman business comes first...' Samms pondered, then brightened. 'Perhaps—probably—I can find somebody on this trip—a Palainian, say—who is better qualified than any of us.'

Kinnison snorted. 'If you can, I'll buy you a week in any Venerian relaxerie you want to name.'

'Better start saving up your credits, then, because from what I know of the Palainian mentality such a development is distinctly more than a possibility.' Samms paused, his eyes narrowing. 'I don't know whether it would make Morgan and his kind more rabid or less so to have a non-Solarian entity possess authority in our affairs political—but at least it would be something new and different. But in spite of what you said about "ducking" politics, what have you got Northrop, Jill and Fairchild doing?'

'Well, we had a couple of discussions. I couldn't give either Jill or Dick orders, of course...'

'Wouldn't, you mean,' Samms corrected.

'Couldn't,' Kinnison insisted. 'Jill, besides being your daughter and Lensman grade, had no official connection with either the Triplanetary Service or the Solarian Patrol. And the Service, including Fairchild, is still Triplanetary; and it will have to stay Triplanetary until you have found enough Lensmen so that you can spring your twin surprises—Galactic Council and Galactic Patrol. However, Northrop and Fairchild are keeping their eyes and ears open and their mouths shut, and Jill is finding out whatever she can about drugs and so on, as well as the various political angles. They'll report to you—facts, deductions, guesses, and recommendations—whenever you say the word.'

'Nice work, Rod. Thanks. I think I'll call Jill now, before I go—wonder where she is?...but I wonder...with the Lens perhaps telephones are superfluous? I'll try it.'

'JILL!' he thought intensely into his Lens, forming as he did so a mental image of his gorgeous daughter as he knew her. But he found, greatly to his surprise, that neither elaboration nor emphasis was necessary.

'Ouch!' came the almost instantaneous answer, long before his thought was complete. 'Don't think so

hard, Dad, it hurts—I almost missed a step.' Virgilia was actually there with him; inside his own mind; in closer touch with him than she had ever before been. 'Back so soon? Shall we report now, or aren't you ready to go to work yet?'

'Skipping for the moment your aspersions on my present activities—not quite.' Samms moderated the intensity of his thought to a conversational level. 'Just wanted to check with you. Come in, Rod.' In flashing thoughts he brought her up to date. 'Jill, do you agree with what Rod here has just told me?'

'Yes. Fully. So do the boys.'

'That settles it, then—unless, of course, I can find a more capable substitute.'

'Of course—but we will believe that when we see it.'

'Where are you and what are you doing?'

'Washington, DC, European Embassy. Dancing with Herkimer Herkimer Third, Senator Morgan's Number One secretary. I was going to make passes at him—in a perfectly lady-like way, of course -but it wasn't necessary. He thinks he can break down my resistance.'

'Careful, Jill! That kind of stuff...'

'Is very old stuff indeed, Daddy dear. Simple. And Herkimer Herkimer Third isn't really a menace; he just thinks he is. Take a look—you can, can't you, with your Lens?'

'Perhaps...Oh, yes. I see him as well as you do.' Fully en rapport with the girl as he was, so that his mind received simultaneously with hers any stimulus which she was willing to share, it seemed as though a keen, handsome, deeply tanned face bent down from a distance of inches towards his own. 'But I don't like it a bit—and him even less.'

'That's because you aren't a girl.' Jill giggled mentally. 'This is fun; and it won't hurt him a bit, except maybe for a slightly bruised vanity, when I don't fall down flat at his feet. And I'm learning a lot that he hasn't any suspicion he's giving away.'

'Knowing you, I believe that. But don't...that is...well, be very careful not to get your fingers burned. The job isn't worth it—yet.'

'Don't worry, Dad.' She laughed unaffectedly. 'When it comes to playboys like this one, I've got millions and skillions and whillions of ohms of resistance. But here comes Senator Morgan himself, with a fat and repulsive Venerian—he's calling my boy-friend away from me, with what he thinks is an imperceptible high-sign, into a huddle—and my olfactory nerves perceive a rich and fruity aroma, as of skunk—so... I hate to seem to be giving a Solarian Councillor the heave-ho, but if I want to read what goes on—and I certainly do—I'll have to concentrate. As soon as you get back give us a call and we'll report. Take it easy, Dad!'

'You're the one to be told that, not me. Good hunting, Jill!'

Samms, still seated calmly at his desk, reached out and pressed a button marked "GARAGE". His office was on the seventieth floor; the garage occupied level after level of sub-basement. The screen brightened; a keen young face appeared.

'Good evening, Jim. Will you please send my car up to the Wright Skyway feeder?'

'At once, sir. It will be there in seventy five seconds.'

Samms cut off; and, after a brief exchange of thought with Kinnison, went out into the hall and along it to the "DOWN" shaft. There, going free, he stepped through a doorless, unguarded archway into over a thousand feet of air. Although it was long after

conventional office hours the shaft was still fairly busy, but that made no difference—inertialess collisions cannot even be felt. He bulleted downward to the sixth floor, where he brought himself to an instantaneous halt.

Leaving the shaft, he joined the now thinning crowd hurrying toward the exit. A girl with meticulously plucked eyebrows and an astounding hair-do, catching sight of his Lens, took her hands out of her breeches pockets—skirts went out, as office dress, when up-and-down open-shaft velocities of a hundred or so miles per hour replaced elevators—nudged her companion, and whispered excitedly:

'Look there! Quick! I never saw one close up before, did you? That's him—himself! First Lensman Samms!'

At the Portal, the Lensman as a matter of habit held out his car-check, but such formalities were no longer necessary, or even possible. Everybody knew, or wanted to be thought of as knowing, Virgil Samms.

'Stall four sixty five, First Lensman, sir,' the uniformed gateman told him, without even glancing at the extended disk.

'Thank you, Tom.'

'This way, please, sir, First Lensman,' and a youth, teeth gleaming white in a startlingly black face, strode proudly to the indicated stall and opened the vehicle's door.

'Thank you, Danny,' Samms said, appreciatively as though he did not know exactly where his ground-car was.

He got in. The door jammed itself gently shut. The runabout—a Dillingham eleven-forty—shot smoothly forward upon its two fat, soft tyres. Half-way to the exit archway he was doing forty; he hit the steeply-banked curve leading into the lofty "street" at ninety.

Nor was there shock or strain. Motorcycle-wise, but automatically, the "Dilly" leaned against its gyroscopes at precisely the correct angle; the huge low-pressure tyres clung to the resilient synthetic of the pavement as though integral with it. Nor was there any question of conflicting traffic, for this thoroughfare, six full levels above Varick Street proper, was not, strictly speaking, a street at all. It had only one point of access, the one which Samms had used; and only one exit—it was simply and only a feeder into Wright Skyway, a limited-access superhighway.

Samms saw, without noting particularly, the maze of traffic-ways of which this feeder was only one tiny part; a maze which extended from ground-level up to a point well above even the towering buildings of New York's metropolitan district.

The way rose sharply; Samms' right foot went down a little farther; the Dillingham began to pick up speed. Moving loud-speakers sang to him and yelled and blared at him, but he did not hear them. Brilliant signs, flashing and flaring all the colours of the spectrum— sheer triumphs of the electrician's art—blazed in or flamed into arresting words and eye-catching pictures, but he did not see them. Advertising—advertising designed by experts to sell everything from aard-varks to Martian zyzmol ("bottled ecstacy")—but the First Lensman was a seasoned big-city dweller. His mind had long since become a perfect filter, admitting to his consciousness only things which he wanted to perceive; only so can big-city life be made endurable.

Approaching the Skyway, he cut in his touring roadlights, slowed down a trifle, and insinuated his low-flyer into the stream of traffic. Those lights threw fifteen hundred watts apiece, but there was no glare— polarised lenses and windshields saw to that.

He wormed his way over to the left-hand, high-speed lane and opened up. At the edge of the

skyscraper district, where Wright Skyway angles sharply downward to ground level, Samms' attention was caught and held by something off to his right—a blue-white, whistling something that hurtled upward into the air. As it ascended it slowed down; its monotone shriek became lower and lower in pitch; its light went down through the spectrum towards the red. Finally it exploded, with an earth-shaking crash; but the lightning-like flash of the detonation, instead of vanishing almost instantaneously, settled itself upon a low-hanging artificial cloud and became a picture and four words—two bearded faces and "SMITH BROS. COUGH CROPS"!

'Well, I'll be damned!' Samms spoke aloud, chagrined at having been compelled to listen to and to look at an advertisement. 'I thought I had seen everything, but that is really new!'

Twenty minutes—fifty miles—later, Samms left the Sky-way at a point near what had once been South Norwalk, Connecticut; an area transformed now into the level square miles of New York Spaceport.

New York Spaceport; then, and until the establishment of Prime Base, the biggest and busiest field in existence upon any planet of Civilisation. For New York City, long the financial and commercial capital of the Earth, had maintained the same dominant position in the affairs of the Solar System and was holding a substantial lead over her rivals, Chicago, London, and Stalingrad, in the race for interstellar supremacy.

And Virgil Samms himself, because of the ever-increasing menace of piracy, had been largely responsible for the policy of basing the war-vessels of the Triplanetary Patrol upon each space-field in direct ratio to the size and importance of that field. Hence he was no stranger in New York Spaceport; in fact, master psychologist that he was, he had made it a

point to know by first name practically everyone connected with it.

No sooner had he turned his Dillingham over to a smiling attendant, however, than he was accosted by a man whom he had never seen before.

'Mr. Samms?' the stranger asked.

'Yes.' Samms did not energise his Lens; he had not yet developed either the inclination or the technique to probe instantaneously every entity who approached him, upon any pretext whatever, in order to find out what that entity really wanted.

'I'm Isaacson...' the man paused, as though he had supplied a world of information.

'Yes?' Samms was receptive, but not impressed.

'Interstellar Spaceways, you know. We've been trying to see you for two weeks, but we couldn't get past your secretaries, so I decided to buttonhole you here, myself. But we're just as much alone here as we would be in either one of our offices—yes, more so. What I want to talk to you about is having our exclusive franchise extended to cover the outer planets and the colonies.'

'Just a minute, Mr. Isaacson. Surely you know that I no longer have even a portfolio in the Council; that practically all of my attention is, and for some time to come will be, directed elsewhere?'

'Exactly—officially.' Isaacson's tone spoke volumes. 'But you're still the Boss; they'll do anything you tell them to. We couldn't try to do business with you before, of course, but in your present position there is nothing whatever to prevent you from getting into the biggest thing that will ever be. We are the biggest corporation in existence now, as you know, and we are still growing—fast. We don't do business in a small way,

or with small men; so here's a cheque for a million credits, or I will deposit it to your account...'

'I'm not interested.'

'As a binder,' the other went on, as smoothly as though his sentence had not been interrupted, 'with twenty-five million more to follow on the day that our franchise goes through.'

'I'm still not interested.'

'No...o...o...?' Isaacson studied the Lensman narrowly: and Samms, Lens now wide awake, studied the entrepreneur. 'Well...I... while I admit that we want you pretty badly, you are smart enough to know that we'll get what we want anyway, with or without you. With you, though, it will be easier and quicker, so I am authorised to offer you, besides the twenty six million credits...' he savoured the words as he uttered them: 'twenty two and one half percent of Spaceways. On today's market that is worth fifty million credits; ten years from now it will be worth fifty billion. That's my high bid; that's as high as we can possibly go.'

'I'm glad to hear that—I'm still not interested,' and Samms strode away, calling his friend Kinnison as he did so.

'Rod? Virgil.' He told the story.

'Whew!' Kinnison whistled expressively. 'They're not pikers, anyway, are they? What a sweet set-up—and you could wrap it up and hand it to them like a pound of coffee...'

'Or you could, Rod.'

'Could be...' The big Lensman ruminated. 'But what a hookup! Perfectly legitimate, and with plenty of precedents—and arguments, of a sort—in its favour. The outer planets. Then Alpha Centauri and Sirius and Procyon and so on. Monopoly—all the traffic will bear...'

'Slavery, you mean!' Samms stormed. 'It would hold Civilisation back for a thousand years!'

'Sure, but what do they care?'

'That's it...and he said—and actually believed—that they would get it without my help...I can't help wondering about that.'

'Simple enough, Virge, when you think about it. He doesn't know yet what a Lensman is. Nobody does, you know, except Lensmen. It will take some time for that knowledge to get around...'

'And still longer for it to be *believed*.'

'Right. But as to the chance of Interstellar Spaceways ever getting the monopoly they're working for, I didn't think I would have to remind you that it was not entirely by accident that over half of the members of the Solarian Council are Lensmen, and that any Galactic Councillor will automatically *have* to be a Lensman. So go right ahead with what you started, my boy, and don't give Isaacson and Company another thought. We'll bend an optic or two in that direction while you are gone.'

'I was overlooking a few things, at that, I guess.' Samms sighed in relief as he entered the main office of the Patrol.

The line at the receptionist's desk was fairly short, but even so, Samms was not allowed to wait. That highly decorative, but far-from-dumb blonde, breaking off in mid-sentence her business of the moment, turned on her charm as though it has been a battery of floodlights, pressed a stud on her desk, and spoke to the man before her and to the Lensman:

'Excuse me a moment, please. First Lensman Samms, sir...?'

'Yes, Miss Regan?' her communicator—"squawk-box", in every day parlance—broke in.

'First Lensman Samms is here, sir,' the girl announced, and broke the circuit.

'Good evening, Sylvia. Lieutenant-Commander Wagner, please, or whoever else is handling clearances,' Samms answered what he though was to have been her question.

'Oh, no, sir; you are cleared. Commodore Clayton has been waiting for you...here he is, now.'

'Hi, Virgil!' Commodore Clayton, a big solid man with a scarred face and a shock of iron-grey hair, whose collar bore the two silver stars which proclaimed him to be the commander-in-chief of a continental contingent of the Patrol, shook hands vigorously. 'I'll zip you out. Miss Regan, call a bug, please.'

'Oh, that isn't necessary, Alex!' Samms protested. 'I'll pick one up outside.'

'Not in any Patrol base in North America, my friend; nor, unless I am very badly mistaken, anywhere else. From now on, Lensmen have absolute priority, and the quicker everybody realises exactly what that means, the better.'

The "bug"—a vehicle something like a jeep, except more so—was waiting at the door. The two men jumped aboard.

'The *Chicago*—and blast!' Clayton ordered, crisply.

The driver obeyed—literally. Gravel flew from beneath skidding tyres as the highly manoeuvrable little ground-car took off. A screaming turn into the deservedly famous Avenue of Oaks. Along the Avenue. Through the Gate, the guards saluting smartly as the bug raced past them. Past the barracks. Past the airport hangars and strips. Out into the space-field, the scarred and blackened area devoted solely to the widely-spaced docks of the tremendous vessels which plied the vacuous reaches of interplanetary and

interstellar space. Spacedocks were, and are, huge and sprawling structures; built of concrete and steel and asbestos and ultra-stubborn refractory and insulation and vacuum-breaks; fully air-conditioned and having refrigeration equipment of thousands of tons per hour of ice; designed not only to expedite servicing, unloading, and loading, but also to protect materials and personnel from the raving, searing blasts of take-off and of landing.

A space-dock is a squat and monstrous cylinder, into whose hollow top the lowermost one-third of a space-ship's bulk fits as snugly as does a baseball into the "pocket" of a veteran fielder's long-seasoned glove. And the tremendous distances between those docks minimise the apparent size, both of the structures themselves and of the vessels surmounting them. Thus, from a distance, the *Chicago* looked little enough, and harmless enough; but as the bug flashed under the overhanging bulk and the driver braked savagely to a stop at one of the dock's entrances, Samms could scarcely keep from flinching. That featureless, grey, smoothly curving wall of alloy steel loomed so incredibly high above them—extended so terrifyingly far outward beyond its visible means of support! It *must* be on the very verge of crashing!

Samms stared deliberately at the mass of metal towering above him, then smiled—not without effort—at his companion.

'You'd think, Alex, that a man would get over being afraid that a ship was going to fall on him, but I haven't—yet.'

'No, and you probably never will. I never have, and I'm one of the old hands. Some claim not to mind it—but not in front of a lie detector. That's why they had to make the passenger docks bigger than the liners—too many passengers fainted and had to be carried aboard on stretchers—or cancelled passage

entirely. However, scaring hell out of them on the ground had one big advantage; they felt so safe inside that they didn't get the colly-wobbles so bad when they went free.'

'Well, I've got over *that*, anyway. Good-bye, Alex; and thanks.'

Samms entered the dock, shot smoothly upward, followed an escorting officer to the captain's own cabin, and settled himself into a cushioned chair facing an ultra-wave view-plate. A face appeared upon his communicator screen and spoke.

'Winfield to First Lensman Samms—you will be ready to blast off at twenty one hundred?'

'Samms to Captain Winfield,' the Lensman replied. 'I will be ready.'

Sirens yelled briefly; a noise which Samms knew was purely a formality. Clearance had been issued; Station P1XNY was filling the air with warnings. Personnel and material close enough to the *Chicago's* dock to be affected by the blast were under cover and safe.

The blast went on; the plate showed, instead of a view of the space-field, a blaze of blue-white light. The warship was inertialiess, it is true; but so terrific were the forces released that incandescent gases, furiously driven, washed the dock and everything for hundreds of yards around it.

The plate cleared. Through the lower, denser layers of atmosphere the *Chicago* bored in seconds; then, as the air grew thinner and thinner, she rushed upward faster and faster. The terrain below became concave...then convex. Being completely without inertia, the ship's velocity was at every instant that at which the friction of the medium through which she blasted her way equalled precisely the force of her driving thrust.

Wherefore, out in open space, the Earth a fast-shrinking tiny ball and Sol himself growing smaller, paler, and weaker at a startling rate, the *Chicago's* speed attained an almost constant value; a value starkly impossible for the human mind to grasp.

CHAPTER 5

For hours Virgil Samms sat motionless, staring almost unseeing into his plate. It was not that the view was not worth seeing—the wonder of space, the ever-changing, constantly-shifting panorama of incredibly brilliant although dimensionless points of light, against that wondrous background of mist-besprinkled black velvet, is a thing that never fails to awe even the most seasoned observer—but he had a tremendous load on his mind. He had to solve an apparently insoluble problem. How...*how*...HOW could he do what he had to do?

Finally, knowing that the time of landing was approaching, he got up, unfolded his fans, and swam lightly through the air of the cabin to a hand-line, along which he drew himself into the control room. He could have made the trip in that room, of course, if he had so chosen; but, knowing that officers of space do not really like to have strangers in that sanctum, he did not intrude until it was necessary.

Captain Winfield was already strapped down at his master conning plate. Pilots, navigators, and computers worked busily at their respective tasks.

'I was just going to call you, First Lensman.' Winfield waved a hand in the general direction of a chair near his own. 'Take the Lieutenant-Captain's station, please.' Then, after a few minutes: 'Go inert, Mr. White.'

'Attention, all personnel,' Lieutenant-Captain White spoke conversationally into a microphone. 'Prepare for inert manoeuvring, Class Three. Off.'

A bank of tiny red lights upon a panel turned green practically as one. White cut the Bergenholm, whereupon Virgil Samms' mass changed instantly from a weight of zero to one of five hundred and twenty five pounds—ships of war then had no space to waste upon such non-essentials as artificial gravity. Although he was braced for the change and cushioned against it, the Lensman's breath *whooshed!* out sharply; but, being intensely interested in what was going on, he swallowed convulsively a couple times, gasped a few deep breaths, and fought his way back up to normalcy.

The Chief Pilot was now at work, with all the virtuoso's skill of his rank and grade; one of the hall-marks of which is to make difficult tasks look easy. He played trills and runs and arpeggios—at times veritable glissades—upon keyboards and pedals, directing with micrometric precision the tremendous forces of the superdreadnought to the task of matching the intrinsic velocity of New York Spaceport at the time of his departure to the I.V. of the surface of the planet so far below.

Samms stared into his plate; first at the incredibly tiny apparent size of that incredibly hot sun, and then at the barren-looking world toward which they were dropping at such terrific speed.

'It doesn't seem possible...' he remarked, half to Winfield, half to himself, 'that a sun could be that big and that hot. Rigel Four is almost two hundred times as far away from it as Earth is from Sol—something like eighteen billion miles—it doesn't look much, if any, bigger than Venus does from Luna—yet this world is hotter than the Sahara Desert.'

'Well, blue giants are both big and hot,' the captain replied, matter-of-factly, 'and their radiation, being mostly invisible, is deadly stuff. And Rigel is about the biggest in this region. There are others a lot worse, though. Doradus S, for instance, would make Rigel,

here, look like a tallow candle. I'm going out there, some of these days, just to take a look at it. But that's enough of astronomical chit-chat—we're down to twenty miles of altitude and we've got your city just about stopped.'

The *Chicago* slowed gently to a halt; perched motionless upon softly hissing jets. Samms directed his visibeam downward and sent along it an exploring, questing thought. Since he had never met a Rigellian in person, he could not form the mental image or pattern necessary to become en rapport with any one individual of the race. He did know, however, the type of mind which must be possessed by the entity with whom he wished to talk, and he combed the Rigellian city until he found one. The rapport was so incomplete and imperfect as to amount almost to no contact at all, but he could, perhaps, make himself understood.

'If you will excuse this possible unpleasant and certainly unwarranted intrusion,' he thought, carefully and slowly, 'I would like very much to discuss with you a matter which should become of paramount importance to all the intelligent peoples of all the planets in space.'

'I welcome you, Tellurian.' Mind fused with mind at every one of uncountable millions of points and paths. This Rigellian professor of sociology, standing at his desk, was physically a monster... the oil-drum of a body, the four blocky legs, the multi-branchiate tentacular arms, that immobile dome of a head, the complete lack of eyes and of ears... nevertheless Samms' mind fused with the monstrosity's as smoothly, as effortlessly, and almost as completely as it had with his own daughter's!

And *what* a mind! The transcendent poise; the staggeringly tremendous range and scope—the untroubled and unshakeable calm; the sublime quietude; the vast and placid certainty; the ultimate

stability, unknown and forever unknowable to any human or near-human race!

'Dismiss all thought of intrusion, First Lensman Samms…I have heard of you human beings, of course, but have never considered seriously the possibility of meeting one of you mind to mind. Indeed, it was reported that none of our minds could make any except the barest and most unsatisfactory contact with any of yours they chance to encounter. It is, I now perceive, the Lens which makes this full accord possible, and it is basically about the Lens that you are here?'

'It is,' and Samms went on to cover in flashing thoughts his conception of what the Galactic Patrol should be and should become. That was easy enough; but when he tried to describe in detail the qualifications necessary for Lensmanship, he began to bog down. 'Force, drive, scope, of course…range…power…but above all, an absolute integrity…an ultimate incorruptibility…' He could recognise such a mind after meeting it and studying it, but as to finding it…It might not be in any place of power or authority. His own, and Rod Kinnison's, happened to be; but Costigan's was not…and both Knobos and DalNalten had made inconspicuousness a fine art…

'I see,' the native stated, when it became clear that Samms could say no more. 'It is evident, of course, that I cannot qualify; nor do I know anyone personally who can. However…'

'What?' Samms demanded. 'I was sure, from the feel of your mind, that you…but with a mind of such depth and breadth, such tremendous scope and power, you must be incorruptible!'

'I am,' came the dry rejoinder. 'We all are. No Rigellian is, or ever will be or can be, what you think of as "corrupt" or "corruptible". Indeed, it is only by the narrowest, most intense concentration upon every line of your thought that I can translate your meaning

into a concept possible for any of us even to understand.'

'Then what...Oh I see. I was starting at the wrong end. Naturally enough, I suppose, I looked first for the qualities rarest in my own race.'

'Of course. Our minds have ample scope and range; and, perhaps, sufficient power. But those qualities which you refer to as "force" and "drive" are fully as rare among us as absolute mental integrity is among you. What you know as "crime" is unknown. We have no police, no government, no laws, no organised armed forces of any kind. We take, practically always, the line of least resistance. We live and let live, as your thought runs. We work together for the common good.'

'Well...I don't know what I expected to find here, but certainly not this...' If Samms had never before been completely thunderstruck, completely at a loss, he was then. 'You don't think, then, that there is any chance?'

'I have been thinking, and there may be a chance...a slight one, but still a chance,' the Rigellian said, slowly. 'For instance, that youth, so full of curiosity, who first visited your planet. Thousands of us have wondered, to ourselves and to each other, about the peculiar qualities of mind which compelled him and others to waste so much time, effort, and wealth upon a project so completely useless as exploration. Why he had even to develop energies and engines theretofore unknown, and which can never be of any real use!'

Samms was shaken by the calm finality with which the Rigellian dismissed all possibility of the usefulness of interstellar exploration, but stuck doggedly to his purpose.

'However slight the chance, I must find and talk to this man. I suppose he is now out in deep space somewhere. Have you any idea where?'

'He is now in his home city, accumulating funds and manufacturing fuel with which to continue his pointless activities. That city is named...that is, in your English you might call it...Suntown? Sunberg? No, it must be more specific... Rigelsville? Rigel City?'

'Rigelston, I would translate it?' Samms hazarded.

'Exactly—Rigelston.' The professor marked its location upon a globular mental map far more accurate and far more detailed than the globe which Captain Winfield and his lieutenant were then studying.

'Thanks. Now, can you and will you get in touch with this explorer and ask him to call a meeting of his full crew and any others who might be interested in the project I have outlined?'

'I can. I will. He and his kind are not quite sane, of course, as you know; but I do not believe that even they are so insane as to be willing to subject themselves to the environment of your vessel.'

'They will not be asked to come here. The meeting will be held in Rigelston. If necessary, I shall insist that it be held there.'

'You would? I perceive that you would. It is strange...yes, fantastic...you are quarrelsome, pugnacious, anti-social, vicious, small-bodied and small-brained; timid, nervous, and highly and senselessly excitable; unbalanced and unsane; as sheerly monstrous mentally as you are physically...' These outrageous thoughts were sent as casually and as impersonally as though the sender were discussing the weather. He paused, then went on: 'And yet, to further such a completely visionary project, you are eager to subject yourself to conditions whose

counterparts I could not force myself, under any circumstances whatever, to meet. It may be…it must be true that there is an extension of the principle of working together for the common good which my mind, for lack of pertinent data, has not been able to grasp. I am now en rapport with Dronvire the explorer.'

'Ask him, please, not to identify himself to me. I do not want to go into that meeting with any preconceived ideas.'

'A balanced thought,' the Rigellian approved. 'Someone will be at the airport to point out to you the already desolated area in which the space-ship of the explorers makes its so-frightful landings; Dronvire will ask someone to meet you at the airport and bring you to the place of meeting.'

The telepathic line snapped and Samms turned a white and sweating face to the *Chicago's* captain.

'God, what a strain! Don't ever try telepathy unless you positively have to—especially not with such an outlandishly *different* race as these Rigellians are!'

'Don't worry; I won't.' Winfield's words were not at all sympathetic, but his tone was. 'You looked as though somebody was beating your brains out with a spiked club. Where next, First Lensman?'

Samms marked the location of Rigelston upon the vessel's chart, then donned ear-plugs and a special radiation-proof suit of armour, equipped with refrigerators and with extra-thick blocks of lead glass to protect the eyes.

The airport, an extremely busy one well outside the city proper, was located easily enough, as was the spot upon which the Tellurian ship was to land. Lightly, slowly, she settled downward, her jets raving out against a gravity fully twice that of her native Earth. Those blasts, however, added little or nothing to the destruction already accomplished by the craft then

lying there—a torpedo-shaped cruiser having perhaps one-twentieth of the *Chicago's* mass and bulk.

The superdreadnought landed, sinking into the hard, dry ground to a depth of some ten or fifteen feet before she stopped. Samms, en rapport with the entity who was to be his escort, made a flashing survey of the mind so intimately in contact with his own. No use. This one was not and never could become Lensman material. He climbed heavily down the ladder. This double-normal gravity made the going a bit difficult, but he could stand that a lot better than some of the other things he was going to have to take. The Rigellian equivalent of an automobile was there, waiting for him, its door invitingly open.

Samms had known—in general—what to expect. The two-wheeled chassis was more or less similar to that of his own Dillingham. The body was a narrow torpedo of steel, bluntly pointed at both ends, and without windows. Two features, however, were both unexpected and unpleasant—the hard tough steel of which that body was forged was an inch and a half thick, instead of one-sixteenth; and even that extraordinarily armoured body was dented and scarred and marred, especially about the fore and rear quarters, as deeply and as badly and as casually as are the fenders of an Earthly jalopy!

The Lensman climbed, not easily or joyously, into that grimly forbidding black interior. Black? It was so black that the port-hole-like doorway seemed to admit no light at all. It was blacker than a witch's cat in a coal cellar at midnight! Samms flinched; then, stiffening, thought at the driver.

'My contact with you seems to have slipped! I'm afraid that I will have to cling to you rather more tightly than may be either polite or comfortable. Deprived of sight, and without your sense of perception, I am practically helpless.'

'Come in, Lensman, by all means. I offered to maintain full engagement, but it seemed to me that you declined it; quite possibly the misunderstanding was due to our unfamiliarity with each others' customary mode of thought. Relax, please, and come in...there! Better?'

'Infinitely better. Thanks.'

And it was. The darkness vanished; through the unexplainable perceptive sense of the Rigellian he could "see" everything—he had a practically perfect three-dimensional view of the entire circumambient sphere. He could see both the inside and the outside of the ground car he was in and of the immense space-ship in which he had come to Rigel IV. He could see the bearings and the wrist-pins of the internal-combustion engine of the car, the interior structure of the welds that held the steel plates together, the busy airport outside, and even deep into the ground. He could see and study in detail the deepest-buried, most heavily shielded parts of the atomic engines of the *Chicago.*

But he was wasting time. He could also plainly see a deeply-cushioned chair, designed to fit a human body, welded to a stanchion and equipped with half a dozen padded restraining straps. He sat down quickly; strapped himself in.

'Ready?'

'Ready.'

The door banged shut with a clangour which burst through the space-suit and ear-plugs with all the violence of a nearby thunderclap. And that was merely the beginning. The engine started—an internal-combustion engine of well over a thousand horsepower, designed for maximum efficiency by engineers in whose lexicon there were no counterparts of any English words relating to noise, or even to

sound. The car took off; with an acceleration which drove the Tellurian backward, deep into the cushions. The scream of tortured tyres and the crescendo bellowing of the engine combined to form an uproar which, amplified by and reverberating within the resonant shell of metal, threatened to addle the very brain inside the Lensman's skull.

'You suffer!' the driver exclaimed, in high concern. 'They cautioned me to start and stop gently, to drive slowly and carefully, to bump softly. They told me you are frail and fragile, a fact which I perceived for myself and which has caused me to drive with the utmost possible care and restraint. Is the fault mine? Have I been too rough?'

'Not at all. It isn't that. It's the ungodly noise.' Then, realising that the Rigellian could have no conception of his meaning, he continued quickly:

'The vibrations in the atmosphere, from sixteen cycles per second up to about nine or ten thousand.' He explained what a second was. 'My nervous system is very sensitive to those vibrations. But I expected them and shielded myself against them as adequately as I could. Nothing can be done about them. Go ahead.'

'Atmospheric vibrations? *Atmospheric* vibrations? Atmospheric *vibrations?*' The driver marvelled, and concentrated upon this entirely new concept while he—

1. Swung around a steel-sheathed concrete pillar at a speed of at least sixty miles per hour, grazing it so closely that he removed one layer of protective coating from the metal.

2. Braked so savagely to miss a wildly careening truck that the restraining straps almost cut Samms' body, space-suit and all, into slices.

3. Darted into a hole in the traffic so narrow that only tiny fractions of inches separated his hurtling

Juggernaut from an enormous steel column on one side and another speeding vehicle on the other.

4. Executed a double-right-angle reverse curve, thus missing by hair's breadths two vehicles travelling in the opposite direction and one in his own.

5. As a grand climax to this spectacular exhibition of insane driving, he plunged at full speed into a traffic artery which seemed so full already that it could not hold even one more car. But it could—just barely could. However, instead of near misses or grazing hits, this time there were bumps, dents—little ones, nothing at all, really, only an inch or so deep—and an utterly hellish concatenation and concentration of noise.

'I fail completely to understand what effect such vibrations could have,' the Rigellian announced finally, sublimely unconscious that anything at all out of the ordinary had occurred. For him, nothing had. 'But surely they cannot be of any use?'

'On this world, I am afraid not. No,' Samms admitted, wearily. 'Here, too, apparently, as everywhere, the big cities are choking themselves to death with their own traffic.'

'Yes. We build and build, but never have roads enough.'

'What are those mounds along the streets?' For some time Samms had been conscious of those long, low, apparently opaque structures; attracted to them because they were the only non-transparent objects within range of the Rigellian's mind. 'Or is it something I should not mention?'

'What? Oh, those? By no means.'

One of the nearby mounds lost its opacity. It was filled with swirling, gyrating bands and streamers of energy so vivid and so solid as to resemble fabric; with wildly hurtling objects of indescribable shapes

and contours; with brilliantly flashing symbols which Samms found, greatly to his surprise, made sense— not through the Rigellian's mind, but through his own Lens:

'EAT TEEGMEE'S FOOD!'

'Advertising!' Samms' thought was a snort.

'Advertising. You do not perceive yours, either, as you drive?' This was the first bond to be established between two of the most highly advanced races of the First Galaxy!

The frightful drive continued; the noise grew worse and worse. Imagine, if you can, a city of fifteen millions of people, throughout whose entire length, breadth, height, and depth no attempt whatever had ever been made to abate any noise, however violent or piercing! If your imagination has been sufficiently vivid and if you have worked understandingly enough, the product may approximate what First Lensman Samms was forced to listen to that day.

Through ever-thickening traffic, climbing to higher and ever higher roadways between towering windowless walls of steel, the massive Rigellian automobile barged and banged its way. Finally it stopped, a thousand feet or so above the ground, beside a building which was still under construction. The heavy door clanged open. They got out.

And then—it chanced to be daylight at the time— Samms saw a tangle of fighting, screaming colours whose like no entity possessing the sense of sight had ever before imagined, Reds, yellows, blues, greens, purples, and every variation and inter-mixture possible; laid on or splashed on or occurring naturally at perfect random, smote his eyes as violently as the all-pervading noise had been assailing his ears.

He realised then that through his guide's sense of perception he had been "seeing" only in shades of

grey, that to these people "visible" light differed only in wave-length from any other band of the complete electromagnetic spectrum of vibration.

Strained and tense, the Lensman followed his escort along a narrow catwalk, through a wall upon which riveters and welders were busily at work, into a room practically without walls and ceiled only by story after story of huge I-beams. Yet *this* was the meeting-place; almost a hundred Rigellians were assembled there!

And as Samms walked towards the group a craneman dropped a couple of tons of steel plate, from a height of eight or ten feet, upon the floor directly behind him.

'I just about jumped right out of my armour,' is the way Samms himself described his reactions; and that description is perhaps as good as any.

At any rate, he went briefly out of control, and the Rigellian sent him a steadying, inquiring, wondering thought. He could no more understand the Tellurian's sensitivity than Samms could understand the fact that to these people, even the concept of physical intrusion was absolutely incomprehensible. These builders were not workmen, in the Tellurian sense. They were Rigellians, each working his few hours per week for the common good. They would be no more in contact with the meeting than would their fellows on the other side of the planet.

Samms closed his eyes to the riot of clashing colours, deafened himself by main strength to the appalling clangour of sound, forced himself to concentrate every fibre of his mind upon his errand.

'Please synchronize with my mind, as many of you as possible,' he thought at the group as a whole, and went en rapport with mind after mind after mind. And mind after mind after mind lacked something. Some

were stronger than others, had more initiative and drive and urge, but none would quite do. Until -

'Thank God!' In the wave of exultant relief, of fulfillment, Samms no longer saw the colours or heard the din. 'You, sir, are of Lensman grade. I perceive that you are Dronvire.'

'Yes, Virgil Samms. I am Dronvire; and at long last I know what it is that I have been seeking all my life. But how of these, my other friends? Are not some of them...?'

'I do not know, nor is it necessary that I find out. You will select...' Samms paused, amazed. The other Rigellians were still in the room, but mentally, he and Dronvire were completely alone.

'They anticipated your thought, and, knowing that it was to be more or less personal, they left us until one of us invites them to return.'

'I like that, and appreciate it. You will go to Arisia. You will receive your Lens. You will return here. You will select and send to Arisia as many or as few of your fellows as you choose. These things I require you, by the Lens of Arisia, to do. Afterward—please note that this is in no sense obligatory—I would like very much to have you visit Earth and accept appointment to the Galactic Council. Will you?'

'I will.' Dronvire needed no time to consider his decision.

The meeting was dismissed. The same entity who had been Samms' chauffeur on the in-bound trip drove him back to the *Chicago*, driving as "slowly" and as "carefully" as before. Nor, this time, did the punishment take such toll, even though Samms knew that each terrific lunge and lurch was adding one more bruise to the already much-too-large collection discolouring almost every square foot of his tough hide.

He had succeeded, and the thrill of success had its usual analgesic effect.

The *Chiacago's* Captain met him in the air-lock and helped him remove his suit.

'Are you *sure* you're all right, Samms?' Winfield was no longer the formal captain, but a friend. 'Even though you didn't call, we were beginning to wonder... you look as though you'd been to a Valerian clambake, and I sure as hell don't like the way you're favouring those ribs and that left leg. I'll tell the boys you got back in A-prime shape, but I'll have the doctors look you over, just to make sure.'

Winfield made the announcement, and through his Lens Samms could plainly feel the wave of relief and pleasure that spread throughout the great ship with the news. It surprised him immensely. Who was *he*, that all these boys should care so much whether he lived or died?

'I'm perfectly all right,' Samms protested. 'There's nothing at all the matter with me that twenty hours of sleep won't fix as good as new.'

'Maybe; but you'll go to the sick-bay first, just the same,' Winfield insisted. 'And I suppose you want me to blast back to Tellus?'

'Right. And fast. The Ambassadors' Ball is next Tuesday evening, you know, and that's one function I can't stay away from, even with a Class A Double Prime excuse.'

CHAPTER 6

The Ambassadors' Ball, one of the most ultra-ultra functions of the year, was well under way. It was not that everyone who was anyone was there; but everyone who was there was, in one way or another, very emphatically someone. Thus, there were affairs at which there were more young and beautiful women, and more young and handsome men; but none exhibiting newer or more expensive gowns, more ribbons and decorations, more or costlier or more refined jewellery, or a larger acreage of powdered and perfumed epidermis.

And even so, the younger set was well enough represented. Since pioneering appeals more to youth than to age, the men representing the colonies were young; and their wives, together with the daughters and the second (or third or fourth, or occasionally the fifth) wives of the human personages practically balanced the account.

Nor was the throng entirely human. The time had not yet come, of course, when warm-blooded, oxygen-breathing monstrosities from hundreds of other solar systems would vie in numbers with the humanity present. There were, however, a few Martians on the floor, wearing their light "robes du convention" and dancing with meticulously mathematical precision. A few Venerians, who did not dance, sat in state or waddled importantly about. Many worlds of the Solarian System, and not a few other systems, were represented.

One couple stood out, even against that opulent and magnificent background. Eyes followed them wherever they went.

The girl was tall, trim, supple; built like a symphony. Her Callistan vexto-silk gown, of the newest and most violent shade of "radioactive" green, was phosphorescently luminous; fluorescent; gleaming and glowing. Its hem swept the floor, but above the waist it vanished mysteriously except for wisps which clung to strategic areas here and there with no support, apparently, except the personal magnetism of the wearer. She, almost alone of all the women there, wore no flowers. Her only jewellery was a rosette of huge, perfectly-matched emeralds, perched precariously upon her bare left shoulder. Her hair, unlike the other women's flawless coiffures, was a flamboyant, artistically-disarranged, red-bronze-auburn mop. Her soft and dewy eyes—Virgilia Samms could control her eyes as perfectly as she could her highly educated hands—were at the moment gold-flecked, tawny wells of girlish innocence and trust.

'But I can't give you this next dance, too, Herkimer—Honestly I can't!' she pleaded, snuggling just a trifle closer into the embrace of the young man who was just as much man, physically, as she was woman. 'I'd just love to, really, but I just simply can't, and you know why, too.'

'You've got some duty-dances, of course...'

'Some? I've got a list as long as from here to there! Senator Morgan first, of course, then Mr. Isaacson, then I sat one out with Mr. Ossmen—I can't stand Venerians, they're so slimy and fat and repulsive!—and that leathery horned toad from Mars and that Jovian hippopotamus...'

She went down the list, and as she named or characterised each entity another finger of her left hand pressed down upon the back of her partner's right, to emphasise the count of her social obligations. But those talented fingers were doing more—far, far more—than that.

Herkimer Herkimer Third, although no little of a Don Juan, was a highly polished, smoothly finished, thoroughly seasoned diplomat. As such, his eyes and his other features—particularly his eyes—had been schooled for years to reveal no trace of whatever might be going on inside his brain. If he had entertained any suspicion of the beautiful girl in his arms, if anyone had suggested that she was trying her best to pump him, he would have smiled the sort of smile which only the top-drawer diplomat can achieve. He was not suspicious of Virgilia Samms. However, simply because she was Virgil Samms' daughter, he took an extra bit of pain to betray no undue interest in any one of the names she recited. And besides, she was not looking at his eyes, nor even at his face. Her glance, demurely downcast, was all too rarely raised above the level of his chin.

There were some things, however, that Herkimer Herkimer Third did not know. That Virgilia Samms was the most accomplished muscle-reader of her times. That she was so close to him, not because of his manly charm, but because only in that position could she do her prodigious best. That she could work with her eyes alone, but in emergencies, when fullest possible results were imperative, she had to use her exquisitely sensitive fingers and her exquisitely tactile skin. That she had studied intensively, and had tabulated the reactions of, each of the entities on her list. That she was now, with his help, fitting those reactions into a pattern. And finally, that that pattern was beginning to assume the grim shape of MURDER!

And Virgilia Samms, working now for something far more urgent and vastly more important than a figmental Galactic Patrol, hoped desperately that this Herkimer was not a muscle-reader too; for she knew that she was revealing her secrets even more completely than was he. In fact, if things got much worse, he could not help but feel the pounding of her

heart...but she could explain that easily enough, by a few appropriate wiggles... No, he wasn't a reader, definitely not. He wasn't watching the right places; he was looking where that gown had been designed to make him look, and nowhere else...and no tell-tale muscles lay beneath any part of either of his hands.

As her eyes and her fingers and her lovely torso sent more and more information to her keen brain, Jill grew more and more anxious. She was sure that murder was intended, but who was to be the victim? Her father? Probably. Pops Kinnison? Possibly. Somebody else? Barely possible. And when? And where? And how? She *didn't know!* And she would have to be *sure*... Mentioning names hadn't been enough, but a personal appearance... Why *didn't* dad show up—or did she wish he wouldn't come at all...?

Virgil Samms entered the ballroom.

'And dad told me, Herkimer,' she cooed sweetly, gazing up into his eyes for the first time in over a minute, 'that I must dance with every one of them. So you see... Oh, there he is now, over there! I've been wondering where he's been keeping himself.' She nodded toward the entrance and prattled on artlessly. 'He's almost *never* late, you know, and I've...'

He looked, and as his eyes met those of the First Lensman, Jill learned three of the facts she needed so badly to know. Her father. Here. Soon. She never knew how she managed to keep herself under control; but, some way and just barely, she did.

Although nothing showed, she was seething inwardly: wrought up as she had never before been. What could she do? She *knew*, but she did not have a scrap or an iota of visible or tangible evidence; and if she made one single slip, however slight, the consequences could be immediate and disastrous.

After this dance might be too late. She could make an excuse to leave the floor, but that would look very bad, later...and none of them would Lens her, she knew, while she was with Herkimer—*damn* such chivalry!...She *could* take the chance of waving at her father, since she hadn't seen him for so long...no, the smallest risk would be with Mase. He looked at her every chance he got, and she'd *make* him use his Lens...

Northrop looked at her; and over Herkimer's shoulder, for one fleeting instant, she allowed her face to reveal the terrified appeal she so keenly felt.

'Want me, Jill?' His Lensed thought touched only the outer fringes of her mind. Full rapport is more intimate than a kiss: no one except her father had ever really put a Lens on Virgilia Samms. Nevertheless:

'*Want* you! I never wanted anybody so much in my life! Come in, Mase—quick—*please!*'

Diffidently enough, he came; but at the first inkling of the girl's news all thought of diffidence or of privacy vanished.

'Jack! Spud! Mr. Kinnison! Mr. Samms!' he Lensed sharp, imperative, almost frantic thoughts. 'Listen in!'

'Steady, Mase, I'll take over,' came Roderick Kinnison's deeper, quieter mental voice. 'First, the matter of guns. Anybody except me wearing a pistol? You are, Spud?'

'Yes, sir.'

'You would be. But you and Mase, Jack?'

'We've got our Lewistons!'

'You would have. Blasters, my sometimes-not-quite-so-bright son, are fine weapons indeed for certain kinds of work. In emergencies, it is of course permissible to kill a few dozen innocent bystanders.

In such a crowd as this, though, it is much better technique to kill only the one you are aiming at. So skip out to my car, you two, right now, and change— and make it *fast*.' Everyone knew that Roderick Kinnison's car was at all times an arsenal on wheels. 'Wish you were in uniform, too, Virge, but it can't be helped now. Work your way—*slowly*—around to the northwest corner. Spud, do the same.'

'It's impossible—starkly unthinkable!' and 'I'm not *sure* of anything, really...' Samms and his daughter began simultaneously to protest.

'Virgil, you talk like a man with a paper nose. Keep still until after you've used your brain. And I'm sure enough of what you know, Jill, to take plenty of steps. You can relax now—take it easy. We're covering Virgil and I called up support in force. You *can* relax a little, I see. Good! I'm not trying to hide from anybody that the next few minutes may be critical. Are you pretty sure, Jill, that Herkimer is a key man?'

'Pretty sure, Pops.' *How* much better she felt, now that the Lensmen were on guard! 'In this one case, at least.'

'Good! Then let him talk you into giving him every dance, right straight through until something breaks. Watch him. He must know the signal and who is going to operate, and if you can give us a fraction of a second of warning it will help no end. Can do?'

'I'll say I can—and I would love to, the big, slimy, stinking skinker!' As transliterated into words, the girl's thought may seem a trifle confused, but Kinnison knew exactly what she meant.

'One more thing, Jill; a detail. The boys are coming back in and are working their partners over this way. See if Herkimer notices that they have changed their holsters.'

'No, he didn't notice,' Jill reported, after a moment. 'But I don't notice any difference, either, and I'm looking for it.'

'Nevertheless, it's there, and the difference between a Mark Seventeen and a Mark Five is something more than that between Tweedledum and Tweedledee,' Kinnison returned, dryly. 'However, it may not be as obvious to non-military personnel as it is to us. That's far enough, boys, don't get too close. Now, Virge, keep solidly en rapport with Jill on one side and with us on the other, so that she won't have to give herself and the show away by yelling and pointing, and...'

'But this is preposterous!' Samms stormed.

'Preposterous, hell,' Roderick Kinnison's thought was still coldly level; only the fact that he was beginning to use non-ballroom language revealed any sign of the strain he was under. 'Stop being so goddam heroic and start using your brain. You turned down fifty billion credits. Why do you suppose they offered that much, when they can get anybody killed for a hundred? And what would they do about it?'

'But they couldn't get away with it, Rod, at an Ambassadors' Ball. They *couldn't*, possibly.'

'Formerly, no. That was my first thought, too. But it was you who pointed out to me, not so long ago, that the techniques of crime have changed of late. In the new light, the swankier the brawl the greater the confusion and the better the chance of getting away clean. Comb *that* out of your whiskers, you red-headed mule!'

'Well...there might be something in it, after all...' Samms' thought showed apprehension at last.

'You know damn well there is. But you boys—Jack and Mase especially—loosen up. You can't do good shooting while you're strung up like a couple of

cocoons. Do something—talk to your partners or think at Jill...'

'That won't be hard, sir.' Mason Northrop grinned feebly. 'And that reminds me of something, Jill. Mentor certainly bracketed the target when he—or she, or it, maybe—said that you would never need a Lens.'

'Huh?' Jill demanded, inelegantly. 'I don't see the connection, if any.'

'No? Everybody else does, I'll bet. How about it?' The other Lensmen, even Samms, agreed enthusiastically. 'Well, do you think that any of those characters, particularly Herkimer Herkimer Third, would let a harness bull in harness—even such a beautiful one as you—get close enough to him to do such a Davey the Dip act on his mind?'

'Oh...I never thought of that, but it's right, and I'm glad...but Pops, you said something about "support in force". Have you any idea how long it will be? I *hope* I can hold out, with you all supporting me, but...'

'You can, Jill. Two or three minutes more, at most.'

'Support? In force? What do you mean?' Samms snapped.

'Just that. The whole damned army,' Kinnison replied. 'I sent Two-Star Commodore Alexander Clayton a thought that lifted him right out of his chair. Everything he's got, at full emergency blast. Armour—mark eighty fours—six by six extra heavies—a ninety sixty for an ambulance—full escort, upstairs and down—way-friskers—'copters—cruisers and big stuff—in short, the works. I would have run with you before this, if I dared; but the minute the relief party shows up, we do a flit.'

'If you *dared*?' Jill asked, shaken by the thought.

'Exactly, my dear. I don't dare. If they start anything we'll do our damndest, but I'm praying they won't.'

But Kinnison's prayers—if he made any—were ignored. Jill heard a sharp, but very usual and insignificant sound; someone had dropped a pencil. She felt an inconspicuous muscle twitch slightly. She saw the almost imperceptible tensing of a neck-muscle which would have turned Herkimer's head in a certain direction if it had been allowed to act. Her eyes flashed along that line, searched busily for milli-seconds. A man was reaching unobtrusively, as though for a handkerchief. But men at Ambassadors' Balls do not carry blue handkerchiefs; nor does any fabric, however dyed, resemble at all closely the blued steel of an automatic pistol.

Jill would have screamed, then, and pointed; but she had time to do neither. Through her rapport with her father the Lensmen saw everything that she saw, in the instant of her seeing it. Hence five shots blasted out, practically as one, before the girl could scream, or point, or even move. She did scream, then; but since dozens of other women were screaming, too, it made no difference—then.

Conway Costigan, trigger-nerved spacehound that he was and with years of gun-fighting and of hand-to-hand brawling in his log, shot first; even before the gunman did. It was Costigan's blinding speed that saved Virgil Samms' life that day; for the would-be assassin was dying, with a heavy slug crashing through his brain, before he finished pulling the trigger. The dying hand twitched upward. The bullet intended for Samms' heart went high; through the fleshy part of the shoulder.

Roderick Kinnison, because of his age, and his son and Northrop, because of their inexperience, were a few milliseconds slow. They, however, were aiming for the body, not for the head; and any of those three resulting wounds would have been satisfactorily fatal. The man went down, and stayed down.

Samms staggered, but did not go down until the elder Kinnison, as gently as was consistent with the maximum of speed, threw him down.

'Stand back! Get Back! Give him air!' Men began to shout, the while pressing closer themselves.

'You men, stand back. Some of you go get a stretcher. You women, come here.' Kinnison's heavy, parade-ground voice smashed down all lesser noises. 'Is there a doctor here?'

There was; and, after being "frisked" for weapons, he went busily to work.

'Joy—Betty—Jill—Clio,' Kinnison called his own wife and their daughter, Virgilia Samms, and Mrs. Costigan. 'You four first. Now you—and you—and you—and you...' he went on, pointing out large, heavy women wearing extremely extreme gowns, 'Stand here, right over him. Cover him up, so that nobody else can get a shot at him. You other women, stand behind and between these—closer yet—fill those spaces up solid—there! Jack, stand there. Mase, there. Costigan, the other end; I'll take this one. Now, everybody, listen. I know damn well that none of you women are wearing guns above the waist, and you've all got long skirts— thank God for ballgowns! Now, fellows, if any one of these women makes a move to lift her skirt, blow her brains out, right then, without waiting to ask questions.'

'Sir, I protest! This is outrageous!' one of the dowagers exclaimed.

'Madam, I agree with you fully. It is.' Kinnison smiled as genuinely as he could under the circumstances. 'It is, however, *necessary*. I will apologise to all you ladies, and to you, doctor—in writing if you like—after we have Virgil Samms aboard the *Chicago*; but until then I would not trust my own grandmother.'

The doctor looked up. 'The *Chicago?* This wound does not appear to be a very serious one, but this man is going to a hospital at once. Ah, the stretcher. So...please...easy...there, that is excellent. Call an ambulance, please, immediately.'

'I did. Long ago. But no hospital, doctor. All those windows—open to the public—or the whole place bombed—by no means. I'm taking no chances whatever.'

'Except with your own life!' Jill put in sharply, looking up from her place at her father's side. Assured that the First Lensman was in no danger of dying, she had begun to take interest in other things. 'You are important, too, you know, and you're standing right out there in the open. Get another stretcher, lie down on it, and we'll guard you, too...and don't be too stiff-necked to take your own advice!' she flared, as he hesitated.

'I'm not, if it were necessary, but it isn't. If they had killed him, yes. I'd probably be next in line. But since he got only a scratch, there'd be no point at all in killing even a *good* Number Two.'

'A *scratch!*' Jill fairly seethed. 'Do you call that horrible wound a *scratch?*'

'Huh? Why, certainly—that's all it is—thanks to you,' he returned, in honest and complete surprise. 'No bones shattered—no main arteries cut—missed the lung—he'll be as good as new in a couple of weeks.'

'And now,' he went on aloud, 'if you ladies will please pick up this stretcher we will move en masse, and *slowly*, toward the door.'

The women, no longer indignant but apparently enjoying the sensation of being the centre of interest, complied with the request.

'Now, boys,' Kinnison Lensed a thought. 'Did any of you—Costigan?—see any signs of a concerted rush, such as there would have been to get the killer away if we hadn't interfered?'

'No, sir,' came Costigan's brisk reply. 'None within sight of me.'

'Jack and Mase—I don't suppose you looked?'

They hadn't—had not thought of it in time.

'You'll learn. It takes a few things like this to make it automatic. But I couldn't see any, either, so I'm fairly certain there wasn't any. Smart operators—quick on the uptake.'

'I'd better get at this, sir, don't you think, and let Operation Boskone go for a while?' Costigan asked.

'I don't think so.' Kinnison frowned in thought. 'This operation was *planned*, son, by people with brains. Any clues you could find now would undoubtedly be plants. No, we'll let the regulars look; we'll stick to our own...'

Sirens wailed and screamed outside. Kinnison sent out an exploring thought.

'Alex?'

'Yes. Where do you want this ninety-sixty with the doctors and nurses? It's too wide for the gates.'

'Go through the wall. Across the lawn. Right up to the door, and never mind the frippery they've got all over the place—have your adjutant tell them to bill us for damage. Samms is shot in the shoulder. Not too serious, but I'm taking him to the Hill, where I know he'll be safe. What have you got on top of the umbrella, the *Boise* or the *Chicago*? I haven't had time to look up yet.'

'Both.'

'Good man.'

Jack Kinnison started at the monstrous tank, which was smashing statues, fountains, and ornamental trees flat into the earth as it moved ponderously across the grounds, and licked his lips. He looked at the companies of soldiers "frisking" the route, the grounds, and the crowd—higher up, at the hovering helicopters—still higher, at the eight light cruisers so evidently and so viciously ready to blast—higher still, at the long streamers of fire which, he now knew, marked the locations of the two most powerful engines of destruction ever built by man—and his face turned slowly white.

'Good Lord, Dad!' he swallowed twice. 'I had no idea...but they might, at that.'

'Not "might", son. They damn well would, if they could get here soon enough with heavy enough stuff.' The elder Kinnison's jaw-muscles did not loosen, his darting eyes did not relax their vigilance for a fraction of a second as he Lensed the thought. 'You boys can't be expected to know it all, but right now you're learning fast. Get this—paste it in your iron hats. *Virgil Samms' life is the most important thing in this whole damned universe!* If they had got him then it would not, strictly speaking, have been my fault, but if they get him now, it will.'

The land cruiser crunched to a stop against the very entrance, and a white-clad man leaped out.

'Let me look at him, please...'

'Not yet!' Kinnison denied, sharply. 'Not until he's got four inches of solid steel between him and whoever wants to finish the job they started. Get your men around him, and get him aboard—fast!'

Samms, protected at every point at every instant, was lifted into the maw of the ninety-sixty; and as the

massive door clanged shut Kinnison heaved a tremendous sigh of relief. The cavalcade moved away.

'Coming with us, Rod?' Commodore Clayton shouted.

'Yes, but got a couple minutes' work here yet. Have a staff car wait for me, and I'll join you.' He turned to the three young Lensmen and the girl. 'This fouls up our plans a little, but not too much—I hope. No change in Mateese or Boskone; you and Costigan, Jill, can go ahead as planned. Northrop, you'll have to brief Jill on Zwilnik and find out what she knows. Virgil was going to do it tonight, after the brawl here, but you know as much about it now as any of us. Check with Knobos, DalNalten, and Fletcher—while Virgil is laid up you and Jack may have to work on both Zabriska and Zwilnik—he'll Lens you. Get the dope, then do as you think best. Get going!' He strode away toward the waiting staff-car.

'Boskone? Zwilnik?' Jill demanded. 'What gives? What are they, Jack?'

'We don't know yet—maybe we're going to name a couple of planets...'

'Piffle!' she scoffed. 'Can *you* talk sense, Mase? What's Boskone?'

'A simple, distinctive, pronounceable coined word; suggested, I believe, by Dr. Bergenholm...' he began.

'You know what I mean, you...' she broke in, but was silenced by a sharply Lensed thought from Jack. His touch was very light, barely sufficient to make conversation possible; but even so, she flinched.

'Use your brain, Jill; you aren't thinking a lick—not that you can be blamed for it. Stop talking; there may be lip-readers or high-powered listeners around. This feels funny, doesn't it? He twitched mentally and went on: 'You already know what Operation Mateese

is, since it's your own dish—politics. Operation Zwilnik is drugs, vice, and so on. Operation Boskone is pirates; Spud is running that. Operation Zabriska is Mase and me checking some peculiar disturbances in the sub-ether. Come in, Mase, and do your stuff—I'll see you later, aboard. Clear ether, Jill!'

Young Kinnison vanished from the fringes of her mind and Northrop appeared. And what a difference! His mind touched hers as gingerly as Jack's had done; as skittishly, as instantaneously ready to bolt away from anything in the least degree private. However, Jack's mind had rubbed hers the wrong way, right from the start—and Mase's didn't!

'Now, about this Operation Zwilnik,' Jill began.

'Something else first. I couldn't help noticing, back there, that you and Jack...well, not out of phase, exactly, or really out of sync, but sort of...well, as though...'

' "Hunting"?' she suggested.

'Not exactly..."forcing" might be better—like holding a tight beam together when it wants to fall apart. So you noticed it yourself?'

'Of course, but I thought Jack and I were the only ones who did. Like scratching a blackboard with your fingernails—you *can* do it, but you're awfully glad to stop...and I *like* Jack, too, darn it—at a distance.'

'And you and I fit like precisely tuned circuits. Jack really meant it, then, when he said that you...that is, he...I didn't quite believe it until now, but if...you know, of course, what you've already done to me.'

Jill's block went on, full strength. She arched her eyebrows and spoke aloud—'why, I haven't the *faintest* idea!'

'Of course not. That's why you're using voice. I've found out, too, that I can't lie with my mind. I feel like

a heel and a louse, with so much job ahead, but you've simply got to tell me something. Then—whatever you say—I'll hit the job with everything I've got. Do I get heaved out between planets without a space-suit, or not?'

'I don't think so.' Jill blushed vividly, but her voice was steady. 'You would rate a space-suit, and enough oxygen to reach another plan—another goal. And now we'd better get to work, don't you think?'

'Yes. Thanks, Jill, a million. I know as well as you do that I was talking out of turn, and how much—but I had to know.' He breathed deep. 'And that's all I ask—for now. Cut your screens.'

She lowered her mental barriers, finding it surprisingly easy to do so in this case; let them down almost as far as she was in the habit of doing with her father. He explained in flashing thoughts everything he knew of the four Operations, concluding:

'I'm not assigned to Zabriska permanently; I'll probably work with you on Mateese after your father gets back into circulation. I'm to act more as a liaison man—neither Knobos nor DalNalten knows you well enough to Lens you. Right?'

'Yes, I've met Mr. Knobos only once, and have never even seen Dr. DalNalten.'

'Ready to visit them, via Lens?'

'Yes. Go ahead.'

The two Lensmen came in. They came into his mind, not hers. Nevertheless their thoughts, superimposed upon Northrop's, came to the girl as clearly as though all four were speaking to each other face to face.

'What a *weird* sensation!' Jill exclaimed. 'Why, I never *imagined* anything like it!'

'We are sorry to trouble you, Miss Samms...' Jill was surprised anew. The silent voice deep within her mind was of characteristically Martian timbre, but instead of the harshly guttural consonants and the hissing sibilants of any Martian's best efforts at English, pronunciation and enunciation were flawless.

'Oh, I didn't mean that. It's no trouble at all, really, I just haven't got used to this telepathy yet.'

'None of us has, to any noticeable degree. But the reason for this call is to ask you if you have anything new, however, slight, to add to our very small knowledge of Zwilnik?'

'Very little I'm afraid; and that little is mostly guesses, deductions, and jumpings at conclusions. Father told you about the way I work, I suppose?'

'Yes. Exact data is not to be expected. Hints. suggestions, possible leads, will be of inestimable value.'

'Well, I met a very short, very fat Venerian, named Ossmen, at a party at the European Embassy. Do either of you know him?'

'I know of him,' DalNalten replied. 'A highly reputable merchant, with such large interests on Tellus that he has to spend most of his time here. He is not in any one of our books...although there is nothing at all surprising in that fact. Go on, please, Miss Samms.'

'He didn't come to the party with Senator Morgan; but he came to some kind of an agreement with him that night, and I am pretty sure that it was about thionite. That's the only new item I have.'

'*Thionite!*' The three Lensmen were equally surprised.

'Yes. Thionite. Definitely.'

'How *sure* are you of this, Miss Samms?' Knobos asked, in deadly earnest.

'I am not *sure* that this particular agreement was about thionite, no; but the probability is roughly nine-tenths. I *am* sure, however, that both Senator Morgan and Ossmen know a lot about thionite that they want to hide. Both gave very high positive reactions—well beyond the six-sigma point of virtual certainty.'

There was a pause, broken by the Martian, but not by a thought directed at any one of the three.

'Sid!' he called, and even Jill could feel the Lensed thought speed.

'Yes, Knobos? Fletcher.'

'That haul-in you made, out in the asteroids. Heroin, hadive, and ladolian, wasn't it? No thionite involved anywhere?'

'No thionite. However, you must remember that part of the gang got away, so all I can say positively is that we didn't see, or hear about, any thionite. There was some gossip, of course: but you know there always is.'

'Of course. Thanks, Sid.' Jill could feel the brilliant Martian's mental gears whirl and click. Then he went into such a flashing exchange of thought with the Venerian that the girl lost track in seconds.

'One more question, Miss Samms?' DalNalten asked. 'Have you detected any indications that there may be some connection between either Ossmen or Morgan and any officer or executive of Interstellar Spaceways?'

'*Spaceways*! Isaacson?' Jill caught her breath. 'Why...nobody even thought of such a thing—at least, nobody ever mentioned it to me—I never thought of making any such tests.'

'The possibility occurred to me only a moment ago, at your mention of thionite. The connection, if any exists, will be exceedingly difficult to trace. But since most, if not all, of the parties involved will probably be included in your Operation Mateese, and since a finding, either positive or negative, would be tremendously significant, we feel emboldened to ask you to keep this point in mind.'

'Why, of course I will. I'll be very glad to.'

'We thank you for your courtesy and your help. One or both of us will get in touch with you from time to time, now that we know the pattern of your personality. May immortal Grolossen speed the healing of your father's wound.'

CHAPTER 7

Late that night—or, rather, very early the following morning—Senator Morgan and his Number One secretary were closeted in the former's doubly spy-ray-proofed office. Morgan's round, heavy, florid face had perhaps lost a little of its usual colour; the fingers of his left hand drummed soundlessly upon the glass top of his desk. His shrewd grey eyes, however, were as keen and as calculating as ever.

'This thing smells, Herkimer...it *reeks*...but I can't figure any of the angles. That operation was *planned*. Sure fire, it *couldn't* miss. Right up to the last split second it worked perfectly. Then—blooie! A flat bust. The Patrol landed and everything was under control. There *must* have been a leak somewhere—but where in hell could it have been?'

'There couldn't have been a leak, Chief; it doesn't make sense.' The secretary uncrossed his long legs, recrossed them in the other direction, threw away a half-smoked cigarette, lit another. 'If there'd been any kind of a leak they would have done a lot more than just kill the low man on the ladder. You know as well as I do that Rocky Kinnison is the hardest-boiled character this side of hell. If he had known anything, he would have killed everybody in sight, including you and me. Besides, if there had been a leak, he would not have let Samms get within ten thousand miles of the place—that's one sure thing. Another thing is he wouldn't have waited until after it was all over to get his army there. No Chief, there couldn't have been a leak. Whatever Samms or Kinnison found out— probably Samms, he's a hell of a lot smarter than Kinnison is, you know—he learned right there and then. He must have seen Brainerd start to pull his gun.'

'I thought of that. I'd buy it, except for one fact. Apparently you didn't time the interval between the shots and the arrival of the tanks.'

'Sorry, Chief.' Herkimer's face was a study in chagrin. 'I made a bad slip there.'

'I'll say you did. One minute and fifty eight seconds.'

'What!'

Morgan remained silent.

'The patrol is fast, of course…and always ready…and they would yank the stuff in on tractor beams, not under their own power…but even so…five minutes is my guess, Chief. Four and a half, absolute minimum.'

'Check. And where do you go from there?

'I see your point. I don't. That blows everything wide open. One set of facts says there was a leak, which occurred between two and a half and three minutes before the signal was given. I ask you, Chief, does that make sense?'

'No. That's what is bothering me. As you say, the facts seem to be contradictory. Somebody must have learned something before anything happened; but if they did, why didn't they do more? And Murgatroyd. If they didn't know about him, why the ships—especially the big battlewagons? If they did think he might be out there somewhere, why didn't they go and find out?'

'Now I'll ask one. Why didn't our Mr. Murgatroyd do something? Or wasn't the pirate fleet supposed to be in on this? Probably not, though.'

'My guess would be the same as yours. Can't see any reason for having a fleet cover a one-man operation, especially as well-planned a one as this was. But that's none of our business. These Lensmen

are. I was watching them every second. Neither Samms nor Kinnison did anything whatever during that two minutes.'

'Young Kinnison and Northrop each left the hall about that time.'

'I know it. So they did. Either one of them *could* have called the Patrol—but what has that to do with the price of beef C.I.F. Valeria?'

Herkimer refrained tactfully from answering the savage question. Morgan drummed and thought for minutes, then went on slowly:

'There are two, and only two, possibilities; neither of which seem even remotely possible. It was—*must* have been—either the Lens or the girl.'

'The girl? Act your age, Senator. I knew where *she* was, and what she was doing, every second.'

'That was evident.' Morgan stopped drumming and smiled cynically. 'I'm getting a hell of a kick out of seeing you taking it, for a change, instead of dishing it out.'

'Yes?' Herkimer's handsome face hardened. 'That game isn't over, my friend.'

'That's what *you* think,' the Senator jibed. 'Can't believe that any woman *can* be Herkimer-proof, eh? You've been working on her for six weeks now, instead of the usual six hours, and you haven't got anywhere yet.'

'I will, Senator.' Herkimer's nostrils flared viciously. 'I'll get her, one way or another, if it's the last thing I ever do.'

'I'll give you eight to five you don't; and a six-month time limit.'

'I'll take five thousand of that. But what makes you think that she's anything to be afraid of? She's a trained psychologist, yes; but so am I; and I'm older and more experienced than she is. That leaves that yoga stuff—her learning how to sit cross-legged, how to contemplate her navel, and how to try to get in tune with the infinite. How do you figure *that* puts her in my class?'

'I told you, I don't. Nothing makes sense. But she *is* Virgil Samms' daughter.'

'What of it? You didn't gag on George Olmstead—you picked him yourself for one of the toughest jobs we've got. By blood he's just about as close to Virgil Samms as Virgilia is. They might as well have been hatched out of the same egg.'

'Physically, yes. Mentally and psychologically, no. Olmstead is a realist, a materialist. He wants his reward in this world, not the next, and is out to get it. Furthermore, the job will probably kill him, and even if it doesn't, he will never be in a position of trust or where he can learn much of anything. On the other hand, Virgil Samms is—but I don't need to tell you what *he* is like. But you don't seem to realise that she's just like him—she isn't playing around with you because of your overpowering charm...'

'Listen, Chief. She didn't know anything and she didn't do anything. I was dancing with her all the time, as close as that,' he clasped his hands tightly together, 'so I know what I'm talking about. And if you think she could *ever* learn anything from me, skip it. You know that nobody on Earth, or anywhere else, can read my face; and besides, she was playing coy right then—wasn't even looking at me. So count her out.'

'We'll have to, I guess.' Morgan resumed his quiet drumming. 'If there were any possibility that she pumped you I'd send you to the mines, but there's no sign...that leaves the Lens. It has seemed, right along,

more logical than the girl—but a lot more fantastic. Been able to find out anything more about it?'

'No. Just what they've been advertising. Combination radio-phone, automatic language-converter, telepath, and so on. Badge of the top skimmings of the top-bracket cops. But I began to think, out there on the floor, that they aren't advertising everything they know.'

'So did I. You tell me.'

'Take the time zero minus three minutes. Besides the five Lensmen—and Jill Samms—the place was full of top brass; scrambled eggs all over the floor. Commodores and Lieutenant-Commodores from all continental governments of the Earth, the other planets, and the colonies, all wearing full-dress side-arms. Nobody knew anything then; we agree on that. But within the next few seconds, somebody found out something and called for help. One of the Lensmen could possibly have done that without showing signs. BUT—at zero time all four Lensmen had their guns out—and *not* Lewistons, please note—and were shooting; whereas none of the other armed officers knew that anything was going on until after it was all over. That puts the finger on the Lens.'

'That's the way I figured it. But the difficulties remain unchanged. *How?* Mind-reading?'

'Space-drift!' Herkimer snorted. 'My mind can't be read.'

'Nor mine.'

'And besides, if they could read minds, they wouldn't have waited until the last possible split second to do it, unless…say, wait a minute!…Did Brainerd act or look nervous, toward the last? I wasn't to look at him, you know.'

'Not nervous, exactly; but he did get a little tense.'

'There you are, then. Hired murderers aren't smart. A Lensman saw him tighten up and got suspicious. Turned in the alarm on general principles. Warned the others to keep on their toes. But even so, it doesn't look like mind-reading—they'd have killed him sooner. They were watchful, and mighty quick on the draw.'

'That could be it. That's about as thin and as specious an explanation as I ever saw cooked up, but it does cover the facts…and the two of us will be able to make it stick…but take notice, pretty boy, that certain parties are not going to like this at all. In fact, they are going to be very highly put out.'

'That's a nice hunk of understatement, boss. But notice one beautiful thing about this story?' Herkimer grinned maliciously. 'It lets us pass the buck to Big Jim Towne. We can be—and will be—sore as hell because he picks such weak-sister characters to do his killings!'

In the heavily armoured improvised ambulance, Virgil Samms sat up and directed a thought at his friend Kinnison, finding his mind a turmoil of confusion.

'What's the matter, Rod?'

'Plenty!' the big Lensman snapped back. 'They were—maybe still are—too damn far ahead of us. Something has been going on that we haven't even suspected. I stood by, as innocent as a three-year-old girl baby, and let you walk right into that one—and I emphatically do not enjoy getting caught with my pants down that way. It makes me jumpy. This may be all, but it may not be—not by eleven thousand light-years—and I'm trying to dope out what is going to happen next.'

'And what have you deduced?'

'Nothing. I'm stuck. So I'm tossing it into your lap. Besides, that's what you are getting paid for, thinking. So go ahead and think. What would you be doing, if you were on the other side?'

'I see. You think, then, that it might not be good technique to take the time to go back to the spaceport?'

'You get the idea. But—can you stand transfer?'

'Certainly. They got my shoulder dressed and taped, and my arm in a sling. Shock practically all gone. Some pain, but not much. I can walk without falling down.'

'Fair enough. Clayton!' He Lensed a vigorous thought.

'Have any of the observers spotted anything, high up or far off?'

'No, sir.'

'Good. Kinnison to Commodore Clayton, orders. Have a 'copter come down and pick up Samms and myself on tractors. Instruct the *Boise* and the cruisers to maintain utmost vigilance. Instruct the *Chicago* to pick us up. Detach the *Chicago* and the *Boise* from your task force. Assign them to me. Off.'

'Clayton to Commissioner Kinnison. Orders received and are being carried out. Off.'

The transfers were made without incident. The two superdreadnoughts leaped into the high stratosphere and tore westward. Halfway to the Hill, Kinnison called Dr. Frederick Rodebush.

'Fred? Kinnison. Have Cleve and Bergenholm link up with us. Now—how are the Geigers on the outside of the Hill behaving?'

'Normal, all of them,' the physicist-Lensman reported after a moment. 'Why?'

Kinnison detailed the happenings of the recent past. 'So tell the boys to unlimber all the stuff the Hill has got.'

'My God!' Cleveland exclaimed. 'Why, that's putting us back to the days of the Interplanetary Wars!'

'With one notable exception,' Kinnison pointed out. 'The attack, if any, will be strictly modern. I hope we'll be able to handle it. One good thing, the old mountain's got a lot of sheer mass. How much radioactivity will it stand?'

'Allotropic iron, U-235, or plutonium?' Rodebush seized his slide-rule.

'What difference does it make?'

'From a practical standpoint...perhaps none. But with a task force defending, not many bombs could get through, so I'd say...'

'I wasn't thinking so much of bombs.'

'What, then?'

'Isotopes. A good, thick blanket of dust. Slow-speed, fine stuff that neither our ships nor the Hill's screens could handle. We've got to decide, first, whether Virgil will be safer there in the Hill or out in space in the *Chicago*; and second, for how long.'

'I see...I'd say here, *under* the Hill. Months, perhaps years, before anything could work down this far. And we can *always* get out. No matter how hot the surface gets, we've got enough screen, heavy water, cadmium, lead, mercury, and everything else necessary to get him out through the locks.'

'That's what I was hoping you'd say. And now, about the defence...I wonder...I don't want everybody to think I've gone completely hysterical, but I'll be damned if I want to get caught again with...' His thought faded out.

'May I offer a suggestion, sir?' Bergenholm's thought broke the prolonged silence.

'I'd be very glad to have it—your suggestions so far haven't been idle vapourings. Another hunch?'

'No, sir, a logical procedure. It has been some months since the last emergency call-out drill was held. If you issue such another call now, and nothing happens, it can be simply another surprise drill; with credit, promotion, and monetary awards for the best performances; Further practice and instruction for the less proficient units.'

'Splendid, Dr. Bergenholm!' Samms' brilliant and agile mind snatched up the thought and carried it along. 'And what a chance, Rod, for something vastly larger and more important than a Continental, or even a Tellurian, drill—make it the first manoeuvre of the Galactic Patrol!'

'I'd like to, Virge, but we can't. My boys are ready, but you aren't. No top appointments and no authority.'

'That can be arranged in a very few minutes. We have been waiting for the psychological moment. This, especially if trouble should develop, is the time. You yourself expect an attack, do you not?'

'Yes. I would not start anything unless and until I was ready to finish it, and I see no reason for assuming that whoever it was that tried to kill you is not at least as good a planner as I am.'

'And the rest of you...? Dr. Bergenholm?'

'My reasoning, while it does not exactly parallel that of Commissioner Kinnison, leads to the same conclusion; that an attack in great force is to be expected.'

'Not *exactly* parallel?' Kinnison demanded. 'In what respects?'

'You do not seem to have considered the possibility, Commissioner, that the proposed assassination of First Lensman Samms could very well have been only the first step in a comprehensive operation.'

'I didn't...and it *could* have been. So go ahead, Virge, with...'

The thought was never finished, for Samms had already gone ahead. Simultaneously, it seemed, the minds of eight other Lensmen joined the group of Tellurians. Samms, intensely serious, spoke aloud to his friend:

'The Galactic Council is now assembled. Do you, Roderick K. Kinnison, promise to uphold, in as much as you conscientiously can and with all that in you lies, the authority of this Council throughout all space?'

'I promise.'

'By virtue of the authority vested in me its president by the Galactic Council, I appoint you Port Admiral of the Galactic Patrol. My fellow councillors are now inducting the armed forces of their various solar systems into the Galactic Patrol...It will not take long...There, you may make your appointments and issue orders for the mobilisation.'

The two superdreadnoughts were now approaching the Hill. The *Boise* stayed "up on top"; the *Chicago* went down. Kinnison, however, paid very little attention to the landing or to Samms' disembarkation, and none whatever to the *Chicago's* reascent into the high heavens. He knew that everything was under control; and, now alone in his cabin, he was busy.

'All personnel of all armed forces just inducted into the Galactic Patrol, attention!' He spoke into an ultra-wave microphone, the familiar parade-ground rasp very evident in his deep and resonant voice. 'Kinnison of Tellus, Port Admiral, speaking. Each of you has taken oath to the Galactic Patrol?'

They had.

'At ease. The organisation chart already in your hands is made effective as of now. Enter in your logs the date and time. Promotions: Commodore Clayton of North America, Tellus...'

In his office at New York Spaceport Clayton came to attention and saluted crisply; his eyes shining, his deeply-scarred face alight.

'...to be Admiral of the First Galactic Region. Commodore Schweikert of Europe, Tellus...'

In Berlin a narrow-waisted, almost foppish-seeming man, with roached blond hair and blue eyes, bowed stiffly from the waist and saluted punctiliously.

'...to be Lieutenant-Admiral of the First Galactic Region.'

And so on, down the list. A marshal and a lieutenant-marshall of the Solarian System; a general and a lieutenant-general of the planet Sol Three. Promotions, agreed upon long since, to fill the high offices thus vacated. Then the list of commodores upon other planets—Guindlos of Redland, Mars; Sesseffsen of Talleron, Venus; Raymond of the Jovian Sub-System; Newman of Alphacent; Walters of Sirius; van-Meeter of Valeria; Adams of Procyon; Roberts of Altair; Barrtell of Fomalhout; Armand of Vega; and Coigne of Aldebaran—each of whom was actually the commander-in-chief of the armed forces of a world. Each of these was made general of his planet.

'Except for lieutenant-commodores and up, who will tune their minds to me—dismissed!' Kinnison stopped talking and went onto his Lens.

'That was for the record. I don't need to tell you, fellows, how glad I am to be able to do this. You're tops, all of you—I don't know of anybody I'd rather have at my back when the ether gets rough...'

'Right back at you, chief!' 'Same to you Rod!' 'Rocky Rod, Port Admiral!' 'Now we're blasting!' came a melange of thoughts. Those splendid men, with whom he had shared so much of danger and of stress, were all as jubilant as schoolboys.

'But the thing that makes this possible may also make it necessary for us to go to work; to earn your extra stars and my wheel.' Kinnison smothered the welter of thoughts and outlined the situation, concluding: 'So you see it may turn out to be only a drill—but on the other hand, since the outfit is big enough to have built a war-fleet alone, if it wanted one, and since it may have had a lot of first-class help that none of us knows anything about, we may be in for the damndest battle that any of us ever saw. So come prepared for *anything*. I am now going back onto voice, for the record.

'Kinnison to the commanding officers of all fleets, sub-fleets, and task-forces of the Galactic Patrol. Information. Subject, tactical problem; defence of the Hill against a postulated Black Fleet of unknown size, strength, and composition; of unknown nationality of origin; coming from an unknown direction in space at an unknown time.

'Kinnison to Admiral Clayton. Orders. Take over. I am relinquishing command of the *Boise* and the *Chicago*.'

'Clayton to Port Admiral Kinnison. Orders received. Taking over. I am at the *Chicago's* main starboard lock. I have instructed Ensign Masterson, the commanding officer of this gig, to wait; that he is to take you down to the Hill.'

'WHAT? Of all the damned...' This was a thought, and unrecorded.

'Sorry, Rod—I'm sorry as hell, and I'd like no end to have you along.' This, too, was a thought. 'But that's

the way it is. Ordinary Admirals ride the ether with their fleets. Port Admirals stay aground. I report to you, and you run things—in broad—by remote control.'

'I see.' Kinnison then Lensed a fuming thought at Samms. 'Alex *couldn't* do this to me—and wouldn't— and knows damn well that I'd burn him to a crisp if he had the guts to try it. So it's *your* doing—what in hell's the big idea?'

'Who's being heroic now, Rod?' Samms asked, quietly. 'Use *your* brain. And then come down here, where you belong.'

And Kinnison, after a long moment of rebellious thought and with as much grace as he could muster, came down. Down not only to the Patrol's familiar offices, but down into the deepest crypts beneath them. He was glum enough, and bitter, at first: but he found much to do. Grand Fleet Headquarters—*his* headquarters—was being organised, and the best efforts of the best minds and of the best technologists of three worlds were being devoted to the task of strengthening the already extremely strong defences of THE HILL. And in a very short time the plates of GFHQ showed that Admiral Clayton and Lieutenant-Admiral Schweikert were doing a very nice job.

All of the really heavy stuff was of Earth, the Mother Planet, and was already in place; as were the less numerous and much lighter contingents of Mars, of Venus, and of Jove. And the fleets of the outlying solar systems—cutters, scouts, and a few light cruisers—were neither maintaining fleet formation nor laying course for Sol. Instead, each individual vessel was blasting at maximum for the position in space in which it would form one unit of a formation englobing at a distance of light-years the entire Solarian System, and each of those hurtling hundreds of ships was literally combing all circumambient space with its furiously-driven detector beams.

'Nice.' Kinnison turned to Samms, now beside him at the master plate. 'Couldn't have done any better myself.'

'After you get it made, what are you going to do with it in case nothing happens?' Samms was still somewhat sceptical. 'How long can you make a drill last?'

'Until all the ensigns have long grey whiskers if I have to, but don't worry—if we have time to get the preliminary globe made I'll be the surprisedest man in the system.'

And Kinnison was not surprised; before full englobement was accomplished, a loudspeaker gave tongue.

'Flagship *Chicago* to Grand Fleet Headquarters!' it blatted, sharply. 'The Black Fleet has been detected. RA twelve hours, declination plus twenty degrees, distance about thirty light-years...'

Kinnison started to say something; then, by main force, shut himself up. He wanted intensely to take over, to tell the boys out there exactly what to do, but he couldn't. He was now a Big Shot—damn the luck! He could be and must be responsible for broad policy and for general strategy, but, once those vitally important decisions had been made, the actual work would have to be done by others. He didn't like it—but there it was. Those flashing thoughts took only an instant of time.

'...which is such extreme range that no estimate of strength or composition can be made at present. We will keep you informed.'

'Acknowledge,' he ordered Randolph; who, wearing now the five silver bars of major, was his Chief Communications Officer. 'No instructions.'

He turned to his plate. Clayton hadn't had to be told to pull in his light stuff; it was all pelting hell-for-leather for Sol and Tellus. Three general plans of battle had been mapped out by Staff. Each had its advantages—and its disadvantages. Operation Acorn—long distance—would be fought at, say, twelve light-years. It would keep everything, particularly the big stuff, away from the Hill, and would make automatics useless...*unless* some got past, or *unless* the automatics were coming in on a sneak course, or *unless* several other things—in any one of which cases what a God-awful shellacking the Hill would take!'

He grinned wryly at Samms, who had been following his thought, and quoted: 'A vast hemisphere of lambent violet flame, through which neither material substance nor destructive ray can pass.'

'Well, that dedicatory statement, while perhaps a bit florid, was strictly true at the time—before the days of allotropic iron and of polycyclic drills. Now I'll quote one: "Nothing is permanent except change".'

'Uh-huh,' and Kinnison returned to his thinking. Operation Adack. Middle distance. Uh-uh. He didn't like it any better now than he had before, even though some of the Big Brains of Staff thought it the ideal solution. A compromise. All of the disadvantages of both of the others, and none of the advantages of either. It *still* stunk, and unless the Black Fleet had an utterly fantastic composition Operation Adack was out.

And Virgil Samms, quietly smoking a cigarette, smiled inwardly. Rod the Rock could scarcely be expected to be in favour of any sort of compromise.

That left Operation Affick. Close up. It has three tremendous advantages. First, the Hill's own offensive weapons—as long as they lasted. Second, the new Rodebush-Bergenholm fields. Third, no sneak attack could be made without detection and interception. It had one tremendous disadvantage; some stuff, and

probably a lot of it, would get through. Automatics, robots, guided missiles equipped with super-speed drives, with polycyclic drills, and with atomic warheads strong enough to shake the whole world.

But with those new fields, shaking the world wouldn't be enough; in order to get deep enough to reach Virgil Samms they would damn near have to destroy the world. Could *anybody* build a bomb that powerful? He didn't think so. Earth technology was supreme throughout all known space; of Earth technologists the North Americans were, and always had been, tops. Grant that the Black Fleet was, basically, North American. Grant further that they had a man as good as Adlington—or that they could spy-ray Adlington's brain and laboratories and shops—a tall order. Adlington himself was several months away from a world-wrecker, unless he could put one a hundred miles down before detonation, which simply was not feasible. He turned to Samms.

'It'll be Affick, Virge, unless they've got a composition that is radically different from anything I ever saw put into space.'

'So? I can't say that I am very much surprised.'

The calm statement and the equally calm reply were beautifully characteristic of the two men. Kinnison had not asked, nor had Samms offered, advice. Kinnison, after weighing the facts, made his decision. Samms, calmly certain that the decision was the best that could be made upon the data available, accepted it without question or criticism.

'We've still got a minute or two,' Kinnison remarked. 'Don't quite know what to make of their line of approach. Coma Berenices. I don't know of anything at all out that way, do you? They could have detoured, though.'

'No, I don't.' Samms frowned in thought. 'Probably a detour.'

'Check.' Kinnison turned to Randolph. 'Tell them to report whatever they know; we can't wait any...'

As he was speaking the report came in.

The Black Fleet was of more or less normal make-up; considerably larger than the North American contingent, but decidely inferior to the Patrol's present Grand Fleet. Either three or four capital ships...

'And we've got six!' Kinnison said, exultantly. 'Our own two, Asia's *Himalaya*, Africa's *Johannesburg*, South America's *Bolivar*, and Europe's *Europa*.'

... Battle cruisers and heavy cruisers, about in the usual proportions; but an unusually high ratio of scouts and light cruisers. There were either two or three large ships which could not be classified definitely at that distance; long-range observers were going out to study them.

'Tell Clayton,' Kinnison instructed Randolph, 'that it is to be Operation Affick, and for him to fly at it.'

'Report continued,' the speaker came to life again. 'There are three capital ships, apparently of approximately the *Chicago* class, but tear-drop-shaped instead of spherical...'

'Ouch!' Kinnison flashed a thought at Samms. 'I don't like that. They can both fight and run.'

'... The battle cruisers are also tear-drops. The small vessels are torpedo-shaped. There are three of the large ships, which we are still not able to classify definitely. They are spherical in shape, and very large, but do not seem to be either armed or screened, and are apparently carriers—possibly of automatics. We are now making contact—off!'

Instead of looking at the plates before them, the two Lensmen went en rapport with Clayton, so that they could see everything he saw. The stupendous Cone of Battle had long since been formed; the word to fire was given in a measured two-second call. Every firing officer in every Patrol ship touched his stud in the same split second. And from the gargantuan mouth of the Cone there spewed a miles-thick column of energy so raw, so stark, so incomprehensibly violent that it must have been seen to be even dimly appreciated. It simply cannot be described.

Its prototype, Triplanetary's Cylinder of Annihilation, had been a highly effective weapon indeed. The offensive beams of the fish-shaped Nevian cruisers of the void were even more powerful. The Cleveland-Rodebush projectors, developed aboard the original *Boise* on the long Nevian way, were stronger still. The composite beam projected by this fleet of the Galactic Patrol, however, was the sublimation and quintessence of each of these, redesigned and redesigned by scientists and engineers of ever-increasing knowledge, rebuilt and rebuilt by technologists of ever-increasing skill.

Capital ships and a few of the heaviest cruisers could mount screen generators able to carry that frightful load; but every smaller ship caught in that semi-solid rod of indescribably incandescent fury simply flared into nothingness.

But in the instant before the firing order was given— as though precisely timed, which in all probability was the case—the ever-watchful observers picked up two items of fact which made the new Admiral of the First Galactic Region cut his almost irresistible weapon and break up his Cone of Battle after only a few seconds of action. One: those three enigmatic cargo scows had fallen apart *before* the beam reached them, and hundreds—yes, thousands—of small objects had hurtled radially outward, out well beyond the field of

action of the Patrol's beam, at a speed many times that of light. Two: Kinnison's forebodings had been prophetic. A swarm of Blacks, all small—must have been hidden right on Earth somewhere!—were already darting at the Hill from the south.

'Cease firing!' Clayton rapped into his microphone. The dreadful beam expired. 'Break cone formation! Independent action—light cruisers and scouts, *get those bombs!* Heavy cruisers and battle cruisers, engage similar units of the Blacks, two to one if possible. *Chicago* and *Boise*, attach Black Number One, *Bolivar* and *Himalaya*, Number Two. *Europa* and *Johannesburg*, Number three!'

Space was full of darting, flashing, madly warring ships. The three Black superdreadnoughts leaped forward as one. Their massed batteries of beams, precisely synchronised and aimed, lashed out as one at the nearest Patrol super heavy, the *Boise*. Under the vicious power of that beautifully-timed thrust that warship's first, second, and third screens, her very wall-shield, flared through the spectrum and into the black. Her Chief Pilot, however, was fast—*very fast*—and he had a fraction of a second in which to work. Thus, practically in the instant of her wall-shield's failure, she went free; and while she was holed badly and put out of action, she was not blown out of space. In fact, it was learned later that she lost only forty men.

The Blacks were not as fortunate. The *Chicago*, now without a partner, joined beams with the *Bolivar* and the *Himalaya* against Number Two; then, a short half-second later, with her other two sister-ships against Number Three. And in that very short space of time two Black superdreadnoughts ceased utterly to be.

But also, in that scant second of time, Black Number One had all but disappeared! Her canny commander, with no stomach at all for odds of five to one against, had ordered flight at max; she was already one-sixtieth

of a light-year—about one hundred thousand million miles—away from the Earth and was devoting her every energy to the accumulation of still more distance.

'*Bolivar! Himalaya*' Clayton barked savagely. 'Get him!' He wanted intensely to join the chase, but he couldn't. He had to stay here. And he didn't have time even to swear. Instead, without a break, the words tripping over each other against his teeth: '*Chicago! Johannesburg! Europa!* Act at will against heaviest craft left. Blast 'em down!'

He gritted his teeth. The scouts and light cruisers were doing their damndest, but they were outnumbered three to one—Christ, what a lot of stuff was getting through! The Blacks wouldn't last long, between the Hill and the heavies...but maybe long enough, at that—the Patrol globe was leaking like a sieve! He voiced a couple of bursts of deep-space profanity and, although he was almost afraid to look, sneaked a quick peek to see how much was left of the Hill. He looked—and stopped swearing in the middle of a four-letter Anglo-Saxon word.

What he saw simply did not make sense. Those Black bombs should have peeled the armour off of that mountain like the skin off of a nectarine and scattered it from the Pacific to the Mississippi. By now there should be a hole a mile deep where the Hill had been. But there wasn't. The Hill was still there! It might have shrunk a little—Clayton couldn't see very well because of the worse-than-incandescent radiance of the practically continuous, sense-battering, world-shaking atomic detonations—*but the Hill was still there!*

And as he stared, chilled and shaken, at that indescribably terrific spectacle, a Black cruiser, holed and helpless, fell toward that armoured mountain with an acceleration starkly impossible to credit. And when it struck it did not penetrate, and splash, and crater,

as it should have done. Instead, it simply spread out, *in a thin layer*, over an acre or so of the fortress' steep and apparently still armoured surface!

'You saw that, Alex? Good. Otherwise you could scarcely believe it,' came Kinnison's silent voice. 'Tell all our ships to stay away. There's a force of over a hundred thousand G's acting in a direction normal to every point of our surface. The boys are giving it all the decrement they can—somewhere between distance cube and fourth power—but even so it's pretty fierce stuff. How about the *Bolivar* and the *Himalaya*? Not having much luck catching Mr. Black, are they?'

'Why, I don't know. I'll check…No. sir, they aren't. They report that they are losing ground and will soon lose trace.'

'I was afraid so, from that shape. Rodebush was about the only one who saw it coming…well, we'll have to redesign and rebuild…'

Port Admiral Kinnison, shortly after directing the foregoing thought, leaned back in his chair and smiled. The battle was practically over. The Hill had come through. The Rodebush-Bergenholm fields had held her together through the most God-awful session of saturation atomic bombing that any world had ever seen or that the mind of man had ever conceived. And the counter-forces had kept the interior rock from flowing like water. So far, so good.

Her original armour was gone. Converted into…what? For hundreds of feet inward from the surface she was hotter than the reacting slugs of the Hanfords. Delousing her would be a project, not an operation; millions of cubic yards of material would have to be hauled off into space with tractors and

allowed to simmer for a few hundred years; but what of that?

Bergenholm had said that the fields would tend to prevent the radioactives from spreading, as they otherwise would—and *Virgil Samms was still safe!*'

'Virge, my boy, come along.' He took the First Lensman by his good arm and lifted him out of his chair. 'Old Doctor Kinnison's peerless prescription for you and me is a big, thick, juicy, porterhouse steak.'

CHAPTER 8

That murderous attack upon Virgil Samms, and its countering by those new super-lawmen, the Lensmen, and by an entire task force of the North American Armed Forces, was news of Civilisation-wide importance. As such, it filled every channel of Universal Telenews for an hour. Then, in stunning and crescendo succession, came the staccato reports of the creation of the Galactic Patrol, the mobilisation—allegedly for manoeuvres—of Galactic Patrol's Grand Fleet, and the ultimately desperate and all-too-nearly successful attack upon The Hill.

'Just a second, folks; we'll have it very shortly. You'll see something that nobody ever saw before and that nobody will ever see again. We're getting in as close as the Law will let us.' The eyes of Telenews' ace reporter and the telephoto lens of his cameraman stared down from a scooter at the furiously smoking, sputteringly incandescent surface of Triplanetary's ancient citadel; while upon dozens of worlds thousands of millions of people packed themselves tighter and tighter around tens of millions of visiplates and loudspeakers in order to see and to hear the tremendous news.

'There it is, folks, look at it—the only really impregnable fortress ever built by man! A good many of our experts had it written off as obsolete, long ago, but it seems these Lensmen had something up their sleeves besides their arms, heh-heh! And speaking of Lensmen, they haven't been throwing their weight around, so most of us haven't noticed them very much, but this reporter wants to go on record right now as saying there must be a lot more to the Lens than any of us has thought, because otherwise nobody would

have gone to all that trouble and expense, to say nothing of the tremendous loss of life, just to kill the Chief Lensman, which seems to have been what they were after.

'We told you a few minutes ago, you know, that every Continent of Civilisation sent official messages denying most emphatically any connection with this outrage. It's still a mystery, folks; in fact, it is getting more and more mysterious all the time. *Not one single man of the Black Fleet was taken alive!* Not even in the ships that were only holed—they blew themselves up! And there were no uniforms or books or anything of the kind to be found in any of the wrecks—no identification whatever!

'And now for the scoop of all time! Universal Telenews has obtained permission to interview the two top Lensmen, both of whom you all know—Virgil Samms and 'Rod the Rock' Kinnison—personally for this beam. We are now going down, by remote control, of course, right into the Galactic patrol office, right in The Hill itself. Here we are. Now if you will step just a little closer to the mike, please, Mr. Samms, or should I say…?'

'You should say "First Lensman Samms",' Kinnison said brusquely.

'Oh, yes. First Lensman Samms. Thank you, Mr. Kinnison. Now, First Lensman Samms, our clients all want to know all about the Lens. We all know what it *does*, but what, really *is* it? Who invented it? How does it work?'

Kinnison started to say something, but Samms silenced him with a thought.

'I will answer those questions by asking you one.' Samms smiled disarmingly. 'Do you remember what happened because the pirates learned to duplicate the golden meteor of the Triplanetary Service?'

'Oh, I see.' The Telenews ace, although brash and not at all thin-skinned, was quick on the uptake. 'Hush-hush? T.S.?'

'Top Secret. Very much so,' Samms confirmed, 'and we are going to keep some things about the Lens secret as long as we possibly can.'

'Fair enough. Sorry folks, but you will agree that they're right on that. Well, then, Mr. Samms, who do you think it was that tried to kill you, and where do you think the Black Fleet came from?'

'I have no idea,' Samms said, slowly and thoughtfully. 'No. No idea whatever.'

'What? Are you *sure* of that? Aren't you holding back maybe just a little bit of a suspicion, for diplomatic reasons?'

'I am holding nothing back; and through my Lens I can make you certain of the fact. Lensed thoughts come from the mind itself, direct, not through such voluntary muscles as the tongue. The mind does not lie—even such lies as you call "diplomacy".'

The Lensman demonstrated and the reporter went on:

'He is *sure*, folks, which fact knocked me speechless for a second or two—which is quite a feat in itself. Now, Mr. Samms, one last question. What is all this Lens stuff really about? What are all you Lensmen—the Galactic Council and so on—really up to? What do you expect to get out of it? And why would anybody want to make such an all-out effort to get rid of you? And give it to me on the Lens, please, if you can do it and talk at the same time—that was a wonderful sensation, folks, of getting the dope straight and *knowing* that it was straight.'

'I can and will answer both by voice and by Lens. Our basic purpose is...' and he quoted verbatim the

resounding sentences which Mentor had impressed so ineradicably upon his mind. 'You know how little happiness, how little real well-being, there is upon any world today. We propose to increase both. What we expect to get out of it is happiness and well-being for ourselves, the satisfaction felt by any good workman doing the job for which he is best fitted and in which he takes pride. As to why anyone should want to kill me, the logical explanation would seem to be that some group or organisation or race, opposed to that for which we Lensmen stand, decided to do away with us and started with me.'

'Thank you, Mr. Samms. I am sure that we all enjoyed this interview very much. Now, folks, you all know "Rocky Rod", "Rod the Rock", Kinnison... just a little closer, please... thank you. I don't suppose you have any suspicions, either, any more than...'

'I certainly have!' Kinnison barked, so savagely that five hundred million people jumped as one. 'How do you want it; voice, or Lens, or both?' Then on the Lens: 'Think it over, son, because *I suspect everybody!*'

'Bub-both, please, Mr. Kinnison.' Even Universal's star reporter was shaken by the quiet but deadly fury of the big Lensman's thought, but he rallied so quickly that his hesitation was barely noticeable. 'Your Lensed thought to me was that you suspect *everybody*, Mr. Kinnison?'

'Just that. Everybody. I suspect every continental government of every world we know, including that of North America of Tellus. I suspect political parties and organised minorities. I suspect pressure groups. I suspect capital and I suspect labour. I suspect an organisation of criminals. I suspect nations and races and worlds that no one of us has as yet heard of—not even you, the top-drawer newshawk of the universe.'

'But you have nothing concrete to go on, I take it?'

'If I did have, do you think I'd be standing here talking to you?'

First Lensman Samms sat in his private quarters and thought.

Lensman Dronvire of Rigel Four stood behind him and helped him think.

Port Admiral Kinnison, with all his force and drive, began a comprehensive programme of investigation, consolidation, expansion, redesigning, and rebuilding.

Virgilia Samms went to a party practically every night. She danced, she flirted, she talked. *How* she talked! Meaningless small talk for the most part—but interspersed with artless questions and comments which, while they perhaps did not put her partner of the moment completely at ease, nevertheless did not quite excite suspicion.

Conway Costigan, Lens under sleeve, undisguised but inconspicuous, rode the ether-lanes; observing minutely and reporting fully.

Jack Kinnison piloted and navigated and computed for this friend and boatmate:

Mason Northrop; who, completely surrounded by breadboard hookups of new and ever-more-fantastic complexity, listened and looked; listened and tuned; listened and rebuilt; listened and—finally—took bearing and bearings and bearings with his ultra-sensitive loops.

DalNalten and Knobos, with dozens of able helpers, combed the records of three worlds in a search which produced as a by-product a monumental "who's who" of crime.

Skilled technicians fed millions of cards, stack by stack, into the most versatile and most accomplished machines known to the statisticians of the age.

And Dr. Nels Bergenholm, abandoning temporarily his regular line of work, devoted his peculiar talents to a highly abstruse research in the closely allied field of organic chemistry.

The walls of Virgil Samms' quarters became covered with charts, diagrams, and figures. Tabulations and condensations piled up on his desk and overflowed into baskets upon the floor. Until:

'Lensman Olmstead, of Alphacent, sir,' his secretary announced.

'Good! Send him in, please.'

The stranger entered. The two men, after staring intently at each other for half a minute, smiled and shook hands vigorously. Except for the fact that the newcomer's hair was brown, they were practically identical!

'I'm certainly glad to see you, George. Bergenholm passed you, of course?'

'Yes. He says that he can match your hair to mine, even the individual white ones. And he has made me a wig-maker's dream of a wig.'

'Married?' Samms' mind leaped ahead to possible complications.

'Widower, same as you. And...'

'Just a minute—going over this once will be enough.' He Lensed call after call. Lensmen in various parts of space became en rapport with him and thus with each other.

'Lensmen—especially you, Rod—George Olmstead is here, and his brother Ray is available. I am going to work.'

'I *still* don't like it!' Kinnison protested. 'It's too dangerous. I told the Universe I was going to keep you covered, and I *meant* it!'

'That's what makes it perfectly safe. That is, if Bergenholm is *sure* that the duplication is close enough...'

'I am sure.' Bergenholm's deeply resonant pseudo-voice left no doubt at all in any one of the linked minds. 'The substitution will not be detected.'

'... and that nobody knows, George, or even suspects, that you got your Lens.'

'I am sure of that.' Olmstead laughed quietly. 'Also, nobody except us and your secretary knows that I am here. For a good many years I have made a specialty of that sort of thing. Photos, fingerprints, and so on have all been taken care of.'

'Good. I simply can not work efficiently here,' Samms expressed what all knew to be the simple truth. 'Dronvire is a much better analyst-synthesist than I am; as soon as any significant correlation is possible he will know it. We have learned that the Towne-Morgan crowd, Mackenzie Power, Ossmen Industries, and Interstellar Spaceways are all tied in together, and that thionite is involved, but we have not been able to get any further. There is a slight correlation—barely significant—between deaths from thionite and the arrival in the Solarian System of certain Spaceways liners. The fact that certain officials of the Earth-Screen Service have been and are spending considerably more than they earn sets up a slight but definite probability that they are allowing space-ships or boats from space-ships to land illegally. These smugglers carry contraband, which may or may not be thionite. In short, we lack fundamental data in every department, and it is high time for me to begin doing my share in getting it.'

'I don't check you, Virge.' None of the Kinnisons ever did give up without a struggle. 'Olmstead is a mighty smooth worker, and you are our prime co-ordinator. Why not let him keep up the counter-espionage—do the job you were figuring on doing yourself—and you stay here and boss it?'

'I have thought of that, a great deal, and have...'

'Because Olmstead can not do it,' a hitherto silent mind cut in, decisively. 'I, Rularion of North Polar Jupiter, say so. There are psychological factors involved. The ability to separate and to evaluate the constituent elements of a complex situation; the ability to make correct decisions without hesitation; as well as many others not as susceptible to concise statement, but which collectively could be called power of mind. How say you, Bergenholm of Tellus? For I have perceived in you a mind approximating in some respects the philosophical and psychological depth of my own.' This outrageously egotistical declaration was, to the Jovian, a simple statement of an equally simple truth, and Bergenholm accepted it as such.

'I agree. Olmstead probably could not succeed.'

'Well, then, can Samms?' Kinnison demanded.

'Who knows?' came Bergenholm's mental shrug, and simultaneously:

'Nobody knows whether I can or not, but I am going to try,' and Samms ended—almost—the argument by asking Bergenholm and a couple of other Lensmen to come into his office and by taking off his Lens.

'And that's another thing I don't like.' Kinnison offered one last objection. 'Without your Lens, *anything* can happen to you.'

'Oh, I won't have to be without it very long. And besides, Virgilia isn't the only one in the Samms family who can work better—sometimes—without a Lens.'

The Lensmen came in and, in a surprisingly short time, went out. A few minutes later, two Lensmen strolled out of Samms' inner office into the outer one.

'Goodbye, George,' the red-headed man said aloud, 'and good luck.'

'Same to you, Chief,' and the brown-haired one strode out.

Norma the secretary was a smart girl, and observant. In her position, she had to be. Her eyes followed the man out, then scanned the Lensman from toe to crown.

'I've never seen anything like it, Mr. Samms,' she remarked then. 'Except for the difference in colouring, and a sort of... well, stoopiness... he could be your identical twin. You two must have had a common ancestor—or several—not too far back, didn't you?'

'We certainly did. Quadruple second cousins, you might call it. We have known of each other for years, but this is the first time we have met.'

'Quadruple second cousins? What does that mean? How come?'

'Well, say that once upon a time there were two men named Albert and Chester...'

'What? Not two Irishmen named Pat and Mike? You're slipping, boss.' The girl smiled roguishly. During rush hours she was always the fast, cool, efficient secretary, but in moments of ease such persiflage as this was the usual thing in the First Lensman's private office. 'Not at all up to your usual form.'

'Merely because I am speaking now as a genealogist, not as a raconteur. But to continue. we will say that Chester and Albert had four children apiece, two boys and two girls, two pairs of identical twins, each. And when they grew up—half way up, that is...'

'Don't tell me that we are going to suppose that all those identical twins married each other?'

'Exactly. Why not?'

'Well, it would be stretching the laws of probability all out of shape. But go ahead—I can see what's coming, I think.'

'Each of those couples had one, and only one, child. We will call those children Jim Samms and Sally Olmstead; John Olmstead and Irene Samms.'

The girl's levity disappeared. 'James Alexander Samms and Sarah Olmstead Samms. Your parents. I didn't see what was coming, after all. This George Olmstead; then, is your...'

'Whatever it is, yes. I can't name it, either—maybe you had better call Genealogy some day and find out. But it's no wonder we look alike. And there are three of us, not two—George has an identical twin brother.'

The red-haired Lensman stepped back into the inner office, shut the door, and Lensed a thought at Virgil Samms.

'It worked, Virgil! I talked to her for five solid minutes, practically leaning on her desk, and she didn't tumble! And if this wig of Bergenholm's fooled *her* so completely, the job he did on you would fool *anybody!*'

'Fine! I've done a little testing myself, on the keenest men I know, without a trace of recognition so far.'

His last lingering doubt resolved, Samms boarded the ponderous radiation-proof, neutron-proof shuttle-scow which was the only possible means of entering or leaving the Hill. A fast cruiser whisked him to Nampa, where Olmstead's "accidentally" damaged transcontinental transport was being repaired, and from which city Olmstead had been gone so briefly that no one had missed him. He occupied Olmstead's space; he surrendered the remainder of Olmstead's

ticket. He reached New York. He took a 'copter to Senator Morgan's office. He was escorted into the private office of Herkimer Herkimer Third.

'Olmstead. Of Alphacent.'

'Yes?' Herkimer's hand moved, ever so little, upon his desk's top.

'Here.' The Lensman dropped an envelope upon the desk in such fashion that it came to rest within an inch of the hand.

'Prints. Here.' Samms made prints. 'Wash your hands over there.' Herkimer pressed a button. 'Check all these prints, against each other and the files. Check the two halves of the torn sheet, fibre to fibre.' He turned to the Lensless Lensman, now standing quietly before his desk. 'Routine; a formality, in your case, but necessary.'

'Of course.'

Then for long seconds the two hard men stared into the hard depths of each other's eyes.

'You may do, Olmstead. We have had very good reports of you. But you have never been in thionite?'

'No. I have never even seen any.'

'What do you want to get into it for?'

'Your scouts sounded me out; what did they tell you? The usual thing—promotion from the ranks into the brass—to get to where I can do myself and the organisation some good.'

'Yourself first, the organisation second?'

'What else? Why should I be different from the rest of you?'

This time the locked eyes held longer; one pair smouldering, the other gold-flecked, tawny ice.

'Why, indeed?' Herkimer smiled thinly. 'We do not advertise it, however.'

'Outside, I wouldn't, either; but here I'm laying my cards flat on the table.'

'I see. You *will* do, Olmstead, if you live. There's a test, you know.'

'They told me there would be.'

'Well, aren't you curious to know what it is?'

'Not particularly. *You* passed it, didn't you?'

'What do you mean by *that* crack?' Herkimer leaped to his feet; his eyes, smouldering before, now ablaze.

'Exactly what I said, no more and no less. You may read into it anything you please.' Samms' voice was as cold as were his eyes. 'You picked me out because of what I am. Did you think that moving upstairs would make a boot-licker out of me?'

'Not at all.' Herkimer sat down and took from a drawer two small, transparent, vaguely capsule-like tubes, each containing a few particles of purple dust. 'You know what this is?'

'I can guess.'

'Each of these is a good, heavy jolt; about all that a strong man with a strong heart can stand. Sit down. Here is one dose. Pull the cover, stick the capsule up one nostril, squeeze the ejector, and sniff. If you can leave this other dose sitting here on the desk you will live, and thus pass the test. If you can't, you die.'

Samms sat, and pulled, and squeezed, and sniffed.

His forearms hit the desk with a thud. His hands clenched themselves into fists, the tight-stretched tendons standing boldly out. His face turned white. His eyes jammed themselves shut; his jaw-muscles

sprang into bands and lumps as they clamped his teeth hard together. Every voluntary muscle in his body went into a rigor as extreme as that of death itself. His heart pounded; his breathing became stertorous.

This was the dreadful "muscle-lock" so uniquely characteristic of thionite; the frenzied immobility of the ultimately passionate satisfaction of every desire.

The Galactic Patrol became for him an actuality; a force for good pervading all the worlds of all the galaxies of all the universes of all existing space-time continua. He knew what the Lens was, and why. He understood time and space. He understood time and space. He knew the absolute beginning and the ultimate end.

He also saw things and did things over which it is best to draw a kindly veil, for every desire—mental or physical, open or sternly suppressed, noble or base— that Virgil Samms had ever had was being *completely satisfied*. EVERY DESIRE.

As Samms sat there, straining motionlessly upon the verge of death through sheer ecstasy, a door opened and Senator Morgan entered the room. Herkimer started, almost imperceptibly, as he turned— had there been, or not, an instantaneously-suppressed flash of guilt in those now completely clear and frank brown eyes?'

'Hi, Chief; come in and sit down. Glad to see you— this is not exactly my idea of fun.'

'No? When did you stop being a sadist?' The senator sat down beside his minion's desk, the fingertips of his left hand began soundlessly to drum. 'You wouldn't have, by any chance, been considering the idea of...?' He paused significantly.

'What an idea.' Herkimer's act—if it was an act— was flawless. 'He's too good a man to waste.'

'I know it, but you didn't act as though you did. I've never seen you come out such a poor second in an interview... and it wasn't because you didn't know to start with just what kind of a tiger he was—that's why he was selected for this job. And it would have been so easy to give him just a wee bit more.'

'That's preposterous, Chief, and you know it.'

'Do I? However, it couldn't have been jealousy, because he isn't being considered for your job. He won't be over you, and there's plenty of room for everybody. What was the matter? Your bloodthirstiness wouldn't have taken you *that* far, under these circumstances. Come clean, Herkimer.'

'Okay—I hate the whole damned family!' Herkimer burst out, viciously.

'I see. That adds up.' Morgan's face cleared, his fingers became motionless. 'You can't make the Samms wench and aren't in a position to skin her alive, so you get allergic to all her relatives. That adds up, but let me tell you something.' His quiet, level voice carried more of menace than most men's loudest threats. 'Keep your love life out of business and keep that sadistic streak under control. Don't let anything like this happen again.

'I won't, Chief. I got off the beam—but he made me so *damn* mad!'

'Certainly. That's exactly what he was trying to do. Elementary. If he could make you look small it would make him look big, and he just about did. But watch now, he's coming to.'

Samms' muscles relaxed. He opened his eyes groggily; then, as a wave of humiliated realisation swept over his consciousness, he closed them again and shuddered. He had always thought himself pretty much of a man; how could he *possibly* have descended to such nauseous depths of depravity, of

turpitude, of sheer moral degradation? And yet every cell of his being was shrieking its demand for more; his mind and his substance alike were permeated by an over-mastering craving to experience again the ultimate thrills which they had so tremendously, so outrageously enjoyed.

There was another good jolt lying right there on the desk in front of him, even though thionite-sniffers always saw to it that no more of the drug could be obtained without considerable physical exertion; which exertion would bring them to their senses. If he took that jolt it would kill him. What of it? What was death? What good was life, except to enjoy such thrills as he had just had and was about to have again? And besides, thionite couldn't kill *him*. He was a super-man; he had just proved it!

He straightened up and reached for the capsule; and that effort, small as it was, was enough to bring First Lensman Virgil Samms back under control. The craving, however, did not decrease. Rather, it increased.

Months were to pass before he could think of thionite, or even of the colour purple, without a spasmodic catching of the breath and a tightening of every muscle. Years were to pass before he could forget, even partially, the theretofore unsuspected dwellers in the dark recesses of his own mind. Nevertheless, from the store of whatever it was that made him what he was, Virgil Samms drew strength. Thumb and forefinger touched the capsule, but instead of picking it up, he pushed it across the desk toward Herkimer.

'Put it away, bub. One whiff of that stuff will last me for life.' He stared unfathomably at the secretary, then turned to Morgan and nodded. 'After all, he did not *say* that he ever passed this or any other test. He just didn't contradict me when I said it.'

With a visible effort Herkimer remained silent, but Morgan did not.

'You talk too much, Olmstead. Can you stand up yet?'

Gripping the desk with both hands, Samms heaved himself to his feet. The room was spinning and gyrating; every individual thing in it was moving in a different and impossible orbit; his already splintered skull threatened more and more violently to emulate a fragmentation bomb; black and white spots and vari-coloured flashes filled his cone of vision. He wrenched one hand free, then the other—and collapsed back into the chair.

'Not yet—quite,' he admitted, through stiff lips.

Although he was careful not to show it, Morgan was amazed—not that the man had collapsed, but that he had been able so soon to lift himself even an inch. "Tiger" was not the word; this Olmstead must be seven-eighths dinosaur.

'It takes a few minutes; longer for some, not so long for others,' Morgan said, blandly. 'But what makes you think Herkimer here never took one of the same?'

'Huh?' Again two pairs of eyes locked and held; and this time the duel was longer and more pregnant. 'What do *you* think? How do you suppose I lived to get as old as I am now? By being dumb?'

Morgan unwrapped a Venerian cigar, settled it comfortably between his teeth, lit it, and drew three slow puffs before replying.

'Ah, a student. An analytical mind,' he said, evenly, and—apparently—irrelevantly. 'Let's skip Herkimer for the moment. Try your hand on me.'

'Why not? From what we hear out in the field, you have always been in the upper brackets, so you

probably never had to prove that you could take it or let it alone. My guess would be, though, that you could.'

'The good old oil, eh?' Morgan allowed his face and voice to register a modicum, precisely metered, of contempt. 'How to get along in the world; Lesson One: Butter up the Boss.'

'Nice try, Senator, but I'll have to score you a clean miss.' Samms, now back almost to normal, grinned companionably. 'We both know that if I were still in the kindergarten I wouldn't be here now.'

'I'll let that one pass—this time.' Under that look and tone Morgan's underlings were wont to cringe, but this Olmstead was not the cringing type. 'Don't do it again. It might not be safe.'

'Oh, it would be safe enough—for today, at least. There are two factors which you are very carefully ignoring. First, I haven't accepted the job yet.'

'Are you innocent enough to think you'll get out of this building alive if I don't accept you?'

'If you want to call it innocence, yes. Oh I know you've got gunnies all over the place, but they don't mean a thing.'

'No?' Morgan's voice was silkily venomous.

'No.' Olmstead was completely unimpressed. 'Put yourself in my place. You know I've been around a long time; and not just around my mother. I was weaned quite a number of years ago.'

'I see. You don't scare worth a damn. A point. And you are testing me, just as I am testing you. Another point. I'm beginning to like you, George. I think I know what your second point is, but let's have it, just for the record.'

'I'm sure you do. Any man, to be my boss, has got to be at least as good a man as I am. Otherwise I take his job away from him.'

'Fair enough. By God, I *do* like you, Olmstead!' Morgan, his big face wreathed in smiles, got up, strode over, and shook hands vigorously; and Samms, scan as he would, could not even hazard a guess as to how much—if any—of this enthusiasm was real. 'Do you want the job? And when can you go to work?'

'Yes, sir. Two hours ago, sir.'

'That's fine!' Morgan boomed. Although he did not comment upon it, he noticed and understood the change in the form of address. 'Without knowing what the job is or how much it pays?'

'Neither is important, sir, at the moment.' Samms, who had got up easily enough to shake hands, now shook his head experimentally. Nothing rattled. Good—he was in pretty good shape already. 'As to the job, I can either do it or find out why it can't be done. As to pay, I've heard you called a lot of things, but "piker" was never one of them.'

'Very well. I predict that you will go far.' Morgan again shook the Lensman's hand; and again Samms could not evaluate the Senator's sincerity. 'Tuesday afternoon. New York Spaceport. Spaceship *Virgin Queen*. Report to Captain Willoughby in the dock office at fourteen hundred hours. Stop at the cashier's office on your way out. Goodbye.'

CHAPTER 9

Piracy was rife. There was no suspicion, however, nor would there be for many years, that there was anything of very large purpose about the business. Murgatroyd was simply a Captain Kidd of space; and even if he were actually connected with Galactic Spaceways, that fact would not be surprising. Such relationships had always existed; the most ferocious and dreaded pirates of the ancient world worked in full partnership with the First Families of that world.

Virgil Samms was thinking of pirates and of piracy when he left Senator Morgan's office. He was still thinking of them while he was reporting to Roderick Kinnison. Hence:

'But that's enough about this stuff and me, Rod. Bring me up to date on Operation Boskone.'

'Branching out no end. Your guess was right that Spaceways' losses to pirates are probably phony. But it wasn't the *known* attacks—that is, those cases in which the ship was found, later, with some or most of the personnel alive—that gave us the real information. They were all pretty much alike. But when we studied the total disappearances we really hit the jack-pot.'

'That doesn't sound just right, but I'm listening.'

'You'd better, since it goes farther than even you suspected. It was no trouble at all to get the passenger lists and the names of the crews of the independent ships that were lost without a trace. Their relatives and friends—we concentrated mostly on wives—could be located, except for the usual few who moved around so much that they got lost. Spacemen average young, you know, and their wives are still younger. Well, these

young women got jobs, most of them remarried, and so on. In short, normal.'

'And in the case of Spaceways, not normal?'

'Decidedly not. In the first place, you'd be amazed at how little publication was ever done of passenger lists, and apparently crew lists were not published at all. No use going into detail as to how we got the stuff, but we got it. However, nine tenths of the wives had disappeared, and none had remarried. The only ones we could find were those who did not care, even when their husbands were alive, whether they ever saw them again or not. But the big break was—you remember the disappearance of that girls'-school cruise ship?'

'Of course. It made a lot of noise.'

'An interesting point in connection with that cruise is that two days before the ship blasted off the school was robbed. The vault was opened with thermite and the whole Administration Building burned to the ground. All the school's records were destroyed. Thus, the list of missing had to be made up from statements made by friends, relatives, and what not.'

'I remember something of the kind. My impression was, though, that the space-ship company furnished... Oh!' The tone of Samms' thought alerted sharply. 'That was Spaceways, under cover?'

'Definitely. Our best guess is that there were quite a few shiploads of women disappeared about that time, instead of one. Austine's College had more students that year than ever before or since. It was the extras, not the regulars, who went on that cruise; the ones who figured it would be more convenient to disappear in space than to become ordinary missing persons.'

'But Rod! That would mean... but where?'

'It means just that. And finding out "where" will run into a project. There are over two thousand million suns in this galaxy, and the best estimate is that there are more than that many planets habitable by beings more or less human in type. You know how much of the galaxy has been explored and how fast the work of exploring the rest of it is going. Your guess is just as good as mine as to where those spacemen and engineers and their wives and girl-friends are now. I am sure, though, of four things; none of which we can ever begin to prove. One; they didn't die in space. Two; they landed on a comfortable and very well equipped Tellurian planet. Three; they built a fleet there. Four; that fleet attacked the Hill.'

'Murgatroyd, do you suppose?' Although surprised by Kinnison's tremendous report, Samms was not dismayed.

'No idea. No data—yet.'

'And they'll keep on building,' Samms said. 'They had a fleet much larger than the one they expected to meet. Now they'll build one larger than all our combined forces. And since the politicians will always know what we are doing... or it might be... I wonder...?'

'You can stop wondering.' Kinnison grinned savagely.

'What do you mean?'

'Just what you were going to think about. You know the edge of the galaxy closest to Tellus, where that big rift cuts in ?'

'Yes.'

'Across that rift, where it won't be surveyed for a thousand years, there's a planet that could be Earth's twin sister. No atomic energy, no space-drive, but heavily industrialised and anxious to welcome us.

Project Bennett. Very, very hush-hush. Nobody except Lensmen know anything about it. Two friends of Dronvire's—smart, smooth operators—are in charge. It's going to be the Navy Yard of the Galactic Patrol.'

'But Rod...' Samms began to protest, his mind leaping ahead to the numberless problems, the tremendous difficulties, inherent in the programme which his friend had outlined so briefly.

'Forget it, Virge!' Kinnison cut in. 'It won't be easy, of course, but we can do anything they can do, and do it better. You can go calmly ahead with your own chores, knowing that when—and notice that I say "when", not "if"—we need it we'll have a fleet up our sleeves that will make the official one look like a task force. But I see you're at the rendezvous, and there's Jill. Tell her "hi" for me. And as the Vegians say— "Tail high, Brother!" '

Samms was in the hotel's ornate lobby; a couple of uniformed "boys" and Jill Samms were approaching. The girl reached him first.

'You had no trouble in recognising me, then, my dear?'

'None at all, Uncle George.' She kissed him perfunctorily, the bell hops faded away. 'So nice to see you—I've heard so much about you. The Marine Room, you said?'

'Yes. I reserved a table.'

And in that famous restaurant, in the unequalled privacy of the city's noisiest and most crowded night spot, they drank sparingly; ate not-so-sparingly; and talked not sparingly at all.

It's perfectly safe here, you think?' Jill asked first.

'Perfectly. A super-sensitive microphone couldn't hear anything, and it's so dark that a lip-reader, even

if he could read us, would need a pair of twelve-inch night-glasses.'

'Goody! They did a marvellous job, Dad. If it weren't for your... well, your personality, I wouldn't recognise you even now.'

'You think I'm safe, then?'

'Absolutely.'

'Then we'll get down to business. You, Knobos, and DalNalten all have keen and powerful minds. You can't all be wrong. Spaceways, then is tied in with both the Towne-Morgan gang and with thionite. The logical extension of that—Dal certainly thought of it, even though he didn't mention it—would be...' Samms paused.

'Check. That the notorious Murgatroyd, instead of being just another pirate chief, is really working for Spaceways and belongs to the Towne-Morgan-Isaacson gang. But Dad—what an idea! Can things be *that* rotten, really?'

'They may be worse than that. Now the next thing. Who, in your opinion, is the real boss?'

'Well, it certainly is not Herkimer Herkimer Third.' Jill ticked him off on a pink forefinger. She had been asked for an opinion; she set out to give it without apology or hesitation. 'He could—just about—direct the affairs of a hot-dog stand. Nor is it Clander. He isn't even a little fish; he's scarcely a minnow. equally certainly it is neither the Venerian nor the Martian. They may run planetary affairs, but nothing bigger. I haven't met Murgatroyd, of course, but I have had several evaluations, and he does not rate up with Towne. And Big Jim—and this surprised me as much as it will you—is almost certainly not the prime mover.' She looked at him questioningly.

'That would have surprised me tremendously yesterday; but after today—I'll tell you about that presently—it doesn't.'

'I'm glad of that. I expected an argument, and I have been inclined to question the validity of my own results, since they do not agree with common knowledge—or, rather, what is supposed to be knowledge. That leaves Isaacson and Senator Morgan.' Jill frowned in perplexity; seemed, for the first time, unsure. 'Isaacson is of course a big man. Able. Well-informed. Extremely capable. A Top-notch executive. Not only *is*, would *have* to be, to run Spaceways. On the other hand, I have always thought that Morgan was nothing but a windbag...' Jill stopped talking; left the thought hanging in air.,

'So did I—until today,' Samms agreed grimly. 'I thought that he was simply an unusually corrupt, greedy, rabble-rousing politician. Our estimates of him may have to be changed very radically.'

Samms' mind raced. From two entirely different angles of approach, Jill and he had arrived at the same conclusion. But, if Morgan were really the Big Shot, would he have deigned to interview personally such small fry as Olmstead? Or was Olmstead's job of more importance than he, Samms, had supposed?

'I've got a dozen more things to check with you,' he went on, almost without a pause, 'but since this leadership matter is the only one in which my experience would affect your judgement, I had better tell you about what happened today...'

Tuesday came, and hour fourteen hundred; and Samms strode into an office. There was a big, clean desk; a wiry, intense, grey-haired man.

'Captain Willoughby?'

'Yes.'

'George Olmstead reporting.'

'Fourth Officer.' The captain punched a button; the heavy, sound-proof door closed itself and locked.

'*Fourth* Officer? New rank, eh? What does the ticket cover?'

'New, and special. Here's the articles; read it and sign it.' He did not add "or else", it was not necessary. It was clearly evident that Captain Willoughby, never garrulous, intended to be particularly reticent with his new subordinate.

Samms read. "…Fourth Officer… shall… no duties or responsibilities in the operation or maintenance of said space-ship… cargo…' Then came a clause which fairly leaped from the paper and smote his eyes: "when in command of a detail outside the hull of said space-ship he shall enforce, by the infliction of death or such other penalty as he deems fit…"

The Lensman was rocked to the heels, but did not show it. Instead, he took the captain's pen—his own, as far as Willoughby was concerned, could have been filled with vanishing ink—and wrote George Olmstead's name in George Olmstead's bold, flowing script.

Willoughby then took him aboard the good ship *Virgin Queen* and led him to his cabin.

'Here you are, Mr. Olmstead. Beyond getting acquainted with the supercargo and the rest of your men, you will have no duties for a few days. You have full run of the ship, with one exception. Stay out of the control room until I call you. Is that clear?'

'Yes, sir.' Willoughby turned away and Samms, after tossing his space-bag into the rack, took inventory.

The room was of course very small; but, considering the importance of mass, it was almost extravagantly supplied. There were shelves, or rather, tight racks, of books; there were sun-lamps and card-shelves and exercisers and games; there was a receiver capable of bringing in programmes from almost anywhere in space. The room had only one lack; it did not have an ultra-wave visiplate. Nor was this lack surprising. "They" would scarcely let George Olmstead know where "they" were taking him.

Samms was surprised, however, when he met the men who were to be directly under his command; for instead of one, or at most two, they numbered exactly forty. And they were all, he thought at first glance, the dregs and sweepings of the lowest dives in space. Before long, however, he learned that they were not all space-rats and denizens of Skid Rows. Six of them— the strongest physically and the hardest mentally of the lot—were fugitives from lethal chambers; murderers and worse. He looked at the biggest, toughest one of the six—a rock-drill-eyed, red-haired giant—and asked:

'What did they tell you, Tworn, that your job was going to be?'

'They didn't say. Just that it was dangerous, but if I done exactly what my boss would tell me to do , and nothing else, I might not even get hurt. An' I was due to take the deep breath the next week, see? That's just how it was, boss.'

'I see,' and one by one Virgil Samms, master psychologist, studied and analysed his motley crew until he was called into the control room.

The navigating tank was covered; no charts were to be seen. The one "live" visiplate showed a planet and a fiercely blue-white sun.

'My orders are to tell you, at this point, all I know about what you've got to do and about that planet down there. Trenco, they call it.' To Virgil Samms, the first adherent of Civilisation ever to hear it, that name meant nothing whatever. 'You are to take about five of your men, go down there, and gather all the green leaves you can. Not green in colour; sort of purplish. What they call broadleaf is the best; leaves about two feet long and a foot wide. But don't be too choosy. If there isn't any broadleaf handy, grab anything you can get hold of.'

'What is the opposition?' Samms asked, quietly. 'And what have they got that makes them so tough?'

'Nothing. No inhabitants, even. Just the planet itself. Next to Arisia, it's the God damndest planet in space. I've never been any closer to it than this, and I never will, so I don't know anything about it except what I hear; but there's something about it that kills men or drives them crazy. We spend seven or eight boats every trip, and thirty-five or forty men, and the biggest load that anybody ever took away from here was just under two hundred pounds of leaf. A good many times we don't get any.'

'They go crazy, eh?' In spite of his control, Samms paled. But it couldn't be like Arisia. 'What are the symptoms? What do they say?'

'Various. Main thing seems to be that they lose their sight. Don't go blind, exactly, but can't see where anything is; or, if they do see it, it isn't there. And it rains over forty feet deep every night, and yet it all dries up by morning. The worst electrical storms in the universe, and wind-velocities—I can show you charts on that—of over eight hundred miles an hour.'

'Whew! How about time? With your permission, I would like to do some surveying before I try to land.'

'A smart idea. A couple of the other boys had the same, but it didn't help—they didn't come back. I'll give you two Tellurian days—no, three—before I give you up and start sending out the other boats. Pick out your five men and see what you can do.'

As the boat dropped away, Willoughby's voice came briskly from a speaker. 'I know that you five men have got ideas. Forget 'em. Fourth Officer Olmstead has the authority and the orders to put a half-ounce slug through the guts of any or all of you that don't jump, and jump fast, to do what he tells you! And if that boat makes any funny moves I blast it out of the ether. Good harvesting!'

For forty-eight Tellurian hours, taking time out only to sleep, Samms scanned and surveyed the planet Trenco; and the more he studied it, the more outrageously abnormal it became.

Trenco was, and is, a peculiar planet indeed. Its atmosphere is not air as we know air; its hydrosphere does not resemble water. Half of that atmosphere and most of that hydrosphere are one chemical, a substance of very low heat of vaporisation and having a boiling point of about seventy five degrees Fahrenheit. Trenco's days are intensely hot; its nights are bitterly cold.

At night, therefore, it rains; and by comparison a Tellurian downpour of one inch per hour is scarcely a drizzle. Upon Trenco it really *rains*—forty seven feet and five inches of precipitation, every night of every Trenconian year. And this tremendous condensation of course causes wind. Willoughby's graphs were accurate. Except at Trenco's very poles there is not a spot in which or a time at which an Earthly gale would not constitute a dead calm; and along the equator, at every sunrise and every sunset, the wind blows from the day side into the night side at a velocity which no

Tellurian hurricane or cyclone, however violent, has even distantly approached.

Also, therefore, there is lightning. Not in the mild and occasional flashes which we of gentle Terra know, but in a continuous, blinding glare which outshines a normal sun; in battering, shattering, multi-billion-volt discharges which not only make darkness unknown there, but also distort beyond recognition and beyond function the warp and the woof of space itself. Sight is almost completely useless in that fantastically altered medium. So is the ultra-beam.

Landing on the daylight side, except possibly at exact noon, would be impossible because of the wind, nor could the ship stay landed for more than a couple of minutes. Landing on the night side would be practically as bad, because of the terrific charge the boat would pick up—unless the boat carried something that could be rebuilt into a leaker. Did it? It did.

Time after time, from pole to pole and from midnight around the clock, Samms stabbed Visibeam and spy-ray down toward Trenco's falsely-visible surface, with consistently and meaninglessly impossible results. The planet tipped, lurched, spun, and danced. It broke up into chunks, each of which began insanely to follow mathematically impossible paths.

Finally, in desperation, he rammed a beam down and held it down. Again he saw the planet break up before his eyes, but this time he held on. He *knew* that he was well out of the stratosphere, a good two hundred miles up. Nevertheless, he *saw* a tremendous mass of jagged rock falling straight down, with terrific velocity, upon his tiny lifeboat!

Unfortunately the crew, to whom he had not been paying overmuch attention of late, saw it, too; and one of them, with a bestial yell, leaped toward Samms and the controls. Samms, reaching for pistol and

blackjack, whirled around just in time to see the big red-head lay the would-be attacker out cold with a vicious hand's-edge chop at the base of the skull.

'Thanks, Tworn. Why?'

'Because I want to get out of this alive, and he'd've had us all in hell in fifteen minutes. You know a hell of a lot more than we do, so I'm playin' it your way. See?'

'I see. Can you use a sap?'

'An artist,' the big man admitted, modestly. 'Just tell me how long you want a guy to be out and I won't miss it a minute, either way. But you'd better blow that crumb's brains out, right now. He ain't no damn good.'

'Not until after I see whether he can work or not. You're a Procian, aren't you?'

'Yeah. Midlands—North Central.'

'What did you do?'

'Nothing much, at first. Just killed a guy that needed killing; but the goddam louse had a lot of money, so they give me twenty five years. I didn't like it very well, and acted rough, so they give me solitary—boot, bandage, and so on. So I tried a break—killed six or eight, maybe a dozen, guards—but didn't quite make it. So they slated me for the big whiff. That's all, boss.'

'I'm promoting you, now, to squad leader. Here's the sap.'

He handed Tworn his blackjack. 'Watch 'em—I'll be too busy to. This landing is going to be tough.'

'Gotcha, boss.' Tworn was calibrating his weapon by slugging himself experimentally on the leg. 'Go ahead. As far as these crumbs are concerned, you've got this air-tank all to yourself.'

Samms had finally decided what he was going to do. He located the terminator on the morning side, poised his little ship somewhat nearer to dawn than to midnight, and "cut the rope". He took one quick reading on the sun, cut off his plates, and let her drop, watching only his pressure gauges and gyros.

One hundred millimetres of mercury. Three hundred. Five hundred. He slowed her down. He was going to hit a thin liquid, but if he hit it too hard he would smash the boat, and he had no idea what the atmospheric pressure at Trenco's surface would be. Six hundred. Even this late at night, it might be greater than Earth's... and it might be a lot less. Seven hundred.

Slower and slower he crept downward, his tension mounting infinitely faster than did the needle of the gauge. This was an instrument landing with a vengeance! Eight hundred. How was the crew taking it? How many of them had Tworn had to disable? He glanced quickly around. None! Now that they could not see the hallucinatory images upn the plates, they were not suffering at all—he himself was the only one aboard who was feeling the strain!

Nine hundred... nine hundred forty. The boat "hit the drink" with a crashing, splashing impact. Its pace was slow enough, however, and the liquid was deep enough, so that no damage was done. Samms applied a little driving power and swung his craft's sharp nose into the line towards the sun. The little ship ploughed slowly forward, as nearly just awash as Samms could keep her; grounded as gently as a river steamboat upon a mud-flat. The starkly incredible downpour slackened; the Lensman knew that the second critical moment was at hand.

'Strap down, men, until we see what this wind is going to do to us.'

The atmosphere, moving at a velocity well above that of sound, was in effect not a gas, but a solid. Even a spaceboat's hard skin of alloy plate, with all its bracing, could not take what was coming next. Inert, she would be split open, smashed, flattened out, and twisted into pretzels. Samms' finger stabbed down; the Berg went into action; the lifeboat went free just as that raging blast of quasi-solid vapour wrenched her into the air.

The second descent was much faster and much easier than the first. Nor, this time, did Samms remain surfaced or drive toward shore. Knowing now that this ocean was not deep enough to harm his vessel, he let her sink to the bottom. More, he turned her on her side and drove her at a flat angle into the bottom; so deep that the rim of her starboard lock was flush with the ocean's floor. Again they waited; and this time the wind did not blow the lifeboat away.

Upon purely theoretical grounds Samms had reasoned that the weird distortion of vision must be a function of distance, and his observations so far had been in accord with that hypothesis. Now, slowly and cautiously, he sent out a visibeam. Ten feet... twenty... forty... all clear. At fifty the seeing was definitely bad; at sixty it became impossible. He shortened back to forty and began to study the vegetation, growing with such fantastic speed that the leaves, pressed flat to the ground by the gale and anchored there by heavy rootlets, were already inches long. There was also what seemed to be animal life, of sorts, but Samms was not, at the moment, interested in Trenconian zoology.

'Are them the plants we're going to get, boss?' Tworn asked, staring into the plate over Samms' shoulder. 'Shall we go out now an' start pickin' 'em?'

'Not yet. Even if we could open the port the blast would wreck us. Also, it would shear your head off, flush with the coaming, as fast as you stuck it out. This

wind should ease off after a while; we'll go out a little before noon. In the meantime we'll get ready. Have the boys break out a couple of spare Number Twelve struts, some clamps and chain, four snatch blocks, and a hundred feet of heavy space-line...

'Good,' he went on, when the order had been obeyed. 'Rig the line from the winch through snatch blocks here, and here, and here, so I can haul you back against the wind. While you are doing that I'll rig a remote control on the winch.'

Shortly before Trenco's fierce, blue-white sun reached meridian, the six men donned space-suits and Samms cautiously opened the air-lock ports. They worked. The wind was now scarely more than an Earthly hurricane; the wildly whipping broadleaf plants, struggling upward, were almost half-way to the vertical. The leaves were apparently almost fully grown.

Four men clamped their suits to the line. The line was paid out. Each man selected two leaves; the largest, fattest, purplest ones he could reach. Samms hauled them back and received the loot; Tworn stowed the leaves away. Again—again—again.

With noon there came a few minutes of "calm". A strong man could stand against the now highly variable wind; could move around without being blown beyond the horizon; and during those few minutes all six men gathered leaves. That time, however, was very short. The wind steadied into the reverse direction with ever-increasing fury; winch and space-line again came into play. And in a scant half hour, when the line began to hum an almost musical note under its load, Samms decided to call it quits.

'That'll be all for today, boys,' he announced. 'About twice more and this line will part. You've done too good a job to lose you. Secure ship.'

'Shall I blow the air, sir?' Tworn asked.

'I don't think so.' Samms thought for a moment. 'No, I'm afraid to take the chance. This stuff, whatever it is, is probably as poisonous as cyanide. We'll keep our suits on and exhaust into space.'

Time passed. "Night" came; the rain and the flood. The bottom softened. Samms blasted the lifeboat out of the mud and away from the planet. He opened the bleeder valves, then both airlock ports; the contaminated air was replaced by the ultra-hard vacuum of the interplanetary void. He signalled the *Virgin Queen*; the lifeboat was taken aboard.

'Quick trip, Olmstead,' Willoughby congratulated him. 'I'm surprised that you got back at all, to say nothing of with so much stuff and not losing a man. Give me the weight, mister, fast!'

'Three hundred and forty eight pounds, sir,' the super-cargo reported.

'My god! And all pure broadleaf! *Nobody* ever did *that* before! How did you do it, Olmstead?'

'I don't know whether that would be any of your business or not.' Samms' mien was not insulting; merely thoughtful. 'Not that I give a damn, but my way might not help anybody else much, and I think I had better report to the main office first, and let them do the telling. Fair enough?'

'Fair enough,' the skipper conceded, ungrudgingly. 'What a load! And no losses!'

'One boatload of air, is all; but air is expensive out here.' Samms made a point, deliberately.

'Air!' Willoughby snorted. 'I'll swap you a hundred flasks of air, any time, for any one of those leaves!' Which was what Samms wanted to know.

Captain Willoughby was smart. He knew that the way to succeed was to use and then to trample upon his inferiors; to toady to such superiors as were too

strong to be pulled down and thus supplanted. He knew this Olmstead had what it took to be a big shot. Therefore:

'They told me to keep you in the dark until we got to Trenco,' he more than half apologised to his Fourth Officer shortly after the *Virgin Queen* blasted away from the Trenconian system. 'But they didn't say anything about afterwards—maybe they figured you wouldn't be aboard any more, as usual—but anyway, you can stay right here in the control room if you want to.'

'Thanks, Skipper, but mightn't it be just as well,' he jerked his head inconspicuously toward the other officers, 'to play the string out, this trip? I don't care where we're going, and we don't want anybody to get any funny ideas.'

'That'd be a lot better, of course—as long as you know that your cards are all aces, as far as I'm concerned.'

'Thanks, Willoughby. I'll remember that.'

Samms had not been entirely frank with the private captain. From the time required to make the trip, he knew to within a few parsecs Trenco's distance from Sol. He did not know the direction, since the distance was so great that he had not been able to recognise any star or constellation. He did know, however, the course upon which the vessel then was, and he would know courses and distances from then on. He was well content.

A couple of uneventful days passed. Samms was again called into the control room, to see that the ship was approaching a three-sun solar system.

'This where we're going to land?' he asked, indifferently.

'We ain't going to land,' Willoughby told him. 'You are going to take the broadleaf down in your boat, close enough so that you can parachute it down to where it has to go. Way 'nuff, pilot, go inert and match intrinsics. Now, Olmstead, watch. You've seen systems like this before?'

'No, but I know about them. Those two suns over there are a hell of a lot bigger and further away than they look, and this one here, much smaller, is in the Trojan position. Have those big suns got any planets?'

'Five or six apiece, they say; all hotter and dryer than the brazen hinges of hell. This sun here has seven, but Number Two—"Cavenda", they call it—is the only Tellurian planet in the system. The first thing we look for is a big diamond-shaped continent... there's only one of that shape... there it is, over there. Notice that one end is bigger than the other—that end is north. Strike a line to split the continent in two and measure from the north end one-third of the length of the line. That's the point we're diving at now... see that crater?'

'Yes.' The *Virgin Queen*, although still hundreds of miles up, was slowing rapidly. 'It must be a big one.'

'It's a good fifty miles across. Go down until you're dead sure that the box will land somewhere inside the rim of that crater. Then dump it. The parachute and the sender are automatic. Understand?'

'Yes, sir; I understand,' and Samms took off.

He was vastly more interested in the stars, however, than in delivering the broadleaf. The constellation directly beyond Sol from wherever he was might be recognisable. Its shape would be smaller and more or less distorted; its smaller stars, brilliant to Earthly eyes only because of their nearness, would be dimmer, perhaps invisible; the picture would be further confused by intervening, nearby, brilliant strangers; but such giants as Canopus and Rigel and Betelgeuse and

Deneb would certainly be highly visible if he could only recognise them. From Trenco his search had failed; but he was still trying.

There was something vaguely familiar! Sweating with the mental effort, he blocked out the too-near, too-bright stars and studied intensively those that were left. A blue-white and a red were most prominent. Rigel and Betelgeuse? Could that constellation be Orion? The Belt was very faint, but it was there. Then Sirius ought to be about there, and Pollux about there; and, at this distance, about equally bright. They were. Aldebaran would be orange, and about one magnitude brighter than Pollux; and Capella would be yellow, and half a magnitude brighter still. There they were! Not too close to where they should be, but close enough—it was Orion! And this thionite way-station, then, was somewhere near right ascension seventeen hours and declination plus ten degrees!

He returned to the *Virgin Queen*. She blasted off. Samms asked very few questions and Willoughby volunteered very little information; nevertheless the First Lensman learned more than anyone of his fellow pirates would have believed possible. Aloof, taciturn, disinterested to a degree, he seemed to spend practically all of his time in his cabin when he was not actually at work; but he kept his eyes and his ears wide open. And Virgil Samms, as has been intimated, had a brain.

The *Virgin Queen* made a quick flit from Cavenda to Vegia, arriving exactly on time; a proud, clean space-ship as high above suspicion as Calpurnia herself. Samms unloaded her cargo; replaced it with one for Earth. She was serviced. She made a fast, eventless run to Tellus. She docked at New York Spaceport. Virgil Samms walked unconcernedly into an ordinary-looking rest-room; George Olmstead, fully informed, walked unconcernedly out.

As soon as he could, Samms Lensed Northrop and Jack Kinnison.

'We lined up a thousand and one signals, sir,' Northrop reported for the pair, 'but only one of them carried a message, and it didn't make sense.'

'Why not?' Samms asked, sharply. 'With a Lens, any kind of a message, however garbled, coded, or interrupted, makes sense.'

'Oh, we understood what it said,' Jack came in, 'but it didn't say enough. Just 'READY—READY—READY'; over and over.'

'What!' Samms exclaimed, and the boys could feel his mind work. 'Did that signal, by any chance, originate anywhere near seventeen hours and plus ten degrees?'

'Very near. Why? How did you know?'

'Then it does make sense!' Samms exclaimed, and called a general conference of Lensmen.

'Keep working along these same lines,' Samms directed, finally. 'Keep Ray Olmstead in the Hill in my place. I am going to Pluto, and—I hope—to Palain Seven.'

Roderick Kinnison of course protested; but, equally of course, his protests were over-ruled.

CHAPTER 10

Pluto is, on the average, about forty times as far away from the sun as is Mother Earth. Each square yard of Earth's surface receives about sixteen hundred times as much heat as does each of Pluto's. The sun as seen from Pluto is a dim, wan speck. Even at perihelion, an event which occurs only once in two hundred forty eight Tellurian years, and at noon and on the equator, Pluto is so bitterly cold that climatic conditions upon its surface simply cannot be described by or to warm-blooded, oxygen-breathing man.

As good an indication as any can be given, perhaps, by mentioning the fact that it had taken the Patrol's best engineers over six months to perfect the armour which Virgil Samms then wore. For no ordinary space-suit would do. Space itself is not cold; the only loss of heat is by radiation into or through an almost perfect vacuum. In contact with Pluto's rocky, metallic soil, however, there would be conduction; and the magnitude of the inevitable heat-loss made the Tellurian scientists gasp.

'Watch your feet, Virge!' had been Roderick Kinnison's insistent last thought. 'Remember those psychologists—if they stayed in contact with that ground for five minutes they froze their feet to the ankles. Not that the boys aren't good, but slipsticks sometimes slip in more ways than one. If your feet ever start to get cold, drop whatever you're doing and drive back here at max!'

Virgil Samms landed. His feet stayed warm. Finally, assured that the heaters of his suit could carry the load indefinitely, he made his way on foot into the settlement

near which he had come to ground. And there he saw his first Palainian.

Or, strictly speaking, he saw part of his first Palainian; for no three-dimensional creature has ever seen or ever will see in entirety any member of any of the frigid-blooded, poison-breathing races. Since life as we know it—organic, three-dimensional life—is based upon liquid water and gaseous oxygen, such life did not and could not develop upon planets whose temperatures are only a few degrees above absolute zero. Many, perhaps most, of these ultra-frigid planets have an atmosphere of sorts; some have no atmosphere at all. Nevertheless, with or without atmosphere and completely without oxygen and water, life—highly intelligent life—did develop upon millions and millions of such worlds. That life is not, however, strictly three-dimensional. Of necessity, even in the lowest forms, it possesses an extension into the hyper-dimension; and it is this metabolic extension alone which makes it possible for life to exist under such extreme conditions.

The extension makes it impossible for any human being to see anything of a Palainian except the fluid, amorphous, ever-changing thing which is his three-dimensional aspect of the moment; makes any attempt at description or portraiture completely futile.

Virgil Samms stared at the Palainian; tried to see what it looked like. He could not tell whether it had eyes or antennae; legs, arms, or tentacles, teeth or beaks, talons or claws or feet; skin, scales, or feathers. It did not even remotely resemble anything that the Lensman had ever seen, sensed, or imagined. He gave up; sent out an exploring thought.

'I am Virgil Samms, a Tellurian,' he sent out slowly, carefully, after he made contact with the outer fringes of the creature's mind. 'Is it possible for you, sir or madam, to give me a moment of your time?'

'Eminently possible, Lensman Samms, since my time is of completely negligible value.' The monster's mind flashed into accord with Samms' with a speed and precision that made him gasp. That is, a part of it became en rapport with a part of his: years were to pass before even the First Lensman would know much more about the Palainian than he learned in that first contact; no human beings except the Children of the Lens ever were to understand even dimly the labyrinthine intricacies, the paradoxical complexities, of the Palainian mind.

' "Madam" might be approximately correct,' the native's thought went smoothly on. 'My name, in your symbology, is Twelfth Pilinipsi; by education, training, and occupation I am a Chief Dexitroboper. I perceive that you are indeed a native of that hellish Planet Three, upon which it was assumed for so long that no life could possibly exist. But communication with your race has been almost impossible heretofore... Ah, the Lens. A remarkable device, truly. I would slay you and take it, except for the obvious fact that only you can possess it.'

'What!' Dismay and consternation flooded Samms' mind. 'You already know the Lens?'

'No. Yours is the first that any of us has perceived. The mechanics, the mathematics, and the basic philosophy of the thing, however, are quite clear.'

'What!' Samms exclaimed again. 'You can, then, produce Lenses yourselves?'

'By no means, any more than you Tellurians can. There are magnitudes, variables, determinants, and forces involved which no Palainian will ever be able to develop, to generate, or to control.'

'I see.' The Lensman pulled himself together. For a First Lensman, he was making a wretched showing indeed...

'Far from it, sir,' the monstrosity assured him. 'Considering the strangeness of the environment into which you have voluntarily flung yourself so senselessly, your mind is well integrated and strong. Otherwise it would have shattered. If our positions were reversed, the mere thought of the raging heat of your Earth would—come no closer, please!' The thing vanished; reappeared many yards away. Her thoughts were a shudder of loathing, of terror, of sheer detestation. 'But to get on. I have been attempting to analyse and to understand your purpose, without success. That failure is not too surprising, of course, since my mind is weak and my total power is small. Explain your mission, please, as simply as you can.

Weak? Small? In view of the power the monstrosity had just shown, Samms probed for irony, for sarcasm or pretence. There was no trace of anything of the kind.

He tried, then, for fifteen solid minutes, to explain the Galactic Patrol, but at the end the Palainian's only reaction was one of blank non-comprehension.

'I fail completely to perceive the use of, or the need for, such an organisation,' she stated flatly. 'This altruism—what good is it? It is unthinkable that any other race would take any risks or exert any effort for us, any more than we would for them. Ignore and be ignored, as you must already know, is the Prime Tenet.'

'But there is a little commerce between our worlds; your people did not ignore our psychologists; and you are not ignoring me,' Samms pointed out.

'Oh, none of us is perfect,' Pilinipsi replied, with a mental shrug and what seemed to be an airy wave of a multi-tentacled member. 'That ideal, like any other, can only be approached asymptotically, never reached; and I, being somewhat foolish and silly, as well as weak and vacillant, am much less perfect than most.'

Flabbergasted, Samms tried a new tack. 'I might be able to make my position clearer if I knew you better. I know your name, and that you are a woman of Palain Seven'—it is a measure of Virgil Samms' real size that he actually thought "woman", and not merely "female"—'but all I can understand of your occupation is the name you have given it. What does a Chief Dexitroboper do?'

'She—or he—or, perhaps, it…is a supervisor of the work of dexitroboping.' The thought, while perfectly clear, was completely meaningless to Samms, and the Palainian knew it. She tried again. 'Dexitroboping has to do with…nourishment? No—with nutrients.'

'Ah. Farming—agriculture,' Samms thought; but this time it was the Palainian who could not grasp the concept. 'Hunting? Fishing?' No better. 'Show me, then, please.'

She tried; but demonstration, too, was useless; for to Samms the Palainian's movements were pointless indeed. The peculiarly flowing subtly changing thing darted back and forth, rose and fell, appeared and disappeared; undergoing the while cyclic changes in shape and form and size, in aspect and texture. It was now spiny, now tentacular, now scaly, now covered with peculiarly repellent feather-like fronds, each oozing a crimson slime. But it apparently did not do anything whatever. The net result of all its activity was, apparently, zero.

'There, it is done.' Pilinipsi's thought again came clear. 'You observed and understood? You did not. That is strange—baffling. Since the Lens did improve communication and understanding tremendously, I hoped that it might extend to the physical as well. But there must be some basic, fundamental difference, the nature of which is at present obscure. I wonder…if I had a Lens, too—but no…'

'But yes!' Samms broke in, eagerly. 'Why don't you go to Arisia and be tested for one? You have a magnificent, a really *tremendous* mind. It is of Lensman grade in every respect except one—you simply don't *want* to use it!'

'Me? Go to Arisia?' The thought would have been, in a Tellurian, a laugh of scorn. 'How utterly silly—how abysmally stupid! There would be personal discomfort, quite possibly personal danger, and two Lenses would be little or no better than one in resolving differences between our two continua, which are probably in fact incommensurable.'

'Well, then,' Samms thought, almost viciously, 'can you introduce me to someone who is stupider, sillier, and more foolish than you are?'

'Not here on Pluto, no.' The Palainian took no offence. 'That was why it was I who interviewed the earlier Tellurian visitors and why I am now conversing with you. The others avoided you.'

'I see.' Samms' thought was grim. 'How about the home planet, then?'

'Ah. Undoubtedly. In fact, there is a group, a club, of such persons. None of them is, of course, as insane—as aberrant—as you are, but they are all much more so than I am.'

'Who of this club would be most interested in becoming a Lensman?'

'Tallick was the least stable member of the New-Thought Club when I left Seven; Kragzex a close second. There may of course have been changes since then. But I cannot believe that even Tallick—even Tallick at his outrageous worst—would be crazy enough to join your Patrol.'

'Nevertheless, I must see him myself. Can you and will you give me a chart of a routing from here to Palain Seven?'

'I can and I will. Nothing you have thought will be of any use to me; that will be the easiest and quickest way of getting rid of you.' The Palainian spread a completely detailed chart in Samms' mind, snapped the telepathic line, and went unconcernedly about her incomprehensible business.

Samms, mind reeling, made his way back to his boat and took off. And as the light-years and the parsecs screamed past, he sank deeper and deeper into a welter of unproductive speculation. What were—really—those Palainians? How could they—really—exist as they seemed to exist? And why had some of that dexitroboper's—whatever *that* meant!—thoughts come in so beautifully sharp and clear and plain while others...?

He knew that his Lens would receive and would convert into his own symbology any thought or message, however coded or garbled or however sent or transmitted. The Lens was not at fault; his symbology was. There were concepts—things—actualities—occurrences—so foreign to Tellurian experience that no referents existed. Hence the human mind lacked the channels, the mechanisms, to grasp them.

He and Roderick Kinnison had glibly discussed the possibility of encountering forms of intelligent life so alien that humanity would have no point whatever of contact with them. After what Samms had just gone through, that was more of a possibility than either he or his friend had believed; and he hoped grimly, as he considered how seriously this partial contact with the Palainian had upset him, that the possibility would never become a fact.

He found the Palainian system easily enough, and Palain Seven. That planet, of course, was almost as

dark upon its sunward side as upon the other, and its inhabitants had no use for light. Pilinipsi's instructions, however, had been minute and exact; hence Samms had very little trouble in locating the principal city— or, rather, the principal village, since there were no real cities. He found the planet's one spaceport. What a thing to call a port! He checked back; recalled exactly this part of his interview with Pluto's Chief Dexitroboper.

'The place upon which space-ships land,' had been her thought, when she showed him exactly where it was in relationship to the town. Just that, and nothing else. It had been his mind, not hers, that had supplied the docks and cradles, the service cars, the officers, and all the other things taken for granted in space-fields everywhere as Samms knew them. Either the Palainian had not perceived the trappings with which Samms had invested her visualisation, or she had not cared enough about his misapprehension to go to the trouble of correcting it; he did not know which.

The whole area was as bare as his hand. Except for the pitted, scarred, slagged-down spots which showed so clearly what driving blasts would do to such inconceivably cold rock and metal, Palainport was in no way distinguishable from any other unimproved portion of the planet's utterly bleak surface.

There were no signals; he had been told of no landing conventions. Apparently it was everyone for himself. Wherefore Samms' tremendous landing lights blazed out, and with their aid he came safely to ground. He put on his armour and strode to the airlock; then changed his mind and went to the cargo-port instead. He had intended to walk, but in view of the rugged and deserted field and the completely unknown terrain between the field and the town, he decided to ride the "creep" instead.

This vehicle, while slow, could go—literally—anywhere. It had a cigar-shaped body of magnalloy; it had big, soft tough tyres; it had cleated tracks; it had air- and water-propellers; it had folding wings; it had driving, braking, and steering jets. It could traverse the deserts of Mars, the oceans and swamps of Venus, the crevassed glaciers of Earth, the jagged, frigid surface of an iron asteroid, and the cratered, fluffy topography of the moon; if not with equal speed, at least with equal safety.

Samms released the thing and drove it into the cargo lock, noting mentally that he would have to exhaust the air of that lock into space before he again broke the inner seal. The ramp slid back into the ship; the cargo port closed. Here he was!

Should he use his headlights, or not? He did not know the Palainians' reaction to or attitude toward light. It had not occurred to him while at Pluto to ask, and it might be important. The landing lights of his vessel might already have done his cause irreparable harm. He could drive by starlight if he had to...but he needed light and he had not seen a single living or moving thing. There was no evidence that there was a Palainian within miles. While he had known, with his brain, that Palain would be dark, he had expected to find buildings and traffic—ground-cars, planes, and at least a few space-ships—and not this vast nothingness.

If nothing else, there *must* be a road from Palain's principal city to its only spaceport; but Samms had not seen it from his vessel and he could not see it now. At least, he could not recognise it. Wherefore he clutched in the tractor drive and took off in a straight line toward town. The going was more than rough—it was really rugged—but the creep was built to stand up under punishment and its pilot's chair was sprung and cushioned to exactly the same degree. Hence,

while the course itself was infinitely worse than the smoothly paved approaches to Rigelston, Samms found this trip much less bruising than the other had been.

Approaching the village, he dimmed his roadlights and slowed down. At its edge he cut them entirely and inched his way forward by starlight alone.

What a town! Virgil Samms had seen the inhabited places of almost every planet of Civilisation. He had seen cities laid out in circles, sectors, ellipses, triangles, squares, parallelo-pipeds—practically every plan known to geometry. He had seen structures of all shapes and sizes—narrow skyscrapers, vast-spreading one-storeys, polyhedra, domes, spheres, semi-cylinders, and erect and inverted full and truncated cones and pyramids. Whatever the plan or the shapes of the component units, however, those inhabited places had, without exception, been understandable. But this!

Samms, his eyes now completely dark-accustomed, could see fairly well, but the more he saw the less he grasped. There was no plan, no coherence or unit whatever. It was as though a cosmic hand had flung a few hundreds of buildings, of incredibly and senselessly varied shapes and sizes and architectures, upon an otherwise empty plain, and as though each structure had been allowed ever since to remain in whatever location and attitude it had chanced to fall. Here and there were jumbled piles of three or more utterly incongruous structures. There were a few whose arrangement was almost orderly. Here and there were large, irregularly-shaped areas of bare, untouched ground. There were no streets—at least, nothing that the man could recognise as such.

Samms headed the creep for one of those open areas, then stopped—declutched the tracks, set the brakes, and killed the engines.

'Go slow, fellow,' he advised himself then. 'Until you find out what a dexitroboper actually does while working at his trade, don't take chances of interfering or of doing damage!'

No Lensman knew—then—that frigid-blooded poison-breathers were not strictly three-dimensional; but Samms did know that he had actually seen things which he could not understand. He and Kinnison had discussed such occurrences calmly enough; but the actuality was enough to shake even the mind of Civilisation's First Lensman.

He did not need to be any closer, anyway. He had learned the Palainians' patterns well enough to Lens them from a vastly greater distance than his present one; this personal visit to Palainopolis had been a gesture of friendliness, not a necessity.

'Tallick? Kragzex?' He sent out the questing, querying thought. 'Lensman Virgil Samms of Sol Three calling Tallick and Kragzex of Palain Seven.'

'Kragzex acknowledging, Virgil Samms,' a thought snapped back, as diamond-clear, as precise, as Pilinipsi's had been.

'Is Tallick here, or anywhere on the planet?'

'He is here, but he is emmfozing at the moment. He will join us presently.'

Damnation! There it was again! First "dexitroboping", and now this!

'So I perceive, the fault is of course mine, in not being able to attune my mind fully to yours. Do not take this, please, as any aspersion upon the character or strength of your own mind.'

'Of course not. I am the first Tellurian you have met?'

'Yes.'

'I have exchanged thoughts with one other Palainian, and the same difficulty existed. I can neither understand nor explain it; but it is as though there are differences between us so fundamental that in some matters mutual comprehension is in fact impossible.'

'A masterly summation and undoubtedly a true one. This emmfozing, then—if I read correctly, your race has only two sexes?'

'You read correctly.'

'I cannot understand. There is no close analogy. However, emmfozing has to do with reproduction.'

'I see,' and Samms saw, not only a frankness brand-new to his experience, but also a new view of both the powers and the limitations of his Lens.

It was, by its very nature, of precisionist grade. It received thoughts and translated them precisely into English. There was some leeway, but not much. If any thought was such that there was no extremely close counterpart or referent in English, the Lens would not translate it at all, but would simply give it a hitherto meaningless symbol—a symbol which would from that time on be associated, by all Lenses everywhere, with that one concept and no other. Samms realised then that he might, some day, learn what a dexitroboper actually did and what the act of emmfozing actually was; but that he very probably would not.

Tallick joined them then, and Samms again described glowingly, as he had done so many times before, the Galactic Patrol of his imaginings and plannings. Kragzex refused to have anything to do with such a thing, almost as abruptly as Pilinipsi had done, but Tallick lingered—and wavered.

'It is widely known that I am not entirely sane,' he admitted, 'which may explain the fact that I would very much like to have a Lens. But I gather, from what you

have said, that I would probably not be given a Lens to use purely for my own selfish purposes?'

'That is my understanding,' Samms agreed.

'I was afraid so.' Tallick's mien was…"woebegone" is the only word for it. 'I have work to do. Projects, you know, of difficulty, of extreme complexity and scope, sometimes even approaching danger. A Lens would be of tremendous use.'

'How?' Samms asked. 'If your work is of enough importance to enough people, Mentor would certainly give you a Lens.'

'This would benefit me; only me. We of Palain, as you probably already know, are selfish, mean-spirited, small-souled, cowardly, furtive, and sly. Of what you call "bravery" we have no trace. We attain our ends by stealth, by indirection, by trickery and deceit.' Ruthlessly the Lens was giving Virgil Samms the uncompromisingly exact English equivalent of the Palainian's every thought. 'We operate, when we must operate at all openly, with the absolute irreducible minimum of personal risk. These attitudes and attributes will, I have no doubt, preclude all possibility of Lensmanship for me and for every member of my race.'

'Not necessarily.'

Not necessarily! Although Virgil Samms did not know it, this was one of the really critical moments in the coming into being of the Galactic Patrol. By a conscious, a tremendous effort, the First Lensman was lifting himself above the narrow, intolerant prejudices of human experience and was consciously attempting to see the whole through Mentor's Arisian mind instead of through his Tellurian own. That Virgil Samms was the first human being to be born with the ability to accomplish that feat even partially was one of the reasons why he was the first wearer of the Lens.

'Not necessarily,' First Lensman Virgil Samms said and meant. He was inexpressibly shocked—revolted in every human fibre—by what this unhuman monster had so frankly and callously thought. There were, however, many things which no human being ever could understand, and there was not the shadow of a doubt that this Tallick had a really tremendous mind. 'You have said that your mind is feeble. If so, there is no simple expression of the weakness of mine. I can perceive only one, the strictly human, facet of the truth. In a broader view it is distinctly possible that your motivation is at least as "noble" as mine. And to complete my argument, you work with other Palainians, do you not, to reach a common goal?'

'At times, yes.'

'Then you can conceive of the desirability of working with non-Palainian entities toward an end which would benefit both races?'

'Postulating such an end, yes; but I am unable to visualise any such. Have you any specific project in mind?'

'Not at the moment.' Samms ducked. He had already fired every shot in his locker. 'I am quite certain, however, that if you go to Arisia you will be informed of several such projects.'

There was a period of silence. Then:

'I believe that I *will* go to Arisia, at that!' Tallick exclaimed, brightly. 'I will make a deal with your friend Mentor. I will give him a share—say fifty percent, or forty—of the time and effort I save on my own projects!'

'Just so you go, Tallick.' Samms concealed right manfully his real opinion of the Palainian's scheme. 'When can you go? Right now?'

'By no means. I must first finish this project. A year, perhaps—or more; or possibly less. Who knows?'

Tallick cut communications and Samms frowned. He did not know the exact length of Seven's year, but he knew that it was long—very long.

CHAPTER 11

A small, black scout-ship, commanded jointly by Master Pilot John K. Kinnison and Master Electronicist Mason M. Northrop, was blasting along a course very close indeed to RA17: D+10. In equipment and personnel, however, she was not an ordinary scout. Her control room was so full of electronics racks and computing machines that there was scarcely footway in any direction; her graduated circles and vernier scales were of a size and a fineness usually seen only in the great vessels of the Galactic Survey. And her crew, instead of the usual twenty-odd men, numbered only seven—one cook, three engineers, and three watch officers. For some time the young Third Officer, then at the board, had been studying something on his plate; comparing it minutely with the chart clipped into the rack in front of him. Now he turned, with a highly exaggerated deference, to the two Lensmen.

'Sirs, which of your Magnificences is officially the commander of this here bucket of odds and ends at the present instant?'

'Him.' Jack used his cigarette as a pointer. 'The guy with the misplaced plucked eyebrow on his upper lip. I don't come on duty until sixteen hundred hours—one precious Tellurian minute yet in which to dream of the beauties of Earth so distant in space and in both past and future time.'

'Huh? Beauties? Plural? Next time I see a party whose pictures are cluttering up this whole ship I'll tell her about your polygamous ideas. I'll ignore that crack about my moustache, though, since you can't raise one of your own. I'm ignoring you, too—like this, see?'

Ostentatiously turning his back upon the lounging Kinnison, Northrop stepped carefully over three or four breadboard hook-ups and stared into the plate over the watch officer's shoulder. He then studied the chart. *'Was ist los,* Stu? I don't see a thing.'

'More Jack's line than yours, Mase. This system we're headed for is a triple, and the chart says it's a double. Natural enough, of course. This whole region is unexplored, so the charts are astronomicals, not surveys. But that makes us Prime Discoverers, and our Commanding Officer—and the book says "Officer", not "Officers"—has got to...'

'That's me, now,' Jack announced, striding grandly toward the plate. 'Amscray, oobsbay. *I* will name the baby. *I* will report. *I* will go down in history...'

'Bounce back, small fry. You weren't at the time of discovery.' Northrop placed a huge hand flat against Jack's face and pushed gently. 'You'll go down, sure enough—not in history, but from a knock on the knob—if you try to steal any thunder away from *me*. And besides, you'd name it *"Dimples"*—what a *revolting* thought!'

'And what would you name it? *"Virgilia"*, I suppose?'

'Far from it, my boy.' He had intended doing just that, but now he did not quite dare. 'After our project, of course. The planet we're heading for will be Zabriska; the suns will be A-, B-, and C-Zabriskae, in order of size; and the watch officer then on duty, Lieutenant L. Stuart Rawlings, will engross these and all other pertinent data in the log. Can you classify 'em from here, Jack?'

'I can make some guesses—close enough, probably, for Discovery work.' Then, after a few minutes: 'Two giants, a blue-white and a bluish yellow; and a yellow dwarf.'

'Dwarf in the Trojan?'

'That would be my guess, since that is the only place it could stay very long, but you can't tell much from one look. I can tell you one thing, though—unless your Zabriska is in a system straight beyond this one, it's got to be a planet of the big fellow himself; and brother, that sun is *hot!*'

'It's got to be here, Jack. I haven't made *that* big an error in reading a beam since I was a sophomore.'

'I'll buy that...well, we're close enough, I guess.' Jack killed the driving blasts, but not the Bergenholm; the inertialess vessel stopped instantaneously in open space. 'Now we've got to find out which one of those twelve or fifteen planets was on our line when that last message was sent... There, we're stable enough, I hope. Open your cameras, Mase. Pull the first plate in fifteen minutes. That ought to give me enough track so I can start the job, since we're at a wide angle to their ecliptic.'

The work went on for an hour or so. Then:

'Something coming from the direction of Tellus,' the watch officer reported. 'Big and fast. Shall I hail her?'

'Might as well,' but the stranger hailed first.

'Space-ship *Chicago*, NA2AA, calling. Are you in trouble? Identify yourself, please.'

'Space-ship NA774J acknowledging. No trouble...'

'Northrop! Jack!' came Virgil Samms' highly concerned thought. The superdreadnought flashed alongside, a bare few hundred miles away, and stopped. 'Why did you stop *here?*'

'This is where our signal came from, sir.'

'Oh.' A hundred thoughts raced through Samms' mind, too fast and too fragmentary to be intelligible. I see you're computing. Would it throw you off too much to go inert and match intrinsics, so that I can join you?'

'No, sir; I've got everything I need for a while.'

Samms came aboard; three Lensmen studied the chart.

'Cavenda is there,' Samms pointed out. 'Trenco is there, off to one side. I felt sure that your signal originated on Cavenda; but Zabriska, here, while on almost the same line, is less than half as far from Tellus.' He did not ask whether the two young Lensmen were sure of their findings. He knew. 'This arouses my curiosity no end—does it merely complicate the thionite problem, or does it set up an entirely new problem? Go ahead, boys, with whatever you were going to do next.'

Jack had already determined that the planet they wanted was the second out; A-Zabriskae Two. He drove the scout as close to the planet as he could without losing complete coverage; stationed it on the line toward Sol.

'Now we wait a bit,' he answered. 'According to recent periodicity, not less than four hours and not more than ten. With the next signal we'll nail that transmitter down to within a few feet. Got your spotting screens full out, Mase?'

'*Recent* periodicity?' Samms snapped. 'It has improved then, lately?'

'Very much, sir.'

'That helps immensely. With George Olmstead harvesting broadleaf, it would. It is still one problem. While we wait, shall we study the planet a little?'

They explored; finding that A-Zabriskae Two was a disappointing planet indeed. It was small, waterless,

airless, utterly featureless, utterly barren. There were no elevations, no depressions, no visible markings whatever—not even a meteor crater. Every square yard of its surface was apparently exactly like every other.

'No rotation,' Jack reported, looking up from the bolometer. 'That sand-pile is not inhabited and never will be. I'm beginning to wonder.'

'So am I, now,' Northrop admitted. 'I still say that those signals came from this line and distance, but it looks as though they must have been sent from a ship. If so, now that we're here—particularly the *Chicago*—there will be no more signals.'

'Not necessarily.' Again Samms' mind transcended his Tellurian experience and knowledge. He did not suspect the truth, but he was not jumping at conclusions. 'There may be highly intelligent life, even upon such a planet as this.'

They waited, and in a few hours a communications beam snapped into life.

'READY—READY—READY...' it said briskly, for not quite one minute, but that was time enough.

Northrop yelped a string of numbers; Jack blasted the little vessel forward and downward; the three watch officers, keen-eyed at their plates, stabbed their visibeams, ultra-beams, and spy-rays along the indicated line.

'And bore straight through the planet if you have to—they may be on the other side!' Jack cautioned, sharply.

'They aren't—it's here, on this side!' Rawlings saw it first. 'Nothing much to it, though...it looks like a relay station.'

'A *relay*! I'll be a...' Jack started to express an unexpurgated opinion, but shut himself up. Young cubs

did not swear in front of the First Lensman. 'Let's land, sir, and look the place over, anyway.'

'By all means.'

They landed, and cautiously disembarked. The horizon, while actually quite a little closer than that of Earth, seemed much more distant because there was nothing whatever—no tree, no shrub, no rock or pebble, not even the slightest ripple—to break the geometrical perfection of that surface of smooth, hard, blindingly reflective, fiendishly hot white sand. Samms was highly dubious at first—a ground-temperature of four hundred seventy-five degrees was not to be taken lightly; he did not at all like the looks of that ultra-fervent blue-white sun; and in his wildest imaginings he had never pictured such a desert. Their space-suits, however, were very well insulated, particularly as to the feet, and highly polished; and in lieu of atmosphere there was an almost perfect vacuum. They could stand it for a while.

The box which housed the relay station was made of non-ferrous metal and was roughly cubical in shape, perhaps five feet on a side. It was so buried that its upper edge was flush with the surface; its top, which was practically indistinguishable from the surrounding sand, was not bolted or welded, but was simply laid on, loose.

Previous spy-ray inspection having proved that the thing was not booby-trapped, Jack lifted the cover by one edge and all three Lensmen studied the mechanisms at close range; learning nothing new. There was an extremely sensitive non-directional receiver, a highly directional sender, a beautifully precise uranium-clock director, and an "eternal" power-pack. There was nothing else.

'What next, sir?' Northrop asked. 'There'll be an incoming signal, probably, in a couple of days. Shall

we stick around and see whether it comes from Cavenda or not?'

'You and Jack had better wait, yes.' Samms thought for minutes. 'I do not believe, now, that the signal will come from Cavenda, or that it will ever come twice from the same direction, but we will have to make sure. But I can't see any *reason* for it!'

'I think I can, sir.' This was Northrop's specialty. 'No space-ship could possibly hit Tellus from here except by accident with a single-ended beam, and they can't use a double-ender because it would have to be on all the time and would be as easy to trace as the Mississippi River. But this planet did all its settling ages ago—which is undoubtedly why they picked it out—and that director in there is a Marchanti—the second Marchanti I have ever seen.'

'Whatever *that* is,' Jack put in, and even Samms thought a question.

'The most precise thing ever built,' the specialist explained. 'Accuracy limited only by that of determination of relative motions. Give me an accurate enough equation to feed into it, like that tape is doing, and two sighting shots, and I'll guarantee to pour an eighteen-inch beam into any two foot cup on Earth. My guess is that it's aimed at some particular bucket-antenna on one of the Solar planets. I could spoil its aim easily enough, but I don't suppose that is what you're after.'

'Decidedly not. We want to trace them, without exciting any more suspicion than is absolutely necessary. How often, would you say, do they have to come here to service this station—change tapes, and whatever else might be necessary?'

'Change tapes, is all. Not very often, by the size of those reels. If they know the relative motions exactly enough, they could compute as far ahead as they care

to. I've been timing that reel—it's got pretty close to three months left on it.'

'And more than that much has been used. It's no wonder we didn't see anything.' Samms straightened up and stared out across the frightful waste. 'Look there—I thought I saw something move—it *is* moving!'

'There's something moving closer than that, and it's really funny.' Jack laughed deeply. 'It's like the paddle-wheels, shaft and all, of an old-fashioned river steamboat, rolling along as unconcernedly as you please. He won't miss me by over four feet, but he isn't swerving a hair. I think I'll block him off, just to see what he does.'

'Be careful, Jack!' Samms cautioned, sharply. 'Don't touch it—it may be charged, or worse.'

Jack took the metal cover, which he was still holding, and by working it back and forth edgewise in the sand, made of it a vertical barrier squarely across the thing's path. The traveller paid no attention, did not alter its steady pace of a couple of miles per hour. It measured about twelve inches long over all; its paddle-wheel-like extremities were perhaps two inches wide and three inches in diameter.

'Do you think it's actually *alive*, sir? In a place like this?'

'I'm sure of it. Watch carefully.'

It struck the barrier and stopped. That is, its forward motion stopped, but its rolling did not. Its rate of revolution did not change; it either did not know or did not care that its drivers were slipping on the smooth, hard sand; that it could not climb the vertical metal plate; that it was not getting anywhere.

'What a brain!' Northrop chortled, squatting down closer. 'Why doesn't it back up or turn around? It may be alive, but it certainly isn't very bright.'

The creature, now in the shadow of the 'Troncist's helmet, slowed down abruptly—went limp—collapsed.

'Get out of his light!' Jack snapped, and pushed his friend violently away; and as the vicious sunlight struck it, the native revived and began to revolve as vigorously as before. 'I've got a hunch. Sounds screwy—never heard of such a thing—but it acts like an energy-converter. Eats energy, raw and straight. No storage capacity—on this world he wouldn't need it—a few more seconds in the shade would probably have killed him, but there's no shade here. Therefore, he can't be dangerous.

He reached out and touched the middle of the revolving shaft. Nothing happened. He turned it at right angles to the plate. The thing rolled away in a straight line, perfectly contented with the new direction. He recaptured it and stuck a test-prod lightly into the sand, just ahead of its shaft and just inside one paddle wheel. Around and around that slim wire the creature went: unable, it seemed, to escape from even such a simple trap; perfectly willing, it seemed, to spend all the rest of its life traversing that tiny circle.

' "What a brain!" is right, Mase,' Jack exclaimed. 'What a brain!'

'This is wonderful, boys, really wonderful; something completely new to our science.' Samms' thought was deep with feeling. 'I am going to see if I can reach its mind or consciousness. Would you like to come along?'

'Would we!'

Samms tuned low and probed; lower and lower; deeper and deeper; and Jack and Mase stayed with him. The thing was certainly alive; it throbbed and vibrated with vitality: equally certainly, it was not very intelligent. But it had a definite consciousness of its own existence; and therefore, however tiny and

primitive, a mind. Although its rudimentary ego could neither receive nor transmit thought, it knew that it was a fontema, that it must roll and roll and roll, endlessly, that by virtue of determined rolling its species would continue and would increase.

'Well, that's one for the book!' Jack exclaimed, but Samms was entranced.

'I would like to find one or two more of them, to find out... I think I'll *take* the time. Can you see any more of them, either of you?'

'No, but we can find some—Stu!' Northrop called.

'Yes?'

'Look around, will you? Find us a couple more of these fontema things and flick them over here with a tractor.'

'Coming up!' and in a few seconds they were there.

'Are you photographing this, Lance?' Samms called the Chief Communications Officer of the *Chicago*.

'We certainly are, sir—all of it. What are they, anyway? Animal, vegetable, or mineral?'

'I don't know. Probably no one of the three, strictly speaking. I'd like to take a couple back to Tellus, but I'm afraid that they'd die, even under an atomic lamp. We'll report to the Society.'

Jack liberated his captive and aimed it to pass within a few feet of one of the newcomers, but the two fontemas did not ignore each other. Both swerved, so that they came together wheel to wheel. The shafts bent toward each other, each into a right angle. The angles touched and fused. The point of fusion swelled rapidly into a double fist-sized lump. The half-shafts doubled in length. The lump split into four; became four perfect paddle-wheels. Four full-grown fontemas rolled away from the spot upon which two had met;

their courses forming two mutually perpendicular straight lines.

'Beautiful!' Samms exclaimed. 'And notice, boys, the method of avoiding inbreeding. Upon a perfectly smooth planet such as this, no two of those four can ever meet, and the chance is almost vanishingly small that any of their first-generation offspring will ever meet. But I'm afraid I've been wasting time. Take me back out to the *Chicago*, please, and I'll be on my way.'

'You don't seem at all optimistic, sir,' Jack ventured, as the NA774J approached the *Chicago*.

'Unfortunately, I am not. The signal will almost certainly come in from an unpredictable direction, from a ship so far away that even a super-fast cruiser could not get close enough to her to detect—just a minute, Rod!' He Lensed the elder Kinnison so sharply that both young Lensmen jumped.

'What is it, Virge?'

Samms explained rapidly, concluding: 'So I would like to have you throw a globe of scouts around this whole Zabriskan system. One detet* out and one detet apart, so as to be able to slap a tracer onto any ship laying a beam to this planet, from any direction whatever. It would not take too many scouts, would it?'

'No; but it wouldn't be worthwhile.'

'Why not?'

'Because it wouldn't prove a thing except what we already know—that Spaceways is involved in the thionite racket. The ship would be clean. Merely another relay.'

* *Detet—The distance at which one space-ship can detect another. EES.*

'Oh. You're probably right.' If Virgil Samms was in the least put out at this cavalier dismissal of his idea, he made no sign. He thought intensely for a couple of minutes. 'You are right. I will have to work from the Cavenda end. How are you coming with Operation Bennett?'

'Nice!' Kinnison enthused. 'When you get a couple of days, come over and see it grow. This is a fine world, Virge—it'll be ready!'

'I'll do that.' Samms broke the connectin and called Dronvire.

'The only change here is for the worse,' the Rigellian reported, tersely. 'The slight positive correlation between deaths from thionite and the arrival of Spaceways vessels has disappeared.'

There was no need to elaborate on that bare statement. Both Lensmen knew what it meant. The enemy, either in anticipation of statistical analysis or for economic reasons, was rationing his small supply of the drug.

And DalNalten was very much unlike his usual equable self. He was glum and unhappy; so much so that it took much urging to make him report at all.

'We have, as you know, put our best operatives to work on the interplanetary lines,' he said finally, half sullenly. 'We have secured quite a little data. The accumulating facts, however, point more and more definitely toward an utterly preposterous conclusion. Can you think of any valid reason why the exports and imports of thionite between Tellus and Mars, Mars and Venus, and Venus and Tellus, should all be exactly equal to each other?'

'What!'

'Precisely. That is why Knobos and I are not yet ready to present even a preliminary report.'

Then Jill. 'I can't prove it, any more than I could before, but I'm pretty sure that Morgan is the Boss. I have drawn every picture I can think of with Isaacson in the driver's seat, but none of them fit?' She paused, questioningly.

'I am already reconciled to adopting that view; at least as a working hypothesis. Go ahead.'

'The fact seems to be that Morgan has always had all the left-wingers of the Nationalists under his thumb. Now he and his man Friday, Representative Flierce, are wooing all the radicals and so-called liberals on our side of both Senate and House—a new technique for him—and they're offering plenty of the right kind of bait. He has the commentators guessing, but there's no doubt whatever in my mind that he is aiming at next Election Day and our Galactic Council.'

'And you and Dronvire are sitting idly by, doing nothing, of course?'

'Of course!' Jill giggled, but sobered quickly. 'He's a smooth, *smooth* worker, Dad. We are organising, of course, and putting out propaganda of our own, but there's so pitifully little that we can actually *do*— look and listen to this for a minute, and you'll see what I mean.'

In her distant room Jill manipulated a reel and flipped a switch. A plate came to life, showing Morgan's big, sweating, passionately earnest face.

'...and who *are* these Lensmen, anyway?' Morgan's voice bellowed, passionate conviction in every syllable. 'They are the hired minions of the classes, stabbers in the back, crooks and scoundrels, TOOLS OF RUTHLESS WEALTH! They are hirelings of the interplanetary bankers, those unspeakable excrescences on the body politic who are still grinding down into the dirt, under an iron heel, the face of the common man! In the guise of democracy they are trying to set up the worst, the most outrageous tyranny

that this universe has ever...' Jill snapped the switch viciously.

'And a lot of people *swallow* that...that *bilge!*' she almost snarled. 'If they had the brains of a...of even that Zabriskan fontema Mase told me about, they wouldn't, but they *do!*'

'I know they do. We have known all along that he is a masterly actor; we now know that he is more than that.'

'Yes, and we're finding out that no appeal to reason, no psychological counter-measures, will work. Dronvire and I agree that you'll *have* to arrange matters so that you can do solid months of stumping yourself. Personally.'

'It may come to that, but there's a lot of other things to do first.'

Samms broke the connection and thought. He did not consciously try to exclude the two youths, but his mind was working so fast and in such a disjointed fashion that they could catch only a few fragments. The incomprehensible vastness of space—tracing—detection—Cavenda's one tiny, fast moving moon—back, and solidly, to DETECTION.

'Mase,' Samms thought then, carefully. 'As a specialist in such things, why is it that the detectors of the smallest scout—lifeboat, even—have practically the same range as those of the largest liners and battleships?'

'Noise level and hash, sir, from the atomics.'

'But can't they be screened out?'

'Not entirely, sir, without blocking reception completely.'

'I see. Suppose, then, that all atomics aboard were to be shut down; that for the necessary heat and light we use electricity, from storage or primary batteries or

from a generator driven by an internal-combustion motor or a heat-engine. Could the range of detection then be increased?'

'Tremendously, sir. My guess is that the limiting factor would then be the cosmics.'

'I hope you're right. While you are waiting for the next signal to come in, you might work out a preliminary design for such a detector. If, as I anticipate, this Zabriska proves to be a dead end, Operation Zabriska ends here—becomes a part of Zwilnik—and you two will follow me at max to Tellus. You, Jack, are very badly needed on Operation Boskone. You and I, Mase, will make appropriate alterations aboard a J-class vessel of the Patrol.'

CHAPTER 12

Approaching Cavenda in his dead-black, converted scout-ship, Virgil Samms cut his drive, killed his atomics, and turned on his super-powered detectors. For five full detets in every direction—throughout a spherical volume over ten detets in diameter—space was void of ships. Some activity was apparent upon the planet dead ahead, but the First Lensman did not worry about that. The drug-runners would of course have atomics in their plants, even if there were no space-ships actually on the planet—which there probably were. What he did worry about was detection. There would be plenty of detectors, probably automatic; not only ordinary sub-ethereals, but electros and radars as well.

He flashed up to within one and a quarter detets, stopped, and checked again. Space was still empty. Then, after making a series of observations, he went inert and established an intrinsic velocity which, he hoped, would be close enough. He again shut off his atomics and started the sixteen-cylinder Diesel engine which would do its best to replace them.

That best was none too good, but it would do. Besides driving the Bergenholm it could furnish enough kilodynes of thrust to produce a velocity many times greater than any attainable by inert matter. It used a lot of oxygen per minute, but it would not run for very many minutes. With her atomics out of action his ship would not register upon the plates of the long-range detectors universally used. Since she was nevertheless travelling faster than light, neither electro-magnetic detector-webs nor radar could "see" her. Good enough.

Samms was not the System's best computer, nor did he have the System's finest instruments. His positional error could be corrected easily enough; but as he drove nearer and nearer to Cavenda, keeping, toward the last, in line with its one small moon, he wondered more and more as to how much of an allowance he should make for error in his intrinsic, which he had set up practically by guess. And there was another variable, the cut-off. He slowed down to just over one light; but even at that comparatively slow speed an error of one millisecond at cut-off meant a displacement of two hundred miles! He switched the spotter into the Berg's cut-off circuit, set it for three hundred miles, and waited tensely at his controls.

The relays clicked, the driving force expired, the vessel went inert. Samms' eyes, flashing from instrument to instrument, told him that matters could have been worse. His intrinsic was neither straight up, as he had hoped, nor straight down, as he had feared, but almost exactly half-way between the two—straight out. He discovered that fact just in time; in another second or two he would have been out beyond the moon's protecting bulk and thus detectable from Cavenda. He went free, flashed back to the opposite boundary of his area of safety, went inert, and put the full power of the bellowing Diesel to the task of bucking down his erroneous intrinsic, losing altitude continuously. Again and again he repeated the manoeuvre; and thus, grimly and stubbornly, he fought his ship to ground.

He was very glad to see that the surface of the satellite was rougher, rockier, ruggeder, and more cratered even than that of Earth's Luna. Upon such a terrain as this, it would be next to impossible to spot even a moving vessel—if it moved carefully.

By a series of short and careful inertialess hops—correcting his intrinsic velocity after each one by an inert collision with the ground—he manoeuvred his

vessel into such a position that Cavenda's enormous globe hung directly overhead. Breathing a profoundly deep breath of relief he killed the big engine, cut in his fully-charged accumulators, and turned on detector and spy-ray. He would see what he could see.

His detectors showed that there was only one point of activity on the whole planet. He located it precisely; then, after cutting his spy-ray to minimum power, he approached it gingerly, yard by yard. Stopped! As he had more than half expected, there was a spy-ray block. A big one, almost two miles in diameter. It would be almost directly beneath him—or rather, almost straight overhead—in about three hours.

Samms had brought along a telescope, considerably more powerful than the telescopic visiplate of his scout. Since the surface gravity of this moon was low—scarcely one-fifth that of Earth—he had no difficulty in lugging the parts out of the ship or in setting the thing up.

But even the telescope did not do much good. The moon was close to Cavenda, as astronomical distances go—but really worthwhile astronomical optical instruments simply are not portable. Thus the Lensman saw something that, by sufficient stretch of the imagination, could have been a factory; and, eyes straining at the tantalising limit of visibility, he even made himself believe that he saw a toothpick-shaped object and a darkly circular blob, either of which could have been the space-ship of the outlaws. He was sure, however, of two facts. There were no real cities upon Cavenda. There were no modern spaceports, or even air-fields.

He dismounted the 'scope, stored it, set his detectors, and waited. He had to sleep at times, of course; but any ordinary detector rig can be set to sound off at any change in its status—and Samms' was no ordinary rig. Wherefore, when the drug-

mongers' vessel took off, Samms left Cavenda as unobtrusively as he had approached it, and swung into that vessel's line.

Samms' strategy had been worked out long since. On his Diesel, at a distance of just over one detet, he would follow the outlaw as fast as he could; long enough to establish his line. He would then switch to atomic drive and close up to between one and two detets; then again go onto Diesel for a check. He would keep this up for as long as might prove necessary.

As far as any of the Lensmen knew, Spaceways always used regular liners or freighters in this business, and this scout was much faster than any such vessel. And even if—highly improbably thought!—the enemy ship was faster than his own, it would still be within range of *those* detectors when it got to wherever it was that it was going. But how wrong Samms was!

At his first check, instead of being not over two detets away the quarry was three and a half; at the second the distance was four and a quarter; at the third, almost exactly five. Scowling, Samms watched the erstwhile brilliant point of light fade into darkness. That circular blob that he had almost seen, then, had been the space-ship, but it had not been a sphere, as he had supposed. Instead, it had been a tear-drop; sticking, sharp tail down, in the ground. Ultra-fast. This was the result. But ideas had blown up under him before, they probably would again. He resumed atomic drive and made arrangements with the Port Admiral to rendezvous with him and the *Chicago* at the earliest possible time.

'What is there along that line?' he demanded of the superdreadnought's Chief Pilot, even before junction had been made.

'Nothing, sir, that we know of,' that worthy reported, after studying his charts.

He boarded the gigantic ship of war, and with Kinnison pored over those same charts.

'Your best bet is Eridan, I think,' Kinnison concluded finally. 'Not too near your line, but they could very easily figure that a one-day dogleg would be a good investment. And Spaceways owns it, you know, from core to planetary limits—the richest uranium mines in existence. Made to order. Nobody would suspect a uranium ship. How about throwing a globe around Eridan?'

Samms thought for minutes. 'No...not yet, at least. We don't know enough yet.'

'I know it—that's why it looks to me like a good time and place to learn something,' Kinnison argued. 'We know—almost know, at least—that a super-fast ship, carrying thionite, has just landed there. This is the hottest lead we've had. I say englobe the planet, declare martial law, and not let anything in or out until we find it. Somebody there must know something, a lot more than we do. I say hunt him out and make him talk.'

'You're just popping off, Rod. You know as well as I do that nabbing a few of the small fry isn't enough. We can't move openly until we can strike high.'

'I suppose not,' Kinnison grumbled. 'But we know so *damned* little, Virge!'

'Little enough,' Samms agreed. 'Of the three main divisions, only the political aspect is at all clear. In the drug division, we know where thionite comes from and where it is processed, and Eridan may be—probably is—another link. On the other end, we know a lot of peddlers and a few middlemen—nobody higher. We have no actual knowledge whatever as to who the higher-ups are or how they work; and it's the bosses we want. Concerning the pirates, we know even

less. 'Murgatroyd' may be no more a man's name than 'zwilnik' is...'

'Before you get too far away from the subject, what are you going to do about Eridan?'

'Nothing, for the moment, would be best, I believe. However, Knobos and DalNalten should switch their attention from Spaceways' passenger liners to the uranium ships from Eridan to all three of the inner planets. Check?'

'Check. Particularly since it explains so beautifully the merry-go-round they have been on so long—chasing the same packages of dope backwards and forwards so many times that the corners of the boxes got worn round. We've got to get the top men, and they're smart. Which reminds me—Morgan as Big Boss does not square up with the Morgan that you and Fairchild smacked down so easily when he tried to investigate the Hill. A loud-mouthed, chiselling politician might have a lock-box full of documentary evidence about party bosses and power deals and chorus girls and Martian tekkyl coats, but the man we're after very definitely would not.'

'You're telling me?' This point was such a sore one that Samms relapsed into idiom. 'The boys should have cracked that box a week ago, but they struck a knot. I'll see if they know anything yet. Tune in, Rod. Ray!' He Lensed a thought at his cousin.

'Yes, Virge?'

'Have you got a spy-ray into that lock-box yet?'

'Glad you called. Yes, last night. Empty. empty as a sub-deb's skull—except for an atomic-powered gimmick that it took Bergenholm's whole laboratory almost a week to neutralise.'

'I see. Thanks. Off.' Samms turned to Kinnison. 'Well?'

'Nice. A mighty smart operator.' Kinnison gave credit ungrudgingly. 'Now I'll buy your picture—what a man! But now—and I've got my ears pinned back— what was it you started to say about pirates?'

'Just that we have very little to go on, except for the kind of stuff they seem to like best, and the fact that even armed escorts have not been able to protect certain types of shipments of late. The escorts, too, have disappeared. But with these facts as bases, it seems to me that we could arrange something, perhaps like this...'

A fast, sleek freighter and a heavy battle-cruiser bored steadily through the inter-stellar void. The merchantman carried a fabulously valuable cargo: not bullion or jewels or plate of price, but things literally above price—machine tools of highest precision, delicate optical and electrical instruments, fine watches and chronometers. She also carried First Lensman Virgil Samms.

And aboard the warship there was Roderick Kinnison; for the first time in history a mere battle-cruiser bore a Port Admiral's flag.

As far as the detectors of those two ships could reach, space was empty of man-made craft; but the two Lensmen knew that they were not alone. One and one-half detets away, loafing along at the freighter's speed and paralleling her course, in a hemispherical formation open to the front, there flew six tremendous tear-drops; superdreadnoughts of whose existence no Tellurian or Colonial government had even an inkling. They were the fastest and deadliest craft yet built by man—the first fruits of Operation Bennett. And they, too, carried Lensmen—Costigan, Jack Kinnison, Northrop, Dronvire of Rigel Four, Rodebush, and Cleveland. Nor was there need of detectors: the eight

Lensmen were in as close communication as though they had been standing in the same room.

'On your toes, men,' came Samms' quiet thought. 'We are about to pass within a few light-minutes of an uninhabited solar system. No Tellurian-type planets at all. This may be it. Tune to Kinnison on one side and to your captains on the other. Take over, Rod.'

At one instant the ether, for one full detet in every direction, was empty. In the next, three intensely brilliant spots of detection flashed into being, in line with the dead planet so invitingly close at hand.

This development came as a surprise, since only two raiders had been expected: a battleship to take care of the escort, a cruiser to take the merchantman. The fact that the pirates had become cautious or suspicious and had sent three superdreadnoughts on the mission, however, did not operate to change the Patrol's strategy; for Samms had concluded, and Dronvire and Bergenholm and Rularion of Jupiter had agreed, that the real commander of the expedition would be aboard the vessel that attacked the freighter.

In the next instant, then—each Lensman saw what Roderick Kinnison saw, in the very instant of his seeing it—six more points of hard, white light sprang into being upon the plates of guileful freighter and decoying cruiser.

'Jack and Mase, take the leader!' Kinnison snapped out the thought. 'Dronvire and Costigan, right wing— he's the one that's going after the freighter. Fred and Lyman, left wing. Hipe!'

The pirate ships flashed up, filling ether and sub-ether alike with a solid mush of interference through which no call for help could be driven; two superdreadnoughts against the cruiser, one against the freighter. The former, of course, had been expected to offer more than a token resistance. Battle-cruisers

of the Patrol were powerful vessels, both on offence and defence, and it was a known and recognised fact that the men of the Patrol were *men*. The pirate commander who attacked the freighter, however, was a surprised pirate indeed. His first beam, directed well forward, well ahead of the precious cargo, should have wrought the same havoc against screens and wall-shields and structure as a white-hot poker would against a pat of luke-warm butter. Practically the whole nose-section, including the control room, should have whiffed outward into space in gobbets and streamers of molten and gaseous metal. But nothing of the sort happened—this merchantman was *no* push-over!'

No ordinary screens protected that particular freighter and the person of First Lensman Samms—Roderick Kinnison had very thoroughly seen to that. In sheer mass her screen generators outweighed her entire cargo, heavy as that cargo was, by more than two to one. Thus the pirate's beams stormed and struck and clawed and clung—uselessly. They did not penetrate. And as the surprised attacker shoved his power up and up, to his absolute ceiling of effort, the only result was to increase the already tremendous pyrotechnic display of energies cascading in all directions from the fiercely radiant defences of the Tellurian freighter.

And in a few seconds the commanding officers of the other two attacking battleships were also surprised. The battle-cruiser's screens did not go down, even under the combined top effort of two superdreadnoughts! And she did not have a beam hot enough to light a match—she must be *all screen!* But before the startled outlaws could do anything about the realisation that they, instead of being the trappers, were in cold fact the trapped, all three of them were surprised again—the last surprise that any of them was ever to receive. Six mighty tear-drops—vastly bigger, faster, more powerful than their own—were

rushing upon them, blanketing all channels of communication as efficiently and as enthusiastically as they themselves had been doing an instant before.

Being out simply and ruthlessly to kill, and not to capture, four of the newcomers from Bennett polished off the cruiser's two attackers in very short order. They simply flashed in, went inert at the four corners of an imaginary tetrahedron, and threw everything they had—and they had plenty. Possibly—just barely possibly—there may have been, somewhere, a space-battle shorter than that one; but there certainly was never one more violent.

Then the four set out after their two sister-ships and the one remaining pirate, who was frantically devoting his every effort to the avoidance of engagement. But with six ships, each one of which was of vastly greater individual power than his own, at the six corners of an octahedron of which he was the geometrical centre, his ability to cut tractor beams and to "squirt out" from between two opposed pressors did him no good whatever. He was englobed; or, rather, to apply the correct terminology to an operation involving so few units, he was "boxed".

To blow the one remaining raider out of the ether would have been easy enough, but that was exactly what the Patrolmen did not want to do. They wanted information. Wherefore each of the Patrol ships directed a dozen or so beams upon the scintillating protective screens of the enemy; enough so that every square yard of defensive web was under direct attack. As rapidly as it could be done without losing equilibrium or synchronisation, the power of each beam was stepped up until the wildly violet incandescence of the pirate screen showed that it was hovering on the very edge of failure. Then, in the instant, needle-beamers went furiously to work. The screen was already loaded to its limit; no transfer of defensive energy was possible. Thus, tremendously

overloaded locally, locally it flared through the ultra-violet into the black and went down; and the fiercely penetrant daggers of pure force stabbed and stabbed and stabbed.

The engine room went first, even though the needlers had to gnaw a hundred-foot hole straight through the pirate craft in order to find the vital installations. Then, enough damage done so that spy-rays could get in, the rest of the work was done with precision and dispatch. In a matter of seconds the pirate hulk lay helpless, and the Patrolmen peeled her like an orange—or, rather, more like an amateur cook very wastefully peeling a potato. Resistless knives of energy sheared off tail-section and nose-section, top and bottom, port and starboard sides; then slabbed off the corners of what was left, until the control room was almost bared to space.

Then, as soon as the intrinsic velocities could possibly be matched, board and storm! With Dronvire of Rigel Four in the lead, closely followed by Costigan, Northrop, Kinnison the Younger, and a platoon of armed and armoured Space Marines!

Samms and the two scientists did not belong in such a melee as that which was to come, and knew it. Kinnison the Elder did not belong, either, but did not know it. In fact, he cursed fluently and bitterly at having to stay out—nevertheless, out he stayed.

Dronvire, on the other hand, did not like to fight. The very thought of actual, bodily, hand-to-hand combat revolted every fibre of his being. In view of what the spy-ray men were reporting, however, and of what all the Lensmen knew of pirate psychology, Dronvire had to get into that control room first, and he had to get there *fast*. And if he *had* to fight, he could; and, physically, he was wonderfully well equipped for just such activity. To his immense physical strength, the natural concomitant of a force of gravity

more than twice Earth's, the armour which so encumbered the Tellurian battlers was a scarcely noticeable impediment. His sense of perception, which could not be barred by any material substance, kept him fully informed of every development in his neighbourhood. His literally incredible speed enabled him not merely to parry a blow aimed at him, but to bash out the brains of the would-be attacker before that blow could be more than started. And whereas a human being can swing only one space-axe or fire only two ray-guns at a time, the Rigellian plunged through space toward what was left of the pirate vessel, swinging not one or two space-axes, but four; each held in a lithe and supple, but immensely strong, tentacular "hand".

Why axes? Why not Lewistons, or rifles, or pistols? Because the space armour of that day could withstand almost indefinitely the output of two or three hand-held projectors; because the resistance of its defensive field varied directly as the cube of the velocity of any material projectile encountering them. Thus, and strangely enough, the advance of science had forced the re-adoption of that long-extinct weapon.

Most of the pirates had died, of course, during the dismemberment of their ship. Many more had been picked off by the needle-beam gunners. In the control room, however, there was a platoon of elite guards, clustered so closely about the commander and his officers that needles could not be used; a group that would have to be wiped out by hand.

If the attack had come by way of the only doorway, so that the pirates could have concentrated their weapons upon one or two Patrolmen, the commander might have had time enough to do what he was under compulsion to do. But while the Patrolmen were still in space a plane of force sheared off the entire side of the room, a tractor beam jerked the detached wall away, and the attackers floated in en masse.

Weightless combat is not at all like any form of gymnastics known to us ground-grippers. It is much more difficult to master, and in times of stress the muscles revert involuntarily and embarrassingly to their wonted gravity-field techniques. Thus the endeavours of most of the battlers upon both sides, while earnest enough and deadly enough of intent, were almost comically unproductive of result. In a matter of seconds frantically-struggling figures were floating from wall to ceiling to wall to floor; striking wildly, darting backward from the violence of their own fierce swings.

The Tellurian Lensmen, however, had had more practice and remembered their lessons better. Jack Kinnison, soaring into the room, grabbed the first solid thing he could reach; a post. Pulling himself down to the floor, he braced both feet, sighted past the nearest foeman, swung his axe, and gave a tremendous shove. Such was his timing that in the instant of maximum effort the beak of his atrociously effective weapon encountered the pirate's helmet—and that was that. He wrenched his axe free and shoved the corpse away in such a direction that the reaction would send him against a wall at the floor line, in position to repeat the manoeuvre.

Since Mason Northrop was heavier and stronger than his friend, his technique was markedly different. He dived for the chart-table, which of course was welded to the floor. He hooked one steel-shod foot around one of the table's legs and braced the other against its top. Weightless but inert, it made no difference whether his position was vertical or horizontal or anywhere between; from this point of vantage with his length of body and arm and axe, he could cover a lot of room. He reached out, hooked bill of axe into belt or line-snap or angle of armour, and pulled; and as the helplessly raging pirate floated past him, he swung and struck. And that, too, was that.

Dronvire of Rigel Four did not rush to the attack. He had never been and was not now either excited or angry. Indeed, it was only empirically that he knew what anger and excitement were. He had never been in any kind of a fight. Therefore he paused for a couple of seconds to analyse the situation and to determine his own most efficient method of operation. He would not have to be in physical contact with the pirate captain to go to work on his mind, but he would have to be closer than this and he would have to be free from physical attack while he concentrated. He perceived what Kinnison and Costigan and Northrop were doing, and knew why each was working in a different fashion. He applied that knowledge to his own mass, to his own musculature, to the length and strength of his arms—each one of which was twice as long and ten times as strong as the trunk of an elephant. He computed forces and leverages, actions and reactions, points of application, stresses and strains.

He threw away two of his axes. The two empty arms reached out, each curling around the neck of a pirate. Two axes flashed, grazing each pinioning arm so nearly that it seemed incredible that the sharp edges did not shear away the Rigellian's own armour. Two heads floated away from two bodies and Dronvire reached for two more. And two—and two—and two. Calm and dispassionate, but not wasting a motion or a millisecond, Dronvire accomplished more, in less time, than all the Tellurians in the room.

'Costigan, Northrop, Kinnison—attend!' he launched a thought. 'I have no time to kill more of them. The commander is dying of a self-inflicted wound and I have important work to do. See to it, please, that these remaining creatures do not attack me while I am doing it.'

Dronvire tuned his mind to that of the pirate and probed. Although dying, the pirate captain offered

fierce resistance, but the Rigellian was not alone. Attuned to his mind, working smoothly with it, giving it strengths and qualities which no Rigellian ever had had or ever would have, were the two strongest minds of Earth: that of Rod the Rock Kinnison, with the driving force, the indomitable will, the transcendent urge of all human heredity; and that of Virgil Samms, with all that had made him First Lensman.

'TELL!' that terrific triple mind demanded, with a force which simply could not be denied. 'WHERE ARE YOU FROM? Resistance is useless; yours or that of those whom you serve. Your bases and powers are smaller and weaker than ours, since Spaceways is only a corporation and we are the Galactic Patrol. TELL! WHO ARE YOUR BOSSES? TELL—TELL!'

Under that irresistible urge there appeared, foggily and without any hint of knowledge of name or of spatial co-ordinates, an embattled planet, very similar in a smaller way to the Patrol's own Bennett, and -

Even more foggily, but still not so blurred but that their features were unmistakably recognisable, the images of two men. That of Murgatroyd, the pirate chief, completely strange to both Kinnison and Samms; and -

Back of Murgatroyd and above him, that of -

BIG JIM TOWNE!

CHAPTER 13

First, about Murgatroyd.' In his office in The Hill Roderick Kinnison spoke aloud to the First Lensman. 'What do you think should be done about him?'

'Murgatroyd. Hm...m...m.' Samms inhaled a mouthful of smoke and exhaled it slowly; watched it dissipate in the air. 'Ah, yes, Murgatroyd.' He repeated the performance. 'My thought, at the moment, is to let him alone.'

'Check,' Kinnison said. If Samms was surprised at his friend's concurrence he did not show it. 'Why? Let's see if we check on that.'

'Because he does not seem to be of fundamental importance. Even if we could find him...and by the way, what do you think the chance is of our spies finding him?'

'Just about the same chance that theirs is of finding out about the Samms-Olmstead switch or our planet Bennett. Vanishingly small. Zero.'

'Right. And even if we could find him—even find their secret base, which is certainly as well hidden as ours is—it would do us no present good, because we could take no positive action. We have, I think, learned the prime fact; that Towne is actually Murgatroyd's superior.'

'That's the way I see it. We can almost draw an organisation chart now.'

'I wouldn't say "almost".' Samms smiled half-ruefully. 'There are gaping holes, and Isaacson is as yet a highly unknown quantity. I've tried to draw one

a dozen times, but we haven't got enough information. An incorrect chart, you know, would be worse than none at all. As soon as I can draw a correct one, I'll show it to you. But in the meantime, the position of our friend James F. Towne is now clear. He is actually a Big Shot in both piracy and politics. That fact surprised me, even though it did clarify the picture tremendously.'

'Me, too. One good thing, we won't have to hunt for him. You've been working on him right along, though, haven't you?'

'Yes, but this new relationship throws light on a good many details which have been obscure. It also tends to strengthen our working hypothesis as to Isaacson—which we can't prove yet, of course—that he is the actual working head of the drug syndicate. Vice-President in charge of Drugs, so to speak.'

'Huh? That's a new one on me. I don't see it.'

'There is very little doubt that at the top there is Morgan. He is, and has been for some time, the real boss of North America. Under him, probably taking orders direct, is President Witherspoon.'

'Undoubtedly. The Nationalist party is strictly a la machine, and Witherspoon is one of the world's slimiest skinkers. Morgan is Chief Engineer of the Machine. Take it from there.'

'We know that Boss Jim is also in the top echelon—quite possibly the Commander-in-Chief—of the enemy's Armed Forces. By analogy, and since Isaacson is apparently on the same level as Towne, immediately below Morgan...'

'Wouldn't there be three? Witherspoon?'

'I doubt it. My present idea is that Witherspoon is at least one level lower. Comparatively small fry.'

'Could be—I'll buy it. A nice picture, Virge; and beautifully symmetrical. His Mightiness Morgan. Secretary of War Towne and Secretary of Drugs Isaacson; and each of them putting a heavy shoulder behind the political bandwagon. Very nice. That makes Operation Mateese tougher than ever—a triple-distilled toughie. Glad I told you it wasn't my dish— saves me the trouble of backing out now.'

'Yes, I have noticed how prone you are to duck tough jobs.' Samms smiled quietly. 'However, unless I am even more mistaken than usual, you will be in it up to your not-so-small ears, my friend, before it is over.'

'Huh? How?' Kinnison demanded.

'That will, I hope, become clear very shortly.' Samms stubbed out the butt of his cigarette and lit another. 'The basic problem can be stated very simply. How are we going to persuade the sovereign countries of Earth—particularly the North American Continent— to grant the Galactic Patrol the tremendous power and authority it will have to have?'

'Nice phrasing, Virge, and studied. Not off the cuff. But aren't you over-drawing a bit? Little if any conflict. The Patrol would be pretty largely inter-systemic in scope...with of course the necessary inter-planetary and inter-continental...and...um...m...'

'Exactly.'

'But it's logical enough, Virge, even at that, and has plenty of precedents, clear back to ancient history 'way back, before space-travel, when they first started to use atomic energy, and the only drugs they had to worry about were cocaine, morphine, heroin, and other purely Tellurian products. I was reading about it just the other day.'

Kinnison swung around, fingered a book out of a matched set, and riffled its leaves. 'Russia was the

world's problem child then—put up what they called an iron curtain—wouldn't play with the neighbours' children, but picked up her marbles and went home. But yet—here it is. Original source unknown—some indications point to a report of somebody named Hoover, sometime in the nineteen forties or fifties, Gregorian calendar. Listen:

' "This protocol"—he's talking about the agreement on world-wide Narcotics Control—"was signed by fifty-two nations, including the USSR"—that was Russia—"and its satellite states. It was the only international agreement to which the Communist countries"—you know more about what Communism was, I supposed, than I do.'

'Just that it was another form of dictatorship that didn't work out.'

' "...to which the Communist countries ever gave more than lip service. This adherence is all the more surprising, in view of the political situation then obtaining, in that all signatory nations obligated themselves to surrender national sovereignty in five highly significant respects, as follows:

' "First, to permit Narcotics agents of all other signatory nations free, secret, and unregistered entry into, unrestricted travel throughout, and exit from, all their lands and waters, wherever situate:

' Second, upon request, to allow known criminals and known contraband to enter and to leave their territories without interference:

' "Third, to co-operate fully, and as a secondary and not as a prime mover, in any Narcotics Patrol program set up by any other signatory nation:

' "Fourth, upon request, to maintain complete secrecy concerning any Narcotics operation: and

' "Fifth, to keep the Central Narcotics Authority fully and continuously informed upon all matters hereinbefore specified."

'And apparently, Virge, it worked. If they could do that, 'way back then, we certainly should be able to make the patrol work now.'

'You talk as though the situations were comparable. They aren't. Instead of giving up an insignificant fraction of their national sovereignty, all nations will have to give up practically all of it. They will have to change their thinking from a National to a Galactic viewpoint; will have to become units in a Galactic Civilisation, just as countries used to be units of states, and states are units of the continents. The Galactic Patrol will not be able to stop at being the supreme and only authority in inter-systemic affairs. It is bound to become intra-systemic, intra-planetary, and intra-continental. Eventually, it must and it shall be the *sole* authority, except for such purely local organisations as city police.'

'*What* a programme!' Kinnison thought silently for minutes. 'But I'm still betting that you can bring it off.'

'We'll keep on driving until we do. What gives us our chance is that the all-Lensman Solarian Council is already in existence and is functioning smoothly; and that the government of North America has no jurisdiction beyond the boundaries of its continent. Thus, and even though Morgan has extra-legal powers both as Boss of North America and as the head of an organisation which is in fact inter-systemic in scope, he can do nothing whatever about the fact that the Solarian Council has been enlarged into the Galactic Council. As a matter of fact, he was and is very much in favour of that particular move—just as much so as we are.'

'You're going too fast for me. How do you figure that?'

'Unlike our idea of the Patrol as a co-ordinator of free and independent races, Morgan sees it as the perfect instrument of a Galactic dictatorship, thus: North America is the most powerful continent of Earth. The other continents will follow her lead—or else. Tellus can very easily dominate the other Solarian planets, and the Solar System can maintain dominance over all other systems as they are discovered and colonised. Therefore, whoever controls the North American Continent controls all space.'

'I see. Could be, at that. Throw the Lensmen out, put his own stooges in. Wonder how he'll go about it? A *tour de force*? No. The next election, would be my guess. If so, that will be the most important election in history.'

'If they decide to wait for the election, yes. I'm not as sure as you seem to be that they will not act sooner.'

'They can't,' Kinnison declared. 'Name me one thing they think they can do, and I'll shoot it fuller of holes than a target.'

'They can, and I am very much afraid that they will,' Samms replied, soberly. 'At any time he cares to do so, Morgan—through the North American Government, of course—can abrogate the treaty and name his own Council.'

'Without my boys—the backbone and the guts of North America, as well as of the Patrol? Don't be stupid, Virge. They're *loyal*.'

'Admitted—but at the same time they are being paid in North American currency. Of course, we will soon have our own Galactic credit system worked out, but...'

'What the hell difference would *that* make? Kinnison wanted savagely to know. 'You think they'd last until the next pay-day if they start playing that kind of ball? What in hell do you think *I'd* be doing?

And Clayton and Schweikert and the rest of the gang? Sitting on our fat rumps and crying into our beers?

'You would do nothing. I could not permit any illegal...'

'Permit!' Kinnison blazed, leaping to his feet. 'Permit—hell! Are you loose-screwed enough to actually think I would ask or need your permission? Listen, Samms!' The Port Admiral's voice took on a quality like nothing his friend had ever before heard. 'The first thing I would do would be to take off your Lens, wrap you up—especially your mouth—in seventeen yards of three-inch adhesive tape, and heave you into the brig. The second would be to call out everything we've got, including every half-built ship on Bennett able to fly, and declare martial law. The third would be a series of summary executions, starting with Morgan and working down. And if he's got any fraction of the brain I credit him with, Morgan knows damned well *exactly* what would happen.'

'Oh.' Samms, while very much taken aback, was thrilled to the centre of his being. 'I had not considered anything so drastic, but you probably would...'

'Not "probably",' Kinnison corrected him grimly. ' "Certainly".'

'...and Morgan does know...except about Bennett, of course...and he would not, for obvious reasons, bring in his secret armed forces. You're right, Rod, it will be the election.'

'Definitely; and it's plain enough what their basic strategy will be.' Kinnison, completely mollified, sat down and lit another cigar. 'His Nationalist party is now in power, but it was our Cosmocrats of the previous administration who so basely slipped one over on the dear pee-pul—who betrayed the entire North American Continent into the claws of rapacious wealth, no less—by ratifying that unlawful, unhallowed,

unconstitutional, and so on, treaty. Scoundrels! Bribe-takers! Betrayers of a sacred trust! *How* Rabble-Rouser Morgan will thump the tub on that theme—he'll make the welkin ring as it never rang before.'

Kinnison mimicked savagely the demagogue's round and purple tones as he went on ' "Since they had no mandate from the pee-pul to trade their birthright for a mess of pottage that nefarious and underhanded treaty is, *a prima vista* and *ipso facto* and a *priori*, completely and necessarily and positively null and void. People of Earth, arouse! Arise! Rise in your might and throw off this stultifying and degrading, this paralysing yoke of the Monied Powers—throw out this dictatorial, autocratic, wealth-directed, illegal, monstrous Council of so-called Lensmen! Rise in your might at the polls! Elect a Council of your own choosing—not of Lensmen, but of ordinary folks like you and me. Throw off this hellish yoke, I say!"—and here he begins to positively froth at the mouth—"so that government of the people, by the people, and for the people shall not perish from the Earth!'

'He has used that exact peroration, ancient as it is, so many times that practically everybody thinks he originated it; and it's always good for so many decibels of applause that he'll keep on using it forever.'

'Your analysis is vivid, cogent, and factual, Rod—but the situation is not at all funny.'

'Did I act as though I thought it was? If so, I'm a damned poor actor. I'd like to kick the bloodsucking leech all the way from here to the Great Nebula in Andromeda, and if I ever get the chance I'm going to!'

'An interesting, but somewhat irrelevant idea.' Samms smiled at his friend's passionate outburst. 'But go on. I agree with you in principle so far, and your viewpoint is—to say the least—refreshing.'

'Well, Morgan will have so hypnotised most of the dear pee-pul that they will think it their own idea when he re-nominates this spineless nincompoop Witherspoon for another term as President of North America, with a solid machine-made slate of hatchet-men behind him. They win the election. Then the government of the North American Continent—not the Morgan-Towne-Isaacson machine, but all nice and legal and by mandate and in strict accordance with the party platform—abrogates the treaty and names its own Council. And right then, my friend, the boys and I will do our stuff.'

'Except that, in such a case, you wouldn't. Think it over, Rod.'

'Why not?' Kinnison demanded, in a voice which, however, did not carry much conviction.

'Because we would be in the wrong; and we are even less able to go against united public opinion than is the Morgan crowd.'

'We'd do *something*—I've got it!' Kinnison banged the desk with his fist. 'That would be a strictly unilateral action. North America would be standing alone.'

'Of course.'

'So we'll pull all the Cosmocrats and all of our friends out of North America—move them to Bennett or somewhere—and make Morgan and Company a present of it. We won't declare martial law or kill anybody, unless they decide to call in their reserves. We'll merely isolate the whole damned continent—throw a screen around it and over it that a microbe won't be able to get through—one that would make that iron curtain I read about look like a bride's veil—and we'll *keep* them isolated until they beg to join up on our terms. Strictly legal, and the perfect solution. How about me giving the boys a briefing on it, right now?'

'Not yet.' Samms' mien, however, lightened markedly. 'I never thought of that way out... It *could* be done, and it would probably work, but I would not recommend it except as an ultimately last resort. It has at least two tremendous drawbacks.'

'I know it, but...'

'It would wreck North America as no nation has ever been wrecked; quite possibly beyond recovery. Furthermore, how many people, including yourself and your children, would like to renounce their North American citizenship and remove themselves, permanently and irrevocably, from North American soil?'

'Um...m...m. Put thataway, it doesn't sound so good, does it? But what the hell else can we do?'

'Just what we have been planning on doing. We must win the election.'

'Huh?' Kinnison's mouth almost fell open. 'You say it easy. How? With whom? By what stretch of the imagination do you figure that you can find anybody with a loose enough mouth to out-lie and out-promise Morgan? And can you duplicate his machine?'

'We can not only duplicate his machine; we can better it. The truth, presented to the people in language they can understand and appreciate, by a man whom they like, admire, and respect, will be more attractive than Morgan's promises. The same truth will dispose of Morgan's lies.'

'Well, go on. You've answered my questions, after a fashion, except the stinger. Does the Council think it's got a man with enough dynage to lift the load?'

'Unanimously. They also agreed unanimously that we have only one. Haven't you any idea who he is?'

'Not a glimmering of one.' Kinnison frowned in thought, then his face cleared into a broad grin and he yelled: 'What a damn fool I am—you, of course!'

'Wrong. I was not even seriously considered. It was the concensus that I could not possibly win. My work has been such as to keep me out of the public eye. If the man in the street thinks of me at all, he thinks that I hold myself apart and above him—the ivory tower concept.'

'Could be, at that; but you've got my curiosity aroused. How can a man of that calibre have been kicking around so long without me knowing anything about him?'

'You do. That's what I've been working around to all afternoon. You.'

'Huh?' Kinnison gasped as though he had received a blow in the solar plexus. 'Me? ME? Hell's—Brazen—Hinges!'

'Exactly. You.' Silencing Kinnison's inarticulate protests, Samms went on: 'First, you'll have no difficulty in talking to an audience as you've just talked to me.'

'Of course not—but did I use any language that would burn out the transmitters? I don't remember whether I did or not.'

'I don't, either. You probably did, but that would be nothing new. Telenews has never yet cut you off the ether because of it. The point is this: while you do not realise it, you are a better tub-thumper and welkin-ringer than Morgan is, when something such as just now—really gets you going. And as for a machine, what finer one is possible than the patrol? Everybody in it or connected with it will support you to the hilt—you know that.'

'Why, I...I suppose so...probably they would, yes.'

'Do you know why?'

'Can't say that I do, unless it's because I treat them fair, so they do the same to me.'

'Exactly. I don't say that everybody likes you, but I don't know of anybody who doesn't respect you. And, most important, everybody—all over space—knows "Rod the Rock" Kinnison, and why he is called that.'

'But that very "man on horseback" thing may backfire on you, Virge.'

'Perhaps—slightly—but we're not afraid of that. And finally, you said you'd like to kick Morgan from here to Andromeda. How would you like to kick him from Panama City to the North Pole?'

'I said it, and I wasn't just warming up my jets, either. I'd like it.' The big Lensman's nostrils flared, his lips thinned. 'By god, Virge, I will!'

'Thanks, Rod.' With no display whatever of the emotion he felt, Samms skipped deliberately to the matter next in hand. 'Now, about Eridan. Let's see if they know anything yet.'

The report of Knobos and DalNalten was terse and exact. They had found—and that finding, so baldly put, could have filled, and should fill a book—that Spaceways' uranium vessels were, beyond any reasonable doubt, hauling thionite from Eridan to the planets of Sol. Spy-rays being useless, they had considered the advisability of investigating Eridan in person, but had decided against such action. Eridan was closely held by Uranium, Incorporated. Its population was one hundred percent Tellurian human. Neither DalNalten nor Knobos could disguise himself well enough to work there. Either would be caught promptly, and as promptly shot.

'Thanks, fellow,' Samms said, when it became evident that the brief report was done. Then, to Kinnison, 'That puts it up to Conway Costigan. And Jack? Or Mase? Or both?'

'Both,' Kinnison decided, 'and anybody else they can use.'

'I'll get them at it.' Samms sent out thoughts. 'And now, I wonder what that daughter of mine is doing? I'm a little worried about her, Rod. She's too cocky for her own good—or strength. Some of these days she's going to bite off more than she can chew, if she hasn't already. The more we learn about Morgan, the less I like the idea of her working on Herkimer Herkimer Third. I've told her so, a dozen times, and why, but of course it didn't do any good.'

'It wouldn't. The only way to develop teeth is to bite with 'em. You had to. So did I. Our kids have got to, too. We lived through it. So will they. As for Herky the Third...' He thought for moments, then went on: 'Check. But she's done a job so far that nobody else could do. In spite of that fact, if it wasn't for our Lenses I'd say to pull her, if you have to heave the insubordinate young jade into the brig. But with the Lenses, and the way you watch her...to say nothing of Mase Northrop, and he's a lot of man... I can't see her getting in either very bad or very deep. Can you?'

'No, I can't.' Samms admitted, but the thoughtful frown did not leave his face. He Lensed her: Finding, as he had supposed, that she was at a party; dancing, as he had feared, with Senator Morgan's Number One Secretary.

'Hi, Dad!' she greeted him gaily, with no slightest change in the expression of the face turned so engagingly to her partner's. 'I have the honour of reporting that all instruments are still dead-centring the green.'

'And have you, by any chance, been paying any attention to what I have been telling you?'

'Oh, lots,' she assured him. 'I've collected reams of data. He could be almost as much of a menace as

he thinks he is, in some cases, but I haven't begun to slip yet. As I have told you all along, this is just a game, and we're both playing it strictly according to the rules.'

'That's good. Keep it that way, my dear.' Samms signed off and his daughter returned her full attention—never noticeably absent—to the handsome secretary.

The evening wore on. Miss Samms danced every dance; occasionally with one or another of the notables present, but usually with Herkimer Herkimer Third.

'A drink?' he asked. 'A small, cold one?'

'Not so small, and *very* cold,' she agreed, enthusiastically.

Glass in hand, Herkimer indicated a nearby doorway. 'I just heard that our host has acquired a very old and very fine bronze—a Neptune. We should run an eye over it, don't you think?'

'By all means,' she agreed again.

But as they passed through the shadowed portal the man's head perked to the right. 'There's something you really ought to see, Jill!' he exclaimed. 'Look!'

She looked. A young woman of her own height and build and with her own flamboyant hair, identical as to hair-do and as to every fine detail of dress and of ornamentation, glass in hand, was strolling back into the ball-room!

Jill started to protest, but could not. In the brief moment of inaction the beam of a snub-nosed P-gun had played along her spine from hips to neck. She did not fall—he had given her a very mild jolt—but, rage as she would, she could neither struggle nor scream. And, after the fact, she knew.

But he *couldn't*—couldn't *possibly!* Nevian paralysis-guns were as outlawed as was Vee Two gas itself! Nevertheless, he had.

And on the instant a woman, dressed in crisp and spotless white and carrying a hooded cloak, appeared—and Herkimer now wore a beard and heavy, horn rimmed spectacles. Thus, very shortly, Virgilia Samms found herself, completely helpless and completely unrecognisable, walking awkwardly out of the house between a businesslike doctor and a solicitous nurse.

'Will you need me any more, Doctor Murray?' The woman carefully and expertly loaded the patient into the rear seat of a car.

'Thank you, no, Miss Childs.' With a sick, cold certainty Jill knew that this conversation was for the benefit of the doorman and the hackers, and that it would stand up under any examination. 'Mrs. Harman's condition is...er...well, nothing at all serious.'

The car moved out into the street and Jill, really frightened for the first time in her triumphant life, fought down an almost overwhelming wave of panic. The hood had slipped down over her eyes, blinding her. She could not move a single voluntary muscle. Nevertheless, she knew that the car travelled a few blocks—six, she thought—west on Bolton Street before turning left.

Why didn't somebody Lens her? Her father wouldn't, she knew, until tomorrow. Neither of the Kinnisons would, nor Spud—they never did except on direct invitation. But Mase would, before he went to bed—or would he? It was past his bed-time now, and she had been pretty caustic, only last night, because she was doing a particularly delicate bit of reading. But he would...he *must!*

'Mase! *Mase!* MASE!'

And, eventually, Mase did.

Deep under The Hill, Roderick Kinnison swore fulminantly at the sheer physical impossibility of getting out of that furiously radiating mountain in a hurry. At New York Spaceport, however, Mason Northrop and Jack Kinnison not only could hurry, but did.

'Where are you, Jill?' Northrop demanded presently. 'What kind of a car are you in?'

'Quite near Stanhope Circle.' In communication with her friends at last, Jill regained a measure of her usual poise. 'Within eight or ten blocks, I'm sure. I'm in a black Wilford sedan, last year's model. I didn't get a chance to see its licence plates.'

'That helps a lot!' Jack grunted, savagely. 'A ten-block radius covers a hell of a lot of territory, and half the cars in town are black Wilford sedans.'

'Shut up, Jack! Go ahead, Jill—tell us all you can, and keep on sending us anything that will help at all.'

'I kept the right and left turns and distance straight for quite a while—about twenty blocks—that's how I know it was Stanhope Circle. I don't know how many times he went around the circle, though, or which way he went when he left it. After leaving the Circle, the traffic was very light, and here there doesn't seem to be any traffic at all. That brings us up to date. You'll know as well as I do what happens next.'

With Jill, the Lensmen knew that Herkimer drove his car up to the kerb and stopped—parked without backing up. He got out and hauled the girl's limp body out of the car, displacing the hood enough to free one eye. Good! Only one other car was visible; a bright yellow convertible parked across the street about half a block ahead. There was a sign—"NO PARKING ON THIS SIDE 7 TO 10". The building toward which

he was carrying her was more than three stories high and had a number—one, four—if he would *only* swing her a little bit more, so that she could see the rest of it—one-four-seven-nine!

'Rushton Boulevard, you think Mase?'

'Could be. Fourteen seventy nine would be on the down-town-traffic side. Blast!'

Into the building, where two masked men locked and barred the door behind them. 'And keep it locked!' Herkimer ordered. 'You know what to do until I come back down.'

Into an elevator, and up. Through massive double doors into a room, whose most conspicuous item of furniture was a heavy steel chair, bolted to the floor. Two masked men got up and placed themselves behind that chair.

Jill's strength was coming back fast; but not fast enough. the cloak was removed. Her ankles were tied firmly, one to each front leg of the chair. Herkimer threw four turns of rope around her torso and the chair's back, took up every inch of slack, and tied a workmanlike knot. Then, still without a word, he stood back and lighted a cigarette. The last trace of paralysis disappeared, but the girl's mad struggles, futile as they were, were not allowed to continue.

'Put a double hammerlock on her,' Herkimer directed, 'but be damned sure not to break anything at this stage of the game. That comes later.'

Jill, more furiously angry than frightened until now, locked her teeth to keep from screaming as the pressure went on. She could not bend forward to relieve the pain; she could not move; she could only grit her teeth and glare. She was beginning to realise, however, what was actually in store; that Herkimer Herkimer Third was in fact a monster whose like she had never known.

He stepped quietly forward, gathered up a handful of fabric, and heaved. The strapless and backless garment, in no way designed to withstand such stresses, parted; squarely across at the upper strand of rope. He puffed his cigarette to a vivid coal—took it in his fingers—there was an audible hiss and a tiny stink of burning flesh as the glowing ember was extinguished in the clear, clean skin below the girl's left armpit. Jill flinched then, and shrieked desperately, but her tormentor was viciously unmoved.

'That was just to settle any doubt as to whether or not I mean business. I'm all done fooling around with you. I want to know two things. first, everything you know about the Lens; where it comes from, what it really is, and what it does besides what your press-agents advertise. Second, what really happened at the Ambassadors' Ball. Start talking. The faster you talk, the less you'll get hurt.'

'You can't get away with this, Herkimer.' Jill tried desperately to pull her shattered nerves together. 'I'll be missed—traced…' She paused, gasping. If she told him that the Lensmen were in full and continuous communication with her—and if he believed it—he would kill her right then. She switched instantly to another track. 'That double isn't good enough to fool anybody who really knows me.'

'She doesn't have to be.' The man grinned venomously. 'Nobody who knows you will get close enough to her to tell the difference. This wasn't done on the spur of the moment, Jill; it was planned—minutely. You haven't got the chance of the proverbial celluloid dog in hell.'

'Jill!' Jack Kinnison's thought stabbed in. 'It isn't Rushton—fourteen seventy nine is a two-storey. What other streets could it be?'

'I don't know…' She was not in very good shape to think.

'Damnation! Got to get hold of somebody who knows the streets. Spud, grab a hacker at the Circle and I'll Lens Parker...' Jack's thought snapped off as he tuned to a local Lensman.

Jill's heart sank. She was starkly certain now that the Lensmen could not find her in time.

'Tighten up a little, Eddie. You, too, Bob.'

'Stop it! Oh, God, STOP IT' The unbearable agony relaxed a little. She watched in horrified fasination a second glowing coal approach her bare right side. 'Even if I do talk you'll kill me anyway. You couldn't let me go now.'

'Kill you, my pet? Not if you behave yourself. We've got a lot of planets the Patrol never heard of, and you could keep a man interested for quite a while, if you really tried. And if you beg hard enough maybe I'll let you try. However, I'd get just as much fun out of killing you as out of the other, so it's up to you. Not sudden death, of course. Little things, at first, like we've been doing. A few more touches of warmth here and there—so...

'Scream as much as you please. I enjoy it, and this room is soundproof. Once more, boys, about half an inch higher this time...up...steady...down. We'll have half an hour or so of this stuff'—Herkimer knew that to the quivering, sensitive, highly imaginative girl his words would be practically as punishing as the atrocious actualities themselves—'then I'll do things to your finger-nails and toe-nails, beginning with burning slivers of double-base flare powder and working up. Then your eyes—or no, I'll save them until last, so you can watch a couple of Venerian slasher-worms work on you, one on each leg, and a Martian digger on your bare belly.'

Gripping her hair firmly in his left hand, he forced her head back and down; down almost to her hard-

held hands. His right hand, concealing something which he had not mentioned and which was probably starkly unmentionable, approached her taut-stretched throat.

'Talk or not, just as you please.' The voice was utterly callous, as chill as the death she now knew he was so willing to deal. 'But listen. If you elect to talk, tell the truth. You won't lie twice. I'll count to ten. One.

Jill uttered a gurgling, strangling noise and he lifted her head a trifle.

'Can you talk now?'

'Yes.'

'Two.'

Helpless, immobile, scared now to a depth of terror she had never imagined it possible to feel, Jill fought her wrenched and shaken mind back from insanity's very edge; managed with a pale tongue to lick bloodless lips. Pops Kinnison always said a man could die only once, but he didn't know...in battle, yes, perhaps...but she had already died a dozen times—but she'd keep on dying forever before she'd say a word. But—

'Tell him, Jill!' Northrop's thought beat at her mind He, her lover, was unashamedly frantic; as much with sheer rage as with sympathy for her physical and mental anguish. 'For the nineteenth time I say *tell him!* We've just located you—Hancock Avenue—we'll be there in two minutes.

'Yes, Jill, quit being a damned stubborn jackass and *tell him!*' Jack Kinnison's thought bit deep; but this time, strangely enough, the girl felt no repugnance at his touch. There was nothing whatever of the lover; nor of the brother, except of the fraternity of arms. She belonged. She would come out of this brawl right side up or none of them would.

'Tell the goddam rat the truth!' Jack's thought drove on. 'It won't make any difference—he won't live long enough to pass it on!'

'But I can't—I won't!' Jill stormed. 'Why, Pops Kinnison would...'

'Not this time I wouldn't, Jill!' Samms' thought tried to come in, too, but the Port Admiral's vehemence was overwhelming. 'No harm—he's doing this strictly on his own—if Morgan had had any idea he'd've killed him first. Start talking or I'll spank you to a rosy blister!'

They were to laugh, later, at the incongruity of that threat, but it did produce results.

'Nine.' Herkimer grinned wolfishly, in sadistic anticipation.

'Stop it—I'll tell!' she screamed. 'Stop it—take that thing away—I can't *stand* it—I'll tell!' She burst into racking, tearing sobs.

'Steady.' Herkimer put something in his pocket, then slapped her so viciously that fingers-long marks sprang into red relief upon the chalk-white background of her cheek. 'Don't crack up; I haven't started to work on you yet. What about that Lens?'

She gulped twice before she could speak. 'It comes from—ulp!—Arisia. I haven't got one myself, so I don't know very much—ulp!—about it at first hand, but from what the boys tell me it must be...'

Outside the building three black forms arrowed downward. Northrop and young Kinnison stopped at the sixth level; Costigan went on down to take care of the guards.

'Bullets, not beams,' the Irishman reminded his younger fellows. 'We'll have to clean up the mess

without leaving a trace, so don't do any more damage to the property than you absolutely have to.'

Neither made any reply; they were both too busy. The two thugs standing behind the steel chair, being armed openly, went first; then Jack put a bullet through Herkimer's head. But Northrop was not content with that. He slid the pin to "full automatic" and ten more heavy slugs tore into the falling body before it struck the floor.

Three quick slashes and the girl was free.

'Jill!'

'Mase!'

Locked in each other's arms, straining together, no by-stander would have believed that this was their first kiss. It was plainly—yes, quite spectacularly—evident, however, that it would not be their last.

Jack, blushing furiously, picked up the cloak and flung it at the oblivious couple.

'P-s-s-t! *P-s-s-t! Jill!* Wrap 'em up!' he whispered, urgently. 'All the top brass in space is coming at full emergency blast—there'll be scrambled eggs all over the place any second now—*Mase! Damn* your thick, hard skull, snap out of it. He's always frothing at the mouth about her running around half naked and if he sees her like this—especially with *you* -he'll simply have a litter of lizards! You'll get a million black spots and seven hundred years in the clink! That's better—'bye now—I'll see you up at New York Spaceport.'

Jack Kinnison dashed to the nearest window, threw it open, and dived headlong out of the building.

CHAPTER 14

The employment office of any concern with personnel running into the hundreds of thousands is a busy place indeed, even when its plants are all on Tellus and its working conditions are as nearly ideal as such things can be made. When that firm's business is Colonial, however, and its working conditions are only a couple of degrees removed from slavery, procurement of personnel is a first-magnitude problem; the Personnel Department, like Alice in Wonderland, must run as fast as it can go in order to stay where it is. Thus the "Help Wanted" advertisements of Uranium, Incorporated covered the planet Earth with blandishment and guile; and thus for twelve hours of every day and for seven days of every week the employment offices of Uranium, Inc. were filled with men—mostly the scum of Earth.

There were, of course, exceptions; one of which strode through the motley group of waiting men and thrust a card through the "Information" wicket. He was a chunky-looking individual, appearing shorter than his actual five feet nine because of a hundred and ninety pounds of weight—even though every pound was placed exactly where it would do the most good. He looked—well, slouchy—and his mien was sullen.

'Birkenfeld—by appointment,' he growled through the wicket, in a voice which could have been pleasantly deep.

The coolly efficient blonde manipulated plugs. 'Mr. George W. Jones, sir, by appointment… Thank you, sir,' and Mr. Jones was escorted into Mr. Birkenfeld's private office.

'Have a chair, please, Mr…er…Jones.'

'So you know?'

'Yes. It is seldom that a man of your education, training, and demonstrated ability applies to us for employment of his own initiative, and a very thorough investigation is indicated.

'What am I here for, then?' the visitor demanded, truculently. 'You could have turned me down by mail. Everybody else has, since I got out.'

'You are here because we who operate on the frontiers cannot afford to pass judgement upon a man because of his past, unless that past precludes the probability of a useful future. Yours does not; and in some cases, such as yours, we are very deeply interested in the future.' The official's eyes drilled deep.

Conway Costigan had never been in the limelight. On the contrary, he had made inconspicuousness a passion and an art. Even in such scenes of violence as that which had occurred at the Ambassadors' Ball he managed to remain unnoticed. His Lens had never been visible. No one except Lensmen—and Clio and Jill—knew that he had one; and Lensmen—and Clio and Jill—did not talk. Although he was calmly certain that this Birkenfeld was not an ordinary interviewer, he was equally certain that the investigators of Uranium, Inc. had found out exactly and only what the Patrol had wanted them to find.

'So?' Jones' bearing altered subtly, and not because of the penetrant eyes. 'That's all I want—a chance. I'll start at the bottom, as far down as you say.'

'We advertise, and truthfully, that opportunity on Eridan is unlimited.' Birkenfeld chose his words with care. 'In your case, opportunity will be either absolutely unlimited or zero, depending entirely upon yourself.'

'I see.' Dumbness had not been included in the fictitious Mr. Jones' background. 'You don't need to draw a blue-print.'

'You'll do, I think.' The interviewer nodded in approval. 'Nevertheless, I must make our position entirely clear. If the slip was—shall we say accidental?—you will go far with us. If you try to play false, you will not last long and you will not be missed.'

'Fair enough.'

'Your willingness to start at the bottom is commendable and it is a fact that those who come up through the ranks make the best executives; in our line at least. Just how far down are you willing to start?'

'How low do you go?'

'A mucker, I think would be low enough; and, from your build, and obvious physical strength, the logical job.'

'Mucker?'

'One who skoufers ore in the mine. Nor can we make any exception in your case as to the routines of induction and transportation.'

'Of course not.'

'Take this slip to Mr. Calkins, in Room 6217. He will run you through the mill.'

And that night, in an obscure boarding-house, Mr. George Washington Jones, after a meticulous Service Special survey in every direction, reached a large and somewhat grimy hand into a screened receptacle in his battered suitcase and touched a Lens.

'Clio?' The lovely mother of their wonderful children appeared in his mind. 'Made it, sweetheart, no suspicion at all. No more Lensing for a while—not too long, I hope—so...so-long, Clio.'

'Take it easy, Spud darling, and *be careful*.' Her tone was light, but she could not conceal a stark background of fear. 'Oh, I *wish* I could go, too!'

'I wish you could, Tootie.' The linked minds flashed back to what the two had done together in the red opacity of Nevian murk; on Nevia's mighty, watery globe—but that kind of thinking would not do. 'But the boys will keep in touch with me and keep you posted. And besides, you know how hard it is to get a baby-sitter!'

It is strange that the fundamental operations of working metalliferous veins have changed so little throughout the ages. Or is it? Ores came into being with the crusts of the planets; they change appreciably only with the passage of geologic time. Ancient mines, of course, could not go down very deep or follow a seam very far; there was too much water and too little air. The steam engine helped, in degree if not in kind, by removing water and supplying air. Tools improved— from the simple metal bar through pick and shovel and candle, through drill and hammer and low explosive and acetylene, through Sullivan slugger and high explosive and electrics, through skoufer and rotary and burley and sourceless glow, to the complex gadgetry of today—but what, fundamentally, is the difference? Men still crawl, snake-like, to where the metal is. Men still, by dint of sheer brawn, jackass the precious stuff out to where our vaunted automatics can get hold of it. And men still die, in horribly unknown fashions and in callously recorded numbers, in the mines which supply the stuff upon which our vaunted culture rests.

But to resume the thread of narrative, George Washington Jones went to Eridan as a common labourer; a mucker. He floated down beside the skip— a "skip" is a mine elevator—some four thousand eight hundred feet. He rode an ore-car a horizontal distance of approximately eight miles to the brilliantly-illuminated cavern which was the Station of the Twelfth

and lowest level. He was assigned to the bunk in which he would sleep for the next fifteen nights: "Fifteen down and three up," ran the standard underground contract.

He walked four hundred yards, yelled "Nothing Down!" and inched his way up a rise—in many places scarcely wider than his shoulders—to the stope some three hundred feet above. He reported to the miner who was to be his immediate boss and bent his back to the skoufer—which, while not resembling a shovel at all closely, still meant hard physical labour. He already knew ore—the glossy, sub-metallic, pitchy black lustre of uraninite or pitchblende; the yellows of autunite and carnotite; the variant and confusing greens of tobernite. No values went from Jones' skoufer into the heavily-timbered, steel-braced waste-pockets of the stope; very little base rock went down the rise.

He became accustomed to the work; got used to breathing the peculiarly lifeless, dry, oily compressed air. And when, after a few days, his stentorian "Nothing Down!" called forth a "Nothing but a little fine stuff!" and a handful of grit and pebbles, he knew that he had been accepted into the undefined, unwritten, and unofficial, yet nevertheless intensely actual, fellowship of hard-rock men. He belonged.

He knew that he must abandon his policy of invisibility; and, after several days of thought, he decided how he would do it. Hence, upon the first day of his "up" period, he joined his fellows in their descent upon one of the rawest, noisiest dives of Danapolis. The men were met, of course, by a bevy of giggling, shrieking, garishly painted and strongly perfumed girls—and at this point young Jones' behaviour became exceedingly unorthodox.

'Buy me a drink, mister? And a dance, huh?'

'On your way, sister.' He brushed the importunate wench aside. 'I get enough exercise underground, an' you ain't got a thing I want.'

Apparently unaware that the girl was exchanging meaningful glances with a couple of husky characters labelled "BOUNCER" in billposter type, the atypical mucker strode up to the long and ornate bar.

'Gimme a bottle of pineapple pop,' he ordered brusquely, 'an' a package of Tellurian cigarettes—Sunshines.'

'P-p-pine... ?' The surprised bartender did not finish the word.

The bouncers were fast, but Costigan was faster. A hard knee took one in the solar plexus; a hard elbow took the other so savagely under the chin as to all but break his neck. A bartender started to swing a bung-starter, and found himself flying through the air toward a table. Men, table, and drinks crashed to the floor.

'I pick my own company an' I drink what I damn please.' Jones announced, grittily. 'Them lunkers ain't hurt none, to speak of...' His hard eyes swept the room malevolently, 'but I ain't in no gentle mood an' the next jaspers that tackle me will wind up in the repair shop, or maybe in the morgue. See?'

This of course was much too much; a dozen embattled roughnecks leaped to mop up on the misguided wight who had so impugned the manhood of all Eridan. Then, while six or seven bartenders blew frantic blasts upon police whistles, there was a flurry of action too fast to be resolved into consecutive events by the eye. Conway Costigan, one of the fastest men with hands and feet the Patrol has ever known, was trying to keep himself alive; and he succeeded.

'What the hell goes on here?' a chorus of raucously authoritative voices yelled, and sixteen policemen—John Law did not travel singly in that district, but in

platoons—swinging clubs and saps, finally hauled George Washington Jones out from the bottom of the pile. He had sundry abrasions and not a few contusions, but no bones were broken and his skin was practically whole.

And since his version of the affair was not only inadequate, but also differed in important particulars from those of several non-participating witnesses, he spent the rest of his holiday in jail; a development with which he was quite content.

The work—and time—went on. He became in rapid succession a head mucker, a miner's pimp (which short and rugged Anglo-Saxon word means simply "helper" in underground parlance) a miner, a top-miner, and then—a long step up the ladder!—a shift-boss.

And then disaster struck; suddenly, paralyzingly, as mine disasters do. Loud-speakers blared briefly— "Explosion! Cave-in! Flood! Fire! Gas! Radiation! Damp!"—and expired. Short-circuits; there was no way of telling which, if any, of those dire warnings were true.

The power failed, and the lights. The hiss of air from valves, a noise which by its constant and unvarying and universal presence soon becomes unheard, became noticeable because of its diminution in volume and tone. And then, seconds later, a jarring, shuddering, rumble was felt and heard, accompanied by the snapping of shattered timbers and the sharper, utterly unforgettable shriek of rending and riven steel. And the men, as men do under such conditions, went wild; yelling, swearing, leaping toward where, in the rayless dark, each thought the rise to be.

It took a couple of seconds for the shift-boss to break out and hook up his emergency battery-lamp; and three or four more seconds, and by dint of fists, feet, and a two-foot length of air-hose, to restore any

degree of order. Four men were dead; but that wasn't too bad—considering.

'Up there! Under the hanging wall!' he ordered, sharply. '*That* won't fall—unless the whole mountain slips. Now, how many of you jaspers have got your emergency kits on you? Twelve—out of twenty-six—what brains! Put on your masks. You without 'em can stay up here—you'll be safe for a while—I hope.'

Then, presently: 'There, that's all for now. I guess.' He flashed his light downward. The massive steel members no longer writhed; the crushed and tortured timbers were still.

'That rise may be open, it goes through solid rock, not waste. I'll see. Wright, you're all in one piece, aren't you?'

'I guess so—yes.'

'Take charge up here. I'll go down to the drift. If the rise is open I'll give you a flash. Send the ones with masks down, one at a time. Take a jolly-bar and bash the brains out of anybody who gets panicky again.'

Jones was not as brave as he sounded: mine disasters carry a terror which is uniquely and peculiarly poignant. Nevertheless he went down the rise, found it open, and signalled. Then, after issuing brief orders, he led the way along the dark and silent drift toward the Station; wondering profanely why the people on duty there had not done something with the wealth of emergency equipment always ready there. The party found some cave-ins, but nothing they could not dig through.

The Station was also silent and dark. Jones, flashing his head-lamp upon the emergency panel, smashed the glass, wrenched the door open, and pushed buttons. Lights flashed on. Warning signals flared, bellowed and rang. The rotary air-pump began again

its normal subdued, whickering whirr. But the water-pump! Shuddering, clanking, groaning, it was threatening to go out any second—but there wasn't a thing in the world Jones could do about it—yet.

The Station itself, so buttressed and pillared with alloy steel as to be little more compressible than an equal volume of solid rock, was unharmed; but in it nothing lived. Four men and a woman—the nurse—were stiffly motionless at their posts; apparently the leads to the Station had been blasted in such fashion that no warning whatever had been given. And smoke, billowing inward from the main tunnel, was growing thicker by the minute. Jones punched another button; a foot-thick barrier of asbestos, tungsten, and vitrified refractory slid smoothly across the tunnel's opening. He considered briefly, pityingly, those who might be outside, but felt no urge to explore. If any lived, there were buttons on the other side of the fire-door.

The eddying smoke disappeared, the flaring lights winked out, air-horns and bells relapsed into silence. The shift-boss, now apparently the Superintendent of the whole Twelfth Level, removed his mask, found the Station walkie-talkie, and snapped a switch. He spoke, listened, spoke again then called a list of names—none of which brought any response.

'Wright, and you five others,' picking out miners who could be depended upon to keep their heads, 'take these guns. Shoot if you have to, but not unless you have to. Have the muckers clear the drift, just enough to get through. You'll find a shift-boss with a crew of nineteen, up in Stope Sixty. Their rise is blocked. They've got light and power again now, and good air, and they're working on it, but opening the rise from the top is a damned slow job. Wright, you throw a chippie into it from the bottom. You others, work back along the drift, clear to the last glory hole. Be sure that all the rises are open—check all the stopes

and glory holes—tell everybody you find alive to report to me here… '

'Aw, what good!' a man shrieked. 'We're all goners anyway—I want *water* an'… '

'Shut up, fool!' There was a sound as of fist meeting flesh, the shriek was stilled. 'Plenty of water—tanks full of the stuff.' A grizzled miner turned to the self-appointed boss and twitched his head toward the labouring pump. 'Too damn much water too soon, huh?'

'I wouldn't wonder—but get busy!'

As his now orderly and purposeful men disappeared, Jones picked up his microphone and changed the setting of a dial.

'On top, somebody,' he said crisply. 'On top…'

'Oh, there's somebody alive down in Twelve, after all!' a girl's voice screamed in his ear. 'Mr. Clancy! Mr Edwards!'

'To hell with Clancy, and Edwards, too,' Jones barked. 'Gimme the Chief Engineer and the Head Surveyor, and gimme 'em *fast.*'

'Clancy speaking, Station Twelve.' If Works Manager Clancy had heard that pointed remark, and he must have, he ignored it. 'Stanley and Emerson will be here in a moment. In the meantime, who's calling? I don't recognise your voice, and it's been so long…'

'Jones. Shift-boss, Stope Fifty Nine. I had a little trouble getting here to the Station.'

'What? Where's Pennoyer? And Riley? And…?'

'Dead. Everybody. Gas or damp. No warning.'

'Not enough to turn on *anything*—not even the purifiers?'

'Nothing.'

'Where were you?'

'Up in the stope.'

'Good God!' That news, to Clancy, was informative enough.

'But to hell with all that. What happened, and where?'

'A skip-load, and then a magazine, of high explosive, right at Station Seven—it's right at the main shaft, you know.'

Jones did not know, since he had never been in that part of the mine, but he could see the picture. 'Main shaft filled up to above Seven, and both emergency shafts blocked. Number One at Six, Number Two at Seven—must have been a fault—But here's Chief Engineer Stanley.' The works manager, not too unwillingly, relinquished the microphone.

A miner came running up and Jones covered his mouthpiece. 'How about the glory holes?'

'Plugged solid, all four of 'em—by the vibro, clear up to Eleven.'

'Thanks.' Then, as soon as Stanley's voice came on:

'What I want to know is, why is this damned water-pump overloading? What's the circuit?'

'You must be…yes, you are pumping against too much head. Five levels above you are dead, you know, so… '

'Dead? Can't you raise *anybody*?'

'Not yet. So you're pumping through dead boosters on Eleven and Ten and so on up, and when your overload-relief valve opens…'

'*Relief* valve!' Jones almost screamed. 'Can I dog the damn thing down?'

'No, it's internal.'

'Christ, what a design—I could eat a handful of iron filings and *puke* a better emergency pump than that!'

'When it opens,' Stanley went stolidly on, 'the water will go through the by-pass back into the sump. So you'd better rod out one of the glory holes and...'

'Get conscious, fat-head!' Jones blazed. 'What would we use for time? Get off the air—gimme Emerson!'

'Emerson speaking.'

'Got your maps?'

'Yes.'

'We got to run a sag up to Eleven—fast—or drown. Can you give me the shortest possible distance?'

'Can do.' The Head Surveyor snapped orders. 'We'll have it for you in a minute. Thank God there was somebody down there with a brain.'

'It doesn't take super-human intelligence to push buttons.'

'You'd be surprised. Your point on glory holes was very well taken—you won't have much time after the pump quits. When the water reaches the Station...'

'Curtains. And it's all done now—running free and easy—recirculating. Hurry that dope!'

';Here it is now. Start at the highest point of Stope Fifty Nine. Repeat.'

'Stope Fifty-Nine.' Jones waved a furious hand as he shouted the words; the tight-packed miners turned and ran. The shift-boss followed them, carrying the

walkie-talkie, aiming an exasperated kick of pure frustration at the merrily-humming water pump as he passed it.

'Thirty two degrees from the vertical—anywhere between thirty and thirty five.'

'Thirty to thirty five off vertical.'

'Direction—got a compass?'

'Yes.'

'Set the blue on zero. Course two hundred seventy five degrees.'

'Blue on zero. Course two seven five.'

'Dex sixty nine point two zero feet. That'll put you into Eleven's class yard—so big you can't miss it.'

'Distance sixty nine point two—*that* all? Fine! Maybe we'll make it, after all. They're sinking a shaft, of course. From where?'

'About four miles in on Six. It'll take time.'

'If we can get up into Eleven we'll have all the time on the clock—it'll take a week or more to flood Twelve's stopes. But this sag is sure as hell going to be touch and go. And say, from the throw of the pump and the volume of the sump, will you give me the best estimate you can of how much time we've got? I want at least an hour, but I'm afraid I won't have it.'

'Yes. I'll call you back.'

The shift-boss elbowed his way through the throng of men and, dragging the radio behind him, wriggled and floated up the rise.

'Wright!' he bellowed, the echoes resounding deafeningly all up and down the narrow tube. 'You up there ahead of me?'

'Yeah!' that worthy bellowed back.

'More men left than I thought—how many—half of 'em?'

'Just about.'

'Good. Sort out the ones you got up there by trades.' Then, when he had emerged into the now brilliantly illuminated stope. 'Where are the timber-pimps?'

'Over there.'

'Rustle timbers. Whatever you can find and wherever you find it, grab it and bring it up here. Get some twelve-inch steel, too, six feet long. Timbermen, grab that stuff off of the face and start your staging right here. You muckers, rig a couple of skoufers to throw muck to bury the base and checkerwork up to the hanging wall. Doze a sluice-way down into that waste pocket there, so we won't clog ourselves up. Work fast, fellows, but make it *solid*—you know the load it'll have to carry and what will happen if it gives.'

They knew. They knew what they had to do and did it; furiously, but with care and precision.

'How wide a sag you figurin' on, Supe?' the boss timberman asked. 'Eight foot checkerwork to the hangin', anyway, huh?'

'Yes. I'll let you know in a minute.'

The surveyor came in. 'Forty one minutes is my best guess.'

'From when?'

'From the time the pump failed.'

'That was four minutes ago—nearer five. And five more before we can start cutting. Forty one less ten is thirty one. Thirty one into sixty nine point two goes...'

'Two point two three feet per minute, my slip-stick says.'

'Thanks. Wright, what would you say is the biggest sag we can cut in this kind of rock at two and a quarter feet a minute?'

'Um...m...m.' The miner scratched his whiskery chin. 'That's a tough one, boss. You'll hafta figure damn close to a hundred pounds of air to the foot on plain cuttin'—that's two hundred and a quarter. But without a burley to pimp for 'er, a rotary can't take that kind of air—she'll foul herself to a standstill before she cuts a foot. An' with a burley riggin' she's got to make damn near a double cut—seven foot inside figger—so any way you look at it you ain't goin' to cut no two foot to the minute.'

'I was hoping you wouldn't check my figures, but you do. So we'll cut five feet. Saw your timbers accordingly. We'll hold that burley by hand.'

Wright shook his head dubiously. 'We don't want to die down here any more than you do, boss, so we'll do our damndest—but how in *hell* do you figure you can hold her to her work?'

'Rig a yoke. Cut a stretcher up for canvas and padding. It'll pound, but a man can stand almost anything, in short enough shifts, if he's got to or die.'

And for a time—two minutes, to be exact, during which the rotary chewed up and spat out a plug of rock over five feet deep—things went very well indeed. Two men, instead of the usual three, could run the rotary; that is, they could tend the complicated pneumatic walking jacks which not only oscillated the cutting demon in a geometrical path, but also rammed it against the face with a steadily held and enormous pressure, even while climbing almost vertically upward under a burden of over twenty thousand pounds.

An armoured hand waved a signal—voice was utterly useless—up! A valve was flipped; a huge, flat, steel foot arose; a timber slid into place, creaking and

groaning as that big flat foot smashed down. Up—again! Up—a third time! Eighteen seconds—less than one-third of a minute—ten inches gained!

And, while it was not easy, two men could hold the burley—in one-minute shifts. As has been intimated, this machine "pimped" for the rotary. It waited on it, ministering to its every need with a singleness of purpose impossible to any except robotic devotion. It picked the rotary's teeth, it freed its linkages, it deloused its ports, it cleared its spillways of compacted debris, it even—and this is a feat starkly unbelievable to anyone who does not know the hardness of neocarballoy and the tensile strength of ultra-special steels—it even changed, while in full operation, the rotary's diamond-tipped cutters.

Both burley and rotary were extremely efficient, but neither was either quiet or gentle. In their quietest moments they shrieked and groaned and yelled, producing a volume of sound in which nothing softer than a cannon-shot could have been heard. But when, in changing the rotary's cutting teeth, the burley's "fingers" were driven into and through the solid rock—a matter of merest routine to both machines—the resultant blasts of sound cannot even be imagined, to say nothing of being described.

And always both machines spewed out torrents of rock, in sizes ranging from impalpable dust up to chunks as big as a fist.

As the sag lengthened and the checkerwork grew higher, the work began to slow down. They began to lose the time they had gained. There were plenty of men, but in that narrow bore there simply was not room for enough men to work. Even through that storm of dust and hurtling rock the timbermen could get their blocking up there, but they could not place it fast enough—there were too many other men in the way. One of them had to get out. Since one man could not

possibly run the rotary, one man would have to hold the burley.

They tried it, one after another. No soap. It hammered them flat. The rotary, fouled in every tooth and channel and vent under the terrific thrust of two hundred thirty pounds of air, merely gnawed and slid. The timbermen now had room—but nothing to do. And Jones, who had been biting at his moustache and ignoring the frantic walkie-talkie for minutes, stared grimly at watch and tape. Three minutes left, and over eight feet to go.

'Gimme that armour!' he rasped, and climbed the blocks. 'Open the air wide open—give 'er the whole two-fifty! Get down, Mac—I'll take it the rest of the way!'

He put his shoulders to the improvised yoke, braced his feet, and heaved. The burley, screaming and yelling and clamouring, went joyously to work—both ways—God, what punishment! The rotary, free and clear, chewed rock more viciously than ever. An armoured hand smote his leg. Lift! He lifted that foot, set it down two inches higher. The other one. Four inches. Six. One foot. Two. Three. Lord of the ancients! Was this lifetime of agony only one minute? Or wasn't he holding her—had the damn thing stopped cutting? No, it was still cutting—the rocks were banging against and bouncing off of his helmet as viciously and as numerously as ever; he could sense, rather than feel, the furious fashion in which the relays of timbermen were labouring to keep those high-stepping jacks in motion.

No, it had been only one minute. Twice that long yet to go. God! Nothing *could* be that brutal—a bull elephant couldn't take it—but by all the gods of space and all the devils in hell, he'd stay with it until that sag broke through. And grimly, doggedly, toward the end

nine-tenths unconsciously, Lensman Conway Costigan stayed with it.

And in the stope so far below, a new and highly authoritative voice blared from the speaker.

'Jones! God damn it, Jones, answer me! If Jones isn't there, somebody else answer me—*anybody!*'

'Yes, sir?' Wright was afraid to answer that peremptory call, but more afraid not to.

'Jones? This is Clancy.'

'No, sir. Not Jones. Wright, sir—top miner.'

'Where's Jones?'

'Up in the sag, sir. He's holding the burley—alone.'

'*Alone!* Hell's purple fires! Tell him to—how many men has he got on the rotary?'

'Two, sir. That's all they's room for.'

'Tell him to quit it—put somebody else on it—I *won't* have him killed, damn it!'

'He's the only one strong enough to hold it, sir, but I'll send up word.' Word went up via sign language, and came back down. 'Beggin' your pardon, sir, but he says to tell you to go to hell, sir. He won't have no time for chit-chat, he says, until this goddam sag is through or the juice goes off, sir.'

A blast of profanity erupted from the speaker, of such violence that the thoroughly scared Wright threw the walkie-talkie down the waste-chute, and in the same instant the rotary crashed through.

Dazed, groggy, barely conscious from his terrific effort, Jones stared owlishly through the heavy, steel-braced lenses of his helmet while the timbermen set a few more courses of wood and the rotary walked itself and the clinging burley up and out of the hole. He

climbed stiffly out, and as he stared at the pillar of light flaring upward from the sag, his gorge began to rise.

'Wha's the idea of that damn surveyor lying to us like that?' he babbled. 'We had oodles an' oodles of time—didn't have to kill ourselves—damn water ain't got there yet—wha's the big...' He wobbled weakly, and took one short step, and the lights went out. The surveyor's estimate had been impossibly, accidentally close. They had had a little extra time; but it was measured very easily in seconds.

And Jones, logical to the end in a queerly addled way, stood in the almost palpable darkness, and wobbled, and thought. If a man couldn't see anything with his eyes wide open, he was either blind or unconscious. He wasn't blind, therefore he must be unconscious and not know it. He sighed, wearily and gratefully, and collapsed.

Battery lights were soon reconnected, and everybody knew that they had holed through. There was no more panic. And, even before the shift-boss had recovered full consciousness, he was walking down the drift toward Station Eleven.

There is no need to enlarge upon the rest of that grim and grisly affair. Level after level was activated; and, since working upward in mines is vastly faster than working downward, the two parties met on the Eighth Level. Half of the men who would otherwise have died were saved, and—much more important from the viewpoint of Uranium, Inc.—the deeper and richer half of the biggest and richest uranium mine in existence, instead of being out of production for a year or more, would be back in full operation in a couple of weeks.

And George Washington Jones, still a trifle shaky from his ordeal, was called into the front office. But before he arrived:

'I'm going to make him Assistant Works Manager,' Clancy announced.

'I think not.'

'But listen, Mr. Isaacson—*please!* How do you expect me to build up a staff if you snatch every good man I find away from me?'

'You didn't find him. Birkenfeld did. He was here only on a test. He is going into Department Q.'

Clancy, who had opened his mouth to continue his protests, shut it wordlessly. He knew that Department Q was -

DEPARTMENT Q.

CHAPTER 15

Costigan was not surprised to see the man he had known as Birkenfeld in Uranium's ornate conference room. He had not expected, however, to see Isaacson. He knew, of course, that Spaceways owned Uranium, Inc., and the planet Eridan, lock, stock, and barrel; but it never entered his modest mind that his case would be of sufficient importance to warrant the personal attention of the Big Noise himself. Hence the sight of that suave and unrevealing face gave the putative Jones a more than temporary qualm. Isaacson was top-bracket stuff, 'way out of his class. Virgil Samms ought to be taking this assignment, but since he wasn't -

But instead of being an inquisition, the meeting was friendly and informal from the start. They complimented him upon the soundness of his judgement and the accuracy of his decisions. They thanked him, both with words and with a considerable sum of expendable credits. They encouraged him to talk about himself, but there was nothing whatever of the star-chamber or of cross-examination. The last question was representative of the whole conference.

'One other thing, Jones, has me slightly baffled,' Isaacson said, with a really winning smile. 'Since you do not drink, and since you were not in search of feminine...er...companionship, just why did you go down to Roaring Jack's dive?'

'Two reasons,' Jones said, with a somewhat shamefaced grin. 'The minor one isn't easy to explain, but...well, I hadn't been having an exactly easy time of it on Earth... You all know about that, I suppose?'

They knew.

'Well, I was taking a very dim view of things in general, and a good fight would get it out of my system. It always does.'

'I see. And the major reason?'

'I knew, of course, that I was on probation. I would have to get promoted, and fast, or stay sunk forever. To get promoted fast, a man can either be enough of a boot-licker to be pulled up from on high, or he can be shoved up by the men he is working with. The best way to get a crowd of hard-rock men to like you is to lick a few of 'em—off hours, of course, and according to Hoyle—and the more of 'em you can lick at once, the better. I'm pretty good at rough-and-tumble brawling, so I gambled that the cops would step in before I got banged up too much. I won.'

'I see,' Isaacson said again, in an entirely different tone. He did see, now. 'The first technique is so universally used that the possibility of the second did not occur to me. Nice work—*very* nice.' He turned to the other members of the Board. 'This, I believe, concludes the business of the meeting?'

For some reason or other Isaacson nodded slightly as he asked the question; and one by one, as though in concurrence, the others nodded in reply. The meeting broke up. Outside the door, however, the magnate did not go about his own business nor send Jones about his. Instead:

'I would like to show you, if I may, the above-ground part of our Works?'

'My time is yours, sir. I am interested.'

It is unnecessary here to go into the details of a Civilisation's greatest uranium operation; the storage bins, the grinders, the Wilfley tables and slime tanks, the flotation sluices, the roasters and reducers, the processes of solution and crystallisation and recrystallisation, of final oxidation and reduction.

Suffice it to say that Isaacson showed Jones the whole immensity of Uranium Works Number One. The trip ended on the top floor of the towering Administration Building, in a heavily-screened room containing a desk, a couple of chairs, and a tremendously massive safe.

'Smoke up.' Isaacson indicated a package of Jones' favourite brand of cigarettes and lighted a cigar. 'You knew that you were under test. I wonder, though, if you knew how much of it was testing?'

'All of it.' Jones grinned. 'Except for the big blow, of course.'

'Of course.'

'There were too many possibilities, of too many different kinds, too pat. I might warn you, though—I could have got away clear with that half-million.'

The possibility existed.' Surprisingly, Isaacson did not tell him that the trap was more subtle than it had appeared to be. 'It was, however, worth the risk. Why didn't you?'

'Because I figure on making more than that, a little later, and I might live longer to spend it.'

'Sound thinking, my boy—really sound. Now—you noticed, of course, the vote at the end of the meeting?'

Jones had noticed it; and although he did not say so, he had been wondering about it ever since. The older man strolled over to the safe and opened it, revealing a single, startlingly small package.

'You passed, unanimously; you are now learning what you have to know. Not that we trust you unreservedly. You will be watched for a long time, and before you can make one false step, you will die.'

'That would seem to be good business, sir.'

'Glad you look at it that way—we thought you would. You saw the Works. Quite an operation, don't you think?'

'Immense, sir. The biggest thing I ever saw.'

'What would you say, then, to the idea of this office being our real headquarters, of that little package there being our real business?' he swung the safe door shut, spun the knob.

'It would have been highly surprising a couple of hours ago.' Costigan could not afford to appear stupid, nor to possess too much knowledge. He had to steer an extremely difficult middle course. 'After the climax of this build-up, though, it wouldn't seem at all impossible. Or that there were wheels—plenty of 'em—within wheels.'

'Smart!' Isaacson applauded. 'And what would you think might be in that package? This room is ray-proof.'

'Against anything the Galactic Patrol can swing?'

'Positively.'

'Well, then, it *might* be something beginning with the letter' he flicked two fingers, almost invisibly fast, into a T and went on without a break 'M, as in morphine.'

Your caution and restraint are commendable. If I had any remaining doubt as to your ability, it is gone.' He paused, frowning. As belief in ability increased, that in sincerity lessened. This doubt, this questioning, existed every time a new executive was initiated into the mysteries of Department Q. The Board's judgement was good. They had slipped only twice, and those two errors had been corrected easily enough. The fellow had been warned once; that was enough. He took the plunge. 'You will work with the Assistant Works Manager here until you understand the duties of the

position. You will be transferred to Tellus as Assistant
Works Manager there. Your principal duties will,
however, be concerned with Department Q—which
you will head up one day if you make good. And, just
incidentally, when you go to Tellus, a package like
that one in the safe will go with you.'

'Oh...I see. I'll make good, sir.' Jones let Isaacson
see his jaw-muscles tighten in resolve. 'It may take a
little time for me to learn my way around, sir, but I'll
learn it.'

'I'm sure you will. And now, to go into greater
detail... '

Virgil Samms had to be sure of his facts. More than
that, he had to be able to prove them; not merely to
the satisfaction of a law-enforcement officer, but
beyond any reasonable doubt of the hardest-headed
member of a cynical and sceptical jury. Wherefore
Jack Kinnison and Mase Northrop took up the thionite
trail at the exact point where, each trip, George
Olmstead had had to abandon it; in the atmosphere
of Cavenda. And fortunately, not too much preparation
was required.

Cavenda was, as has been intimated, a primitive
world. Its native people, humanoid in type, had
developed a culture approximating in some respects
that of the North American Indian at about the time of
Columbus, in others that of the ancient Nomads of
Araby. Thus a couple of wandering natives,
unrecognisable under their dirty stormproof blankets
and their scarcely thinner layers of grease and grime,
watched impassively, incuriously, while a box floated
pendant from its parachute from sky to ground.
Mounted upon their uncouth steeds, they followed that
box when it was hauled to the white man's village.
Unlike many of the other natives, these two did not

shuffle into that village, to lean silently against a rock or a wall awaiting their turn to exchange a few hours of simple labour for a container of a new and highly potent beverage. They did, however, keep themselves constantly and minutely informed as to everything these strange, devil-ridden white men did. One of these pseudo-natives wandered off into the wilderness two or three days before the huge thing-which-flies-without-wings left ground; the other immediately afterward.

Thus the departure of the space-ship from Cavenda was recorded, as was its arrival at Eridan. It had been extremely difficult for the Patrol's engineers to devise ways and means of tracing that ship from departure to arrival without exciting suspicion, but it had not proved impossible.

And Jack Kinnison, lounging idly and elegantly in the concourse of Danapolis Spaceport, seethed imperceptibly.

Having swallowed a tiny Service Special capsule that morning, he knew that he had been under continuous spy-ray inspection for over two hours. He had not given himself away—practically everybody screened their inside coat pockets and hip pockets, and the cat-whisker lead from Lens to leg simply could not be seen—but for all the good they were doing him his ultra-instruments might just as well have been back on Tellus.

'Mase!' he sent, with no change whatever in the vapid expression then on his face. 'I'm still covered. Are you?'

'Covered!' the answering thought was a snort. 'They're covering me like water covers a submarine!'

'Keep tuned. I'll call Spud. Spud!'

'Come in, Jack.' Conway Costigan, alone now in the sanctum of Department Q, did not seem to be busy, but he was.

'That red herring they told us to drag across the trail was too damned red. They must be touchier than fulminate to spy-work on their armed forces—neither Mase nor I can do a lick of work. Anybody else covered?'

'No. All clear.'

'Good. Tell them the zwilnik blockers took us out.'

'I'll do that. Distance only, or is somebody on your tail?'

'Somebody; and I mean *some body*. A slick chick with a classy chassis; a blonde, with great, big come-hither eyes. Too good to be true; especially the falsies. Wiring, my friend—and I haven't been able to get a close look, but I wouldn't wonder if her nostrils had a skillionth of a whillimetre too much expansion. I want a spy-ray op—is it safe to use Fred?' Kinnison referred to the grizzled engineer now puttering about in a certain space-ship; not the one in which he and Northrop had come to Eridan.

'Definitely not. I can do it myself and still stay very much in character... No, I don't know her. Not surprising, of course, since the policy here is never to let the right hand know what the left is doing. How about you, Mase? Have you got a little girl-friend, too?'

'Yea, verily, brother; but not little. More my size.' Northrop pointed out a tall, trim brunette, strolling along with the effortless, consciously unconscious poise of the professional model.

'Hm...m...m. I don't know her, either,' Costigan reported, 'but both of them are wearing four-inch spy-ray blocks and are probably wired up like Christmas trees. By inference, P-gun proof. I can't penetrate, of

course, but maybe I can get a viewpoint... You're right, Jack. Nostrils plugged. Anti-thionite, anti-Vee-Two, anti-everything. In fact, anti-social. I'll spread their pictures around and see if anybody knows either of them.'

He did so, and over a hundred of the Patrol's shrewdest operatives—upon this occasion North America had invaded Eridan in force—studied and thought. No one knew the tall brunette, but -

'I know the blonde.' This was Parker of Washington, a Service ace for twenty five years. ' "Hell-cat Hazel" DeForce, the hardest-boiled babe unhung. Watch your step around her; she's just as handy with a knife and knock-out drops as she is with a gun.'

'Thanks, Parker. I've heard of her.' Costigan was thinking fast. 'Free-lance. No way of telling who she's working for at the moment.' This was a statement not a question.

'Only that it would have to be somebody with a lot of money. Her price is high. That all?'

'That's all, fellows.' Then, to Jack and Northrop: 'My thought is that you two guys are completely out-classed—out-weighed, out-numbered, out-manned, and out-gunned. Undressed, you're sitting ducks; and if you put out any screens it'll crystallise their suspicions and they'll grab you right then—or maybe even knock you off. You'd better get out of here at full blast; you can't do any more good here, the way things are.'

'Sure we can!' Kinnison protested. 'You wanted a diversion, didn't you?'

'Yes, but you already...'

'What we've done already isn't a patch to what we can do next. We can set up such a diversion that the boys can walk right on the thionite-carrier's heels

without anybody paying any attention. By the way, you don't know yet who is going to carry it, do you?'

'No. No penetration at all.'

'You soon will, bucko. Watch our smoke!'

'What do you think you're going to do?' Costigan demanded, sharply.

'This.' Jack explained. 'And don't try to say no. We're on our own, you know.'

'We...I...I...it sounds good, and if you can pull it off it will help no end. Go ahead.'

The demurely luscious blonde stared disconsolately at the bulletin board, upon which another thirty minutes was being added to the time of arrival of a ship already three hours late. She picked up a book, glanced at its cover, put it down. Her hand moved toward a magazine, drew back, dropped idly into her lap. She sighed, stifled a yawn prettily, leaned backward in her seat—in such a position, Jack noticed, that he could not see into her nostrils—and closed her eyes. And Jack Kinnison, coming visibly to a decision, sat down beside her.

'Pardon me, miss, but I feel just like you look. Can you tell me why convention decrees that two people, stuck in this concourse by arrivals that nobody knows when will arrive, have got to suffer alone when they could have so much more fun suffering together?'

The girl's eyes opened slowly; she was neither startled, nor afraid, nor—it seemed—even interested. In fact, she gazed at him with so much disinterest and for so long a time that he began to wonder—was she going to play sweet and innocent to the end?

'Yes, conventions are stupid, sometimes,' she admitted finally, her lovely lips curving into the beginnings of a smile. Her voice, low and sweet, matched perfectly the rest of her charming self. 'After

all, perfectly nice people do meet informally on shipboard; why not in concourses?'

'Why not, indeed? And I'm perfectly nice people, I assure you. Willi Borden is the name. My friends call me Bill. And you?'

'Beatrice Bailey; Bee for short. Tell me what you like, and we'll talk about it.'

'Why talk, when we could be eating? I'm with a guy. He's out on the field somewhere—a big bruiser with a pencil-stripe black moustache. Maybe you saw him talking to me a while back?'

'I think so, now that you mention him. Too big - *much* too big.' The girl spoke carelessly, but managed to make it very clear that Jack Kinnison was just exactly the right size. 'Why?'

'I told him I'd have supper with him. Shall we hunt him up and eat together?'

'Why not? Is he alone?'

'He was, when I saw him last.' Although Jack knew exactly where Northrop was, and who was with him, he had to play safe; he did not know how much this "Bee Bailey" really knew. 'He knows a lot more people around here than I do, though, so maybe he isn't now. Let me carry some of that plunder?'

'You might carry those books—thanks. But the field is so *big*—how do you expect to find him? Or do you know where he is?'

'Oh-oh!' he denied, vigorously. This was the critical moment. She certainly wasn't suspicious—yet—but she was showing signs of not wanting to go out there, and if she refused to go... 'To be honest, I don't care whether I find him or not—the idea of ditching him appeals to me more and more. So how about this? We'll dash out to the third dock—just so I won't have

to actually lie about looking for him—and dash right back here. Or wouldn't you rather have it a two-some.

'I refuse to answer, by advice of counsel.' The girl laughed gaily, but her answer was plain enough.

Their rate of progress was by no means a dash, and Kinnison did not look—with his eyes—for Northrop. Nevertheless, just south of the third dock, the two young couples met.

'My cousin, Grace James,' Northrop said, without a tremor or a quiver. 'Wild Willi Borden, Grace—usually called Baldy on account of his hair.'

The girls were introduced; each vouchsafing the other a completely meaningless smile and a colourlessly conventional word of greeting. Were they, in fact as in seeming, total strangers? Or were they in fact working together as closely as were the two young Lensmen themselves? If that was acting, it was a beautiful job; neither man could detect the slightest flaw in the performance of either girl.

'Whither away, pilot?' Jack allowed no lapse of time. 'You know all the places around here. Lead us to a good one.'

'This way, my old and fragrant fruit.' Northrop led off with a flourish, and again Jack tensed. The walk led straight past the third-class, apparently deserted dock of which a certain ultra-fast vessel was the only occupant. If nothing happened for fifteen more seconds...

Nothing did. The laughing, chattering four came abreast of the portal. The door swung open and the Lensmen went into action.

They did not like to strong-arm women, but speed was their first consideration, with safety a close second; and it is impossible for a man to make speed while carrying a conscious, lithe, strong, heavily-armed

woman in such a position that she cannot use fists, feet, teeth, gun or knife. An unconscious woman, on the other hand, can be carried easily and safely enough. Therefore Jack spun his partner around, forced both of her hands into one of his. The free hand flashed upward toward the neck; a hard finger pressed unerringly against a nerve; the girl went limp. The two victims were hustled aboard and the spaceship, surrounded now by full-coverage screen, took off.

Kinnison paid no attention to ship or course; orders had been given long since and would be carried out. Instead, he lowered his burden to the floor, spread her out flat, and sought out and removed item after item of wiring, apparatus, and offensive and defensive armament. He did not undress her—quite—but he made completely certain that the only weapons left to the young lady were those with which Nature had endowed her. And, Northrop having taken care of his alleged cousin with equal thoroughness, the small-arms were sent out and both doors of the room were securely locked.

'Now, Hellcat Hazel DeForce,' Kinnison said, conversationally, 'You can snap out of it any time— you've been back to normal for at least two minutes. You've found out that your famous sex-appeal won't work. There's nothing loose you can grab, and you're too smart an operator to tackle me bare-handed. Who's the captain of your team—you or the clothes-horse?'

'Clothes-horse!' the statuesque brunette exclaimed, but her protests were drowned out. The blonde could— and did—talk louder, faster, and rougher.

'Do you think you can get away with *this*?' she demanded. 'Why, you... ' and the unexpurgated, trenchant, brilliantly detailed characterisation could

have seared its way through four-ply asbestos. 'And just what do you think you're going to do with me?'

'As to the first, I think so,' Kinnison replied, ignoring the deep-space verbiage. 'As to the second—as of now I don't know. What would you do if our situations were reversed?'

'I'd blast you to a cinder—or else take a knife and...'

'Hazel!' the brunette cautioned sharply. 'Careful! You'll touch them off and they'll...'

'Shut up, Jane! They won't hurt us any more than they have already; it's psychologically impossible. Isn't that true, copper?' Hazel lighted a cigarette, inhaled deeply, and blew a cloud of smoke at Kinnison's face.

'Pretty much so, I guess,' the Lensman admitted, frankly enough, 'but we can put you away for the rest of your lives.'

'Space-happy? Or do you think I am?' she sneered. 'What would you use for a case? We're as safe as if we were in God's pocket. And besides, our positions *will* be reversed pretty quick. You may not know it, but the fastest ships in space are chasing us, right now.'

'For once you're wrong. We've got plenty of legs ourselves and we're blasting for rendezvous with a task-force. But enough of this chatter. I want to know what job you're on and why you picked on us. Give.'

'Oh, does 'oo?' Hazel cooed, venomously. 'Come and sit on mama's lap, itty bitty soldier boy, and she'll tell you everything you want to know.'

Both Lensmen probed, then, with everything they had, but learned nothing of value. The women did not know what the Patrolmen were trying to do, but they were so intensely hostile that their mental blocks, unconscious although they were, were as effective as

full-driven thought screens against the most insidious approaches the men could make.

'Anything in their hand-bags, Mase?' Jack asked, finally.

'I'll look... Nothing much—just this,' and the very tonelessness of Northrop's voice made Jack look up quickly.

'Just a letter from the boy-friend.' Hazel shrugged her shoulders. Nothing hot—not even warm—go ahead and read it.'

'Not interested in what it says, but it might be smart to develop it, envelope and all, for invisible ink and whatnot.' He did so, deeming it a worthwhile expenditure of time. He already knew what the hidden message was; but no one not of the Patrol should know that no transmission of intelligence, however coded or garbled or disguised or by whatever means sent, could be concealed from any wearer of Arisia's Lens.

'Listen, Hazel,' Kinnison said, holding up the now slightly stained paper. ' "Three six two"—that's you, I suppose, and you're the squad leader—"Men mentioned previously being investigated stop assign three nine eight"—that must be you, Jane—"and make acquaintance stop if no further instructions received by eighteen hundred hours liquidate immediately stop party one".'

The blonde operative lost for the first time her brazen control. 'Why...that code is *unbreakable!*' she gasped.

'Wrong again, Gentle Alice. Some of us are specialists.' He directed a thought at Northrop. 'This changes things slightly, Mase. I was going to turn them loose, but now I don't know. Better we take it up with the boss, don't you think?'

'Pos-i-*tive*-ly!'

Samms was called, and considered the matter for approximately one minute. 'Your first idea was right, Jack. Let them go. The message may be helpful and informative, but the women would not. They know nothing. Congratulations, boys, on the complete success of Operation Red Herring.'

'Ouch!' Jack grimaced mentally to his partner after the First Lensman had cut off. 'They know enough to be in on bumping you and me off, but that ain't important, says he!'

'And it ain't, bub,' Northrop grinned back. 'Moderately so, maybe, if they had got us, but not at all now they can't. The Lensmen have landed and the situation is well in hand. It is written. Selah.'

'Check. Let's wrap it up.' Jack turned to the blonde. 'Come on, Hazel. Out. Number Four lifeboat. Do you want to come peaceably or shall I work on your neck again?'

'You could think of other places that would be more fun.' She got up and stared directly into his eyes, her lip curling. 'That is, if you were a *man* instead of a sublimated Boy Scout.'

Kinnison, without a word, wheeled and unlocked a door. Hazel swaggered forward, but the taller girl hung back. 'Are you sure there's air—and they'll pick us up? Maybe they're going to make us breathe space...'

'Huh? They haven't got the guts,' Hazel sneered. 'Come on, Jane. Number Four, you said, darling?'

She led the way. Kinnison opened the portal. Jane hurried aboard, but Hazel paused and held out her arms.

'Aren't you even going to kiss mama goodbye, baby boy?' she taunted.

'Better not waste much more time. We blow this boat, sealed or open, in fifteen seconds.' By what effort Kinnison held his voice level and expressionless, he hoped the wench would never know.

She looked at him, started to say something, looked again. She had gone just about as far as it was safe to go. She stepped into the boat and reached for the lever. And as the valve was swinging smoothly shut the men heard a tinkling laugh, reminiscent of icicles breaking against steel bells.

'Hell's—Brazen—Hinges!' Kinnison wiped his forehead as the lifeboat shot away. Hazel was something brand new to him; a phenomenon with which none of his education, training, or experience had equipped him to cope. 'I've heard about the guy who got hold of a tiger by the tail, but...' His thought expired on a wondering, confused note.

'Yeah.' Northrop was in no better case. 'We won—technically—I guess—or did we? That was a God-awful drubbing we took, mister.'

'Well, we got away alive, anyway... We'll tell Parker his dope is correct to the proverbial twenty decimals. And now that we've escaped, let's call Spud and see how things came out.'

And Costigan-Jones assured them that everything had come out very well indeed. The shipment of thionite had been followed without any difficulty at all, from the space-ship clear through to Jones' own office, and it reposed now in Department Q's own safe, under Jones' personal watch and ward. The pressure had lightened tremendously, just as Kinnison and Northrop had thought it would, when they set up their diversion. Costigan listened impassively to the whole story.

'Now *should* I have shot her, or not?' Jack demanded. 'Not whether I *could* have or not—I couldn't—but *should* I have, Spud?'

'I don't know.' Costigan thought for minutes. 'I don't think so. No—not in cold blood. I couldn't have, either, and wouldn't if I could. It wouldn't be worth it. Somebody will shoot her some day, but not one of us—unless, of course, it's in a fight.'

'Thanks, Spud; that makes me feel better. Off.'

Costigan-Jones' desk was already clear, since there was little or no paper-work connected with his position in Department Q . Hence his preparations for departure were few and simple. He merely opened the safe, stuck the package into his pocket, closed and locked the safe, and took a company ground-car to the spaceport.

Nor was there any more formality about his leaving the planet. Eridan had, of course, a Customs frontier of sorts; but since Uranium Inc. owned Eridan in fee simple, its Customs paid no attention whatever to company ships or to low-number, gold-badge company men. Nor did Jones need ticket, passport, or visa. Company men rode company ships to and from company plants, wherever situated, without let or hindrance. Thus, wearing the aura of power of his new position—and Gold Badge Number Thirty Eight—George W. Jones was whisked out to the uranium ship and was shown to his cabin.

Nor was it surprising that the trip from Eridan to Earth was completely without incident. This was an ordinary freighter, hauling uranium on a routine flight. Her cargo was valuable, of course—the sine qua non of inter-stellar trade—but in no sense precious. Not pirate-bait, by any means. And only two men knew that this flight was in any whit different from the one which had preceded it or the one which would follow it. If this ship was escorted or guarded the fact was not

apparent: and no Patrol vessel came nearer to it than four detets—Virgil Samms and Roderick Kinnison saw to that.

The voyage, however, was not tedious. Jones was busy every minute. In fact, there were scarcely minutes enough in which to assimilate the material which Isaacson had given him—the layouts, flow-sheets, and organisation charts of Works Number Eighteen, on Tellus.

And upon arrival at the private spaceport which was an integral part of Works Number Eighteen, Jones was not surprised (he knew more now than he had known a few weeks before; and infinitely more than the man on the street) to learn that the Customs men of this particular North American Port of Entry were just as complaisant as were those of Eridan. They did not bother even to count the boxes, to say nothing of inspecting them. They stamped the ship's papers without either reading or checking them. They made a perfunctory search, it is true, of crewmen and quarters, but a low number gold badge was still a magic talisman. Unquestioned, sacrosanct, he and his baggage were escorted to the ground-car first in line.

'Administration Building,' Jones-Costigan told the hacker, and that was that.

CHAPTER 16

It has been said that the basic drive of the Eddorians was a lust for power; a thought which should be elucidated and perhaps slightly modified. Their warrings, their strifes, their internecine intrigues and connivings were inevitable because of the tremendousness and capability—and the limitations—of their minds. Not enough *could* occur upon any one planet to keep such minds as theirs even partially occupied; and, unlike the Arisians, they could not satiate themselves in a static philosophical study of the infinite possibilities of the Cosmic All. They had to be *doing* something; or, better yet, making other and lesser beings do things to make the physical universe conform to their idea of what a universe should be.

Their first care was to set up the various echelons of control. The second echelon, immediately below the Masters, was of course the most important, and after a survey of both galaxies they decided to give this high honour to the Ploorans. Ploor, as is now well known, was a planet of a sun so variable that all Plooran life had to undergo radical cyclic changes in physical form in order to live through the tremendous climatic changes involved in its every year. Physical form, however, meant nothing to the Eddorians. Since no other planet even remotely like theirs existed in this, our normal plenum, physiques like theirs would be impossible; and the Plooran mentality left very little to be desired.

In the third echelon there were many different races, among which the frigid-blooded, poison-breathing Eich were perhaps the most efficient and most callous; and in the fourth there were millions upon millions of entities representing thousands upon thousands of wide-variant races.

Thus, at the pinpoint in history represented by the time of Virgil Samms and Roderick Kinnison, and Eddorians were busy; and if such a word can be used, happy. Gharlane of Eddore, second in authority only to the All-Highest, His Ultimate Supremacy himself, paid little attention to any one planet or to any one race. Even such a mind as his, when directing the affairs of twenty million and then sixty million and then a hundred million worlds, can do so only in broad, and not in fine.

And thus the reports which were now flooding in to Gharlane in a constantly increasing stream concerned classes and groups of worlds, and solar systems, and galactic regions. A planet might perhaps be mentioned as representative of a class, but no individual entity lower than a Plooran was named or discussed. Gharlane analysed those tremendous reports; collated, digested, compared, and reconciled them; determined trends and tendencies and most probable resultants. Gharlane issued orders, the carrying out of which would make an entire galactic region fit more and ever more exactly into the Great Plan.

But, as has been pointed out, there was one flaw inherent in the Boskonian system. Underlings, then as now, were prone to gloss over their own mistakes, to cover up their own incompetences. Thus, since he had no reason to inquire specifically, Gharlane did not know that anything whatever had gone amiss on Sol Three, the pestiferous planet which had formerly caused him more trouble than all the rest of his worlds combined.

After the fact, it is easy to say that he should have continued his personal supervision of Earth, but can that view be defended? Egotistical, self-confident, arrogant, Gharlane *knew* that he had finally whipped Tellus into line. It was the same now as any other planet of its class. And even had he thought it worthwhile to

make such a glaring exception, would not the fused Elders of Arisia have intervened?

Be those things as they may, Gharlane did not know that the new-born Galactic Patrol had been successful in defending Triplanetary's Hill against the Black Fleet. Nor did the Plooran Assistant Director in charge. Nor did any member of that dreadful group of Eich which was even then calling itself the Council of Boskone. The highest-ranking Boskonian who knew of the fiasco, calmly confident of his own ability, had not considered this minor reverse of sufficient importance to report to his immediate superior. He had already taken steps to correct the condition. In fact, as matters now stood, the thing was more fortunate than otherwise, in that it would lull the Patrol into believing themselves in a position of superiority—a belief which would, at election time, prove fatal.

This being, human to the limit of classification except for a faint but unmistakable blue coloration, had been closeted with Senator Morgan for a matter of two hours.

'In the matters covered, your reports have been complete and conclusive,' the visitor said finally, 'but you have not reported on the Lens.'

'Purposely. We are investigating it, but any report based upon our present knowledge would be partial and inconclusive.'

'I see. Commendable enough, usually. News of this phenomenon has, however, gone farther and higher than you think and I have been ordered to take cognisance of it; to decide whether or not to handle it myself.'

'I am thoroughly capable of...'

'I will decide that, not you.' Morgan subsided. 'A partial report is therefore in order. Go ahead.'

'According to the procedure submitted and approved, a Lensman was taken alive. Since the Lens has telepathic properties, and hence is presumably operative at great distances, the operation was carried out in the shortest possible time. The Lens, immediately upon removal from the Patrolman's arm, ceased to radiate and the operative who held the thing died. It was then applied by force to four other men—workers, these, of no importance. All four died, thus obviating all possibility of coincidence. An attempt was made to analyse a fragment of the active material, without success. It seemed to be completely inert. Neither was it affected by electrical discharges or by sub-atomic bombardment, nor by any temperatures available. Meanwhile, the man was of course being questioned, under truth-drug and beams. His mind denied any knowledge of the nature of the Lens; a thing which I am rather inclined to believe. His mind adhered to the belief that he obtained the Lens upon the planet Arisia. I am offering for your consideration my opinion that the high-ranking officers of the Patrol are using hypnotism to conceal the real source of the Lens.'

'Your opinion is accepted for consideration.'

'The man died during examination. Two minutes after his death his Lens disappeared.'

'Disappeared? What do you mean? Flew away? Vanished? Was stolen? Disintegrated? Or what?

'No. More like evaporation or sublimation, except that there was no gradual diminution in volume, and there was no detectable residue, either solid, liquid, or gaseous. The platinum-alloy bracelet remained intact.'

'And then?'

'The Patrol attacked in force and our expedition was destroyed.'

'You are sure of these observational facts?'

'I have the detailed records. Would you like to see them?'

'Send them to my office. I hereby relieve you of all responsibility in the matter of the Lens. In fact, even I may decide to refer it to a higher echelon. Have you any other material, not necessarily facts, which may have bearing?'

'None,' Morgan replied; and it was just as well for Virgilia Samms' continued well-being that the Senator did not think it worthwhile to mention the traceless disappearance of his Number One secretary and a few members of a certain unsavoury gang. To his way of thinking, the Lens was not involved, except perhaps very incidentally. Herkimer, in spite of advice and orders, had probably got rough with the girl, and Samms' mob had rubbed him out. Served him right.

'I have no criticism of any phase of your work. You are doing a particularly nice job on thionite. You are of course observing all specified precautions as to key personnel?'

'Certainly. Thorough testing and unremitting watchfulness. Our Mr. Isaacson is about to promote a man who has proved very satisfactory. Keep them that way. Goodbye.' The visitor strode out.

Morgan reached for a switch, then drew his hand back. No. He would like to sit in on the forthcoming interview, but he did not have the time. He had tested Olmstead repeatedly and personally; he knew what the man was. It was Isaacson's department; let Isaacson handle it. He himself must work full time at the job which only he could handle; the Nationalists must and would win this forthcoming election.

And in the office of the president of Interstellar Spaceways, Isaacson got up and shook hands with George Olmstead.

'I called you in for two reasons. First, in reply to your message that you were ready for a bigger job. What makes you think that any such are available?'

'Do I need to answer that?'

'Perhaps not... no.' The magnate smiled quietly. Morgan was right; this man could not be accused of being dumb. 'There is such a job, you are ready for it, and you have your successor trained in the work of harvesting. Second, why did you cut down, instead of increasing as ordered, the weight of broadleaf per trip? This, Olmstead, is really serious.'

'I explained why. It would have been more serious the other way. Didn't you believe I knew what I was talking about?'

'Your reasoning may have been distorted in transmittal. I want it straight from you.'

'Very well. It isn't smart to be greedy. There's a point at which something that has been merely a nuisance becomes a thing that *has* to be wiped out. Since I didn't want to be in that ferry when the Patrol blows it out of the ether, I cut down the take, and I advise you to keep it down. What you're getting now is a lot more than you ever got before, and a *hell* of a lot more than none at all. Think it over.'

'I see. Upon what basis did you arrive at the figure you established?'

'Pure guesswork, nothing else. I guessed that about three hundred percent of the previous average per month ought to satisfy anybody who wasn't too greedy to have good sense, and that more than that would ring a loud, clear bell right where we don't want any noise made. So I cut it down to three, and advised Ferdy either to keep it at three or quit while he was still all in one piece.'

'You exceeded your authority...and were insubordinate...but it wouldn't surprise me if you were right. You are certainly right in principle, and the poundage can be determined by statistical and psychological analysis. But in the meantime, there is tremendous pressure for increased production.'

'I know it. Pressure be damned. My dear cousin Virgil is, as you already know, a crackpot. He is visionary, idealistic, full of sweet and beautiful concepts of what the universe would be like if there weren't so many people like you and me in it; but don't ever make the mistake of writing him off as anybody's fool. And you know, probably better than I do, what Rod Kinnison is like. If I were you I'd tell whoever is doing the screaming to shut their damn mouths before they get their teeth kicked down their throats.'

'I'm very much inclined to take your advice. And now as to this proposed promotion. You are of course familiar in a general way with our operation at Northport?'

I could scarcely help knowing *something* about the biggest uranium works on Earth. However, I am not well enough qualified in detail to make a good technical executive.'

'Nor is it necessary. Our thought is to make you a key man in a new and increasingly important branch of the business, known as Department Q. It is concerned neither with production nor with uranium.'

'Q as in "quiet", eh? I'm listening with both ears. What duties would be connected with this...er...position? What would I really do?'

Two pairs of hard eyes locked and held, staring yieldlessly into each other's depths.

'You would not be unduly surprised to learn that substances other than uranium occasionally reach Northport?'

'Not *too* surprised, no,' Olmstead replied dryly. 'What would I do with it?'

'We need not go into that here or now. I offer you the position.'

'I accept it.'

'Very well. I will take you to Northport, and we will continue our talk en route.'

And in a spy-ray-proof, sound-proof compartment of a Spaceways-owned stratoliner they did so.

'Just for my information, Mr. Isaacson, how many predecessors have I had on this particular job, and what happened to them? The Patrol get them?'

'Two. No; we have not been able to find any evidence that the Samms crowd has any suspicion of us. Both were too small for the job; neither could handle personnel. One got funny ideas, the other couldn't stand the strain. If you don't get funny ideas, and don't crack up, you will make out in a big—and I mean *really* big—way.'

'If I do either I'll be more than somewhat surprised.' Olmstead's features set themselves into a mirthless, uncompromising, somehow bitter grin.

'So will I.' Isaacson agreed.

He knew what this man was, and just how case-hardened he was. He knew that he had fought Morgan himself to a scoreless tie after twisting Herkimer—and he was no soft touch—into a pretzel in nothing flat. At the thought of the secretary, so recently and so mysteriouslsy vanished, the magnate's mind left for a moment the matter in hand. What was at the bottom of that affair—the Lens or the woman? Or both? If he were in Morgan's shoes...but he wasn't. He had enough grief of his own, without worrying about any of Morgan's stinkeroos. He studied Olmstead's

inscrutable, subtly sneering smile and knew that he had made a wise decision.

'I gather that I am going to be one of the main links in the primary chain of deliveries. What's the technique, and how do I cover up?'

'Technique first. You go fishing. You are an expert at that, I believe?'

'You might say so. I won't have to do any faking there.'

'Some weekend soon, and every weekend later on, we hope, you will indulge in your favourite sport at some lake or other. You will take the customary solid and liquid refreshments along in a lunch-box. When you have finished eating you will toss the lunch-box overboard.'

'That all?'

'That's all.'

'The lunch-box, then, will be slightly special?'

'More or less, although it will look ordinary enough. Now as to the cover-up. How would "Director of Research" sound?'

'I don't know. Depends on what the researchers are doing. Before I became an engineer I was a pure scientist of sorts; but that was quite a while ago and I was never a specialist.'

'That is one reason why I think you will do. We have plenty of specialists—too many, I often think. They dash off in all directions, without rhyme or reason. What we want is a man with enough scientific training to know in general what is going on, but what he will need most is hard common sense, and enough ability—mental force, you might call it—to hold the specialists down to earth and make them pull together. If you can do it—and if I didn't think you could I

wouldn't be talking to you—the whole force will know that you are earning your pay; just as we could not hide the fact that your two predecessors weren't.'

'Put that way it sounds good. I wouldn't wonder if I could handle it.'

The conversation went on, but the rest of it is of little importance here. The plane landed. Isaacson introduced the new Director of Research to Works Manager Rand, who in turn introduced him to a few of his scientists and to the svelte and spectacular redhead who was to be his private secretary.

It was clear from the first that the Research Department was not going to be an easy one to manage. The top men were defiant, the middle ranks were sullen, the smaller fry were apprehensive as well as sullen. The secretary flaunted chips on both shapely shoulders. Men and women alike expected the application of the old wheeze "a new broom sweeps clean" for the third time in scarcely twice that many months, and they were defying him to do his worst. Wherefore they were very much surprised when the new boss did nothing whatever for two solid weeks except read reports and get acquainted with his department.

'How d'ya like your new boss, May?' another secretary asked, during a break.

'Oh, not too bad...I guess.' May's tone was full of reservations. 'He's quiet—sort of reserved—no passes or anything like that—it'd be funny if I finally got a boss that has something on the ball, wouldn't it? But you know what, Molly?' The redhead giggled suddenly. 'I had a camera-fiend first, you know, with a million credits' worth of stereo-cams and such stuff, and then a golf-nut. I wonder what this Dr. Olmstead does with his spare cash?'

'You'll find out, dearie, no doubt.' Molly's tone gave the words a meaning slightly different from the semantic one of their arrangement.

'I intend to, Molly—I *fully* intend to.' May's meaning, too, was not expressed exactly by the sequence of words used. 'It must be tough, a boss's life. Having to sit at a desk or be in conference six or seven hours a day—when he isn't playing around somewhere—for a measley thousand credits or so a month. How do they get that way?'

'You said it, May. You *really* said it. But we'll get ours, huh?'

Time went on. George Olmstead studied reports, and more reports. He read one, and re-read it, frowning. He compared it minutely with another; then sent redheaded May to hunt up one which had been turned in a couple of weeks before. He took them home that evening, and in the morning he punched three buttons. Three stiffly polite young men obeyed his summons.

'Good morning, Doctor Olmstead.'

'Morning, boys. I'm not up on the fundamental theory of any one of these three reports, but if you combine this, and this, and this,' indicating heavily-pencilled sections of the three documents, 'would you, or would you not, be able to work out a process that would do away with about three-quarters of the final purification and separation processes?'

They did not know. It had not been the business of any one of them, or all of them collectively, to find out.

'I'm making it your business as of now. Drop whatever you're doing, put your heads together, and find out. Theory first, then a small-scale laboratory experiment. Then come back here on the double.'

'Yes, sir,' and in a few days they were back.

'Does it work?'

'In theory it should, sir, and on a laboratory scale it does.'

The three young mèn were, if possible, even stiffer than before. It was not the first time, nor would it be the last, that a Director of Research would seize credit for work which he was not capable of doing.

'Good. Miss Read, get me Rand... Rand? Olmstead. Three of my boys have just hatched out something that may be worth quite a few million credits a year to us... Me? Hell, no! Talk to them. I can't understand any one of the three parts of it, to say nothing of inventing it. I want you to give 'em a class AAA priority on the pilot plant, as of right now. If they can develop it, and I'm betting they can, I'm going to put their pictures in the Northport News and give 'em a couple of thousand credits apiece and a couple of weeks vacation to spend it in... Yeah, I'll send 'em in.' He turned to the flabbergasted three. 'Take your dope in to Rand—now. Show him what you've got; then tear into that pilot plant.'

And, a little later, Molly and May again met in the powder room.

'So your new boss is a *fisherman!*' Molly snickered. 'And they say he paid over *two hundred credits* for a *reel!* You were right, May; a boss's life must be mighty hard to take. And he sits around more and does less, they say, than any other exec in the plant.'

'*Who* says so, the dirty, sneaking liars?' The redhead blazed, completely unaware that she had reversed her former position. 'And even if it *was* so, which it isn't, he can do more work sitting perfectly still than any other boss in the whole Works can do tearing around at forty parsecs a minute, so there!'

George Olmstead was earning his salary.

His position was fully consolidated when, a few days later, a tremor of excitement ran through the Research Department. 'Heads up, everybody! Mr. Isaacson—himself—is coming—*here!* What for, I wonder? Y'don't s'pose he's going to take the Old Man away from us already, do you?'

He came. He went through, for the first time, the entire department. He observed minutely, and he understood what he saw.

Olmstead led the Big Boss into his private office and flipped the switch which supposedly rendered that sanctum proof against any and all forms of spying, eavesdropping, intrusion and communication. It did not, however, close the deeper, subtler channels which the Lensmen used.

'Good work, George. So *damned* good that I'm going to have to take you out of Department Q entirely and make you Works Manager of our new plant on Vegia. Have you got a man you can break in to take your place here?'

'Including Department Q? No.' Although Olmstead did not show it; he was disappointed at hearing the word "Vegia". He had been aiming much higher than that—at the secret planet of the Boskonian Armed Forces, no less—but there might still be enough time to win a transfer there.

'Excluding. I've got another good man here now for that. Jones. Not heavy enough, though, for Vegia.'

'In that case, yes. Dr. Whitworth, one of the boys who worked out the new process. It'll take a little time, though. Three weeks minimum.'

'Three weeks it is. Today's Friday. You've got things in shape, haven't you, so that you can take the weekend off?'

'I was figuring on it. I'm not going where I thought I was, though, I imagine.'

'Probably not. Lake Chesuncook, on Route 273. Rough country, and the hotel is something less than fourth rate, but the fishing can't be beat.'

'I'm glad of that. When I fish, I like to catch something.'

'It would smell if you didn't. They stock lunch-boxes in the cafeteria, you know. Have your girl get you one, full of sandwiches and stuff. Start early this afternoon, as soon as you can after I leave. Be sure and see Jones, with your lunch-box, before you leave. Goodbye.'

'Miss Reed, please send Whitworth in. Then skip down to the cafeteria and get me a lunch-box. Sandwiches and a thermos of coffee. Provender suitable for a wet and hungry fisherman.'

'Yes, *sir!*' There were no chips now; the redhead's boss was the top ace of the whole plant.

'Hi, Ned. Take the throne.' Olmstead waved his hand at the now vacant chair behind the big desk. 'Hold it down 'til I get back. Monday, maybe.'

'Going fishing, huh?' Gone was all trace of stiffness, of reserve, of unfriendliness. 'You big, lucky stiff!'

'Well, my brilliant young squirt, maybe you'll get old and fat enough to go fishing yourself some day. Who knows? 'Bye.'

Lunch-box in hand and encumbered with tackle, Olmstead walked blithely along the corridor to the office of Assistant Works Manager Jones. While he had not known just what to expect, he was not surprised to see a lunch-box exactly like his own upon the side-table. He placed his box beside it.

'Hi, Olmstead.' By no slightest flicker of expression did either Lensman step out of character. Shoving off early?'

'Yeah. Dropped by to let the Head Office know I won't be in 'til Monday.'

'OK. So'm I, but more speed for me. Chemquassabamticook Lake.'

'Do you pronounce that or sneeze it? But have fun, my boy. I'm combining business with pleasure, though—breaking in Whitworth on my job. That Fairplay thing is going to break in about an hour, and it'll scare the pants off of him. But it'll keep until Monday, anyway, and if he handles it right he's just about in.'

Jones grinned. 'A bit brutal, perhaps, but a sure way to find out. 'Bye.'

'So long.,' Olmstead strolled out, nonchalantly picking up the wrong lunch-box on the way, and left the building.

He ordered his Dillingham, and tossed the lunch-box aboard as carelessly as though it did not contain an unknown number of millions of credits' worth of clear-quill, uncut thionite.

'I hope you have a nice weekend, sir,' the yard-man said, as he helped stow baggage and tackle.

'Thanks, Otto. I'll bring you a couple of fish Monday, if I catch that many,' and it should be said in passing that he brought them. Lensmen keep their promises, under whatever circumstances or however lightly given.

It being mid-afternoon of Friday, the traffic was already heavy. Northport was not a metropolis, of course; but on the other hand it did not have metropolitan multi-tiered, one-way, non-intersecting streets. But Olmstead was in no hurry. He inched his

spectacular mount—it was a violently iridescent chrome green in colour, with highly polished chromium gingerbread wherever there was any excuse for gingerbread to be—across the city and into the north-bound side of the super-highway. Even then, he did not hurry. He wanted to hit the inspection station at the edge of the Preserve at dusk. Ninety miles an hour would do it. He worked his way into the ninety-mile lane and became motionless relative to the other vehicles on the strip.

It was a peculiar sensation; it seemed as though the cars themselves were stationary, with the pavement flowing backward beneath them. There was no passing, no weaving, no cutting in and out. Only occasionally would the formation be broken as a car would shift almost imperceptibly to one side or the other; speeding up or slowing down to match the assigned speed of the neighbouring way.

The afternoon was bright and clear, neither too hot nor too cold. Olmstead enjoyed his drive thoroughly, and arrived at the turn-off right on schedule. Leaving the wide, smooth way, he slowed down abruptly; even a Dillingham Super-Sporter could not make speed on the narrow, rough, and hilly road to Chesuncook Lake.

At dusk he reached the Post. Instead of stopping on the pavement he pulled off the road, got out, stretched hugely, and took a few drum-major's steps to take the kinks out of his legs.

'A lot of road, eh?' the smartly-uniformed trooper remarked. 'No guns?'

'No guns.' Olmstead opened up for inspection. 'From Northport. Funny, isn't it, how hard it is to stop, even when you aren't in any particular hurry? Guess I'll eat now—join me in a sandwich and some hot coffee or a cold lemon sour or cherry soda?'

'I've got my own supper, thanks; I was just going to eat. But did you say a *cold* lemon sour?'

'Uh-huh. Ice-cold. Zero degrees Centigrade.'

'I *will* join you, in that case. Thanks.'

Olmstead opened a frost-lined compartment; took out two half-litre bottles; placed them and his open lunch-box invitingly on the low stone wall.

'Hm…m…m. Quite a zipper you got there, mister.'

The trooper gazed admiringly at the luxurious, two-wheeled monster; listened appreciatively to its almost inaudible hum. 'I've heard about those new supers, but that is the first one I ever saw. Nice. All the comforts of home, eh?'

'Just about. Sure you won't help me clean up on those sandwiches, before they get stale?'

Seated on the wall, the two men ate and talked. If that trooper had known what was in the box beside his leg he probably would have fallen over backward; but how was he even to suspect? There was nothing crass or rough or coarse about any of the work of any of Boskone's high-level operators.

Olmstead drove on to the lake and took up his reservation at the ramshackle hotel. He slept, and bright and early the next morning he was up and fishing—and this part of the performance he really enjoyed. He knew his stuff and the fish were there; bit, wary, and game. He loved it.

At noon he ate, and quite openly and brazenly consigned the "empty" box to the watery deep. Even if he had not had so many fish to carry, he was not the type to lug a cheap lunch-box back to town. He fished joyously all afternoon, without getting quite the limit, and as the sun grazed the horizon he started his putt-putt and skimmed back to the dock.

The thing hadn't sent out any radiation yet, Northrop informed him tensely, but it certainly would, and when it did they'd be ready. There were Lensmen and Patrolmen all over the place, thicker than hair on a dog.

And George Olmstead, sighing wearily and yet blissfully anticipatory of one more day of enthralling sport, gathered up his equipment and his fish and strolled toward the hotel.

CHAPTER 17

Forty thousand miles from Earth's centre the *Chicago* loafed along a circular arc, inert, at a mere ten thousand miles an hour; a speed which, and not by accident, kept her practically stationary above a certain point on the planet's surface. Nor was it by chance that both Virgil Samms and Roderick Kinnison were aboard. And a dozen or so other craft, cruisers and such, whose officers were out to put space-time in their logs, were flitting aimlessly about; but never very far away from the flagship. And farther out—well out—a cordon of diesel-powered detector ships swept space to the full limit of their prodigious reach. The navigating officers of those vessels knew to a nicety the place and course of every ship lawfully in the ether, and the appearance of even one unscheduled trace would set in motion a long succession of carefully-planned events.

And far below, grazing atmosphere, never very far from the direct line between the *Chicago* and Earth's core, floated a palatial pleasure yacht. And this craft carried not one Lensman, or two, but eight; two of whom kept their eyes fixed upon their observation plates. They were watching a lunch-box resting upon the bottom of a lake.

'Hasn't it radiated yet?' Roderick Kinnison demanded. 'Or been approached, or moved?'

'Not yet,' Lyman Cleveland replied, crisply. 'Neither Northrop's rig nor mine has shown any sign of activity.'

He did not amplify the statement, nor was there need. Mason Northrop was a Master Electronocist; Cleveland was perhaps the world's greatest living

expert. Neither of them had detected radiation. Ergo, none existed.

Equally certainly the box had not moved, or been moved, or approached. 'No change, Rod,' Doctor Frederick Rodebush Lensed the assured thought. 'Six of us have been watching the plates in five-minute shifts.'

A few minutes later, however: 'Here is a thought which may be of interest,' DalNalten the Venerian announced, spraying himself with a couple pints of water. 'It is natural enough, of course, for any Venerian to be in or on any water he can reach—I would enjoy very much being on or in that lake myself—but it may not be entirely by coincidence that one particular Venerian, Ossmen, is visiting this particular lake at this particular time.'

'What!' Nine Lensmen yelled the thought practically as one.

'Precisely. Ossmen.' It was a measure of the Venerian Lensman's concern that he used only two words instead of twenty or thirty. 'In the red boat with the yellow sail.'

'Do you see any detector rigs?' Samms asked.

'He wouldn't need any,' DalNalten put in. 'He will be able to see it. Or, if a little colane had been rubbed on it which no Tellurian could have noticed, any Venerian could smell it from one end of that lake to the other.'

'True. I didn't think of that. It may not have a transmitter after all.'

'Maybe not, but keep on listening, anyway,' The Port Admiral ordered. 'Bend a plate on Ossmen, and a couple more on the rest of the boats. But Ossmen is clean, you say, Jack? Not even a spy-ray block?'

'He couldn't have a block, Dad. It'd give too much away, here on our home grounds. Like on Eridan, where their ops could wear anything they could lift, but we had to go naked.' He flinched mentally as he recalled his encounter with Hazel the Hell-cat, and Northrop flinched with him.

'That's right, Rod,' Olmstead in his boat below agreed, and Conway Costigan, in his room in Northport, concurred. The top-drawer operatives of the enemy depended for safety upon perfection of technique, not upon crude and dangerous mechanical devices.

'Well, since you're all so sure of it, I'll buy it,' and the waiting went on.

Under the slight urge of the light and vagrant breeze, the red boat moved slowly across the water. A somnolent, lackadaisical youth, who very evidently cared nothing about where the boat went, sat in its stern, with his left arm draped loosely across the tiller. Nor was Ossmen any more concerned. His only care, apparently, was to avoid interference with the fishermen; his under-water jaunts were long, even for a Venerian, and he entered and left the water as smoothly as only a Venerian—or a seal—could.

'However, he could have, and probably has got, a capsule spy-ray detector,' Jack offered, presently. 'Or, since a Venerian can swallow anything one inch smaller than a kitchen stove, he could have a whole analysing station stashed away in his stomach. Nobody's put a beam on him yet, have you?'

Nobody had.

'It might be smart not to. Watch him with 'scopes… and when he gets up close to the box, better pull your beams off of it. DalNalten, I don't suppose it would be quite bright for you to go swimming down there too, would it?'

'Very definitely not, which is why I am up here and dry. None of them would go near it.'

They waited, and finally Ossmen's purposeless wanderings brought him over the spot on the lake's bottom which was the target of so many Tellurian eyes. He gazed at the discarded lunch-box as incuriously as he had looked at so many other sunken objects, and swam over it as casually—and only the ultra-cameras caught what he actually did. He swam serenely on.

'The box is still there,' the spy-ray men reported, 'but the package is gone.'

'Good!' Kinnison exclaimed. 'Can you 'scopists see it on him?'

'Ten to one they can't,' Jack said. 'He swallowed it. I expected him to swallow it box and all.'

'We can't see it, sir. He must have swallowed it.'

'Make sure.'

'Yes, sir... He's back on the boat now and we've shot him from all angles. He's clean—nothing outside.'

'Perfect! That means he isn't figuring on slipping it to somebody else in a crowd. This will be an ordinary job of shadowing from here on in, so I'll put in the umbrella.'

The detector ships were recalled. The *Chicago* and the various other ships of war returned to their various bases. The pleasure craft floated away. But on the other hand there were bursts of activity throughout the forest for a mile or so back from the shores of the lake. Camps were struck. Hiking parties decided that they had hiked enough and began to retrace their steps. Lithe young men, who had been doing this and that, stopped doing it and headed for the nearest trails.

For Kinnison *pre* had erred slightly in saying that the rest of the enterprise was to be an ordinary job of shadowing. No ordinary job would do. With the game this nearly in the bag it must be made absolutely certain that no suspicion was aroused, and yet Samms had to have *facts*. Sharp, hard, clear facts; facts so self-evidently facts that no intelligence above idiot grade could possibly mistake them for anything but facts.

Wherefore Ossmen the Venerian was not alone thenceforth. From lake to hotel, from hotel to car, along the road, into and in and out of train and plane, clear to an ordinary-enough-looking building in an ordinary business section of New York, he was *never* alone. Where the travelling population was light, the Patrol operatives were few and did not crowd the Venerian too nearly; where dense, as in a metropolitan station, they ringed him three deep.

He reached his destination, which was of course spy-ray proofed, late Sunday night. He went in, remained briefly, came out.

'Shall we spy-ray him, Virge? Follow him? Or what?'

'No spy-rays. Follow him. Cover him like a blanket. At the usual time give him the usual spy-ray going-over, but not until then. This time, make it *thorough*. Make certain that he hasn't got it on him, in him, or in or around his house.'

'There'll be nothing doing here tonight, will there?'

'No, it would be too noticeable. So you, Fred, and Lyman, take the first trick; the rest of us will get some sleep.'

When the building opened Monday morning the Lensmen were back, with dozens of others, including Knobos of Mars. There were also present or nearby literally hundreds of the shrewdest, most capable detectives of Earth.

'So *this* is their headquarters—one of them at least,' the Martian thought, studying the trickle of people entering and leaving the building. 'It is as we thought, Dal, why we could never find it, why we could never trace any wholesaler backward. None of us has ever seen any of these persons before. Complete change of personnel per operation; probably interplanetary. Long periods of quiescence. Check?'

'Check: but we have them now.'

'Just like that, huh?' Jack Kinnison jibed; and from his viewpoint his idea was the more valid, for the wholesalers were very clever operators indeed.

From the more professional viewpoint of Knobos and DalNalten, however, who had fought a steadily losing battle so long, the task was not too difficult. Their forces were beautifully organised and synchronised; they were present in such overwhelming numbers that "tails" could be changed every fifteen seconds; long before anybody, however suspicious, could begin to suspect any one shadow. Nor was it necessary for the tails to signal each other, however inconspicuously, or to indicate any suspect at change-over time. Lensed thoughts directed every move, without confusion or error.

And there were tiny cameras with tremendous, protuberant lenses, the "long eyes" capable of taking wire-sharp close ups from five hundred feet; and other devices and apparatus and equipment too numerous to mention here.

Thus the wholesalers were traced and their transactions with the retail peddlers were recorded. And from that point on, even Jack Kinnison had to admit that the sailing was clear. These small fry were not smart, and their customers were even less so. None had screens or detectors or other apparatus; their every transaction could be and was recorded from a distance of many miles by the ultra-instruments of the Patrol.

And not only the transactions. Clearly, unmistakably, the purchaser was followed from buying to sniffing; nor was the time intervening ever long. Thionite, then as now, was bought at retail only to use, and the whole ghastly thing went down on tape and film. The gasping, hysterical appeal; the exchange of currency for drug; the headlong rush to a place of solitude; the rigid muscle-lock and the horribly ecstatic transports; the shaken, soul-searing recovery or the entranced death. It all went on record. It was sickening to have to record such things. More than one observer did sicken in fact, and had to be relieved. But Virgil Samms had to have concrete, positive, irrefutable evidence. He got it. Any possible jury, upon seeing that evidence, would know it to be the truth; no possible jury, after seeing that evidence, could bring in any verdict other than "guilty".

Oddly enough, Jack Kinnison was the only casualty of that long and hectic day. A man—later proved to be a middle-sized potentate of the underworld—who was not even under suspicion at the time, for some reason or other got the idea that Jack was after him. The Lensman had, perhaps, allowed some part of his long eye to show; a fast and efficient long-range telephoto lens is a devilishly awkward thing to conceal. At any rate the racketeer sent out a call for help, just in case his bodyguards would not be enough, and in the meantime his personal attendants rallied enthusiastically around.

They had two objects in view; One, to pass a knife expeditiously and quietly through young Kinnison's throat from ear to ear; and: Two, to tear the long eye apart and subject a few square inches of super-sensitive emulsion to the bright light of day. And if the Big Shot had known that the photographer was not alone, that the big, hulking bruiser a few feet away was also a bull, they might have succeeded.

Two of the four hoods reached Jack just fractionally ahead of the other two; one to seize the camera, the other to swing the knife. But Jack Kinnison was fast; fast of brain and nerve and muscle. He saw them coming. In three flashing motions he bent the barrel of the telephoto into a neat arc around the side of the first man's head, ducked frantically under the fiercely-driven knife, and drove the toe of his boot into the spot upon which prize-fighters like to have their rabbit-punches land. Both of those attackers lost interest promptly. One of them lost interest permanently; for a telephoto lens in barrel is heavy, very rigid, and very, very hard.

While Battling Jack was still off balance, the other two guards arrived—but so did Mason Northrop. Mase was not quite as fast as Jack was; but, as has been pointed out, he was bigger and much stronger. When he hit a man, with either hand, that man dropped. It was the same as being on the receiving end of the blow of a twenty-pound hammer falling through a distance of ninety seven and one-half feet.

The Lensmen had of course also yelled for help, and it took only a split second for a Patrol speedster to travel from any given point to any other in the same county. It took no time at all for that speedster to fill a couple of square blocks with patterns of force through which neither bullets nor beams could be driven. Therefore the battle ended as suddenly as it began; before more thugs, with their automatics and portables, could reach the scene.

Kinnison *fils* cursed and damned fulminantly the edict which had forbidden arms that day, and swore that he would never get out of bed again without strapping on at least two blasters; but he had to admit finally that he had nothing to squawk about. Kinnison *pre* explained quite patiently—for him—that all he had got out of the little fracas was a split lip, that young Northrop's hair wasn't even mussed, and that if

everybody had been packing guns some scatter-brained young damn fool like him would have started blasting and blown everything higher than up—would have spoiled Samms' whole operation maybe beyond repair. Now would he please quit bellyaching and get to hell out?

He got.

'That buttons thionite up, don't you think?' Rod Kinnison asked. 'And the lawyers will have plenty of time to get the case licked into shape and lined up for trial.'

'Yes and no.' Samms frowned in thought. 'The *evidence* is complete, from original producer to ultimate consumer; but our best guess is that it will take years to get the really important offenders behind bars.'

'Why? I thought you were giving them altogether too much time when you scheduled the blow-off for three weeks ahead of election.'

'Because the drug racket is only a small part of it. We're going to break the whole thing at once, you know, and Mateese covers a lot more ground—murder, kidnapping, bribery, corruption, misfeasance—practically everything you can think of.'

'I know. What of it?'

'Jurisdiction, among other things. With the President, over half of the Congress, much of the judiciary, and practically all of the political bosses and police chiefs of the Continent under indictment at once, the legal problem becomes incredibly difficult. The Patrol's Department of Law has been working on it twenty four hours a day, and the only thing they seem

sure of is a long succession of bitterly-contested points of law. There are no precedents whatever.'

'Precedents be damned! They're guilty and everybody knows it. We'll change the laws so that...'

'We will *not!*' Samms interrupted, sharply. 'We want and we will have government by law, not by men. We have had too much of that already. Speed is not of the essence; justice very definitely is.'

' "Crusader" Samms, now and forever! But I'll buy it, Virge—now let's get back down to earth. Operation Zwilnik. That leaves Operation Boskone, which is, I suppose, still getting nowhere fast.'

The First Lensman did not reply. It was, and both men knew it. The shrewdest, most capable and experienced operatives of the Patrol had hit that wall with everything they had, and had simply bounced. Low-level trials had found no point of contact, no angle of approach. Middle level, ditto. George Olmstead, working at the highest possible level, was morally certain that he had found a point of contact, but had not been able to do anything with it.

'How about calling a Council conference on it?' Kinnison asked finally. 'Or Bergenholm at least? Maybe he can get one of his hunches on it.'

'I have discussed it with them all, just as I have with you. No one had anything constructive to offer, except to go ahead with Bennett as you are doing. The consensus is that the Boskonians know just as much about our military affairs as we know about theirs— no more.'

'It *would* be too much to expect them to be dumb enough to figure us as dumb enough to depend only on our visible Grand Fleet, after the warning they gave us at The Hill,' Kinnison admitted.

'Yes. What worries me most is that they had a running start.'

'Not enough to count,' the Port Admiral declared. 'We can out-produce 'em and out-fight 'em.'

'Don't be over-optimistic. You can't deny them the possession of brains, ability, man-power and resources at least equal to ours.'

'I don't have to.' Kinnison remained obstinately cheerful. 'Morale, my boy, is what counts. Man-power and tonnage and fire-power are important, of course, but morale has won every war in history. And our morale right now is higher than a cat's back—higher than any time since John Paul Jones—and getting higher by the day.'

'Yes?' The question was monosyllabic but potent.

'Yes. I mean just that -yes. From what we know of their system they *can't* have the morale we've got. Anything they can do we can do more of and better. What you've got, Virge, is a bad case of ingrowing nerves. You've never been to Bennett, in spite of the number of times I've asked you to. I say take time right now and come along—it'll be good for what ails you. It will also be a very fine thing for Bennett and for the Patrol—you'll find yourself no stranger there.'

'You may have something there... I'll do it.'

Port Admiral and First Lensman went to Bennett, not in the *Chicago* or other superdreadnought, but in a two-man speedster. This was necessary because space-travel, as far as that planet was concerned, was a strictly one-way affair except for Lensmen. Only Lensmen could leave Bennett, under any circumstances or for any reason whatever. There was no outgoing mail, express, or freight. Even the war-vessels of the Fleet, while on practice manoeuvres outside the bottle-tight envelopes surrounding the system, were so

screened that no unauthorised communication could possible be made.

'In other words,' Kinnison finished explaining, 'we slapped on everything anybody could think of, including Bergenholm and Rularion; and believe me, brother, that was a lot of stuff.'

'But wouldn't the very fact of such rigid restrictions operate against morale? It is a truism of psychology that imprisonment, like everything else, is purely relative.'

'Yeah, that's what I told Rularion, except I used simpler and rougher language. You know how sarcastic and superior he is, even when he's wrong?'

'How I know!'

'Well, when he's right he's too damned insufferable for words. You'd've thought he was talking to the prize boob of a class of half-wits. As long as nobody on the planet knew that there was any such thing as space-travel, or suspected that they were not the only form of intelligent life in the universe, it was all right. No such concept as being planet-bound could exist. They had all the room there was. But after they met us, and digested all the implications, they would develop the colly-wobbles no end. This, of course, is an extreme simplification of the way the old coot poured it into me; but he came through with the solution, so I took it like a little man.'

'What was the solution?'

'It's a shame you were too busy to come in on it. You'll see when we land.'

But Virgil Samms was quick on the uptake. Even before they landed, he understood. When the speedster slowed down for atmosphere he saw blazoned upon the clouds a welter of one many-times repeated signal; as they came to ground he saw that

the same set of symbols was repeated, not only upon every available cloud, but also upon airships, captive balloons, streamers, roofs and sides of buildings— even, in multi-coloured rocks and flower-beds, upon the ground itself.

'Twenty Haress,' Samms translated, and frowned in thought. 'A date of the Bennettan year. Would it by any chance happen to coincide with our Tellurian November fourteenth of this present year?'

'Bright boy!' Kinnison applauded. 'I thought you'd get it, but not so fast. Yes—election day.'

'I see. They know what is going on, then?'

'Everything that counts. They know what we stand to win—and lose. They've named it Liberation Day, and everything on the planet is building up to it in a grand crescendo. I was a little afraid of it at first, but if the screens are really tight it won't make any difference how many people know it, and if they aren't the beans would all be spilled anyway. And it really works—I get a bigger thrill every time I come here.'

'I can see where it might work.'

Bennett was a fully Tellurian world in mass, in atmosphere and in climate; her native peoples were human to the limit of classification, both physically and mentally. And first Lensman Samms, as he toured it with his friend, found a world aflame with a zeal and an ardour unknown to bless Earth since the days of the Crusades. The Patrol's cleverest and shrewdest psychologists, by merely sticking to the truth, had done a marvellous job.

Bennett knew that it was the Arsenal and the Navy Yard of Civilisation, and it was proud of it. Its factories were humming as they had never hummed before; every industry, every business, every farm was operating at one hundred percent of capacity. Bennett was dotted and spattered with spaceports already built,

and hundreds more were being rushed to completion. The already staggering number of ships of war operating out of those ports was being augmented every hour by more and ever more ultra-modern, ultra-fast, ultra-powerful shapes.

It was an honour to help build those ships; it was a still greater one to help man them. Competitive examinations were being held constantly, nor were all or even most of the applicants native Bennettans.

Samms did not have to ask where these young people were coming from. He knew. From all the planets of Civilisation, attracted by carefully-worded advertisements of good jobs at high pay on new and highly secret projects on newly discovered planets. There were hundreds of such ads. Most were probably the Patrol's and led here; many were of Spaceways, Uranium Incorporated, and other mercantile firms. The possibility that some of them might lead to what was now being called Boskonia had been tested thoroughly, but with uniformly negative results. Lensmen had applied by scores for those non-Patrol jobs and had found them bona-fide. The conclusion was unavoidable—Boskone was doing its recruitment on planets unknown to any wearer of Arisia's Lens. On the other hand, more than a trickle of Boskonians were applying for Patrol jobs, but Samms was almost certain that none had been accepted. The final screening was done by Lensmen, and in such matters Lensmen did not make many or serious mistakes.

Bennett had been informed of the First Lensman's arrival, and Kinnison had been guilty of a gross understatement indeed in telling Samms that he would not be regarded as a stranger. Wherever Samms went he was met by wildly enthusiastic crowds. He had to make speeches, each of which was climaxed by a tremendous roar of 'TO LIBERATION DAY!'

'No Lensman material here, you say, Rod?' Samms asked, after the first city-shaking demonstration was over. One of his prime concerns, throughout his life, was this. 'With all this enthusiasm? Sure?'

'We haven't found any good enough to refer to you yet. However, in a few years, when the younger generation gets a little older, there certainly will be.'

'Check.' The tour of inspection and acquaintance was finished, the two Lensmen started back to Earth.

'Well, my sceptical and pessimistic friend, was I lying, or not?' Kinnison asked, as soon as the speedster's ports were sealed. 'Can they match that or not?'

'You weren't—and I don't believe they can. I have never seen anything like it. Autocracies have parades and cheers and demonstrations, of course, but they have always been forced—artificial. Those were spontaneous.'

'Not only that, but the enthusiasm will carry through. We'll be piping hot and ready to go. But about this stumping—you said I'd better start as soon as we get back?'

'Within a few days, I'd say.'

'I wouldn't wonder, so let's use this time in working out a plan of campaign. My idea is to start out like this…'

CHAPTER 18

Conway Costigan, leaving behind him scores of clues, all highly misleading, severed his connection with Uranium, Inc. as soon as he dared after Operation Zwilnik had been brought to a successful close. The technical operation, that is; the legal battles in which it figured so largely were to run on for enough years to make the word "zwilnik" a common noun and adjective in the language.

He came to Tellus as unobtrusively as was his wont, and took an inconspicuous but very active part in Operation Mateese, now in full swing.

'Now is the time for all good men and true to come to the aid of the party, eh?' Clio Costigan giggled.

'You can play that straight across the keyboard of your electric, pet, and not with just two fingers, either. Did you hear what the boss told 'em today?'

'Yes.' The girl's levity disappeared. 'They're so *dirty*, Spud—I'm really afraid.'

'So am I. But we're not too lily-fingered ourselves if we have to be and we're covering 'em like a blanket—Kinnison and Samms both.'

'Good.'

'And in that connection, I'll have to be out half the night again tonight. All right?'

'Of course. It's so nice having you home at all, darling, instead of a million light-years away, that I'm practically delirious with delight.'

It was sometimes hard to tell what impish Mrs. Costigan meant by what she said. Costigan looked at

her, decided she was taking him for a ride, and smacked her a couple of times where it would do the most good. He then kissed her thoroughly and left. He had very little time, these days, either to himself or for his lovely and adored wife.

For Roderick Kinnison's campaign, which had started out rough and not too clean, became rougher and rougher, and no cleaner, as it went along. Morgan and his crew were swinging from the heels, with everything and anything they could dig up or invent, however little of truth or even of plausibility it might contain, and Rod the Rock had never held in principle with the gentle precept of turning the other cheek. He was rather an Old Testamentarian, and he was no neophyte at dirty fighting. As a young operative, skilled in the punishing, maiming techniques of hand-to-hand rough-and-tumble combat, he had brawled successfully in most of the dives of most of the solarian planets and of most of their moons. With this background, and being a quick study, and under the masterly coaching of Virgil Samms, Nels Bergenholm, and Rularion of North Polar Jupiter, it did not take him long to learn the various gambits and ripostes of this non-physical, but nevertheless no-holds-barred, political mayhem.

And the "boys and girls" of the Patrol worked like badgers, digging up an item here and a fact there and a bit of information somewhere else, all for the day of reckoning which was to come. They used ultra-wave scanners, spy-rays, long eyes, stool-pigeons— everything they could think of to use—and they could not *always* be blocked out or evaded.

'We've got it, boss—now let's *use* it!'

'No. Save it! Nail it down, solid! Get the facts— names, dates, places, and amounts. Prove it first— then save it!'

Prove it! Save it! The joint injunction was used so often that it came to be a slogan and was accepted as such. Unlike most slogans, however, it was carefully and diligently put to use. The operatives proved it and saved it, over and over, over and over again; by dint of what unsparing effort and self-less devotion only they themselves ever fully knew.

Kinnison stumped the Continent. He visited every state, all of the big cities, most of the towns, and many villages and hamlets; and always, wherever he went, a part of the show was to demonstrate to his audiences how the Lens worked.

'Look at me. You know that no two individuals are or ever can be alike. Robert Johnson is not like Fred Smith; Joe Jones is entirely different from John Brown. Look at me again. Concentrate upon whatever it is in your mind that makes me Roderick Kinnison, the individual. That will enable each of you to get into as close touch with me as though our two minds were one. I am not talking now; you are reading my mind. Since you are reading my very mind, you know exactly what I am *really* thinking, for better or for worse. It is impossible for my mind to lie to yours, since I can change neither the basic pattern of my personality nor my basic way of thought; nor would I if I could. Being in my mind, you know that already; you know what my basic quality is. My friends call it strength and courage; Pirate Chief Morgan and his cut-throat crew call it many other things. Be that as it may, you now know whether or not you want me for your President. I can do nothing whatever to sway your opinion, for what your minds have perceived you know to be the truth. That is the way the Lens works. It bares the depths of my mind to yours, and in return enables me to understand your thoughts.

'But it is in no sense hypnotism, as Morgan is so foolishly trying to make you believe. Morgan knows as well as the rest of us do that even the most

accomplished hypnotist, with all his apparatus, CAN NOT AFFECT A STRONG AND DEFINITE OPPOSED WILL. He is therefore saying that each and every one of you now receiving this thought is such a spineless weakling that—but you may draw your own conclusions.

'In closing, remember—nail this fact down so solidly that you will never forget it—a sound and healthy mind CAN NOT LIE. The Mouth can, and does. So does the typewriter. But the mind—NEVER! I can hide my thoughts from you, even while we are en rapport, like this...but I CAN NOT LIE TO YOU. That is why, some day, all of your highest executives will have to be Lensmen, and not politicians, diplomats, crooks and boodlers. I thank you.'

As that long, bitter, incredibly vicious campaign neared its vitriolic end tension mounted higher and ever higher: and in a room in the Samms home three young Lensmen and a red-haired girl were not at ease. All four were lean and drawn. Jack Kinnison was talking.

'...not the party, so much, but Dad. He started out with bare fists, and now he's wading into 'em with spiked brass knuckles.'

'You can play *that* across the board,' Costigan agreed.

'He's really giving 'em hell,' Northrop said, admiringly.

'Did you boys listen in on his Casper speech last night?'

They hadn't; they had been too busy.

'I could give it to you on your Lenses, but I couldn't reproduce the tone—the exquisite way he lifted large pieces of hide and rubbed salt into the raw places. When he gets excited you know he can't help but use

voice, too, so I got some of it on a record. He starts out on voice, nice and easy, as usual; then goes onto his Lens without talking; then starts yelling as well as thinking. Listen:'

'You ought to have a Lensman president. You may not believe that any Lensman is, and as a matter of fact *must* be incorruptible. That is my belief, as you can feel for yourselves, but I cannot *prove* it to you. Only time can do that. It is a self-evident fact, however, which you can feel for yourselves, that a Lensman president could not lie to you except by word of mouth or in writing. You could demand from him at any time a Lensed statement upon any subject. Upon some matters of state he could and should refuse to answer; but not upon any question involving moral turpitude. If he answered, you would know the truth. If he refused to answer, you would know why and could initiate impeachment proceedings then and there.

'In the past there have been presidents who used that high office for low purposes; whose very memory reeks of malfeasance and corruption. One was impeached, others should have been. Witherspoon never should have been elected. Witherspoon should have been impeached the day after he was inaugurated. Witherspoon should be impeached now. We know, and at the Grand Rally at New York Spaceport three weeks from tonight we are going to PROVE, that Witherspoon is simply a minor cog-wheel in the Morgan-Towne-Isaacson machine, "playing footsie" at command with whatever group happens to be the highest bidder at the moment, irrespective of North America's or the System's good. Witherspoon is a gangster, a cheat, and a God Damn liar, but he is of very little actual importance; merely a boodling nincompoop. Morgan is the real boss and the real menace, the Operating Engineer of the lowest-down, lousiest, filthiest, rottenest, most corrupt machine of murderers, extortionists, bribe-takers, panderers,

perjurers, and other pimples on the body politic that has ever disgraced any so-called civilised government. Good night.'

'Wow!' Jack Kinnison yelped. 'That's high, even for him!'

'Just a minute, Jack,' Jill cautioned. 'The other side, too. Listen to this choice bit from Senator Morgan.'

'It is not exactly hypnotism, but something infinitely worse; something that steals away your very minds; that makes anyone listening believe that white is yellow, red, purple, or pea-green. Until our scientists have checked this menace, until we have every wearer of that cursed Lens behind steel bars, I advise you in all earnestness not to listen to them at all. If you do listen your minds will surely be insidiously decomposed and broken; you will surely end your days gibbering in a padded cell.

'And murders? *Murders!* The feeble remnants of the gangs which our government has all but wiped out may perhaps commit a murder or so per year; the perpetrators of which are caught, tried, and punished. But how many of your sons and daughters has Roderick Kinnison murdered, either personally or through his uniformed slaves? Think! Read the record! Then make him explain, if he can; but do not listen to his lying, mind-destroying Lens.

'Democracy? Bah! What does "Rod the Rock" Kinnison—the hardest, most vicious tyrant, the most relentless and pitiless martinet ever known to any Armed Force in the long history of our world—know of democracy? Nothing! He understands only force. All who oppose him in anything, however small, or who seek to reason with him, die without record or trace; and if he is not arrested, tried, and executed, all such will continue, tracelessly and without any pretence of trial, to die.

'But at bottom, even though he is not intelligent enough to realise it, he is merely one more in the long parade of tools of ruthless and predatory wealth, the MONIED POWERS. *They*, my friends, never sleep; they have only one God, one tenet, one creed—the almighty CREDIT. *That* is what they are after, and note how craftily, how stealthily, they have done and are doing their grabbing. Where is your representation upon that so-called Galactic Council? How did this criminal, this vicious, this outrageously unconstitutional, this irresponsible, uncontrollable, and dictatorial monstrosity come into being? How and when did you give this bloated colossus the right to establish its own currency—to have the immeasurable effrontery to debar the solidest currency in the universe, the credit of North America, from interplanetary and interstellar commence? Their aim is clear; they intend to tax you into slavery and death. Do not forget for one instant, my friends, that the power to tax is the power to destroy. THE POWER TO TAX IS THE POWER TO DESTROY. Our forefathers fought and bled and died to establish the principle that taxation without rep...'

'And so on, for one solid hour!' Jill snarled, as she snapped the switch viciously. 'How do you like *them* potatoes?'

'Hell's—Blazing—Pinnacles!' This from Jack, silent for seconds, and:

'Rugged stuff...very, *very* rugged.' from Northrop. 'No wonder you look sort of pooped, Spud. Being Chief Bodyguard must have developed recently into quite a chore.'

'You ain't just snapping your choppers, bub,' was Costigan's grimly flippant reply. 'I've yelled for help—in force.'

'So have I, and I'm going to yell again, right now,' Jack declared. 'I don't know whether Dad is going to

kill Morgan or not—and don't give a damn—but if Morgan isn't going all out to kill Dad it's because they've forgotten how to make bombs.'

He Lensed a call to Bergenholm.

'Yes, Jack?...I will refer you to Rularion, who has had this matter under consideration.'

'Yes, John Kinnison, I have considered the matter and have taken action,' the Jovian's calmly assured thought rolled into the minds of all, even Lensless Jill's. 'The point, youth, was well taken. It was your thought that some thousands—perhaps five—of spy-ray operators and other operatives will be required to insure that the Grand Rally will not be marred by episodes of violence.'

'It was,' Jack said, flatly. 'It still is.'

'Not having considered all possible contingencies nor the extent of the field of necessary action, you err. The number will approach nineteen thousand very nearly. Admiral Clayton has been so advised and his staff is now at work upon a plan of action in accordance with my recommendation. Your suggestions, Conway Costigan, in the matter of immediate protection of Roderick Kinnison's person, are now in effect, and you are hereby relieved of that responsibility. I assume that you four wish to continue at work?'

The Jovian's assumption was sound.

'I suggest, then, that you confer with Admiral Clayton and fit yourselves into his programme of security. I intend to make the same suggestion to all Lensmen and other qualified persons not engaged in work of more pressing importance.'

Rularion cut off and Jack scowled blackly. 'The Grand Rally is going to be held three weeks before election day. I *still* don't like it. I'd save it until the

night before election—knock their teeth out with it at the last possible minute.'

'You're wrong, Jack; the Chief is right,' Costigan argued. 'Two ways. One, we can't play that kind of ball. Two, this gives them just enough rope to hang themselves.'

'Well...maybe.' Kinnison-like, Jack was far from being convinced. 'But that's the way it's going to be, so let's call Clayton.'

'First,' Costigan broke in. 'Jill, will you please explain why they have to waste as big a man as Kinnison on such a piffling job as president? I was out in the sticks, you know—it doesn't make sense.'

'Because he's the only man alive who can lick Morgan's machine at the polls,' Jill stated a simple fact. 'The Patrol can get along without him for one term, after that it won't make any difference.'

'But Morgan works from the side-lines. Why couldn't he?'

'The psychology is entirely different. Morgan *is* a boss. Pops Kinnison isn't. He's a leader. See?'

'Oh...I guess so...Yes. Go ahead.'

Outwardly, New York Spaceport did not change appreciably. At any given moment of day or night there were so many hundreds of persons strolling aimlessly or walking purposefully about that an extra hundred or so made no perceptible difference. And the spaceport was only the end-point. The Patrol's activities began hundreds of thousands or millions or billions of miles away from Earth's metropolis.

A web was set up through which not even a grain-of-sand meteorite could pass undetected. Every space-

ship bound for Earth carried at least one passenger who would not otherwise have been aboard; passengers who, if not wearing Lenses, carried Service Special equipment amply sufficient for the work in hand. Geigers and other vastly more complicated mechanisms flew toward Earth from every direction in space; streamed toward New York in Earth's every channel of traffic. Every train and plane, every bus and boat and car, every conveyance of every kind and every pedestrian approaching New York City was searched; with a search as thorough as it was unobtrusive. And every thing and every entity approaching New York Spaceport was combed, literally by the cubic millimetre.

No arrests were made. No package was confiscated, or even disturbed, throughout the ranks of public check boxes, in private offices, or in elaborate or casual hiding-places. As far as the enemy knew, the Patrol had no suspicion whatever that anything out of the ordinary was going on. That is, until the last possible minute. Then a tall, lean, space-tanned veteran spoke softly aloud, as though to himself:

'Spy-ray blocks—interference—umbrella—on. Report.'

That voice, low and soft as it was, was picked up by every Service Special receiver within a radius of a thousand miles, and by every Lensman listening, wherever he might be. So were, in a matter of seconds, the replies.

'Spy-ray blocks on, sir.'

'Interference on, sir.'

'Umbrella on, sir.'

No spy-ray could be driven into any part of the tremendous port. No beam, communicator or detonating, could operate anywhere near it. The enemy would now know that something had gone

wrong, but he would not be able to do anything about it.

'Reports received,' the tanned man said, still quietly. 'Operation Zunk will proceed as scheduled.'

And four hundred seventy one highly skilled men, carrying duplicate keys and/or whatever other specialised apparatus and equipment would be necessary, quietly took possession of four hundred seventy one objects, of almost that many shapes and sizes. And, out in the gathering crowd, a few disturbances occurred and a few ambulances dashed busily here and there. Some women had fainted, no doubt, ran the report. They always did.

And Conway Costigan, who had been watching, without seeming even to look at him, a porter loading a truck with opulent-looking hand-luggage from a locker, followed man and truck out into the concourse. Closing up, he asked:

'Where are you taking that baggage, Charley?'

'Up Ramp One, boss,' came the unflurried reply. 'Flight ninety will be late taking off, on accounta this jamboree, and they want it right up there handy.'

'Take it down to the...'

Over the years a good many men had tried to catch Conway Costigan off guard or napping, to beat him to the punch or to the draw—with a startlingly uniform lack of success. The Lensman's fist travelled a bare seven inches: the supposed porter gasped once and travelled—or rather, staggered backward—approximately seven feet before he collapsed and sprawled unconscious upon the pavement.

'Decontamination,' Costigan remarked, apparently to empty air, as he picked the fellow up and draped him limply over the truckful of suitcases. 'Deke. Front

and centre. Area forty-six. Class Eff-ex—hotter than the middle tailrace of hell.'

'You called Deke?' A man came running up. 'Eff-ex six—nineteen. This it?'

'Check. It's yours, porter and all. Take it away.'

Costigan strolled on until he met Jack Kinnison, who had a rapidly-developing mouse under his left eye.

'How did *that* happen, Jack?' he demanded sharply. 'Something slip?'

'Not exactly.' Kinnison grinned ruefully. 'I have the *damndest* luck! A woman—an old lady at that—thought I was staging a hold-up and swung on me with her hand-bag—southpaw and from the rear. And if you laugh, you untuneful harp, I'll hang one right on the end of your chin, so help me.

'Far be it from such,' Costigan assured him, and did not—quite—laugh. 'Wonder how we came out? They should have reported before this—p-s-s-t! Here it comes!'

Decontamination was complete; Operation Zunk had been a one-hundred-percent success; there had been no casualties.

'Except for one black eye,' Costigan could not help adding; but his Lens and his Service Specials were off. Jack would have brained him if any of them had been on.

Linking arms, the two young Lensmen stroke away toward Ramp Four, which was to be their station.

This was the largest crowd Earth had ever known. Everybody, particularly the Nationalists, had wondered why this climactic political rally had been set for three full weeks ahead of the election, but their curiosity had not been satisfied. Furthermore, this meeting had

been advertised as no previous one had ever been; neither pains nor cash had been spared in giving it the greatest build-up ever known. Not only had every channel of communication been loaded for weeks, but also Samms' workers had been very busily engaged in starting rumours; which grew, as rumours do, into things which their own fathers and mothers could not recognise. And the baffled Nationalists, trying to play the whole thing down, made matters worse. Interest spread from North America to the other continents, to the other planets, and to the other solar systems.

Thus, to say that everybody was interested in, and was listening to, the Cosmocrats' Grand Rally would not be too serious an exaggeration.

Roderick Kinnison stepped up to the battery of microphones; certain screens were cut.

'Fellow entities of Civilisation and others: while it may seem strange to broadcast a political rally to other continents and to beam it to other worlds, it was necessary in this case. The message to be given, while it will go into the political affairs of the North American Continent of Tellus, will deal primarily with a far larger thing; a matter which will be of paramount importance to all intelligent beings of every inhabited world. You know how to attune your minds to mine. Do it now.'

He staggered mentally under the shock of encountering practically simultaneously so many minds, but rallied strongly and went on, via Lens:

'My first message is not to you, my fellow Cosmocrats, nor to you, my fellow dwellers on Earth, nor even to you, my fellow adherents to Civilisation; but to THE ENEMY. I do not mean my political opponents, the Nationalists, who are almost all loyal fellow North Americans. I mean the entities who are using the leaders of that Nationalist party as pawns in a vastly larger game.

'I know, ENEMY, that you are listening. I know that you had goon squads in this audience, to kill me and my superior officer. Know now that they are impotent. I know that you had atomic bombs, with which to obliterate this assemblage and this entire area. They have been disassembled and stored. I know that you had large supplies of radio-active dusts. They now lie in the Patrol vaults near Weekhauken. All the devices which you intended to employ are known, and all save one have been either nullified or confiscated.

'That one exception is your war-fleet, a force sufficient in your opinion to wipe out all the Armed Forces of the Galactic Patrol. You intended to use it in case we Cosmocrats win this forthcoming election; you may decide to use it now. Do so if you like; you can do nothing to interrupt or to affect this meeting. This is all I have to say to you, Enemy of Civilisation.

'Now to you, my legitimate audience. I am not here to deliver the address promised you, but merely to introduce the real speaker—First Lensman Virgil Samms...'

A mental gasp, millions strong, made itself tellingly felt.

'...Yes—First Lensman Samms, of whom you all know. He has not been attending political meetings because we, his advisers, would not let him. Why? Here are the facts. Through Archibald Isaacson, of Interstellar Spaceways, he was offered a bribe which would in a few years have amounted to some fifty billion credits; more wealth than any individual entity has ever possessed. Then there was an attempt at murder, which we were able—just barely—to block. Knowing there was no other place on Earth where he would be safe, we took him to The Hill. You know what happened; you know what condition The Hill is in now. This warfare was ascribed to pirates.

'The whole stupendous operation, however, was made in a vain attempt to kill one man—Virgil Samms. The Enemy knew, and we learned, that Samms is the greatest man who has ever lived. His name will last as long as Civilisation endures, for it is he, and *only* he, who can make it possible for Civilisation *to* endure.

'Why was I not killed? Why was I allowed to keep on making campaign speeches? Because I do not count. I am of no more importance to the cause of Civilisation than is my opponent Witherspoon to that of the Enemy.

'I am a wheel-horse, a plugger. You all know me— "Rocky Rod" Kinnison, the hard-boiled egg. I've got guts enough to stand up and fight for what I *know* is right. I've got the guts and the inclination to stand up and slug it out, toe to toe, with man, beast, or devil. I would make and WILL MAKE a good president; I've got the guts and inclination to keep on slugging after you elect me; before God I promise to smash down every machine-made crook who tries to hold any part of our government down in the reeking muck in which it now is.

'I am a plugger and a slugger, with no spark of the terrific flame of inspirational genius which makes Virgil Samms what he so uniquely is. My *kind* may be important, but I individually am not. There are *so* many of us! If they had killed me another slugger would have taken my place and the effect upon the job would have been nil.

'Virgil Samms, however, *can not be replaced* and the Enemy knows it. He is unique in all history. No one else can do his job. If he is killed before the principles for which he is working are firmly established Civilisation will collapse back into barbarism. It will not recover until another such mind comes into existence, the probability of which occurrence I will let you compute for yourselves.

'For those reasons Virgil Samms is not here in person. Nor is he in The Hill, since the Enemy may now possess weapons powerful enough to destroy not only that hitherto impregnable fortress, but also the whole Earth. And they would destroy Earth, without a qualm, if in so doing they could kill the First Lensman.

'Therefore Samms is now out in deep space. Our fleet is waiting to be attacked. If we win, the Galactic Patrol will go on. If we lose, we hope you shall have learned enough so that we will not have died uselessly.'

'Die? Why should *you* die? *You* are safe on Earth!'

'Ah, one of the goons sent that thought. If our fleet is defeated no Lensman, anywhere, will live a week. The Enemy will see to that.

'That is all from me. Stay tuned. Come in, First Lensman Virgil Samms—take over, sir.'

It was psychologically impossible for Virgil Samms to use such language as Kinnison had just employed. Nor was it either necessary or desirable that he should; the ground had been prepared. Therefore—coldly, impersonally, logically, tellingly—he told the whole terrific story. He revealed the most important things dug up by the Patrol's indefatigable investigators, reciting names, places, dates, transactions, and amounts. Only in the last couple of minutes did he warm up at all.

'Nor is this in any sense a smear campaign or a bringing of baseless charges to becloud the issue or to vilify without cause and upon the very eve of election a political opponent. These are facts. Formal charges are now being preferred; every person mentioned, and many others, will be put under arrest as soon as possible. If any one of them were in any degree innocent our case against him could be made to fall in less than the three weeks intervening before election day. That is why this meeting is being held at this time.

'Not one of them is innocent. Being guilty, and knowing that we can and will prove guilt, they will adopt a policy of delay and recrimination. Since our courts are, for the most part, just, the accused will be able to delay the trials and the actual presentation of evidence until after election day. Forewarned, however, you will know exactly why the trials will have been delayed, and in spite of the fog of misrepresentation you will know where the truth lies. You will know how to cast your votes. You will vote for Roderick Kinnison and for those who support him.

There is no need for me to enlarge upon the character of Port Admiral Kinnison. You know him as well as I do. Honest, incorruptible, fearless, you know that he will make the best president we have ever had. If you do not already know it, ask any one of the hundreds of thousands of strong, able, clear-thinking young men and women who have served under him in our Armed Forces.

'I thank you, everyone who has listened, for your interest.'

CHAPTER 19

As long as they were commodores, Clayton of North America and Schweikert of Europe had stayed fairly close to the home planet except for infrequent vacation trips. With the formation of the Galactic Patrol, however, and their becoming Admiral and Lieutenant-Admiral of the First Galactic Region, and their acquisition of Lenses, the radius of their sphere of action was tremendously increased. One or the other of them was always to be found in Grand Fleet Headquarters at New York Spaceport, but only very seldom were both of them there at once. And if the absentee were not to be found on Earth, what of it? The First Galactic Region included all of the solar systems and all of the planets adherent to Civilisation, and the absentee could, as a matter of business and duty, be practically anywhere.

Usually, however, he was not upon any of the generally-known planets, but upon Bennett—getting acquainted with the officers, supervising the drilling of Grand Fleet in new manoeuvres, teaching classes in advanced strategy, and holding skull-practice generally. It was hard work, and not too inspiring, but in the end it paid off big. They knew their men; their men knew them. They could work together with a snap, a smoothness, a precision otherwise impossible; for imported top brass, unknown to and unacquainted with the body of command, can not have and does not expect the deep regard and the earned respect so necessary to high morale.

Clayton and Schweikert had both. They started early enough, worked hard enough, and had enough stuff, to earn both. Thus it came about that when, upon a scheduled day, the two admirals came to Bennett

together, they were greeted as enthusiastically as though they had been Bennettans born and bred; and their welcome became a planet-wide celebration when Clayton issued the orders which all Bennett had been waiting so long and so impatiently to hear. Bennettans were at last to leave Bennett!

Group after group, sub-fleet after sub-fleet, the component units of the Galactic Patrol's Grand Fleet took off. They assembled in space; they manoeuvred enough to shake themselves down into some semblance of unity; they practised the new manoeuvres; they blasted off in formation for Sol. And as the tremendous armada neared the Solar System it met—or, rather, was joined by—the Patrol ships about which Morgan and his minions already knew; each of which fitted itself into its long-assigned place. Every planet of Civilisation had sent its every vessel capable of putting out a screen or of throwing a beam, but so immense was the number of warships in Grand Fleet that this increment, great as it intrinsically was, made no perceptible difference in its size.

On Rally Day Grand Fleet lay poised near Earth. As soon as he had introduced Samms to the intensely interested listeners at the Rally, Roderick Kinnison disappeared. Actually, he drove a bug to a distant corner of the spaceport and left the Earth in a light cruiser, but to all intents and purposes, so engrossed was everyone in what Samms was saying, Kinnison simply vanished. Samms was already in the *Boise*; the Port Admiral went out to his old flagship, the *Chicago*. Nor, in case any observer of the Enemy should be trying to keep track of him, could his course be traced. Cleveland and Northrop and Rularion and all they needed of the vast resources of the Patrol saw to that.

Neither Samms nor Kinnison had any business being with Grand Fleet in person, of course, and both knew it; but everyone knew why they were there and were glad that the two top Lensmen had decided to

live or die with their Fleet. If Grand Fleet won, they would probably live; if Grand Fleet lost they would certainly die—if not in the pyrotechnic dissolution of their ships, then in a matter of days upon the ground. With the Fleet their presence would contribute markedly to morale. It was a chance very much worth taking.

Nor were Clayton and Schweikert together, or even near each other. Samms, Kinnison, and the two admirals were as far away from each other as they could get and still remain in Grand Fleet's fighting cylinder.

Cylinder? Yes. The Patrol's Board of Strategy, assuming that the enemy would attack in conventional cone formation and knowing that one cone could defeat another only after a long and costly engagement, had long since spent months and months at war-games in their tactical tanks, in search of a better formation. They had found it. Theoretically, a cylinder of proper composition could defeat, with negligible loss and in a very short time, the best cones they were able to devise. The drawback was that the ships composing a theoretically efficient cylinder would have to be highly specialised and vastly greater in number than any one power had ever been able to put into the ether. However, with all the resources of Bennett devoted to construction, this difficulty would not be insuperable.

This of course, brought up the question of what would happen if cylinder met cylinder—if the Black strategists should also have arrived at the same solution—and this question remained unanswered. Or, rather, there were too many answers, no two of which agreed; like those to the classical one of what would happen if an irresistible force should strike an immovable object. There would be a lot of intensely interesting by-products!

Even Rularion of Jove did not come up with a definite solution. Nor did Bergenholm; who, although a comparatively obscure young Lensman-scientist and not a member of the Galactic Council, was frequently called into consultation because of his unique ability to arrive at correct conclusions via some obscurely short-circuiting process of thought.

'Well,' Port Admiral Kinnison had concluded, finally, 'If they've got one, too, we'll just have to shorten ours up, widen it out, and pray.'

'Clayton to Port Admiral Kinnison,' came a communication through channels. 'Have you any additional orders or instructions?'

'Kinnison to Admiral Clayton. None,' the Port Admiral replied, as formally, then went on via Lens: 'No comment or criticism to make, Alex. You fellows have done a job so far and you'll keep on doing one. How much detection have you got out?'

'Twelve detets—three globes of diesels. If we sit here and do nothing the boys will get edgy and go stale, so if you and Virge agree we'll give 'em some practice. Lord knows they need it, and it'll keep 'em on their toes. But about the Blacks—they may be figuring on delaying any action until we've had time to crack from boredom. What's your idea on that?'

'I've been worried about the same thing. Practice will help, but whether enough or not I don't know. What do you think, Virge? Will they hold it up deliberately or strike fast?'

'Fast,' the First Lensman replied, promptly and definitely. 'As soon as they possibly can, for several reasons. They don't know our real strength, any more than we know theirs. They undoubtedly believe, however, the same as we do, that they are more efficient than we are and have the larger force. By their own need of practice they will know ours. They

do not attach nearly as much importance to morale as we do; by the very nature of their regime they can't. Also, our open challenge will tend very definitely to force their hands, since face-saving is even more important to them than it is to us. They will strike as soon as they can and as hard as they can.'

Grand Fleet manoeuvres were begun, but in a day or so the alarms came blasting in. The enemy had been detected; coming in, as the previous Black Fleet had come, from the direction of Coma Berenices. Calculating machines clicked and whirred; orders were flashed, and a brief string of numbers; ships by the hundred and the thousands flashed into their assigned positions.

Or, more precisely, *almost* into them. Most of the navigators and pilots had not had enough practice yet to hit their assigned positions exactly on the first try, since a radical change in axial direction was involved, but they did pretty well; a few minutes of juggling and jockeying were enough. Clayton and Schweikert used a little caustic language—via Lens and to their fellow Lensmen only, of course—but Samms and Kinnison were well enough pleased. The time of formation had been very satisfactorily short and the cone was smooth, symmetrical, and of beautifully uniform density.

The preliminary formation was a cone, not a cylinder. It was not a conventional Cone of Battle in that it was not of standard composition, was too big, and had altogether too many ships for its size. It was, however, of the conventional shape, and it was believed that by the time the enemy could perceive any significant differences it would be too late for him to do anything about it. The cylinder would be forming about that time, anyway, and it was almost believed— at least it was strongly hoped—that the enemy would not have the time or the knowledge or the equipment to do anything about that, either.

Kinnison grinned to himself as his mind, en rapport with Clayton's, watched the enemy's Cone of Battle enlarge upon the Admiral's conning plate. It was big, and powerful; the Galactic Patrol's publicly-known forces would have stood exactly the chance of the proverbial snowball in the nether regions. It was not, however, the Port Admiral thought, big enough to form an efficient cylinder, or to handle the Patrol's real force in any fashion—and unless they shifted within the next second or two it would be too late for the enemy to do anything at all.

As though by magic about ninety five percent of the Patrol's tremendous cone changed into a tightly-packed double cylinder. This manoeuvre was much simpler than the previous one, and had been practised to perfection. The mouth of the cone closed in and lengthened; the closed end opened out and shortened. Tractors and pressors leaped from ship to ship, binding the whole myriad of hitherto discrete units into a single structure as solid, even comparatively as to size, as a cantilever bridge. And instead of remaining quiescent, waiting to be attacked, the cylinder flashed forward, inertialess, at maximum blast.

Throughout the years the violence, intensity, and sheer brute power of offensive weapons had increased steadily. Defensive armament had kept step. One fundamental fact, however, had not changed throughout the ages and has not changed yet. Three or more units of given power have always been able to conquer one unit of the same power, if engagements could be forced and no assistance could be given; and two units could practically always do so. Fundamentally, therefore, strategy always had been and still is the development of new artifices and techniques by virtue of which two or more of our units may attack one of theirs; the while affording the minimum of opportunity for them to retaliate in kind.

The Patrol's Grand Fleet flashed forward, almost exactly along the axis of the Black cone; right where the enemy wanted it—or so he thought. Straight into the yawning mouth, erupting now a blast of flame beside which the wildest imaginings of Inferno must pale into insignificance; straight along that raging axis toward the apex, at the terrific speed of the two directly opposed velocities of flight. But, to the complete consternation of the Black High Command, nothing much happened. For, as has been pointed out, that cylinder was not of even approximately normal composition. In fact, there was not a normal war-vessel in it. The outer skin and both ends of the cylinder were purely defensive. Those vessels, packed so closely that their repellor fields actually touched, were all screen; none of them had a beam hot enough to light a match. Conversely, the inner layer, or "Liner", was composed of vessels that were practically all offence. They had to be protected at every point—but *how* they could ladle it out!

The leading and trailing edges of the formation— the ends of the gigantic pipe, so to speak—would of course bear the brunt of the Black attack, and it was this factor that had given the Patrol's strategists the most serious concern. Wherefore the first ten and the last six double rings of ships were special indeed. They were *all* screen—nothing else. They were drones, operated by remote control, carrying no living thing. If the Patrol losses could be held to eight double rings of ships at the first pass and four at the second— theoretical computations indicated losses of six and two—Samms and his fellows would be well content.

All of the Patrol ships had, of course, the standard equipment of so-called "violet", "green" and "red" fields, as well as duodecaplylatomate and ordinary atomic bombs, dirigible torpedoes and transporters, slicers, polycyclic drills, and so on; but in this battle the principal reliance was to be placed upon the sheer,

brutal, overwhelming power of what had been called the "macro beam"—now simply the "beam". Furthermore, in the incredibly incandescent frenzy of the chosen field of action—the cylinder was to attack the cone at its very strongest part—no conceivable material projectile could have lasted a single microsecond after leaving the screens of force of its parent vessel. It could have flown fast enough; ultra-beam trackers could have steered it rapidly enough and accurately enough; but before it could have travelled a foot, even at ultra-light speed, it would have ceased utterly to be. It would have been resolved into its sub-atomic constituent particles and waves. Nothing material could exist, except instantaneously, in the field of force filling the axis of the Black's Cone of Battle; a field beside which the exact centre of a multi-billion-volt flash of lightning would constitute a dead area.

That field, however, encountered no material object. The Patrol's "screeners", packed so closely as to have a four hundred percent overlap, had been designed to withstand precisely that inconceivable environment. Practically all of them withstood it. And in a fraction of a second the hollow forward end of the cylinder engulfed, pipe-wise, the entire apex of the enemy's war-cone, and the hitherto idle "sluggers" of the cylinder's liner went to work.

Each of those vessels had one heavy pressor beam, each having the same push as every other, directed inward, toward the cylinder's axis, and backward at an angle of fifteen degrees from the perpendicular line between ship and axis. Therefore, wherever any Black ship entered the Patrol's cylinder or however, it was driven to and held at the axis and forced backward along that axis. None of them, however, got very far. They were perforce in single file; one ship opposing at least one solid ring of giant sluggers who did not have to concern themselves with defence, but could

pour every iota of their tremendous resources into offensive beams. Thus the odds were not merely two or three to one; but never less than eighty, and very frequently over two hundred to one.

Under the impact of those unimaginable torrents of force the screens of the engulfed vessels flashed once, practically instantaneously through the spectrum, and went down. Whether they had two or three or four courses made no difference—in fact, even the ultra-speed analysers of the observers could not tell. Then, a couple of microseconds later, the wall-shields—the strongest fabrics of force developed by man up to that time—also failed. Then those ravenous fields of force struck bare, unprotected metal, and every molecule, inorganic and organic, of ships and contents alike, disappeared in a bursting flare of energy so raw and so violent as to stagger even those who had brought it into existence. It was certainly vastly more than a mere volatilisation; it was deduced later that the detonating unstable isotopes of the Black's own bombs, in the frightful temperatures already existing in the Patrol's quasi-solid beams, had initiated a chain reaction which had resulted in the fissioning of a considerable proportion of the atomic nuclei of usually completely stable elements!

The cylinder stopped; the Lensmen took stock. The depth of erosion of the leading edge had averaged almost exactly six double rings of drones. In places the sixth ring was still intact; in others, which had encountered unusually concentrated beaming, the seventh was gone. Also, a fraction of one percent of the manned war-vessels had disappeared. Brief though the time of engagement had been, the enemy had been able to concentrate enough beams to burn a few holes through the walls of the attacking cylinder.

It had not been hoped that more than a few hundreds of Black vessels could be blown out of the ether at this first pass. General Staff had been sure,

however, that the heaviest and most dangerous ships, including those carrying the enemy's High Command, would be among them. The mid-section of the apex of the conventional Cone of Battle had always been the safest place to be; therefore that was where the Black admirals had been and therefore they no longer lived.

In a few seconds it became clear that if any Black High Command existed, it was not in shape to function efficiently. Some of the enemy ships were still blasting, with little or no concerted effort, at the regulation cone which the cylinder had left behind; a few were attempting to get into some kind of a formation, possibly to attack the Patrol's cylinder. Indecision was visible and rampant.

To turn that tremendous cylindrical engine of destruction around would have been a task of hours, but it was not necessary. Instead, each vessel cut its tractors and pressors, spun end for end, re-connected, and retraced almost exactly its previous course; cutting out and blasting into nothingness another "plug" of Black warships. Another reversal, another dash; and this time, so disorganised were the foes and so feeble the beaming, not a single Patrol vessel was lost. The Black fleet, so proud and so conquering of mien a few minutes before, had fallen completely apart.

'That's enough, Rod, don't you think?' Samms thought then. 'Please order Clayton to cease action, so that we can hold a parley with their senior officers.'

'Parley, hell!' Kinnison's answering thought was a snarl. 'We've got 'em going—mop 'em up before they can pull themselves together! Parley be damned!'

'Beyond a certain point military action becomes indefensible butchery, of which our Galactic Patrol will never be guilty. That point has now been reached. If you do not agree with me. I'll be glad to call a Council meeting to decide which of us is right.'

'That isn't necessary. You're right—that's one reason I'm not First Lensman.' The Port Admiral, fury and fire ebbing from his mind, issued orders; the Patrol forces hung motionless in space. 'As President of the Galactic Council, Virge, take over.'

Spy-rays probed and searched; a communicator beam was sent. Virgil Samms spoke aloud, in the lingua franca of deep space.

'Connect me, please, with the senior officer of your fleet.'

There appeared upon Samms' plate a strong, not unhandsome face; deep-stamped with the bitter hopelessness of a strong man facing certain death.

'You've got us. Come on and finish us.'

'Some such indoctrination was to be expected, but I anticipate no trouble in convincing you that you have been grossly misinformed in everything you have been told concerning us; our aims, our ethics, our morals, and our standards of conduct. There are, I assume, other surviving officers of your rank, although of lesser seniority?'

'There are ten other vice-admirals, but I am in command. They will obey my orders or die.'

'Nevertheless, they shall be heard. Please go inert, match our intrinsic velocity, and come aboard, all eleven of you. We wish to explore with all of you the possibilities of a lasting peace between our worlds.'

'Peace? Bah! Why lie?' The Black commander's expression did not change. 'I know what you are and what you do to conquered races. We prefer a clean, quick death in your beams to the kind you deal out in your torture rooms and experimental laboratories. Come ahead—I intend to attack you as soon as I can make a formation.'

'I repeat, you have been grossly, terribly, *shockingly* misinformed.' Samms' voice was quiet and steady; his eyes held those of the other. 'We are civilised men, not barbarians or savages. Does not the fact that we ceased hostilities so soon mean anything to you?'

For the first time the stranger's face change subtly, and Samms pressed the slight advantage.

'I see it does. Now if you will converse with me mind to mind...' The First Lensman felt for the man's ego and began to tune to it, but this was too much.

'I will not!' The Black put up a solid block. 'I will have nothing to do with your cursed Lens. I know what it is and will have none of it!'

'Oh, what's the use, Virge!' Kinnison snapped. 'Let's get on with it!'

'A great deal of use, Rod,' Samms replied, quietly. 'This is a turning-point. I *must* be right—I *can't* be that far wrong,' and he again turned his attention to the enemy commander.

'Very well, sir, we will continue to use spoken language. I repeat, please come aboard with your ten fellow vice-admirals. You will not be asked to surrender. You will retain your side-arms—as long as you make no attempt to use them. Whether or not we come to any agreement, you will be allowed to return unharmed to your vessels before the battle is resumed.'

'What? Side-arms? Returned? You swear it?'

'As President of the Galactic Council, in the presence of the highest officers of the Galactic Patrol as witnesses, I swear it.'

'We will come aboard.'

'Very well. I will have ten other Lensmen and officers here with me.'

The *Boise*, of course, inerted first; followed by the *Chicago* and nine of the tremendous tear-drops from Bennett. Port Admiral Kinnison and nine other Lensmen joined Samms in the *Boise's* con room; the tight formation of eleven Patrol ships blasted in unison in the space-courtesy of meeting the equally tight formation of Black warships half-way in the matter of intrinsic velocity.

Soon the two little sub-fleets were motionless in respect to each other. Eleven Black gigs were launched. Eleven Black vice-admirals came aboard, to the accompaniment of the full military honours customarily granted to visiting admirals of friendly powers. Each was armed with what seemed to be an exact duplicate of the Patrol's own current blaster; Lewiston, Mark Seventeen. In the lead strode the tall, heavy, grey-haired man with whom Samms had been dealing; still defiant, still sullen, still concealing sternly his sheer desperation. His block was still on, full strength.

The man next in line was much younger than the leader, much less wrought up, much more intent. Samms felt for this man's ego, tuned to it, and got the shock of his life. This Black vice-admiral's mind was not at all what he had expected to encounter—it was, in every respect, of Lensman grade!

'Oh...how? You are not speaking, and...I see...the Lens...THE LENS!' The stranger's mind was for seconds an utterly indescribable turmoil in which relief, gladness, and high anticipation struggled for supremacy.

In the next few seconds, even before the visitors had reached their places at the conference table, Virgil Samms and Corander of Petrine exchanged thoughts which would require many thousands of words to express; only a few of which are necessary here.

'The LENS...I have dreamed of such a thing, without hope of realisation or possibility. *How* we have been

misled! They are, then, actually available upon your world, Samms of Tellus?'

'Not exactly, and not at all generally,' and Samms explained as he had explained so many times before. 'You will wear one sooner than you think. But as to ending this warfare. You survivors are practically all natives of your own world. Petrine?'

'Not "practically", we are Petrinos all. The "teachers" were all in the Centre. Many remain upon Petrine and its neighbouring worlds, but none remain alive here.'

'Ohlanser, then, who assumed command, is also a Petrino? So hard-headed, I had assumed otherwise. He will be a stumbling-block. Is he actually in supreme command?'

'Only by and with our consent, under such astounding circumstances as these. He is a reactionary, of the old, die-hard, war-dog school. He would ordinarily be in supreme command and would be supported by the teachers if any were here; but I will challenge his authority and theirs; standing upon my right to command my own fleet as I see fit. So will, I think, several others. So go ahead with your meeting.'

'Be seated, Gentlemen.' All saluted punctiliously and sat down. 'Now, Vice-Admiral Ohlanser...'

'How do you, a stranger, know my name?'

'I know many things. We have a suggestion to offer which, if you Petrinos will follow it, will end this warfare. First, please believe that we have no designs upon your planet, nor any quarrel with any of its people who are not hopelessly contaminated by the ideas and the culture of the entities who are back of this whole movement; quite possibly those who you refer to as the "teachers". You did not know whom you were to fight, or why.' This was a statement with no hint of question about it.

'I see now that we did not know all the truth,' Ohlanser admitted, stiffly. 'We were informed, and given proof sufficient to make us believe, that you were monsters from outer space—rapacious, insatiable, senselessly and callously destructive to all other forms of intelligent life.'

'We suspected something of the kind. Do you others agree? Vice-Admiral Corander?'

'Yes. We were shown detailed and documented proofs; stereos of battles, in which no quarter was given. We saw system after system conquered, world after world laid waste. We were made to believe that our only hope of continued existence was to meet you and destroy you in space; for if you were allowed to reach Petrine every man, woman, and child on the planet would either be killed outright or tortured to death. I see now that those proofs were entirely false; completely vicious.'

'They were. Those who spread that lying propaganda and all who support their organisation must be and shall be weeded out. Petrine must be and shall be given her rightful place in the galactic fellowship of free, independent, and co-operative worlds. So must any and all planets whose peoples wish to adhere to Civilisation instead of to tyranny and despotism. To further these ends, we Lensmen suggest that you re-form your fleet and proceed to Arisia...'

'Arisia!' Ohlanser did not like the idea.

'Arisia,' Samms insisted. 'Upon leaving Arisia, knowing vastly more than you do now, you will return to your home planet, where you will take whatever steps you will then know to be necessary.'

'We were told that your Lenses are hypnotic devices,' Ohlanser sneered, 'designed to steal away and destroy the minds of any who listen to you. I believe

that, fully. I will not go to Arisia, nor will any part of Petrine's Grand Fleet. I will not attack my home planet. I will not do battle against my own people. This is final.'

'I am not saying or implying that you should. But you continue to close your mind to reason. How about you, Vice-Admiral Corander? And you others?'

In the momentary silence Samms put himself en rapport with the other officers, and was overjoyed at what he learned.

'I do not agree with Vice-Admiral Ohlanser,' Corander said, flatly. 'He commands, not Grand Fleet, but his sub-fleet merely, as do we all. I will lead my sub-fleet to Arisia.'

'Traitor!' Ohlanser shouted. He leaped to his feet and drew his blaster, but a tractor beam snatched it from his grasp before he could fire.

'You were allowed to wear side-arms, not to use them.' Samms said, quietly. 'How many of you others agree with Corander; how many with Ohlanser?'

All nine voted with the younger man.

'Very well. Ohlanser, you may either accept Corander's leadership or leave this meeting now and take your sub-fleet directly back to Petrine. Decide now which you prefer to do.'

'You mean you aren't going to kill me, even now? Or even degrade me, or put me under arrest?'

'In that case...I was—must have been—wrong. I will follow Corander.'

'A wise choice. Corander, you already know what to expect; except that four or five other Petrinos now in this room will help you, not only in deciding what must be done upon Petrine, but also in the doing of it. This meeting will adjourn.'

'But...no reprisals?' Corander, in spite of his newly acquired knowledge, was dubious, almost dumbfounded. 'No invasion or occupation? No indemnities to your Patrol, or reparations? No punishment of us, our men, or our families?'

'None.'

'That does not square up even with ordinary military usage.'

'I know it. It does conform, however, to the policy of the Galactic Patrol which is to spread throughout our island universe.'

'You are not even sending your fleet, or heavy units of it, with us, to see to it that we follow your instructions?'

'It is not necessary. If you need any form of help you will inform us of your requirements via Lens, as I am conversing with you now, and whatever you want will be supplied. However, I do not expect any such call. You and your fellows are capable of handling the situation. You will soon know the truth, and know that you know it; and when your house-cleaning is done we will consider your application for representation upon the Galactic Council. Goodbye.'

Thus the Lensmen—particularly First Lensman Virgil Samms—brought another sector of the galaxy under the aegis of Civilisation.

CHAPTER 20

After the Rally there were a few days during which neither Samms nor Kinnison was on Earth. That the Cosmocrats' presidential candidate and the First Lensman were both with the Fleet was not a secret; in fact, it was advertised. Everyone was told why they were out there, and almost everyone approved.

Nor was their absence felt. Developments, fast and terrific, were slammed home. Cosmocratic spellbinders in every state of North America waved the flag, pointed with pride, and viewed with alarm, in the very best tradition of North American politics. But above all, there appeared upon every news-stand and in every book-shop of the Continent, at opening time of the day following Rally Day, a book of over eighteen hundred pages of fine print; a book the publication of which had given Samms himself no little concern.

'But I'm afraid of it!' he had protested. 'We know it's true; but there's material on almost every page for the biggest libel and slander suits in history!'

'I know it,' the bald and paunchy Lensman-attorney had replied. 'Fully. I hope they *do* take action against us, but I'm absolutely certain they won't.'

'You hope they do?'

'Yes. If they take the initiative they can't prevent us from presenting our evidence in full; and there is no court in existence, however corrupt, before which we could not win. What they want and must have is delay; avoidance of any issue until after the election.'

'I see.' Samms was convinced.

The location of the Patrol's Grand Fleet had been concealed from all inhabitants of the Solarian system, friends and foes alike; but the climactic battle—liberating as it did energies sufficient to distort the very warp and woof of the fabric of space itself—could not be hidden or denied, or even belittled. It was not, however, advertised or blazoned abroad. Then as now the newshawks wanted to know, instantly and via long-range communicators, vastly more than those responsible for security cared to tell; then as now the latter said as little as it was humanly possible to say.

Everyone knew that the Patrol had won a magnificent victory; but nobody knew who or what the enemy had been. Since the rank and file knew it, everyone knew that only a fraction of the Black fleet had actually been destroyed; but nobody knew where the remaining vessels went or what they did. Everyone knew that about ninety five percent of the Patrol's astonishingly huge Grand Fleet had come from, and was on its way back to, the planet Bennett, and knew—since Bennettans would in a few weeks be scampering gaily all over space—in general *what* Bennett was; but nobody knew *why* it was.

Thus, when the North American Contingent landed at New York Spaceport, everyone whom the newsmen could reach was literally mobbed. However, in accordance with the aphorism ascribed to the wise old owl, those who knew the least said the most. But the Telenews ace who had once interviewed both Kinnison and Samms wasted no time upon small fry. He insisted on seeing the two top Lensmen, and kept on insisting until he did see them.

'Nothing to say,' Kinnison said curtly, leaving no doubt whatever that he meant it. 'All talking—if any—will be done by First Lensman Samms.'

'Now, all you millions of Telenews listeners, I am interviewing First Lensman Samms himself. A little

closer to the mike, please, First Lensman. Now, sir, what everybody wants to know is—who are the Blacks?'

'I don't know.'

'You don't know? On the Lens, sir?'

'On the Lens. I still don't know.'

'I see. But you have suspicions or ideas? You can guess?'

'I can guess; but that's all it would be—a guess.'

'And my guess, folks, is that his guess would be a very highly informed guess. Will you tell the public, First Lensman Samms, what your guess is?'

'I will.' If this reply astonished the newshawk, it staggered Kinnison and the others who knew Samms best. It was, however, a coldly calculated political move. 'While it will probably be several weeks before we can furnish detailed and unassailable proof, it is my considered opinion that the Black fleet was built and controlled by the Morgan-Towne-Isaacson machine. That they, all unknown to any of us, enticed, corrupted, and seduced a world, or several worlds, to their programme of domination and enslavement. That they intended by armed force to take over the Continent of North America and through it the whole earth and all the other planets adherent to Civilisation. That they intended to hunt down and kill every Lensman, and to subvert the Galactic Council to their own ends. This is what you wanted?'

That's fine, sir—*just* what we wanted. But just one more thing, sir.' The newsman had obtained infinitely more than he had expected to get, yet, good newsmanlike, he wanted more. 'Just a word, if you will, Mr. Samms, as to these trials and the White Book?'

'I can add very little, I'm afraid, to what I have already said and what is in the book; and that little can be classed as "I told you so". We are trying, and

will continue to try, to force those criminals to trial; to break up, to prohibit, an unending series of hair-splitting delays. We want, and are determined to get, legal action; to make each of those we have accused defend himself in court and under oath. Morgan and his crew, however, are working desperately to avoid any action at all, because they know that we can and will prove every allegation we have made.'

The Telenews ace signed off, Samms and Kinnison went to their respective offices, and Cosmocratic orators throughout the nation held a field-day. They glowed and scintillated with triumph. They yelled themselves hoarse, leather-lunged tub-thumpers though they were, in pointing out the unsullied purity, the spotless perfection of their own party and its every candidate for office; in shuddering revulsion at the never-to-be-sufficiently-condemned, proved and demonstrated villainy and blackguardy of the opposition.

And the Nationalists, although they had been dealt a terrific and entirely unexpected blow, worked near-miracles of politics with what they had. Morgan and his minions ranted and raved. They were being jobbed. They were being crucified by the Monied Powers. All those allegations and charges were sheerest fabrications—false, utterly vicious, containing nothing whatever of truth. They, not the Patrol, were trying to force a show-down; to vindicate themselves and to confute those unspeakably unscrupulous Lensmen before Election Day. And they were succeeding! Why, otherwise, had not a single one of the thousands of accused even been arrested? Ask that lying First Lensman, Virgil Samms! Ask that rock-hearted, iron-headed, conscienceless murderer, Roderick Kinnison! But do not, at peril of your sanity, submit your minds to their Lenses!

And why, the reader asks, were not at least some of those named persons arrested before Election Day?

And your historian must answer frankly that he does not know. He is not a lawyer. It would be of interest—to some few of us—to follow in detail at least one of those days of legal battling in one of the high courts of the land; to quote verbatim at least a few of the many thousands of pages of transcript: but to most of us the technicalities involved would be boring in the extreme.

But couldn't the voters tell easily enough which side was on the offensive and which on the defensive? Which pressed for action and which insisted on postponement and delay? They could have, easily enough, if they had cared enough about the basic issues involved to make the necessary mental effort, but almost everyone was too busy doing something else. And it was so much easier to take somebody else's word for it. And finally, *thinking* is an exercise to which all too few brains are accustomed.

But Morgan neither ranted nor raved nor blustered when he sat in conference with his faintly-blue superior, who had come storming in as soon as he had learned of the crushing defeat of the Black fleet. The Kalonian was very highly concerned; so much so that the undertone of his peculiar complexion was slowly turning to a delicate shade of green.

'How did *that* happen? How *could* it happen? Why was I not informed of the Patrol's real power—how could you be guilty of such stupidity? Now I'll have to report to Scrwan of the Eich. He's pure, undiluted poison—and if word of this catastrophe ever gets up to Ploor…!!!'

'Come down out of the stratosphere, Fernald,' Morgan countered, bitingly. 'Don't try to make *me* the goat—I won't sit still for it. It happened because they could build a bigger fleet than we could. You were in on that—all of it. You knew what we were doing, and approved it—all of it. You were as badly fooled as I

was. You were not informed because I could find out nothing—I could learn no more of their Bennett than they could of our Petrine. As to reporting, you will of course do as you please; but I would advise you not to cry too much before you're really hurt. This battle isn't over yet, my friend.'

The Kalonian had been a badly shaken entity; it was a measure of his state of mind that he did not liquidate the temerarious Tellurian then and there. But since Morgan was as undisturbed as ever, and as sure of himself, he began to regain his wonted aplomb. His colour became again its normal pale blue.

'I will forgive your insubordination this time, since there were no witnesses, but use no more such language to me,' he said, stiffly. 'I fail to perceive any basis for your optimism. The only chance now remaining is for you to win the election, and how can you do that? You are—must be—losing ground steadily and rapidly.'

'Not as much as you might think.' Morgan pulled down a large, carefully-drawn chart. 'This line represents the hide-bound Nationalists, whom nothing we can do will alienate from the party; this one the equally hide-bound Cosmocrats. The balance of power lies, as always, with the independents—these here. And many of them are not as independent as is supposed. We can buy or bring pressure to bear on half of them—that cuts them down to this size here. So, no matter what the Patrol does, it can affect only this relatively small block here, and it is this block we are fighting for. We are losing a little ground, and steadily, yes; since we can't conceal from anybody with half a brain the fact that we're doing our best to keep the cases from ever coming to trial. But here's the actual observed line of sentiment, as determined from psychological indices up to yesterday; here is the extrapolation of that line to Election Day. It forecasts us to get just under forty nine percent of the total vote.'

'And is there anything cheerful about that?' Fernald asked frostily.

'I'll say there is!' Morgan's big face assumed a sneering smile, an expression never seen by any voter. 'This chart deals only with living, legally registered, bona-fide voters. Now if we can come that close to winning an absolutely honest election, how do you figure we can possibly lose the kind this one is going to be? We're in power, you know. We've got this machine and we know how to use it.'

'Oh, yes, I remember—vaguely. You told me about North American politics once, a few years ago. Dead men, ringers, repeaters, ballot-box stuffing, and so on, you said?'

' "And so on" is right, Chief!' Morgan assured him, heartily. 'Everything goes, this time. It'll be one of the biggest landslides in North American history.'

'I will, then defer any action until after the election.'

'That will be the smart thing to do, Chief; then you won't have to take any, or make any report at all,' and upon this highly satisfactory note the conference closed.

And Morgan was actually as confident as he had appeared. His charts were actual and factual. He knew the power of money and the effectiveness of pressure; he knew the capabilities of the various units of his machine. He did not, however, know two things: Jill Samms' insidious, deeply-hidden Voters' Protective League and the bright flame of loyalty pervading the Galactic Patrol. Thus, between times of bellowing and screaming his carefully-prepared, rabble-rousing speeches, he watched calmly and contentedly the devious workings of his smooth and efficient organisation.

Until the day before election, that is. Then hordes of young men and young women went suddenly and

briefly to work; at least four in every precinct of the entire nation. They visited, it seemed, every residence and every dwelling unit, everywhere. They asked questions, and took notes, and vanished; and the machine's operatives, after the alarm was given, could not find man or girl or notebook. And the Galactic Patrol, which had never before paid any attention to elections, had given leave and ample time to its every North American citizen. Vessels of the North American Contingent were grounded and practically emptied of personnel; bases and stations were depopulated; and even from every distant world every Patrolman registered in any North American precinct came to spend the day at home.

Morgan began then to worry, but there was nothing he could do about the situation—or was there? If the civilian boys and girls were checking the registration books—and they were—it was as legally-appointed checkers. If the uniformed boys and girls were all coming home to vote—and they were—that, too, was their inalienable right. But boys and girls were notoriously prone to accident and to debauchery... but again Morgan was surprised; and, this time, taken heavily aback. The web which had protected Grand Rally so efficiently, but greatly enlarged now, was functioning again; and Morgan and his minions spent a sleepless and thoroughly uncomfortable night.

Election Day dawned clear, bright, and cool; auguring a record turn-out. Voting was early and extraordinarily heavy; the polls were crowded. There was, however, very little disorder. Surprisingly little, in view of the fact that the Cosmocratic watchers, instead of being the venal wights of custom, were cold-eyed, unreachable men and women who seemed to know by sight every voter in the precinct. At least they spotted on sight and challenged without hesitation every ringer, every dead one, every repeater, and every impostor who claimed the right to vote. And those

challenges, being borne out in every case by the carefully-checked registration lists, were in every case upheld.

Not all of the policemen on duty, especially in the big cities, were above suspicion, of course. But whenever any one of those officers began to show a willingness to play ball with the machine a calm, quiet-eyed Patrolman would remark, casually:

'Better see that this election stays straight, bud, and strictly according to the lists and signatures—or you're apt to find yourself listed in the big book along with the rest of the rats.'

It was not that the machine liked the way things were going, or that it did not have goon squads on the job. It was that there were, everywhere and always, more Patrolmen than there were goons. And those Patrolmen, however young in years some of them might have appeared to be, were space-bronzed veterans, space-hardened fighting men, armed with the last word in blasters—Lewiston, Mark Seventeen.

To the boy's friends and neighbours, of course, his Lewiston was practically invisible. It was merely an article of clothing, the same as his pants. It carried not more of significance, of threat or of menace, than did the pistol and the club of the friendly Irish cop on the beat. But the goon did not see the Patrolman as a friend. He saw the keen, clear, sharply discerning eyes; the long, strong fingers; the smoothly flowing muscles, so eloquent of speed and of power. He saw the Lewiston for what it was; the deadliest, most destructive hand-weapon known to man. Above all he saw the difference in numbers: six or seven or eight Patrolmen to four or five or six of his own kind. If more hoods arrived, so did more spacemen; if some departed, so did a corresponding number of the wearers of the space-black and silver.

'Ain't you getting tired of sticking around here, George?' One mobster asked confidentially of one Patrolman. 'I am. What say we and some of you fellows round up some girls and go have us a party?'

'Uh-uh,' George denied. His voice was gay and careless, but his eyes were icy cold. 'My uncle's cousin's stepson is running for second assistant dog-catcher, and I can't leave until I find out whether he wins or not.'

Thus nothing happened; thus the invisible but nevertheless terrific tension did not erupt into open battle; and thus, for the first time in North America's long history, a presidential election was ninety nine and ninety nine one-hundredths percent pure!

Evening came. The polls closed. The Cosmocrats' headquarters for the day, the Grand Ballroom of the Hotel van der Voort, became the goal of every Patrolman who thought he stood any chance at all of getting in. Kinnison had been there all day, of course. So had Joy, his wife, who for lack of space has been sadly neglected in these annals. Betty, their daughter, had come in early, accompanied by a husky and personable young lieutenant, who has no other place in this story. Jack Kinnison arrived, with Dimples Maynard—dazzlingly blonde, wearing a screamingly red wisp of silk. She too, has been shamefully slighted here, although she was never slighted anywhere else.

'The first time I ever saw her,' Jack was wont to say, 'I went right into a flat spin, running around in circles and biting myself in the small of the back, and couldn't pull out of it for four hours!'

That Miss Maynard should be a very special item is not at all surprising, in view of the fact that she was to become the wife of one of THE Kinnisons and the mother of another.

The First Lensman, who had been in and out, came in to stay. So did Jill and her inseparable, Mason Northrop. And so did others, singly or by twos and threes. Lensmen and their wives. Conway and Clio Costigan, Dr. and Mrs. Rodebush, and Cleveland, Admiral and Mrs. Clayton, ditto Schweikert, and Dr. Nels Bergenholm. And others. Nor were they all North Americans, or even human. Rularion was there; and so was blocky, stocky Dronvire of Rigel Four. No outsider could tell, ever, what any Lensman was thinking, to say nothing of such a monstrous Lensman as Dronvire—but that hotel was being covered as no political headquarters had ever been covered before.

The returns came in, see-sawing maddeningly back and forth. Faster and faster. The Maritime Provinces split fifty-fifty. Main, New Hampshire, and Vermont, Cosmocrat. New York, upstate, Cosmocrat. New York City, on the basis of incomplete but highly significant returns, was piling up a huge Nationalist majority. Pennsylvania—labour—Nationalist. Ohio—farmers—Cosmocrat. Twelve southern states went six and six. Chicago, as usual, solidly for the machine; likewise Quebec and Ottawa and Montreal and Toronto and Detroit and Kansas City and St. Louis and New Orleans and Denver.

Then northern and western and far southern states came in and evened the score. Saskatchewan, Alberta, Britcol, and Alaska, all went Cosmocrat. So did Washington, Idaho, Montana, Oregon, Nevada, Utah, Arizona, Newmex, and most of the states of Mexico.

At three o'clock in the morning the Cosmocrats had a slight but definite lead and were, finally, holding it. At four o'clock the lead was larger, but California was still an unknown quantity—California could wreck everything. How would California go? Especially, how would California's two metropolitan districts—the two most independent and free-thinking and least

predictable big cities of the nation—how *would* they go?

At five o'clock California seemed safe. Except for Los Angeles and San Francisco, the Cosmocrats had swept the state, and in those two great cities they held a commanding lead. It was still mathematically possible, however, for the Nationalists to win.

'It's in the bag! Let's start the celebration!' someone shouted, and others took up the cry.

'Stop it! No!' Kinnison's parade-ground voice cut through the noise. 'No celebration is in order or will be held until the result becomes certain or Witherspoon concedes!'

The two events came practically together: Witherspoon conceded a couple of minutes before it became mathematically impossible for him to win. Then came the celebration, which went on and on interminably. At the first opportunity, however, Kinnison took Samms by the arm, led him without a word into a small office, and shut the door. Samms, also saying nothing, sat down in the swivel chair, put both feet up on the desk, lit a cigarette, and inhaled deeply.

'Well, Virge—satisfied?' Kinnison broke the silence at last. His Lens was off. 'We're on our way.'

'Yes, Rod. Fully. At last.' No more than his friend did he dare to use his Lens; to plumb the depths he knew so well were there. 'Now it will roll—under its own power—no one man now is or ever will be indispensable to the Galactic Patrol—*nothing* can stop it now!'

EPILOGUE

The murder of Senator Morgan, in his own private office, was never solved. If it had occurred before the election, suspicion would certainly have fallen upon Roderick Kinnison, but as it was it did not. By no stretch of the imagination could anyone conceive of 'Rod the Rock' kicking a man after he had knocked him down. Not that Morgan did not have powerful and vindictive enemies in the underworld: he had so many that it proved impossible to fasten the crime to any one of them.

Officially, Kinnison was on a five-year leave of absence from the Galactic Patrol, the office of Port Admiral had been detached entirely from the fleet and assigned to the Office of the President of North America. Actually, however, in every respect that counted, Roderick Kinnison was still Port Admiral, and would remain so until he died or until the Council retired him by force.

Officially, Kinnison was taking a short, well-earned vacation from the job in which he had been so outstandingly successful. Actually, he was doing a quick flit to Petrine, to get personally acquainted with the new Lensmen and to see what kind of a job they were doing. Besides, Virgil Samms was already there.

He arrived. He got acquainted. He saw. He approved.

'How about coming back to Tellus with me, Virge?' he asked, when the visiting was done. 'I've got to make a speech, and it'd be nice to have you hold my hand.'

'I'd be glad to,' and the *Chicago* took off.

Half of North America was dark when they neared Tellus; all of it, apparently, was obscured by clouds. Only the navigating officers of the vessel knew where they were, nor did either of the two Lensmen care. They were having too much fun arguing about the talents and abilities of their respective grandsons.

The *Chicago* landed. A bug was waiting. The two Lensmen, without an order being given, were whisked away. Samms had not asked where the speech was to be given, and Kinnison simply did not realise that he had not told him all about it. Thus Samms had no idea that he was just leaving Spokane Spaceport, Washington.

After a few miles of fast, open-country driving the bug reached the city. It slowed down, swung into brightly-lighted Maple Street, and passed a sign reading "Cannon Hill" something-or-other—neither of which names meant anything to either Lensman.

Kinnison looked at his friend's red-thatched head and glanced at his watch.

'Looking at you reminds me—I need a haircut,' he remarked. 'Should have got one aboard, but didn't think of it. Joy told me if I come home without it she'll braid it in pigtails and tie it up with pink ribbons, and you're shaggier than I am. You've got to get one or else buy yourself a violin. What say we do it now?'

'Have we got time enough?'

'Plenty.' Then, to the driver: 'Stop at the first barber shop you see, please.'

'Yes, sir. There's a good one a few blocks further along.'

The bug sped down Maple Street, turned sharply into plainly-marked Twelfth Avenue. Neither Lensman saw the sign.

'Here you are, sir.'

'Thanks.'

There were two barbers and two chairs, both empty. The Lensmen, noticing that the place was neatly kept and meticulously clean, sat down and resumed their discussion of two extremely unusual infants. The barbers went busily to work.

'Just as well, though—better, really—that the kids didn't marry each other, at that,' Kinnison concluded finally. 'The way it is, we've each got a grandson— it'd be tough to have to share one with *you*.'

Samms made no reply to this sally, for something was happening. The fact that this fair-skinned, yellow-haired blue-eyed barber was left-handed had not rung any bells—there were lots of left-handed barbers. he had neither seen nor heard the cat—a less-than-half-grown, grey, tiger-striped kitten—which, after standing up on its hind legs to sniff ecstatically at his nylon-clad ankles, had uttered a couple of almost inaudible "meows" and had begun to purr happily. Crouching, tensing its strong little legs, it leaped almost vertically upward. Its tail struck the barber's elbow.

Hastily brushing the kitten aside, and beginning profuse apologies both for his awkwardness and for the presence of the cat—he had never done such a thing before and he would drown him forthwith—the barber applied a styptic pencil and recollection hit Samms a pile-driver blow.

'Well, I'm a...!' He voiced three highly un-Samms-like, highly specific expletives which, as Mentor had foretold so long ago, were both self-derogatory and profane. Then as full realisation dawned, he bit a word squarely in two.

'Excuse me, please, Mr. Carbonero, for this outrageous display. It was not the scratch, nor was

any of it your fault. Nothing you could have done would have…'

'You know my name?' the astonished barber interrupted.

'Yes. You were…ah…recommended to me by a…a friend…' Whatever Samms could say would make things worse. The truth, wild as it was, would have to be told, at least in part. 'You do not look like an Italian, but perhaps you have enough of that racial heritage to believe in prophecy?'

'Of course, sir. There have always been prophets— *true* prophets.'

'Good. This event was foretold in detail; in such complete detail that I was deeply, terribly shocked. Even to the kitten. You call it Thomas.'

'Yes, sir. Thomas Aquinas.'

'It is actually a female. In here, Thomasina!' The kitten had been climbing enthusiastically up his leg; now, as he held a pocket invitingly open, she sprang into it, settled down, and began to purr blissfully. While the barbers and Kinnison stared pop-eyed Samms went on:

'She is determined to adopt me, and it would be a shame not to requite such affection. Would you part with her—for, say, ten credits?'

'*Ten credits!* I'll be glad to give her to you for nothing!'

'Ten it is, then. One more thing. Rod, you always carry a pocket rule. Measure this scratch, will you? You'll find it's mighty close to three millimetres long.'

'Not "close", Virge—it's *exactly* three millimetres, as near as this vernier can scale it.'

'And just above and parallel to the cheek-bone.'

'Check. Just above and as parallel as though it had been ruled there by a draughtsman.'

'Well, that's that. Let's get finished with the haircuts, before you're late for your speech,' and the barbers, with thoughts which will be left to the imagination, resumed their interrupted tasks.

'Spill it, Virge!' Kinnison Lensed the pent-up thought. If Carbonero, who did not know Samms at all, had been amazed at what had been happening, Kinnison, who had known him so long and so well, had been literally and completely dumb-founded. 'What in hell's behind this? What's the story? GIVE!'

Samms told him, and a mental silence fell; a silence too deep for intelligible thought. Each was beginning to realise that he never would and never could know what Mentor of Arisia really was.

So ends E.E 'Doc' Smith's classic
First Lensman

**The famous Lensman series
continues in book three—**
Galactic Patrol

E.E. 'Doc' Smith's classic Lensman series

Triplanetary

The planets Arisia and Eddore were at war for control of the Universe. The battleground was a tiny backward planet in a remote galaxy called Earth!

Only a few Earthlings knew of the titanic struggle, and of the strange, decisive role they were to play in the war of the super-races.

ISBN 1899884 12 2

First Lensman

No human had ever landed on the hidden planet of Arisia. A mysterious space barrier turned back both men and ships. Then Samms of the Galactic Patrol got through—and came back with the Lens, the strange device which gave its wearer powers no man had ever possessed before.

ISBN 1899884 13 0

Galactic Patrol

The pirates of Boskone raided at will, menacing the whole of interstellar civilisation. Masterminded by a super-scientist, their fleets out-gunned even the mighty cruisers of the Galactic Patrol.

When Kim Kinnison of the Patrol found the secret Boskonian base, it was impregnable to outside attack. But a single infiltrator might penetrate its defenses—if he wanted to take on million-to-one odds!

ISBN 1899884 14 9

Gray Lensman

Somewhere among the galaxies was the stronghold of Boskone—a network of brilliant interplanetary criminals whose mania for conquest threatened the future of all civilisation.

But where?

Boskonian bases dotted the universe—shielded by gigantic thought-screens that defied penetration. It was up to Lensman Kin Kinnison, using his fantastic mental powers, to infiltrate the Boksonian strongholds and learn the location of the enemy's Grand Base—and smash it forever!

ISBN 1899884 15 7

Second Stage Lensman

Kim Kinnison had the incredible assignment of infiltrating the inner circle of Boskone. His job was to become a Boskonian in every gesture, thought and deed. He had to work himself up through the ranks of an alien enemy organisation, into the highest echelons of power—until it was he who would be issuing the orders that would destroy his own civilisation!

ISBN 1899884 16 5

Children of the Lens

It was beginning to look as though no one could prevent the annihilation of the civilised Universe. For a weird intelligence was directing the destruction of all civilisation from the icy depths of outer space.

Kin Kinnison of the Galactic Patrol was one of the few men who knew how near the end was. And in the last

desperate stratagem to save the Universe from total destruction, he knew he had to use his children as bait for the evil powers of the hell-planet Ploor…

ISBN 1899884 21 1

Masters of the Vortex

A churning nuclear fireball, appearing out of nowhere, bringing utter destruction—and countless numbers of them were menacing planets throughout the Galaxy!

'Storm' Cloud, nucleonic genius, set out in his spaceship 'Vortex Blaster' to track and destroy the mysterious vortices—and embarked on a saga of adventure, discovery and conflict among the far stars.

ISBN 18899884 17 3

All titles are available from all good bookshops or by direct mail from Macmillan Direct on

01256 302699 (code 160)

Cheques should be made payable to Macmillan Direct, Houndmills, Basingstoke, Hampshire, RG21 6XS

You can also contact us at our website—

Ripping.com.UK

Ripping

Minds of the Empire
by Warren James Palmer

'For a moment Moss stood rooted to the spot staring down the muzzle of the rifle pointed at his head. Then without any conscious thought, pure power and anger surged down his back from his head into his arm and then to his hand. It felt as if his whole body was charged with a million volts of pure energy, like some huge capacitor. Where that power came from he couldn't say, it was as if it came from the very roots of his soul. From head to toe every hair on his body stood stock upright as if charged with static electricity. Without even knowing the reason why, he raised his hand and pointed at the guard with one finger.'

By the year 2020 the United Nations World Defence Force can finally guarantee the security of every nation on the planet through the use of orbital laser battle stations.

That is until the day the Dyason arrived. The Dyason are humanoid, but not from our star system. In a blitzkrieg attack they wipe out the World Defence Force and within days, force worldwide capitulation. except for a few renegades, mankind is enslaved.

Out of the prison ghettos of London a new hero emerges, a youth with exceptional mental powers. Minds of the Empire follows Moss as he struggles to escape the rubble of London and flee from both the Dyason and the Resistance.

The first book in the Dyason series spans space, time and legend in a fast moving adventure that keeps the adrenaline pumping.

ISBN 1899884-00-9   £4.99

THE DARK LAGOON

BY SIMON M. SHINEROCK

Rex Proctor has a problem—off the coast of Florida, for a thousand years he built his fantasy island out of the goodness he stole from the souls of his victims. Now the Dark Lagoon has burst its banks, threatening to destroy everything—washing his ambitions away forever. Only a soul untainted by life can neutralise the evil waters and not only restore his powers, but enable him to disturb the equilibrium of the whole world.

Jack Simmons and Tom Kidman met at college in London. After a shaky start they became best friends and decided to celebrate their graduation together with a year-long working holiday in America. Even before they started their journey, fate intervened to complicate what was supposed to have been the ultimate boy's-own adventure. Jack met Ruth, the girl of his dreams and fell in love. Of course, he couldn't let Tom down, but the seed of betrayal was sown; lying there waiting for a rainstorm to set it growing out of control.

They had no way of knowing how over the next twenty years their lives would become inextricably bound up with Proctor's plan. They had no way of imagining the final confrontation, in which each would play their part and help determine the fate of all mankind.

ISBN 1899884 18 1   £5.99

MERCER'S WHORE

BY J.K HADERACK

'Mercer raised the shield bearing the cross of Christa in his almost useless left arm as the cruel barbs of the demon's hooks attempted to rip at his flesh. Once more he struck with his broadsword and sparks flashed in the night as he struck the creature's heavy armour. His energy was all but spent; Mercer had never planned to meet his opponent in the dark of night. The demagogue should have been destroyed by the flames which devoured the temple. His parries were getting weaker and weaker, soon he would make a fatal mistake and that would be the end of it. It was then that Haye, his whore leapt up from the edge of the river and struck the demagogue with incredible strength and ferocity. It was as if she was possessed by the soul of Christa!'

The temple of cards conceals many dark secrets but, far beyond its warped and twisted wall, men whisper of the Slow Room which dilates time extending pleasure or pain infinitely.

But, for those who enter that room, there is sometimes a terrible price to be paid when human flesh is wagered upon the outcome of the barbaric combat ritual of Chain, Hook and Blade.

Facing Kum, the demonic Temple Guardian, many warriors have died in slow agony. But now, as clouds of war darken the land, a new challenger approaches from the East. His name is Mercer, a man who is perhaps the greatest horse-warrior of that age.

Yet, at the centre of it all is a woman who must finally stand between the forces of light and the powers of ultimate darkness. Her name is Haye but to others, she is known simply as Mercer's Whore.

ISBN 1899884 19 X   £5.99

FOR AUTUMN 1997
RIPPING Is also proud to present...

Brilliant novels from exciting new authors...

Brian Hughes's Hobson & Co (paranormal investigators)

A story of incredible and inventive imagination. Our unlikely heroes live in a northern town somewhere in England.

Until recently Hobson & Co, have had but one single case! However, a spate of bizarre and highly unlikely incidents occur in their street, beginning with the mysterious disappearance of their neighbours newborn child.

Their unorthodox investigations span time and space in an addictive, off-beat novel. Superbly illustrated by the author

ISBN 1899884 11 4   £5.99

Hunter Tremayne's Archangels

What happens when a group of complete strangers are hunted by a psychopath demanding 'The Wolf is Coming—Who shall protect the Lambs!'?

The answer is wrapped up in mythology, religious chronicles and ancient legend. The time is coming when the Archangels will have to face the Fallen Angel for the final battle. With the fate of mankind in the balance. Who will prevail?

A thoughtful but fast moving adventure which takes the reader across continents to the arctic north.

1899884 24 6 £5.99

New for autumn 1997...

Sports Bikes!

In today's world of air-bags, crumple zones, safety catches, stay-pressed slacks and fluff removers, motorcycling is an ever-swelling oasis of adrenaline adventures and insanity.

Whether you're a knee-scraping, buzz-bomber or a would-be rider who never actually makes it out of the armchair, this pioneering book will tell you all about choosing your dream bike, what to wear and how to get faster.

It's stuffed full of true stories, narrow misses, top tips and some of the best biking photos ever taken. Oh, and plenty of terrifying crash pics!

Written by Jill Strong, staff writer for the bikers bible—Performance Bike Magazine—this lavishly illustrated, witty hardback book, is going to be THE essential purchase for all street racers.

Go on, buy it! You know you want to...

ISBN-1899884 22 x

£19.99 Hardback. 150pages. Approx 200 colour photos.